TAMING

OF THE

FEW

Guardians of the PHAE
Book One

ROWAN DILLON

GREEN DRAGON PUBLISHING

Published by Green Dragon Publishing
Beacon Falls, CT
www.GreenDragonArtist.com

Dedication:

As this is my first foray into urban fantasy, I'd like to thank my fantastic critique group for all their help keeping me on-genre, especially authors Mattea Orr and MA Hoyler. And sincere thanks go to my publisher, editors, and beta readers, including Christina Lalama and Ian Erik Morris—without your help, this never would have happened!

I also dedicate it to those who face prejudice, hatred, and bigotry in any form.

Pronunciation Guide

Below is a list of some of the words and names in the story that are in other languages:

Al'ama—(al-a-MAH) An exclamation in Arabic
Amadán—(ah-mah-DAWN) A foolish or silly person
Asa—(ah-SAH) A god of protection in the Bantu tradition
Bintou—(bin-TOO)
Chikushou! —(cheek-a-SHAW) A Japanese curse
Ciara—(KEE-rah)
Dobhar-chú—(DOHVer KHU) King Otter in Irish folklore
Eithne—(ENya)
Gaotha Na Chósta Copair—(GWEEha na KHOstah COPPer) Winds of the copper coast
Hiroki—(hih-ROW-kee)
Hy-Brasil—(HI-brass-ILL) A mythical island off the coast of Ireland
Immram—(im-RAHM) Sea journey tales in Irish folklore
Inis Meáin—(INish MEEN) Middle Island (one of the Aran Islands of Ireland)
Inis Mór—(INish MORE) Big Island (one of the Aran Islands of Ireland)
Inis Oírr—(INishEER) East Island (one of the Aran Islands of Ireland)
Kami—(kah-mee) Spirit or deity in Japanese folklore
Khánh Hòa—(kahn hwa) A province in Vietnam
Ki—(KEE) The heart or spirit in Japanese belief
Mag Mell—(meg mel) A name for the Otherworld in Irish folklore
Magh Tuireadh—(moy TOUR-ah) A set of battles in Irish the Mythological Cycle
Ogham—(OW-uhm) A medieval Irish alphabet
Oireachtas—(ERR-ek-tes) The Irish legislature body
Qacha—(KAH-chah)
Róisín—(row-SHEEN)
Sídhe—(SHEE) the Faery Folk
Taishitsu—(tieSHEETsoo) Constitution (Japanese)
Teachta Dála—(TYOKHtah DAWlah) An Irish legislator
Tír na nÓg—(CHEER nuh NOHG) the world of the afterlife
Tuatha Dé Danann—(TOOha day DAHnen) Deities of pre-Christian Ireland

Chapter One

"If there is magic on this planet, it is contained in water."
– Loren Eiseley

Latest CNN *Update: A new study has proposed an explanation for the rise in unusual powers in a small percentage of the human population in the last six months. Scientists have posited that the shift in the magnetic poles may have been a factor in this phenomenon. Further studies have been planned to determine the extent of such powers and the range of those affected. Initial results suggest higher concentrations in certain populations, including those with Irish, Peruvian, Hawaiian, and Siberian ancestry. From reports across the world, cases appear to be increasing.*

We here at CNN *are committed to bringing you the latest on this story as it develops. This article has been updated to reflect the inclusion of those with Siberian ancestry.*

Anna:

Anna Taylor stayed behind after the girls' swim team shuffled out of the locker room. The heavy scent of chlorine grew stronger as the echo of water slapping the edge of the pool fell into silence. She pulled off the clothing hiding her scaly skin, leaving only her one-piece. As a coach, she had to remain conservative in her plain blue swimsuit, but she longed for a shiny, iridescent one.

She stepped to the deep end and dove in, relishing her privacy as she cut the water with her hands. It enveloped her like a comfortable lover, caressing her reddened hands and soothing her pain. Now her skin glowed with delight, the only irritation coming from heavy levels of chlorine in her beloved water.

Swimming several laps, Anna lost track of time as she communed with her element, delighting in her solitude. After a blissful eternity, she stood in the shallow end and examined her arms. Painful flakes had faded into an even pattern, like the scales of a snake or fish. As soon as she pulled her hand out of the water, the angry redness returned.

Anna moved her hand just under the surface, forming eddies in the water. She did it again, hoping to make stronger eddies, and she coaxed a small waterspout in the pool. Raising her hands, the waterspout rose, hovering over the surface. She'd never been able to do that before. Her abilities had grown over the last month, which both excited and frightened her.

Just as she made the waterspout as big as her head, someone gasped and Anna glanced up, her heart in her throat. The tall, blonde freshman's eyes grew wide.

With growing dread, Anna dropped the waterspout back into the pool and dragged herself away from the water's embrace. The air stung her skin and made her wince as she climbed the shallow-end stairs. She grabbed her towel and wrapped it around her body, pulling her black hair away from her red, scaly forearms.

"Coach Taylor? What is that? What did you do? And what happened to your arms?"

The harsh scent of chlorine burned her nose. "It's nothing, Tanya. Just a flare-up of my eczema. Nothing to get excited over."

The girl swallowed but didn't take her eyes off Anna's arms. Maybe she'd forget the waterspout. "What did you need, Tanya? Did you forget something in the locker room?"

Tanya's eyes grew wide as she shook her head.

Full of self-conscious dread, Anna strode past the girl with apparent confidence and dried off. Then she pulled on her shirt and gloves, covering her blemishes. By the time she'd finished dressing, Tanya had disappeared. Anna's skin crawled with anxiety. She'd have to be more careful in the future. She didn't want to get fired.

Once back in her office, Anna pulled her gloves back off to examine her skin. The lotion helped keep the rest supple, but the flaky bits had gotten worse. They itched like the devil, and she craved a long, satisfying scratch. Instead, she pulled the gloves on again and strode to her office, turning on her computer.

She'd meant to look up the address and hours of the closest urgent care clinic, but when she opened her browser, a headline caught her eye.

Demonstration in Washington, D.C. Turns to Violence as Several are Arrested.

Panic seized her as she remembered her brother, Joel, had traveled to DC that weekend. She opened the article to watch the video, straining to see if she recognized his face in the crowd. Vile, hateful words filled the various banners and signs.

Unnaturals, Go Away!

No Mutants Wanted!

Pure Humans Only!

Anna glimpsed several young men with dark, curly hair, similar to Joel's, but none bore his round face and freckles. Then his face popped up behind a man with an American Flag wrapped around his shoulders. Her brother held a sign scrawled with red paint. "Pure Blood or Nothing." Fuckabiscuit.

Well, if Joel had gotten arrested, he would have called her. He'd have hated it, but he had no one else, as far as she knew. Since she'd received no calls, he must be safe.

The bus home seemed lonelier tonight. The college town emptied as people fled to weekend destinations. They ran to their families and their loved ones. She had no loved ones left. Only her brother remained, someone she barely liked. She entered her apartment, the empty rooms silent and judging. Her second-hand furniture was comfortable, though, and she had plenty of books to keep her company.

In her evening routine, she put the kettle on and snuggled into the overstuffed armchair next to the window. She leaned against the sill, sipping her tea, and watched the cars drive by on the street below. The motors whined as they passed, drowning out the more delicate noises of birdsong and insects as they called out for love in the night.

The next day, the rain made everything a muddy mess. As she got to her office by the university pool, Anna took off her jacket just as her intra-office chat dinged. When she opened the app, her boss' face appeared, and he didn't look pleased. "Anna, we need to discuss something. Can you come now?"

Dread knotted her stomach as she walked down the lime green hall to the administrative offices. The image of Tanya's wide eyes followed her. She swallowed hard as the assistant waved her in. When Anna sat at the desk, her boss looked up and entwined his fingers. Never a good sign.

He raised his eyebrows. "Anna, an incident after swimming practice last night has been brought to my attention. Would you like to tell me what happened?"

Anna cleared her throat. How would she explain this without sounding like a nut, without revealing her secret? She cleared her throat again, this time coughing before she spoke, staring at the bookcase filled with dusty, leatherbound volumes rather than at him. "I'm not sure what you mean. One of my students came back after practice while I did laps. Surely that's not an issue?"

He didn't respond at first but stared at her with those piercing eyes. She knew damn well he used it as a tactic to unsettle people. That didn't make it any less effective. She continued to study the books, counting the red and green volumes.

Her boss gave her a nod. "The young lady mentioned an unusual rash you have on your arms. Now," he held up his hand, "I'm not allowed to ask about any medical conditions, unless it poses a danger to our students. In which case, you must let the nurse know."

For a moment, Anna dared to breathe. Without a medical examination, which they couldn't insist upon, the university wouldn't know otherwise. She'd assure them she had nothing contagious.

"In addition, she mentioned you playing with the water."

The brief bloom of hope disappeared. *Fuckabiscuit.* Anna cocked her head, feigning innocence and meeting his gaze for the first time. Anna forced herself to give a smile. "I played with the water? I didn't realize I broke any regulations by splashing."

He pressed his lips together, again letting the silence lengthen. "Splashing would not be an offense. However, this young lady claimed she witnessed you performing magic."

Anna forced herself to laugh. "Magic? That's silly." For a moment, she considered asking if the girl had been drunk, but she refused to malign Tanya that way, not even to save her own skin.

He settled back in his chair. "Not so silly, lately. You must have seen the news. It's hard to miss the stories about these Unhidden talents all over the world. She claims what she saw must be magic, that you created a whirlpool floating above the water as clear as day. While this is hearsay," he cleared his throat, "I'm afraid recent events have necessitated a hard line when it comes to allegations of such powers."

As hard as Anna tried, she couldn't think of any mundane explanation to his accusation. Her forced smile faded into dread.

Ciara:

In the suburbs of Dublin

When her phone rang, Ciara let out a colorful curse and almost dropped her tea on the office carpet. When she saw who it was, she cursed again before glancing around to ensure she was alone. "Yes, this is Ciara."

Justine's voice sounded annoyed. "Why aren't you at the bunker?"

She swallowed. "Was I supposed to be? I never got notification. I'm at headquarters. If you need me there, I can be there in about forty-five minutes, depending on traffic."

"No, no, that'll be too late. Stay where you are. But next time, let us know you won't be coming."

Ciara gritted her teeth against her angry retort. It wouldn't do to argue back with Justine. That never worked out for the better. "Understood."

"I wanted to give you the heads up, though. We've got more talents coming through. Some heavy-hitters, too. At least four, possibly more. You'll need to get them placed and traced as soon as possible."

She chewed her lip. "That might be tricky. The Limerick Centre just graduated their lot, and they usually like some breathing room between classes. Wexford and Donegal are full. Drogheda isn't online yet."

"Then you'll have to convince the Limerick family to take them more quickly." Justine paused for so long Ciara thought the call had dropped. "Just make it happen, aye? We need this group to be effective, and fast."

Someone walked down the hallway. It must have been Martin, by the heaviness of the tread. She waited until the footsteps faded. "What's going on, Justine?"

"Nothing I can tell you. Nothing I know for certain, even. But there has been some intelligence that we need to be on our guard."

"On our guard? Against what? Are the Russians attacking? Do we have Nazis on our doorstep?"

She meant it as a joke, anything to lighten the mood, but Justine didn't cooperate with a chuckle. Instead, her tone turned even more grim.

"Don't rule anything out. Not now. Our organization is much too young to handle any sort of crisis yet."

Ciara swallowed and nodded, then realized Justine couldn't hear a nod. "Understood. I'll get things taken care of when the class arrives."

"See that you do."

Anna:

As Anna placed her personal items in a box, she glanced at the wall behind her desk. Photographs of her students over the years filled every space. Dozens of smiling faces, triumphant celebrations, and sweet personalities. She'd coached at the university for five years and loved the job with all her heart. To be dismissed over a few moments of unguarded play made her rage inside.

Anna slid her framed copy of Middle Earth into the box, beside her notebooks, Legolas mousepad, and ceramic Prancing Pony mug. As she did so, she noticed the webbing between her fingers had thickened. When she held her hand up to the light, the skin looked translucent.

She left the photos.

The university had no proof of any wrongdoing. She hadn't broken the law by having an Unhidden talent. But she worked in an at-will employment state so, in reality, they could dismiss anyone for any reason unless she proved discrimination against a protected class of citizen. And the Unhidden weren't a protected class.

Anna didn't know for certain if she even qualified as Unhidden. She suspected, of course. Normal people didn't make waves without touching the water or dry their hair instantly without a towel.

However, she'd need a lawyer to argue her case, and with her measly salary, she'd never be able to afford one. She glanced out the window at the rain. This would be a long, wet bus ride home. Anna covered the box with her waterproof jacket. She'd survive getting wet, but her things wouldn't.

As she exited the building to cross a field to the parking lot, someone hissed behind her. Anna turned, only to get hit in the forehead with a ball of mud. Startled and shocked, she stumbled back, dropping her box. The mug, the one her mother gave her before the accident, shattered. Anna sniffed back sudden tears. Her things scattered on the wet pavement as someone shouted in triumph. As a man shouted "mutant!", another mudball smacked her in the chest.

Anna gritted her teeth and stooped to gather her notebooks and keepsakes. Jeers and yells pounded against her head with raindrops. Another student threw mud, but it missed, smearing across her Middle Earth map. While glass covered the parchment, the cardboard backing already soaked up water.

As she swallowed a sob of frustration, Anna glanced up at her tormentors just as more mud flew toward her. This time, it hit her full in the face.

With a growl, Anna stood, facing the ring of over twenty people, both students and adults. Anna recognized one, a woman whose child she used to babysit, Marian, a secretary to one of the Deans. The savage rage on the woman's face shook Anna to her core. This attack just grew more personal.

Marian bent to pick up something from the field. Not mud this time, but a stone. Flashes of *The Crucible* ran through Anna's head, angry mobs hunting witches. Before Marian could fling her missile, Anna pointed at her. At first, she'd only meant to delay the woman long enough for her to pick up her things and escape. But when Anna saw anger and fright flicker on her face, something snapped inside.

The pounding rain ceased abruptly. A few people glanced up, confusion clear on their expressions. As the wind whistled in a sudden burst, a torrent of water slammed Marian's head. Pounded by the barrage of water, the woman screamed as she crumpled in the mud. Anna gulped, frightened by her own power.

The rain returned to normal, but astonishment, horror, and rage bloomed on the surrounding faces. Three people crowded close. One man grabbed her coat, yanking it half off, exposing her red, scaly arms.

Frantic now, Anna tore herself from his grip and shrugged her coat back on. She scrambled to gather stuff into the sodden cardboard box. She left her notebooks and concentrated on the items she couldn't replace, like the map. After clutching the disintegrating box to her chest, she pelted down the path to the bus stop, leaving enraged shouts and curses behind her. A thrown stone whistled past her ear.

She got to the stop just as the bus turned the corner. Thankful for wonderful coincidences, Anna glanced over her shoulder. The mob rushed toward her, but the bus arrived first. Her breath rasped in her throat and her lungs heaved as she scrambled on, the door shutting on her attackers. She'd make it. She'd escaped.

Anna stayed in her apartment that night and all the next day, but by the following evening, she needed to get outside. With a deep breath, she glanced out of her window first, to make sure no one gathered on the street. She'd woken from nightmares several times last night, and still had a hard time believing what had happened at the university.

She walked the three blocks to her favorite teashop, the place with old brick walls, fancy hats hanging on the wall, and so thick with old-world charm, she felt transported to another place and time. After placing her order for vanilla tea, she sat down and gazed out the window. The aroma of hot tea salved her soul, almost as much as the rain healed her skin.

Anna cradled her warm cup in the corner. Her hands no longer flaked, but a hint of fish-like scales rimmed the edge of her knuckles.

Instead of red, angry skin, they tinged greenish-blue, a lovely ocean color. She admired them as if she'd just gotten her nails done. They shimmered with iridescence.

A man stood next to her table. Anna glanced up as she hid her hands in her lap, but a hoodie shrouded his face. Hastily, she pulled her sleeves down to cover the damning scales, but he just dropped a pamphlet on her table and marched out the door.

Curious, she glanced at the title. A glossy picture of a stone castle and the word "Ireland" in a Celtic font emblazoned the front. Anna ran her hand over the shiny paper as she opened it. Inside the three-fold brochure, photographs of happy, freckled redheads beamed. She dismissed it as typical touristy crap until the word "Unhidden" jumped out. She forced herself to read the words.

"In Ireland, ten percent of the population show signs of Unhidden blood. As a result, it's become a haven for Unhidden around the world, those driven out of their homes and families. We welcome those with this gift to come home and be a part of a society which celebrates and cherishes our powers."

Anna's spine tingled with sudden longing. Ireland. Home to the PHAE, the Protectorate for unHidden Advancement and Education. *It sounds innocuous enough, but what would I do for a living?* If her body continued to change, she might become more than a swimming coach. She might even turn into something useful. She might even find a family who didn't detest her.

With the brochure spread out in front of her, she sipped her tea and studied the glossy pictures. Castles and pints of Guinness stared back at her.

She glanced out the window again, at the street sign. University Drive. She'd lost her job here. There didn't seem to be much point in trying to find another nearby. No other colleges in the area were large enough to need a swim coach, so she'd have to move regardless. And if she had to move, she could move anywhere.

How much would it cost to fly to Ireland?

The brochure had a website. She pulled it up on her phone and stared at the photographs and slick web design before any of the information registered.

According to the PHAE, they reimbursed travel costs for qualifying immigrants. What determined qualification? They funded research for a DNA blood test to determine who had Unhidden genes.

Testable DNA and pure-human protests didn't sound like a great combination. If the protesters had their way, they might use such tests for a more sinister purpose. This country had a horrible history with genetic racism, eugenics, and things like forced sterilization of anyone they deemed *undesirable.* Not quite as bad as Nazi Germany, but Anna had read about such things even into the 1980s, in living memory. If she could escape that, she would.

A bang made her jump, but it was only the door. A woman stepped in and glanced around. Her gaze fell on Anna and a small smile played across her lips. Anna didn't recognize her, but her blood chilled. The woman left, and Anna bolted the rest of her tea, practically running back to her apartment. Even if she didn't go to Ireland, this place was no longer safe for her.

Anna's footsteps echoed in the stark, empty apartment. She'd donated all her furniture to Goodwill. She refused to sell the last few boxes, her treasured Tolkien books and memorabilia. Her best friend said she'd keep them and would come collect them later, and then drop the key with the landlord. Anna didn't want to risk another day here. Marian knew her address. Anna had to leave town.

She wished she had more time to plan, but the scene at the university haunted her. No time to plan meant the only person she could talk to was her brother, Joel, and he wasn't a great option even in the best of times.

Anna hefted her stuffed purse and pulled out the handle of both her carry-on and her larger suitcase. She gave a last glance at the place she'd lived in for five years, ever since she took the job at SUNY Empire State in Rochester. While living alone had been a new adventure, at least she knew upstate New York. Anna had grown up here. She'd gone to college here. Now she'd leave here, perhaps forever. Her heart grew heavy as she shut the door behind her.

She spun around and ran back into the living room. Anna touched the windowsill where she watched the world, sipping her tea on rainy days. The paint along the edge had worn away from her leaning on it. After wiping away a recalcitrant tear, she sniffed. She stared at the shadowy corner where things moved in her imagination on dark nights, and at the sheer curtain that would brush her arm as she dozed off, startling her awake. Anna let out a ragged breath.

This time, when she closed the door, it remained shut.

The bus reeked of urine. Anna expected that, but the expectation didn't make the reality any nicer. Her sense of smell had dulled as her webbing grew. She counted that as a blessing.

She'd gotten into the habit of wearing long sleeves and gloves all the time. She wore those nylon things that looked like tattoos so if someone caught a glimpse of her hands, they might assume she wore some cosplay thing instead of actual scales.

Joel hadn't wanted to meet with her. Despite being her only sibling, they seldom visited since their parents died. But he'd agreed to be home when she arrived in Albany. He'd gotten back from the protest the day before, safe and sound.

The bus ride would take two hours. Anna prayed the seat next to her would remain open, but when an older woman sat next to her, she let out her breath in relief. An older woman would be much easier to deal with than a lecherous man. In all her thirty years, she'd never gotten the meet-cute bus companion romantic comedies insisted she deserved. This woman pulled out a book as soon as she settled into her seat. Anna pulled a book up on her phone, plugged her earbuds in, and played the *Hamilton* soundtrack as the bus rolled down the road.

It felt like only a few minutes had passed when they pulled into the Albany station. The rain slammed against the pavement outside, but she didn't mind. She'd always loved the rain, almost as much as she loved swimming, even before the changes came. That adoration made more sense now. Anna shoved that thought away and pulled up her brother's address on her phone.

One taxi later and a mad dash into the apartment building lobby, Anna shook the excess rain off her coat. She climbed the stairs to the second floor while dragging her luggage behind her, then rapped out their childhood knock on his door. Three knocks, a pause, and three more.

Just as she finished the last tap, her brother flung the door open, glared at her, and turned back into the apartment, trusting her to follow. She did, dropping her bag and coat near the door.

He crossed his arms, glaring at her with judging brown eyes. "Well? Is it cold enough for tea? Or do you want a Coke?"

"Tea, please. Do you have lemon?"

He held up a golden plastic bear. "Just honey."

"Blech. Just regular, then."

As Joel went through the motions of putting the teakettle on the stove, arranging the cups and the teabags, Anna studied him, especially his hands. She didn't notice a flaky rash or any webbing, but maybe his Unhidden blood manifested elsewhere.

World Health Organization bulletins said Unhidden people's powers grew over several months. However, some might take years to show. Her changes might have revealed themselves earlier than his, or he kept his hidden. Common consensus said the changes were genetic, but no one knew for certain.

The pundits made a game of guessing which talented people had these powers. Everyone agreed Freddie Mercury must have had siren blood. And who could deny Michael Phelps's ancestry now, with his full merman tail? Cleopatra must have been a succubus, at least on most bookie lists, because Heaven forbid a woman be so influential without supernatural beauty.

Not everyone had earth-shattering powers. Some minor talents had been discovered, like the ability to change ones' eye color, or to make a pencil spin on the table. She wished she had something to spin right now as her nervousness grew. Anna fidgeted with her webbed fingers and sighed.

As the teakettle screeched, Anna folded her hands in plain sight, waiting for her brother to comment on them. He didn't comply with her obvious invitation. Instead, he poured the tea and sat across from her at the kitchen island, his shoulders tense. "So. Anna. Say your piece."

Anna rolled her eyes. "Really? I travel two hours to talk to my brother, and you start with that? Cheesus Crisps."

He gave her a shrug. "What do you want me to say, Anna? Would you prefer an engraved invitation?"

With a cock of her head, Anna raised her eyebrows. "Maybe start with why the hell you went to a pure-human supremacist protest?"

His gaze dropped to his cup. "Just checking things out. They aren't bad people. They just want to make things better for the rest of us."

Anna splayed her hands on the counter. "The rest of whom, Joel?"

While staring at her hands, he furrowed his brow. His lip curled up as he leaned closer. "That's disgusting. What the hell happened to you? Did you have some sort of chemical accident?"

Unconsciously, she covered one hand with the other, and then forced herself to stop. "No. My skin is changing."

Joel drew back, shaking his head. "Gross. Your skin isn't changing, it's peeling off. What is that, leprosy? Do you need to go to the doctor? Is that why you came? Do you need money?"

Anna clenched her teeth so hard her jaw ached. "Joel. Stop looking at my hands. Look at me. This isn't some chemical accident. I don't have a disease. This is me. My blood. Your blood. We've got Unhidden blood. You know that stuff you just spent several days protesting against? That march filled with Nazis and eugenics and hate? Yeah. That's against us. We're Unhidden."

Her brother stared at her with a blank expression. Her older brother who'd always been so clever. Better at math and science, always able to beat her on trivia night. The brother who willingly threw himself into a fight with three bigger guys when they gave her a hard time during her senior year. The only relative she had left.

Joel, whose lip curled up again in growing disgust as he stared at the webbing between her fingers.

Her brother, who pulled away from her as if she held a ticking bomb about to explode all over his minimalist apartment. His expression of revulsion stabbed at Anna's heart.

"What the Hell is this crap? Are you one of those freaks?"

She wanted to yell at him, scream at him, make him face what he denied. Her own brother, the guy who'd taught her how to swim, who had helped her move into her first apartment. The guy who'd held her tight when her first boyfriend cheated on her.

But Joel was the only family she had left, so she tried once again. "We're family, whether you like it or not!"

"Get out, Anna. I don't even want to see you right now."

He wouldn't listen, not yet. Later, he might be willing to hear her. Now, escape seemed best.

Anna grabbed her bag, purse, and jacket, fleeing from the judgment and censure of her only family, feeling like she'd abandoned the fight. But she'd only launched the first shot across the bow. The next move was up to him.

She stared outside at the deluge. She should just call a taxi, but she needed the rain right then and, besides, what was the use of having waterproof luggage if she never needed the feature? Her body and blood craved clean water against her skin, with no chlorine or chemicals. She tied her jacket around her waist, pushed up her sleeves, and marched into the torrent.

The wetness sluiced down, and her skin sang. She tilted her head back to catch some drops in her mouth and spun in the delightful coolness of pure water.

Anna sauntered along the street, energized by the rain. She wished Joel lived near a lake or ocean, someplace she might dive into and swim free but, then again, she'd never liked swimming in a place where she couldn't see the bottom. Streets and buildings crowded around her as the rain soaked her to the bone. Everything in her purse would get ruined if she stayed out, so she ducked into the first cafe she found, one Joel had taken her to on her last visit.

She took the PHAE brochure out, staring again at the glossy photos. Maybe she should send them an email and ask some questions. What if they didn't want her? She'd have to describe her power, to make sure they'd be willing to take her in. Moving to another county, another continent, seemed impossible, but so did staying here.

The door to the cafe swung open, and the sound of whooshing tires in the rain intruded on her thoughts. Joel shook the water from his coat. His face didn't look sorry, but at least he wore a half-smile. Anna motioned for him to sit.

No other customers had remained in the coffee shop as the rain pelted down outside. Joel ordered his tea and sat down opposite her.

"How did you find me?"

"The only place that serves tea in the neighborhood? Give me some credit. And we've been here before."

Their conversation stuttered, full of awkward pauses and feigned pleasantries. Then he noticed the brochure and picked it up. "What fresh idiocy is this?"

With a shrug, Anna gave him a rueful smile. "Some guy dropped it off. I'm thinking about checking it out."

Joel's voice grew angry and dismissive. "You have got to be the most gullible person in the world, Anna. How do you know these aren't some sort of human traffickers?"

She let out a snort. "I'm not exactly a nubile teenager, ripe for some rich pedophile to rape, Joel. I turned thirty last month."

Her brother waved his hand. "Whatever. Do you think there aren't disgusting men out there willing to pay to get a drugged woman no matter how she looks? Your age doesn't matter."

With a roll of her eyes, she ignored his backhanded insult and snatched the brochure from his hand. "Don't you *whatever* me. When are you going to open your own eyes?"

Joel threw a cagey glance around the empty café. "Keep your damned voice down, Anna! Do you want someone to hear you? We can't talk about that here."

She blinked in mock innocence, cocking her head and keeping her voice at a normal volume. "Talk about what, Joel? Are you concerned about something?"

He glowered over his teacup. "Later, Anna. Later."

"Later, when?"

With a scowl, he took a gulp of tea, then slammed the cup down with a clatter. He clenched his jaw. "Why is it you're always asking me to do things?"

Anna furrowed her brow. "What are you talking about?"

"You always come to me for help. Joel, help me move. Joel, help me with my homework. When have I ever asked for your help, Anna?"

There must have been times, but not a single one came to mind. She furrowed her brow, trying to recall any example.

Joel rolled his eyes. "Exactly. You may be my sister but, in reality, all you are is dead weight."

After more regrettable conversation, Joel refused to let her stay with him, refused to admit he had Unhidden blood, and when she brandished the brochure as her only option left, refused to even take her to the bus station. Anna was on her own, leaping into a new life.

She picked up her phone and typed out an email before she could think, before she could reconsider, before she could talk herself out of it. Her finger hovered over the *send* button before she mashed it hard.

Anna swallowed. *There.* Now they know about her and what she could do. And since she told them she was coming to Ireland, they'd be expecting her.

Once her brother left, Anna trudged three blocks to the Greyhound station, dragging her luggage behind her.

The cheapest tickets, both bus and plane, forced her to travel mid-week. After the incident at the university, she didn't want to deal with crowds, but even mid-week, the station seemed full of people. The acrid scent of antiseptic cleaner assaulted her as she opened the door and wrestled her bags inside. When she checked the boards, she found her bus listed, but she'd arrived way early. Her anxiety about being late meant she came too early to everything.

The bus to Newark would arrive at terminal two. She settled into a plastic seat with the bus space in view and arranged her bags. Anna double checked the e-ticket on her phone and tried to quell the butterflies dancing in her stomach.

She'd have been less nervous with Joel by her side despite his tendency to bring out the worst in her. His betrayal still itched at her soul, much like her skin itched right now. She glanced at her hands, peeking under the gloves. The scaliness had faded, but it still burned red with irritation.

The announcement for her bus interrupted Anna's stewing. She sprang up and gathered her bag. After striding to the bus with all the confidence she didn't have, she waited in line as each passenger checked their luggage into the hold. When she climbed in, the stink of mildew and old sweat enveloped her. She breathed through her mouth and found a window seat near the back. If she kept her earbuds in, no one would speak to her.

A young man sat next to her, all elbows and angles. He wore earbuds as well, so she looked forward to a peaceful ride. She queued up the *Hamilton* soundtrack again and closed her eyes until the bus engine roared to life, startling her out of her trance.

She peered out the window and noticed one last passenger rushing for the doors. An older man, perhaps mid-fifties, panting, sweating, with a thinning comb-over. He hauled himself up the steps, glancing around the full bus for a seat. Grateful she already had a seating companion, she closed her eyes again until a hiss made her open them.

One beefy passenger stood, a frown creasing the lines of his saturnine face. "Where do you think you're going, freak?"

Anna stared at the newcomer, noticing his cat-slit yellow eyes. *He must be an Unhidden, unless he cosplayed with trick contact lenses.*

The man stammered, glancing down at his shoes. "I…I'm going to New York, just like everyone else here. Is there…is there a seat in the back?"

Two other passengers stood. A bleached blonde woman wearing a red T-shirt and a middle-aged man with a beer-belly. The woman sneered. "There's no room for you on this bus. Only humans get to ride. Freaks walk."

Her seatmate glanced at Anna, then back at the scene unfolding. She twitched her long sleeves down, though they hadn't ridden up enough to show her scaly skin. Anna shrank deeper into her seat and replaced one earbud, which had fallen out. She didn't put on her music, though, wanting to hear how this played out despite the fear hammering at her heart.

The newcomer's eyes flicked to each person confronting him. "I paid for my ticket. I deserve a seat."

The first passenger blocked his way. "Not on this bus. Try the next one. They might have room for freaks and animals." He stepped forward and the Unhidden man stepped back. Two steps, three steps, four, back to the door. He glared at the bus driver, who gave an apologetic shrug and placed his hands on the steering wheel.

With a disgusted huff, the Unhidden man climbed down the steps into the terminal. The three standing passengers followed him out. Anna tugged her gloves and sleeves into place again.

The bus driver stood, a scowl on his face, but the third man shoved him back down. "You'd better not leave us, either."

Anna didn't see what happened. She turned on her music and squeezed her eyes shut. But even with her music on, the sound of punching and kicking filtered in. They must have been right below her window. Grunts, cries of pain, angry shouts, and derisive laughter wove in a horrible counterpoint to her soundtrack. Sharp banging against the thin metal exterior of the bus made her jump, fear rushing through her veins. She dropped her phone and it hit the wheel well. An audible *crack* made her suck in her breath. Another bang against the side of the bus made her let out a whimper, which earned her another glance from her seatmate.

The aggressors re-entered the bus and sat in their seats, the first man's hair mussed. Only once the bus pulled away did Anna risk a glance back. The Unhidden man lay in a crumpled heap on the ground, smears of blood on his clothes and the concrete. He moved his arm, and she let out a breath of relief. At least they hadn't killed him. Anna swallowed hard, shoving back her own cowardice at not speaking up. But if she had, there'd be two beaten, bloody bodies on that terminal rather than one. No other passengers had spoken up, either.

With shaking hands, she retrieved her phone from the bus floor. A long crack across the face made her want to cry. At least it still turned on. The crack seemed like yet another betrayal in her life.

The screen flickered a few times before her music displayed. After cursing under her breath, she powered it down. Perhaps it just needed a rest. A few moments in silence made her change her mind and try it again. This time, it reluctantly flashed to life. Anna switched the music to *Hadestown* and let the familiar songs drown out her fears. Heavy raindrops pelted the window as they barreled down the highway toward New York City, her breath clouding the glass further, occluding her view.

The bus lurched, yanking Anna out of her doze. The young man next to her jerked awake and they exchanged a shy smile. She mustn't take safety for granted. As the man at the terminal showed, that naïveté might prove dangerous. Without her long-sleeved shirts and gloves, they'd accuse her of being a freak, too. They'd beat her into a quivering hulk of pain. Anna clasped her fingers tight to keep them from shaking, visions of mudballs flying at her face flickering in her memory.

The rain increased to a deluge. Sheets of water sluiced against the windows and the driver slowed. This part of the highway climbed hills and mountains, treacherous even in dry weather. Anna held her breath as the back of the bus fishtailed on a washout. Several other passengers let out gasps. If only she could make the rain stop, just until they passed. Then she might feel a little less like they would die in a fiery crash any minute.

A bump in the wheels and another slide made her grip the seat arms, her nails digging into the thin-padded plastic. For someone who didn't own a car, Anna hated not being in control of the vehicle.

Anna wished with all her might for the rain to stop. She wished hard, like when she tried to bring back Tinkerbell as a child. She clamped her eyes shut so tight, she grew dizzy, and the bus swirled in a whirlpool of possibilities. Light danced at the corner of her vision.

When Anna blinked her eyes open, the rain had lessened. Even if the change was coincidental, she'd distracted herself long enough for the worst to be over.

When the bus pulled into the massive airport complex, Anna waited until everyone got off before she rose. She'd already had enough of people to last her a week, and her journey had barely begun.

The man who'd been sitting next to her flashed a smile as she retrieved her bags. His freckles made him cute in an Ed Sheeran sort of way. "Where are you headed?"

Really? Four hours sitting next to me in silence, and now he wants to chat? "I think I'm in terminal four." He pulled her bag from the bus hold. Anna shouldered her purse and nodded thanks, reaching for the handle.

"Here, I can carry that for you. I think terminal four is this way. What's your name?" He grabbed the handle of one roller bag.

She ignored the question and pulled it out of his grip. "No, that's fine. I can carry my stuff. Don't you have your own luggage to carry?"

He shrugged and patted the duffel on his back. "Just this. I'm not flying international, so I don't need as much. Are you moving or something? That's a lot of stuff."

Too much information. She'd given away too much just with the terminal. With a smile, Anna walked toward the Aer Lingus check-in desk. The guy followed her. "Hey, don't be like that! Here, let me buy you a drink once we check in?"

Anna didn't want a drink. She didn't want to be sociable, not with thousands of strangers teeming around her. Her vision tilted and dizziness surrounded her. Shouting echoed in the back of her mind. She stopped walking and adjusted her grip on the luggage as if her hand slipped.

"If you just let me help you, you wouldn't have to drag all this." He put a hand on her shoulder and started to pull the bag off.

Anna shrugged away his hand, glaring at him. "Listen, I don't need any help, okay? I just want to get to my flight."

"Why are you being so weird? C'mon, I'm a nice guy. I promise." He flashed her another smile, all teeth and sincerity. It made her skin crawl.

A Native American woman came up behind him, wearing faded jeans, a white button-down shirt, and a formidable frown. "I believe the young lady asked you to leave her alone, young man. Take the hint. You wouldn't want to miss your flight, would you?"

As the jerk stalked away, flashing her a resentful glare, Anna swallowed her fear and smiled at her rescuer. "Thank you."

The other woman shrugged. "He had trouble written all over him. I'm Komie. Are you traveling alone?"

While alarm bells started ringing again, Anna felt gratitude for Komie's help. "Yeah. I'm Anna. Pleased to meet you."

"Well, Anna, I'm traveling to Ireland." She glanced at the check-in counter. "Are you flying Aer Lingus, as well?"

Anna nodded, willing herself not to blurt out anything. But the promise of protection called to her so strongly she ached to feel that warmth.

The woman patted her arm. "Then we can travel together. Once we check in, I sure could use a nice cup of hot tea. Will you join me?"

Perhaps being sociable wouldn't be so difficult with this woman. They checked in their luggage, got their boarding passes, and turned to find some tea just as shouts rang out. Anna's heart seized as she focused on the crowd near the TSA checkpoint. Banners and signs like those at the Washington DC protest shot up through the sea of people.

Anna halted, her legs no longer able to move. Komie had kept walking but turned back when she noticed she was alone. "Anna?"

She swallowed, pointing to the signs. When Komie followed her gesture, she shook her head. "Those are ignorant idiots. Don't let them bother you. Besides, we can go around them. There's plenty of room."

Even as Komie tugged on her arm, one face peeked out from the crowd. A face she knew well. Joel's mouth curled up in a satisfied grin as he pointed to her. "There's one, now!"

Chapter Two

"A happy family is but an earlier heaven."
– George Bernard Shaw

Michelle:

A farm near Limerick, Ireland

Michelle Byrne scrubbed a pan while staring out her kitchen window. The twins should be weeding, but they'd staged a battle with dueling water hoses. She smiled to herself, allowing them time for chaos before she imposed order upon their day. Last month had been rough for them all, and they needed a bit of play.

Music drifted from the hallway, so she shut off the faucet. Yes, that was her ringtone. With a sigh, she dried her hands and fetched the phone just as her husband, Colin, rushed in, brushing a hand through his short black hair.

She patted his hand as she answered the phone. "Hello, Byrne Farm."

"Michelle? This is Ciara. Have you got a couple minutes? I need to come by to discuss a few things."

Michelle pursed her lips. Ciara only ever wanted to discuss a new class, and they'd barely recovered from the last lot. But she had a duty, and she knew it. As her stress level rose, her hair curled, an annoying but mostly unconscious result of her Unhidden talent. "Sure and we're about to have tea. You're welcome to join us."

The lines of Colin's face grew deeper as he frowned. "Headquarters?"

Michelle nodded and leaned on the kitchen table. "Of course. I'll lay long odds she wants us to host another group."

Colin placed an arm around her shoulders and squeezed. "And you, so fond of gambling."

She let out a snort. "Aye, well, this pace would drive me to a flutter if nothing else did. Does she see us as some sort of talent factory? What does she think we are, Ireland's Next Top PHAE Talent?"

He pulled out a chair and sat next to her. "And if that is what she wants, will we say yes?"

Shaking her head, she gave a shrug. "Do we really have a choice? We told the PHAE we'd be willing to be an education center. But then, they'd get two or three a month. Now, they get that many a week. Many of them have dangerous powers and need to learn how to deal with them."

Colin rose, strode to the kitchen window, and stared out at the garden. "PHAE has three other centers and a fourth gearing up. We don't have to say yes."

"We made a promise. A vow. A contract," Michelle spat out the words.

He turned to her with pursed lips. "You don't need to snap at me, Michelle. I'm just offering valid alternatives. You're taking on too much. *We're* taking on too much. We are allowed to say no."

"And do you trust the PHAE to ensure this latest batch has the right support for their gifts? Or will they simply shuffle them off into field work without proper education? You remember what happened to that one poor lad."

Colin clenched his jaw but didn't answer.

In about twenty minutes, when the tall, elegant brunette arrived in her tailored suit and high heels, Michelle squared her shoulders. She'd always envied the other woman's sophistication. Michelle may not be big-city elegant, but she doubted Ciara could handle her farm.

After Ciara asked her expected question, though, Michelle's envy turned to frustration. She crossed her arms and took strength from her discussion with Colin. "No, we're not ready for another class yet. We've barely cleaned up from the last one! That boy who could turn water into chlorine wreaked havoc on the river before he learned how to control his talent. We're still finding dead fish all along the bank. And the neighbors are in a fine fettle."

Ciara paced around the dining room. "The Shannon's a big river. It'll be fine. How about a smaller class? We've four ready to send on. Anna's got power over water and can help with your cleanup. Max can talk to the wind. Nokomis makes plants grow, and Hiroki can convince people to do things."

Michelle choked out a laugh. "'Power over water'? You're not being too vague, are you? Like that lad who could make sparks? Sure and he burnt down the whole education center in Westmeath, with himself besides. You keep throwing these poor, lost souls into the ocean and hoping they learn how to swim. And they don't have minor talents, like ours. They need time, Ciara. Time to learn their powers, their capabilities, and how to control them."

While she took a deep breath to control her temper, Colin squeezed her shoulder. "Perhaps we should consider them, Michelle."

Michelle took a deep breath and locked gazes with her husband. His mouth said yes, but his eyes said no. Of course, he wanted to be polite to Ciara, to preserve his own position at PHAE, but Michelle had more leeway. Four would be too many. She might be able to take two, but that needed some negotiation tricks.

With a shake of her head, Michelle sliced her hand through the air. "No! They can go up to the Donegal farm if you need to place them so fast. And don't you have a new place in Drogheda now?"

Ciara picked her teacup up from the enormous woodblock kitchen table, cradling the bottom on her palm. She stared out the window at the ornamental and kitchen herbs growing in the garden. Bees buzzed around the flowers as she sipped her tea. "I wish I could. They just took three minor talents. Drogheda isn't ready for anyone yet. And the Wexford farm took another four. The Unhidden are flooding in faster than we can place them."

Michelle clasped her hands and spoke in a firm voice. "And we won't agree to take on students before we're ready. That was our agreement with the PHAE. If they wish to sign a new contract, they're welcome to offer one. I can't guarantee we'll sign it."

The Dublin woman stopped her pacing, her brown ponytail swishing over her shoulder. "Is that what you really want? To be removed from our list of education centers? I can do that if you want out. That'll hurt because you're our best teachers, but we don't want you teaching resentment to new recruits."

Colin let out a sigh and refilled his own cup with half tea, half cream. "Ciara, you know we love teaching new members. We just need to be able to define our pace. This is too quick for a full class. Sure and send over your first member. Let's see how she does, aye? Give us a day before sending the second one."

Michelle gave a sullen nod. "Fine. We can teach her how to clean the river first. Then we'll set her to cleaning the rooms. The last class left them in a disaster, and our own children are wrecked keeping up with them."

Ciara gave a sly smile. "What if I send over Paul and Martin to help with the cleaning tomorrow, and send Max and Anna together the next day?"

With a roll of her eyes, Michelle said, "Fine. Make sure they bring cleaning supplies. And no pranks this time! My rosebushes have only just recovered from last time."

Colin gave Michelle a kiss on her cheek, which earned him a wrinkled nose and a smile. He drank down the rest of his milky tea. "What're the new students' stories?"

With a sigh of relief, Ciara sat with her hands flat on the table. Perfectly manicured maroon nails contrasted with the rough blond wood. "Anna Taylor. She's just flown in from Rochester, New York. She can literally lift water into the air, but with very little control or finesse. She still needs a thorough assessment of her capabilities. And Max…" Ciara paused and rolled her eyes, "well, Max Hurley is a bit of a handful. Mid-sixties, a Vietnam vet from Australia. Let's just say he has some authority issues. He talks to the winds, and they listen."

Michelle cocked her head. "Offensive talents? We don't get many of those. Have they explored their limitations?"

Ciara shook her head. "Not yet. Anna's wary of her own power, and doesn't like deep water, ironically enough. But she's a sweet lass. She worked as a swimming coach at university, but she's people-shy. Max has been using his power to help with his Outback flying tour business, but not much more. I'll send them over tomorrow, then?"

Michelle rose, rinsing her cup out in the sink. "No. Send Paul and Martin first. Give us a day to finish cleaning. I'll send my Róisín to headquarters to get her measure and make friends. The lass will feel more comfortable if she's met one of us first. Max sounds like he will arrive prickly no matter what."

Anna:

Komie yanked her arm to pull her away from the crowd of protesters. Anna's eyes locked with Joel's, and she wanted to scream, to ask him why, maybe even to punch him in the nose.

The native woman kept pulling her down a hallway. "This way!"

Tearing her eyes from Joel, Anna moved her feet and ran, dragging her bag behind her. "Where are we going?"

"I don't know, but anywhere is better than there. Look! Employees only."

Anna drew back. "We can't go in there!"

"Of course, we can. We're in danger, and they will help us."

She wished she had Komie's confidence, and her heart raced as they opened the forbidden door. They stepped into an empty lounge, a round table in the middle, with a fridge and a coffee pot along one wall. After the noise and danger, this felt oppressively silent. "Now what?"

Komie pointed at another door on the far wall. "We go through there." Anna followed with reluctance but also budding curiosity. What happened if someone found them? Would Komie be able to talk them out of getting arrested? Or was this how her adventure would end, being put in jail for trespassing in off-limits airport areas?

The day's events suddenly slumped on her shoulders, and she wanted nothing more than to curl up and take a long nap. Komie led her through several empty halls, past a few closed doors, and then through another door.

They'd made it into the main terminal, and the angry protesters were nowhere to be seen. Anna let out a deep sigh of relief tinged with hysteria. They'd made it.

She let Komie get her on board the airplane, even let her put the carryons away. Finally, as the plan glided into the atmosphere, Anna closed her eyes and slept. When she woke, she'd be in Ireland. A new life, a new world, a new chance.

Anna:

Anna stared at the massive Irish mansion covered in ivy. Its imposing grandeur made every muscle in her body scream to run away, run back to the plane, back to Rochester, back to her efficiency apartment, and back to the dean to beg for her job back. But the angry faces of the mob that drove her off campus haunted her memory, and her brother's betrayal at the airport made it hurt even more. Komie had helped her scoot out of that situation, and she thanked whatever providence had brought them together at the right time. She squared her shoulders to face her new life. Would these new people welcome her? Would they become her new family? Or would she have to escape again?

Behind her, the other passengers disembarked and the minibus from the Dublin airport drove away. They had no escape now. Her own face dripped from humidity and nerves. For a moment, she considered wiping away the moisture with her water magic, but the last time she'd tried that, her skin almost cracked from dryness, and her skin tended to get red and scaly anyhow, especially on her arms. She hadn't learned to use her power with finesse yet.

Anna glanced back at the other passengers. They were folks like her, those who had left their homes around the world to come to Ireland, at the vague promise of sanctuary from a world turning against them. Other talents no longer welcome in their old lives. Komie, of course, with long braids shot with silver. An older Australian man named Max with his sun-dark face and a long ponytail. A Japanese man named Hiroki, who looked younger than her own thirty years.

Unhidden.

At least here, she didn't have to hide her strangeness. They wouldn't be chased away by an angry mob. Here, they could be who they were. Even more, they'd be encouraged, taught, nurtured for their abilities, or so she'd been told. Anna heartily prayed that these assurances were true.

Together, they grabbed their luggage and marched to the solid wooden double doors with ornate ironwork hinges. The Aussie man pounded the knocker three times.

Almost immediately, the door swung open, revealing a tall, elegant woman with straight brown hair and a huge smile. "Welcome, all of you! I'm Ciara Doherty, head of the admissions department, and I'll be your PHAE liaison. Come into reception and we'll get you sorted straight away. Paul, here, will take your bags to your rooms. You should only be with us a few days as we get you assigned to one of our centers."

As Ciara's gaze fell upon Max, he groaned. A knowing grin spread across her face. "Fancy seeing you here, Max."

He raised his eyebrows. "Fancy that, pet. Dropped your husband in the ocean, then?"

She gave him a shrug. "Brian's at the Belfast office."

A young man with long straight hair and a scruffy goatee, looking like a grinning Jesus, grabbed her suitcase. She didn't want to let go, but she forced her fingers to uncurl, ignoring their itching skin. That bag represented all her remaining worldly goods. She'd sold or given away all her stuff, furniture, everything but the books she left with her best friend. Letting go of her suitcase felt like the last bit of her comfortable life being ripped away.

As Paul disappeared around a corner, Anna crossed the threshold into the mansion. The spacious entry hall, flanked by two curved staircases, looked straight out of a period drama. Plush red carpeting led to a library on the left and a drawing room on the right.

The others shuffled in behind her, and Anna hastily stepped to the side, chiding herself for acting like a country bumpkin amazed by opulence. Still, she admired the gilt cornices and carved banisters. When Ciara led the group through the library, she ached to explore the floor-to-ceiling bookcases, with a warm cup of tea and some cucumber sandwiches with the crusts cut off.

Past the library, a study had been set up like a classroom. A screen dominated one wall, with a half-dozen chairs and tables. Ciara took her position at the screen, gesturing at each of them to find a seat. Anna took a seat on the end and folded her hands under the table, scratching the skin on her hands. She wished she'd thought to pull the lotion from her bag.

Paul entered, pushing a cart loaded with coffee, tea, and sandwiches, so echoing her wish in the library, Anna wondered if he could read minds. But no, the food must have been prepared before their arrival. She waited until the others got their refreshments before pouring a cup of tea and taking an egg salad sandwich as she spied no cucumber ones.

While she nibbled her sandwich, Ciara turned on the screen. A photograph of the house they'd just entered almost glowed golden in a late afternoon light. "The house you're in is the international headquarters for PHAE, the Protectorate for unHidden Advancement and Education. You will be here for a few days, learning about the organization, while we sort out long-term accommodation for each of you. You will also be given a DNA test. Just a cheek swab, mind you, no needles involved. This will help us in our research to discover a genetic marker for Unhidden talents."

She took a sip from her water bottle before continuing. "Once that's done, we will send you to one of several education centers located throughout the country, where you will learn about your talents, how to use them, their limitations, and how you might be part of the organization."

Komie raised her hand. "Will we be assigned positions? Or will we be able to choose?"

"You will be given a wide array of choices. This is a volunteer organization not a work camp." Ciara grinned, lessening the harshness of her words, but Komie didn't return the smile.

"And what of those Unhidden who are unable to work? Those too old, ill, or disabled? Are they also accepted in your organization?"

Ciara's grin disappeared. "We accept all with talent, Komie. If they cannot work, then we find a place for them to live. We take care of our own." She pressed a button on her laptop. The image shifted to a large farmhouse, more ivy covering the façade, and a smiling family out front, waving to the camera. "This is one of our centers in Limerick. We have others in Drogheda, Donegal, and Wexford, with more being organized. As Unhidden make their way to Ireland, the need rises each month."

The Australian man snorted. "Why's everyone coming here, then? I'm only here because this bloke insisted." He pointed his thumb at Hiroki, who tried to shrink into his seat. "That and my plane burnt up."

Ciara gave a patient smile. "Excellent question, Max. From what we can tell, while Unhidden are a very small percentage of the world's population, the Irish have demonstrated a higher incidence of these powers.

Therefore, this has become the natural choice for headquarters. We've been working closely with the government of the Republic of Ireland to ensure we have the resources we need while being respectful of their sovereignty. Our folktale tradition is strong, and we've always been believers in the strange and unusual."

"And the locals accept that?"

"Well, some folks are protesting in the city, people who would rather us go elsewhere, but we'll never please everyone."

Max let out another snort, and Komie shot him a quelling glare, but he ignored her and knocked back half his cup of black coffee.

Ciara squared her shoulders. "Once you have explored the extent of your powers, we will evaluate your talents and offer a range of possible positions within PHAE."

As Ciara continued, Anna wondered what she might do with her talent. While she had power over water, she hadn't had time to explore the practical aspects. Why would anyone need to create hand-sized waterspouts? And she harbored a deep fear of water, especially anything she couldn't see the bottom of, so working in the ocean or rivers would be right out.

The image switched to one of a busy city harbor. "This is Dublin Harbour. We have our administrative complex located in a secure underground bunker. That's where the majority of our operations are managed, safe from prying eyes."

As Hiroki let out a soft sigh at the engineering marvel, Anna hoped they wouldn't send her to a bunker. That seemed so horribly World War II. Scenes from grainy, black and white movies her father used to watch flickered through her mind, each one full of old, serious white men. Beachhead invasions, submarines, and Pearl Harbor images melded into each other. Eventually, they merged into an image of Winston Churchill, and then faded into darkness, like the ending of a film.

The PHAE representative switched off the screen and opened her arms. "And that's everything you need to know at the moment. Any questions?"

Anna realized she'd zoned out and missed a good chunk of Ciara's presentation. She glanced at the other inductees, silently begging them to ask Ciara to repeat herself, but they didn't listen.

Michelle:

Fire crackled in the pit, hissing at the damp firewood. Colin and Michelle held hands as they sat on their bench. Brendan sat next to his sister, Róisín, while Liam, Hugh, and Fiona sat on the third bench.

As each of their children each settled with juice, cider, or tea, Michelle cleared her throat. "You must have heard that Ciara rang today. She's gathering a new group of students to join us."

Fiona clapped with glee and let out a yelp of excitement. Liam rolled his eyes at his younger sister, but Róisín's eyes sparkled. "Will I go fetch them from Dublin, then?"

"Maybe. Ciara said that depends on when they fill the class. They've got an American woman and an older man from Australia due in a few days. I've asked Ciara to give each new set of entrants some time to settle in before sending another pair." She glared at Liam and Hugh. "This time, the two of you had best behave. None of your shenanigans like the last time. Do you understand?"

Hugh glanced at his twin, their expressions a mixture of chagrin and mischief.

"I'm serious. If you can't follow the rules, you won't be allowed to help at all. Not even during the evening stories."

They both lowered their gaze and nodded. Michelle narrowed her eyes but took their assent at face value. For now.

Colin swigged his cider. "Remember, no arguing about chores or who gets assigned to whom." He glared at Liam and Hugh, who made faces back at him.

Michelle turned to Róisín. "They'll send a few folks to help us clean, and then you can go get the newbies. Call us if you need anything, understand? Anything at all."

"I'll be fine, Mam. Really, I will. I'm excited to go."

"Dublin is a much bigger city than Limerick."

Róisín rolled her eyes. "I know, Mam. I've been to Galway and Cork. I'll be fine in Dublin. Besides, it's not like HQ is downtown. It's a good twenty minutes into the suburbs."

Colin crossed his arms, giving his eldest daughter a stern look. "Call us when you arrive, mind."

After the children went to bed, Michelle left the kitchen, drying her hands on a kitchen towel. Colin sat in his chair, staring at the peat fire. "Colin? Are you okay?"

He turned with a half-smile. "Well enough, my love. Just thinking about Róisín. Are you sure it's wise to let her go to Dublin?"

After rolling her eyes, Michelle sat on the arm of the faded overstuffed chair, rubbing her husband's back with one hand. "She's twenty-seven years old and a grown woman. We raised her to be sensible and capable. Besides, what else can she learn here? She needs experience at headquarters. She needs to learn more about her healing powers. Do you want to keep her stuck in the west country forever?"

"No, of course not. But Brendan doesn't want to leave, and he's just a year younger."

"Brendan loves teaching whenever a new class comes in. Of course, he doesn't want to leave. They may be siblings, but they have different lives and different drives."

"Fair enough. I just worry."

She kissed him on his forehead and smoothed his hair. "If you didn't worry, I'd know the fairies had taken you away. I'd expect nothing else. The hour's getting late, now. Come to bed."

Max:

Maximilian Hurley waited his turn for a DNA test with poor patience. His hands grew slick with sweat, and he wiped them on his jeans. Whispers in the back of his skull tickled, but he pushed them away. He resisted the urge to run out the door, down the road, and all the way to the airport. Bloody hell, he'd run back to Australia if he wouldn't drown first.

He glanced at the young woman next to him. She'd arrived the day before, helping them with their orientation. Her constant sunniness annoyed Max, but her pretty smile made up for it. Róisín broke into his thoughts by placing a gentle hand on his arm. "This'll be quick and painless. They just need to swab your cheek. It won't hurt in the slightest."

He glanced at her and back at his hands, now clasped tight in his lap. Memories of too many white coats and grim expressions flashed in his mind from his stint in Vietnam. He shoved those away, too, along with the rage and frustration that always followed. "Doctors are fucking sadists."

Róisín gifted him a brilliant smile and, for a moment, he forgot she was young enough to be his granddaughter. Well, maybe his daughter. "They'll be gentle, I assure you. Dr. Claire's fantastic and kind."

He swallowed and glanced at the ornate door, willing it to remain closed. This PHAE group had repurposed an enormous manor house into their headquarters. Eighteenth century oil portraits looked surreal while he waited for a DNA test. He stared at a war scene filled with fantasy creatures.

Róisín poked him in the ribs and pointed at the painting. "That's the Battle of Magh Tuireadh."

"The what of what?"

She let out a giggle. "An Irish battle from our ancient myths, between the Fir Bolg and the Tuatha Dé Danann."

"If you say so." That sounded just as unintelligible as the Aboriginal myths he'd been taught as a child. He wiped his hands on his jeans again as the door opened. Róisín offered a hand to help him to his feet. He jerked his hand away and rose himself. With a deep breath, he pushed back the clamoring fears and entered the room.

A metal examination table covered with tissue paper stood along one wall, next to a coffee table covered in specimen bottles, swabs, and pre-printed labels. At least the wood-paneled room bore no resemblance to that hospital in Adelaide. The doctor, a striking woman his own age, with blue eyes and gray hair pulled back in a severe bun, glanced up from her clipboard. "Mr. Maximilian Hurley?"

He pushed the words through a dry throat. "That's me, luv."

"Have a seat, Mr. Hurley. I'm Dr. Claire, and this won't take long at all. Now, can you verify your date of birth for me?"

He sat on the metal table and didn't know what to do with his hands, so he wiped them again. "April 1st, 1951. I was my own mother's April Fools joke."

She ignored the banter, made a note, and picked up a blood pressure cuff. "Can you hold out an arm? Either one will do."

Max stared at the cuff as she tightened it and pumped air in. Her stethoscope stabbed like ice on his skin despite his perspiration. Then she took his temperature, clicking a bit when she got the results. "Hmm. A little high, but not unusual for a man of your age. Now, open your mouth wide."

Max opened his mouth, holding back a sarcastic remark about his age. He wanted to wipe away the sweat dribbling down his cheek. His heartbeat raced as she approached with a cotton swab. His memory flashed to the doctor in Khánh Hòa and the pain that came from that visit. He fought the urge to shove her away and flee.

Sounds hammered at his memory, sounds he didn't want to hear. Helicopters diving into a village. Screams. Fire. Pain. He wished the whispering voices plaguing him since he arrived in Ireland would return just long enough to drown out the screams but, perversely, they remained silent. *Bloody lot of good they are, then.*

He needed something, anything, to anchor him in the here and now rather than the pain and fear of his past. Max shut his eyes and thought of Róisín's sweet smile. But her smile morphed into Trina's. Her long, thick, black hair, with a tinge of red when she stood in the sun. Her lilting French-Vietnamese accent. Her soft cheek as he caressed her skin. Max fought back tears of loss and regret.

"Grand, you can shut your mouth now. All done. Thank you, Mr. Hurley."

He caught his breath and jumped down from the table. His legs threatened to buckle, so he held himself steady before allowing the doctor to lead him out. Róisín took his arm. "Now, that wasn't so bad, right?"

Chapter Three

"Call it a clan, call it a network, call it a tribe, call it a family.
Whatever you call it, whoever you are, you need one." – Jane Howard

Anna:

Leaving headquarters in Dublin

After she'd packed that afternoon, and Paul helped her bring her bags to the door, an Irish woman about her own age, with shoulder-length honey-blonde hair, introduced herself as Róisín Byrne. "I'll be taking you to my parents' farm. Don't worry, they don't bite. And it's a lovely drive, about two hours. We should arrive just in time for tea."

As she settled in the car, Anna gave Róisín a shy smile. The Irish woman seemed really sweet, but Anna's stomach still roiled from fear and anxiety. All afternoon, she'd debated just leaving PHAE headquarters and taking her chances in Dublin, but that notion frightened her even more. What had possessed her to drop her entire life and move to a new country? Sure, she'd had that nasty fight with Joel. But she'd quit her job because of the angry mob not her brother.

Anna shuddered as she remembered the frightening violence that had prompted the move but still hadn't processed the reality. Almost as if Róisín read her mind, the Irish woman asked, "Do you regret leaving your home? You lived in New York, right?"

With a swallow, Anna glanced into the back seat at Max, but he'd fallen asleep with his head against the window, a line of drool already dripping from the corner of his mouth. "Yeah, but upstate, in Rochester.

Not New York City." Everyone always assumed she meant the city when she mentioned New York, as if that was the only part of the state.

"What made you take the plunge, if you'll pardon the pun?"

Anna let out a humorless chuckle. *Plunge. Water. Very clever.* "I got fired after someone caught me making a tiny water funnel with my mind in the college pool. I fell into some ugliness after that."

Unhidden they'd shrieked at her, like a vicious epithet. When she got to Ireland, the label didn't seem so bad, as lots of people had these strange new talents, and they wore the epithet as an honor.

"And you came straight to headquarters when you arrived? Or did you explore Dublin first?"

"No, I headed to PHAE first. I didn't want to get lost." Or run into another mob. Instead of a mob, PHAE offered her endless forms to fill out. As a teacher, she understood paperwork. It gave her something to concentrate on rather than the fear screaming in the back of her mind.

After filling in all the forms, having a lovely meal, and meeting the staff, they'd shown her to a room. Still in shock from all the changes in her life, Anna had stared at the four-poster canopy bed. "That settles it. I'm officially in a freaking fairy tale."

She imagined herself as a princess waiting for Prince Charming and laughed at her silly fancies. That's what she got for tossing her entire life away and moving to Ireland based on the promises of a glossy brochure.

Now, just a few days later, this mysterious agency was shipping her off to some farm on the west coast for education and training with a family. Their family? PHAE as a whole? Anna didn't know and didn't have enough gumption to ask.

Knots returned to Anna's stomach. Not as bad as the bus ride to the airport, where she had to escape a group of protestors, including her own brother. Nor as bad as the flight to Ireland or arriving at headquarters. Still, the rapid succession of trying situations had exhausted her both mentally and physically. She adjusted her long sleeves and gloves to cover her scales and glanced at the countryside flying by the car window.

Róisín chattered as she drove down the two-lane highway. "I trained to be a vet, as I've always had a bit of a healing touch, and I love animals. Grew up on a farm. They don't keep animals now, but we had scads of them growing up. Horses, cows, pigs, chickens, ducks. Now, we just have the woods and Mam's garden. Which is good, because I quit the vet's office when Mam and Da joined up with PHAE. I help them out at home and at headquarters. They've got me shuttling folks around lately, now that more and more Unhidden are arriving all the time."

After they passed Limerick, the road narrowed to one lane, with tight hedgerows on either side, the trees forming a canopy above. They came to the literal end of the road, driving up to a large gate with iron horses, flanked by a decorative stone wall. Róisín opened an app on her phone, and the gates opened inward.

The driveway wended through thick pine woods, revealing a beautiful farmhouse, the one Ciara had shown them in the introductory presentation. A three-story gray stone building with arched windows, bright red shutters, and ivy clinging to the façade. Anna counted ten windows in the front, but as they pulled around, it looked at least two rooms deep. Outbuildings lined one side of the back garden while two barns and a stable loomed on the other side, with several trails winding into the surrounding woods.

She'd definitely fallen into a storybook.

A mature woman with reddish-brown hair and laugh lines emerged as the car stopped. Róisín hopped out and gave the older woman a fierce hug, so Anna assumed this to be Róisín's mother, Michelle Byrne, which would make the tall man with dark hair Colin, Róisín's father. After that, the gaggle of children running out to meet the bus became too much for Anna, so she concentrated on retrieving her bag. Max yanked his duffel bag out and, with a grunt, handed her the other.

Róisín set up a line for the host family and led Anna past them, like a reception line at a wedding. After Colin and Michelle, Róisín introduced her eldest brother, Brendan, tall like their father, with dark hair down to his chin, reminding her of Keanu Reeves. She gave him a shy smile, and he returned it with a grin before turning to shake Max's hand.

Next came the twin blond boys, aged ten as announced with pleased expressions, Liam and Hugh. Róisín had confided tales of these two hellions and their hijinks on the drive down. The youngest daughter, Fiona, had red hair and freckles shining bright against her pale Irish complexion.

By the time Róisín led Anna down the reception line, she repeated the names to herself until she had them pat, though telling the twins apart would be a challenge.

With the introductions finished, Michelle clapped her hands. "All right, everyone inside! We've laid out a welcome tea for you both. Brendan will carry your bags to your rooms, and you can settle in when the meal's over. This way!"

Anna didn't want to give up her purse, but Brendan insisted. "Don't worry, Anna. I'll bring them to your room upstairs. I'll take good care of your things, I promise." He flashed her a warm smile. She got tongue-tied and surrendered her belongings even as she tweaked her sleeves down to cover her arms. Róisín gave her a wink as she took Max's duffel and followed her brother inside.

They walked through the front room into the kitchen, complete with a thick wooden table, like in the servants' kitchen in *Downton Abbey*. The rustic table, despite its sturdiness, almost creaked with the dishes upon it. A whole ham, lamb, with an enormous bowl of potatoes. Then carrots, onions, and other mixed root vegetables in the middle. The other end had bread, butter, honey, several cheeses, and a bowl of apples. The feast looked large enough to feed an entire swim team.

For a flash, she missed her job coaching the swim team. Then the image of mudballs being thrown at her face reminded her that she'd left for a very good reason.

Michelle held up her hands. "Plates are here on the sideboard. Take a plate, take some silverware, and choose what you like. Napkins and drinks are in the dining room, just through that door. Save room for dessert!"

Anna's stomach rumbled. When she reached for a cup, her long sleeve rode up her arm. She glanced to either side to see if anyone noticed the slip. After she tugged it back down to cover her scales, she filled her plate and found a place at the table. One by one, the family sat. Once again, she repeated their names in her head to keep her memory sharp.

Anna had never tasted lamb, so she took a small slice and chewed. Not quite like beef, but not like venison, either. She tried another bite and decided she liked the taste. The bread, potatoes, and dessert all tasted equally delicious. Her student budget had never allowed such rich food, and her salary as a swimming coach hadn't been much better. At least she wouldn't have to subsist on cheap ramen noodles every night.

The family chatted of things to be done the next day, such as weeding the garden or chopping wood for the firepit. Anna's anxiety drained her energy, and she fought to keep her eyes open despite being early evening. When she stifled a yawn, Brendan appeared at her shoulder again, taking her plate and bowl. "Here, I'll take those into the kitchen. Be right back."

When he returned to collect her, she gave the room a hasty wave as he led her up the stairs and to the left. They walked by white-plastered walls with dark wood beams. As they passed several open doors, she peered inside. A different color scheme decorated each room, which had a sink and a double bed.

Halfway down the hall, Brendan turned into one with pale green walls, flower borders near the ceiling, and green satin covers on the bed. "This'll be your room. I've set your bags in the closet, and there's a press for your clothes. You'll have to share the toilet down the hall when the others arrive."

A toilet down the hall might also mean a bathtub, something she could soak in to relieve her itchy skin. But with a shared bathroom, soaking would be hogging the facilities. She might ask Brendan for a bucket, and she'd just plunge her arms into it whenever she felt the need.

"Others?"

He opened her window a crack, letting in the cool breeze. "Well, Max is down in the outbuildings, but Ciara mentioned others in a few days. You might have met them already at HQ. Hiroki and Nokomis, I think. That should keep you comfortable through the night, but if the night gets too chilly, the window's easy to close. You must be tired after a long day."

Once again tongue-tied, Anna nodded thanks and walked to the window, rubbing her sleeves. She sat in the window seat as Brendan sat beside her. The evening sun painted the back garden orange. Near midsummer, the nights seemed to come late in Ireland, even later than in upstate New York. She drew in a breath at the manicured beauty, several benches and walkways winding amongst two fountains.

Brendan followed her gaze and let out a chuckle. "That's Mam's pride and joy, that is. She said you can spend all summer growing food and animals but, at the end of the day, you need to enjoy the beauty of growing things. She's planned that entire thing out, and we built it for her." His grin showed he didn't resent the labor.

Then he clapped his hands on his thighs and rose. "Right, I'm off, then. Take some time to settle in and come down to the orientation meeting in the morning. Mam rings a big bell for meals and meetings. If you need anything, I'm two doors down on your left. Come into the hall, and I'll show you." He pointed at a red door. "Mam had them all painted different colors to keep the confusion down. Yours is green, like your décor."

"Does that mean your room is painted red?"

He rolled his eyes. "So it is, though I've covered the walls with posters. Gave me nightmares once or twice after I watched a horror movie."

Anna giggled as he left. She retreated to her new sanctuary and closed the door. Brendan seemed so helpful and adorable. Best not to let herself get too attached, though. She had a horrible habit of developing a crush on any young man who showed her kindness, and she'd probably not be here long. He must help a new batch of recruits every few weeks, from what Róisín said. And that lingering worry about being run out of yet another home still hovered in her mind.

Anna arranged her clothes in the chest of drawers, placed her toiletries on the sink counter, and sat on the bed, her hands folded. This room seemed homier than a dorm, but not as comfortable as her own place.

She leaned against the windowsill to enjoy the garden, letting out a deep sigh and trying to calm her beating heart. Her first night in a strange place always triggered her anxiety. She'd just gotten used to the place in Dublin after a few days, but now she needed to start all over.

For a moment, her mind flashed back to her old apartment and watching the world while sipping tea. In Rochester, she lived on a busy street, and loved watching the cars drive past. She especially liked when it rained, with the *whoosh* of tires on wet pavement. This window had a much better view.

As she studied the garden, she spied Michelle and Colin sitting on a bench, holding hands. How sweet to be married for so long and still be so affectionate.

What was it like to live with someone for so many years? Róisín must be almost her own age. That meant, what, thirty years of marriage? Anna couldn't get her head around that. If her parents still lived, the concept might not seem so alien.

After swallowing down a knot of envy, Anna pulled out her cracked phone, peeled off her gloves, and set an alarm for the morning. Once she removed her shirt, she rubbed her forearms, now almost fully scaled. Their smooth coolness felt like snakeskin but sensitive to the touch, as if she still had skin. They sparkled in the fading sunlight slanting through the window.

Her eyelids drooped, and she let out a jaw-cracking yawn. Today had been so eventful, filled with more drastic changes. She looked forward to a time when she could stay in one place again and not travel halfway across the world.

Anna curled up on top of the duvet, praying she'd fall asleep quickly, but her mind raced with all the new people, places, and ideas.

Max:

The next morning, Max stretched and cracked awake. He'd slept well enough, and his normal nightmares had taken a welcome holiday, at least for now. This place seemed too bloody sweet and sickly to be real, but at least the bed felt comfy. A vast improvement on the lumpy thing he'd called a mattress back home.

After dinner, Róisín had led him into the garden. Suspicious, he glanced around and halted. "You got me in a tent or something?"

She'd shaken her head with a chuckle. "No, no, nothing so primitive. We've four outbuildings made into guest quarters. They used to be for the staff. You'll have to share a shower but other than that, they're lovely."

When she'd brought him to the second one, he had to admit the flat looked loads better than his barracks had in the war. To be fair, more luxurious than his own trailer back in Coober Pedy. That thing had seen better days. Hell, it'd seen better decades. But if his plane hadn't been destroyed, he'd still be happily taking cheap tourists on third-rate plane tours across the Outback.

But his plane *had* been burnt, so here he stood, halfway across the world and completely lost. *God, but I need a drink.* As lovely as she looked, he couldn't wait until Róisín left him alone so he could knock back a slug from his flask.

Once alone, he'd drunk half the contents and frowned. He'd have to find a re-supply right quick. They'd passed a pub in town, which didn't seem too far down the road.

He scrubbed his face, sniffed under his arms, and then scrubbed those as well. Travel always made him sweat, and this trip had been rough.

Even before the poking and prodding at headquarters, he'd been a mess after the flights from Australia. Max had issues flying commercial. Not being in control usually gave him a fit, and this trip had been no exception.

He still ached to be up in his plane, and he'd been promised a new one to join this freak show, but Hiroki'd warned him he'd need to jump through some hoops first. Fine, he'd jump. But only so far and so high before he'd raise a stink. He'd gotten pretty good at raising a stink, with plenty of practice.

He sort of missed Hiroki, but the Japanese man had said he had to stay in Dublin for a while. "I have been assured I can join you later, Max. I've some other tasks they wish me to complete before I join you at the Byrne Farm."

"So, they take the only bloke I know on the whole island and send me somewhere else? I already don't like this deal."

"They will take excellent care of you. They have assured me of this."

"Yeah, I've been assured of that before. Never bloody comes true, though."

With a deep sigh, he pulled on his shorts and walked outside, searching for the shared bathroom. Róisín had pointed the door out last night, but the whole yard looked different in the morning light. Once inside, he took a quick shower, blessing the hot water in this cold, damp place. After brushing his teeth and hair, he returned to his rustic cabin room.

After dressing, he slid his half-full flask into a pocket and entered the main house in search of coffee. He needed plenty of that before folks started talking to him. As soon as he opened the back door, however, Róisín's smiling face made him stumble back. "Max! We've been expecting you!"

His mood improved immediately, and his lined face cracked a wide grin. "Well, my day's looking up already. What's the story, luv?"

"Please, come right in! We had breakfast laid out a while ago. Didn't you hear the bell?"

Max shrugged. "Not really hungry, luv, and do I look like Pavlov's dog? I am thirsty, though. I saw a pub in town?"

The Irish woman's sunny smile slipped a notch. "Not at this time of the morning, not even in Ireland. Besides, Mam has information to share, and she expects you to be at breakfast."

"She can go right on expecting. It's good practice."

The girl pursed her lips. "She's got important data, and you don't want to cross her. Trust me on this."

He rolled his eyes and followed her to the dining room. As he took his seat, their hostess gave him a stern stare, nodding for him to take a seat. "In the future, Mr. Hurley, please endeavor to be on time. I do not tolerate gratuitous disrespect. And now that everyone has *finally* joined us, we can proceed." She glanced at the twin boys, Liam and Hugh, who hit the table in a drumroll, which ended in a raspberry. She glared at them both.

Max poured himself a cup of coffee from the tray in the middle of the table and shot a glance at Anna, his fellow inductee. The American girl sipped her tea while keeping her eyes on their hostess, playing the dutiful guest. Max damped his own irritation at her subservience. How she behaved was her own business.

Michelle pulled her long hair back and tied the mass into a loose knot at the back of her neck. "Ciara will have already acquainted you with the basics, but we wanted to dive into some of the details behind the PHAE, the Unhidden, and how we believe these powers work. We've been trying to discover why so many Unhidden are Irish. While other countries have strong numbers, Ireland seems to have the highest percentage.

"Those countries with a more recent tradition of magical people, such as fairies, sprites, hidden folk, seem to have higher populations of Unhidden. This power might come from interbreeding with the ancient, sometimes legendary beings of those lands. This isn't common knowledge, as the idea is past the bounds of provable science, but that's the current theory.

"Ireland's fairy tradition is strong, and despite modern society's refusal to believe, that may be the cause of so many Unhidden. Now, many of these talents are incidental. Some are as simple as changing eye color or pulling back time two seconds. My own is curling my hair, a talent with no practical application." She stopped to demonstrate, her hair pulling into tight curls and then straightening again. "Strong talents are rare. Yours are among the strongest we've yet seen."

Max glanced around, and each of these sycophantic people appeared glued to her words as if she were the bloody Dalai Lama.

"Reports of violence due to fear and hate are making headlines across the world. People are protesting against our folk despite evidence they are genetic. People fear what they don't understand, and no one understands the Unhidden, who we are, or what we can do."

Max's mind drifted as she parroted the same information Ciara had pushed down their throat yesterday. He'd been out of school for decades and had no wish to re-enroll. Instead, he peered into the kitchen, trying to see if the shelves held any booze bottles.

The Irish woman swept over them with a genuine smile. "And that's where you come in. You're the latest class of applicants to come to PHAE. Our purpose here is to first, assess your talents and desires, second, to teach you about PHAE, and third, to train you in your new positions, should you wish to remain."

Max let out a snort of derision. Michelle frowned and stared straight at him. "If you are not interested, you're free to leave. This is not an armed services corps where you enlist in a contract. I can also dismiss you from my household if you should prove intransigent or uncooperative. Do I make myself clear?"

Max swallowed the coffee he'd just sipped and mumbled, "Clear."

Michelle's frown relaxed back into her habitual smile. "Excellent. Next, a helper is assigned to each of you. One of us will be your guide and mentor in all things PHAE. Each of us is well-versed in protocols and the organization. Max, your helper is my daughter, Róisín. Brendan will help

Anna. The younger children can also help and answer questions but take their information with a grain of salt." She frowned at Liam and Hugh, who both giggled. The youngest girl, Fiona, held her head up in a solemn manner, but her eyes glistened with excitement and mischief.

Michelle nodded and clasped her hands. "Now, for the curriculum. We will assess your talents and determine your limitations. We've some PHAE representatives arriving soon, and they'll work with you to find a position within the organization, or within Ireland, that might interest you and benefit from your talents."

Max let out a huff. Michelle sent him another quelling look, one designed to make children shake, but he ignored her. Then Róisín raised one eyebrow at him, and he desisted.

Anna raised her hand. "Excuse me for the question, Mrs. Byrne, but how long will the assessments take?"

"Please, call me Michelle, Anna, thank you. And the assessments, testing, and placement should take a few days. After that, we'll have education and training, which will last several weeks, perhaps a month."

Once again, Anna raised her hand. "Will you pace the training on the position or the individual's speed at learning?"

"A bit of both. Now, in return for your training, room, and board, we ask that each guest help with chores. This is a working farm, and many hands make light work. We will do our best to accommodate preferences and physical limitations, but we will not tolerate shirking."

She drank the last of her tea, placed the cup down, and took a deep breath. "Now, any further questions?"

Max held up his cup. "Oi. Where's the nearest pub?"

Michelle pursed her lips. "A five kilometer walk into the village. If you should venture in that direction, please let one of us know so we won't worry."

He gave a snort. "Five klicks! Fuck me dead. I can't walk that long sober much less after a night at the pub. Where's your car?"

His language and request earned him glares and a surreptitious giggle.

Colin piped up. "Drink-driving is illegal here, Mr. Hurley."

"Then a horse? A donkey? A goat? Anything? Work with me here, luv."

Michelle glared at Max, her lips pressed in a thin line. She reminded Max of his grandmother for a moment, not a complimentary comparison. "Our livestock are not for your convenience. I mentioned this is a working farm. I must add, I don't approve of strong drink, and drunken hooligans are not welcome here."

Max gave a huge grin and turned to Róisín. "Then would you drive me up tonight? All single ladies love a good night out at the pub!"

Only silence greeted his request. He sat back in defeat. "Tough crowd, mates."

He needed some sort of bolster against all this institutional crap. He didn't care for the prospect of being poked, prodded, and tested like a raw recruit again.

Anna placed a hand on his arm. "This shouldn't be too bad. We aren't children. They need to figure out what we can do before we go any further. As a teacher, I'm familiar with placement tests. They're helpful."

Max pulled away from the younger woman's hand. "Well, there's helpful, and then there's punitive. Trouble is, we each draw the line in a different place."

Anna:

That morning, Anna had faced the day with trepidation. While she wanted to discover where she fit into this organization, a nagging worry scraped at the back of her mind. What if they couldn't find something for her to do?

She'd left a decent job in New York. To be fair, they'd let her go with prejudice. Anna still couldn't believe the Dean had done that, but she couldn't do much about it. She might complain to the teacher's union, but she didn't even know if that would work. Prejudice had been running high, judging from the mob who had chased her away. But she couldn't dwell on that now. She had a new day to face.

Anna had chosen her outfit to be professional, comfortable, and simple. If she didn't have to adjust her clothing every five minutes, she'd seem less physically nervous, if not mentally. Her blouse had the advantage of long sleeves and buttoned cuffs to cover her scales. The beige cotton gloves became a Godsend, as they covered her hands without bringing attention to them. Unless someone looked closely, they might just be her uncovered hands.

Róisín had met her as she left her room. "Good morning, Anna! You look delightful today. But those long sleeves look uncomfortable. The day's going to be warm. Why don't you wear something with short sleeves?"

Anna swallowed, unconsciously rubbing her arms. "I don't like to show them."

The other woman gave a reassuring smile. "I caught a glimpse earlier, and they looked gorgeous. Please?"

Anna swallowed and unbuttoned one sleeve, revealing her scales.

While shaking her head, the Irish woman chuckled. "Why should you hide them? They're stunning, and they shine in the sunlight. You have magical skin."

With a nervous nod, Anna walked downstairs with her, but she couldn't believe Róisín's compliments. The other woman just had a kind nature. Still, Anna hid a private smile at the warm glow she felt.

When Michelle entered, she frowned and scanned the room. Then she sent Róisín out the back door. When the young woman returned a few minutes later, she had a sullen-looking Max in tow. Red creases marred one side of his face under his sleep-matted hair. He must have slept through the bell.

Michelle launched into another detailed description of what their next few days would entail. As a teacher, Anna appreciated having the itinerary spelled out for her.

The twins and Fiona brought in plates piled high with scrambled eggs, sausage, and toast. She helped herself as Michelle finished her presentation.

Anna tried to imagine what job might suit her, but her mind blanked. Small things niggled at her concentration, like Max tapping on his coffee cup and Liam's fork scraping his plate. Even chewing seemed very loud. Anna glanced up when three new people entered the room, her toast now a dry mass in her mouth.

She recognized two of them from headquarters, Ciara and Paul. She hadn't met the third man, a bulky dark man who stood almost as tall as Max. They each wore suits and carried briefcases and e-pads but placed them on a table in the corner as they took plates and served themselves breakfast. Anna's stomach growled, and she grabbed another piece of toast to quiet her pangs.

Once Ciara set her plate down, she gave a haughty smile. "Along with my colleagues, Martin Angolo and Paul Finglas, I will interview each of you. Now, I want to assure both of you that these interviews are nothing formal. They're just a way for you to tell us what you want. We then take that information and try to find a place within the PHAE where you can be happy and useful."

Max slapped his hands on the table. "Useful, huh? And what if we can't find a *useful* spot?"

The new man, Martin, addressed Max with a Caribbean lilt. "We'll find something for you, mate."

"But what if I don't want to be *used?* I had enough of being useful, *mate*, back in the Royal Air Force. Orders from people with less soul than this mug of coffee. Orders to destroy entire villages with no warning. That's not what I want. That's not what any of us want." He swept back with his arm, encompassing the entire room. While Anna resented him speaking for her, she couldn't let him stand alone.

Anna cast a nervous glance Max. "He's got a point. We aren't in the military."

Michelle pressed her lips thin. "I've already told you, Mr. Hurley. We are not here to command you. However, your talent is strong and has the potential to commit much damage if unchecked. Letting you run amok without giving you the chance to channel that power for the greater good would be irresponsible of us."

Róisín pulled at Max's sleeve, pleading with him to sit. Brendan spoke in a low voice to Colin, who glanced at Ciara. After rolling his eyes and letting out a dramatic sigh, Max also sat.

Ciara clapped her hands. "Grand, then. Two of the outbuildings are set up for us. Enjoy your breakfast."

Michelle:

A high-pitched squeal outside made Michelle put the teapot down and rush out. What fresh chaos had her children created? Just as she reached the garden, Liam darted out from the pine trees and pelted toward the stable. His twin, Hugh, came hot on his heels. Fiona, the youngest, brought up the rear, rage burning on her freckled face. A mess of mud in her clothing and hair gave a clue to her anger.

With raised eyebrows, Michelle crossed her arms as the twins tried to scramble up the ladder into the hayloft. The corner of her mouth twitched up as she realized they wouldn't be fast enough.

Just as Hugh reached the top, Fiona barreled into Liam, dragging him to the ground with a primal scream of triumph. Though she was nine and they were eleven, her fury gave her strength. Good thing for the boys

Fiona hadn't shown any Unhidden talents yet. At that age, she'd use it without compunction.

With a suppressed chuckle, Michelle went to break up the fight. She couldn't blame them for being bored. With new students in residence, they always got more restless. Maybe when they got older, they wouldn't get so unsettled with the constant change. Keeping her brood of five children occupied had always been a challenge, especially with the three youngest.

She pulled Fiona off her brother and yelled up at the loft. "Hugh, get down here. Now." To his credit, her son scrambled down the ladder so fast she suspected he might have some sort of super-speed Unhidden talent. As she glared at her children, their flushed faces showed a mixture of fear, triumph, and anger.

"Now, what happened?"

All three tried to speak at once, but she held up her hands. "One at a time. Liam, you first."

As Liam got tongue-tied trying to explain the sequence of events, Hugh interjected to fill in the missing bits. Fiona vibrated with wanting to argue, but she held her tongue, and Michelle gave her a tiny smile. "Now, Fiona, what's your story?"

The redhead girl barely breathed as she launched into a step-by-step description of how the brothers ambushed her in the woods, rubbed mud into her hair and face, and would die a horrible death from a thousand paper cuts, and that she'd take pleasure in rubbing lemon juice on each and every one for weeks.

Michelle affixed a glare on her youngest for her zeal at the planned torture, but she had to admit, the boys had definitely earned her wrath. While half-tempted to let Fiona have her way, that wouldn't be wise or fair. Still, they had bullied their sister and must pay penance for such acts. Luckily, after raising their two older siblings, she had a way to defuse the situation and hopefully teach them better.

"Liam, I want you to tell me know what you could have done better."

Anna:

After breakfast, Brendan and Anna followed the tree-covered flagstone path to the water's edge. The River Shannon ran wide, deep, and fast. Water slipped over half-submerged rocks, opaque brown with recent rains. A large branch swirled past, caught in the rippling current.

Anna swallowed. The ocean both beckoned and terrified her. To be fair, she didn't fear the water itself, just whatever dangerous creatures hid below the surface, waiting to attack her dangling feet the moment she entered.

She turned to her minder, thankful that Brendan rather than the sterner Michelle would be giving her this exam. "Are you sure I have to do this? Can't I just tell you what I can do? Does Max need to do this, too?"

With a lopsided grin, Brendan clapped his hand on her shoulder. "That would only tell me what you've tried. It'd be no good whatsoever at finding what else you can do, what your limits are, or where your strengths lie. And yes, you both need to be tested, but Da will be working with him. We're supposed to do this one-on-one, so you don't feel intimidated by a group of people, like in an examination or interview. More homey and friendly, right?"

"Friendly?"

He gave her a warm smile. "Absolutely. I'm here to help you, not judge you."

Her doubts didn't melt away, but they did thaw. Maybe this family would like her after all. Or at least this member of the family. She swallowed back on her budding crush again. "And I have to get in the water?"

He quirked an eyebrow. "That'd be best, don't you think?"

Anna gulped again, staring as the water lapped against the flagstone steps. As a delaying tactic, she stepped out of her shoes and placed them neatly to the side, rolling her socks up into each one. She'd worn a simple skirt she wouldn't mind getting wet and a thick T-shirt.

She didn't want to show her scales or admit her fear in front of Brendan, but she also couldn't bear the thought of putting her bare legs into the water. Tensing her entire body, she touched her toe to the surface, then pulled back from the chilly water.

Brendan placed a hand on her shoulder. "Here, I'll go in with you. Will that help? I know a strange river must seem daunting. Did you swim in New York rivers? If you've ever swam in any river, this one'll be no different." The Irish man removed his socks and shoes, rolling up his slacks. Then he slapped his hands on his knees. "Ready?"

"Brendan…"

"The water's not scary, really! Here, I'll hold your hand. One step at a time." He offered his hand and she stared at the offered body part like she spied a venomous snake. Then, ashamed of both her dread and distrust, she grasped it. His skin felt warm and calloused and her skin tingled where they touched.

Brendan stared at her hand, at the scales peeking from under her long sleeve. She gulped, waiting for him to yank in horror. When he didn't, Anna took a deep breath and stood with him. He gave her hand a squeeze, flashed her a roguish grin, and stepped in. She matched his step as her blood turned cold.

They took one step. Then another. The chilly river lapped her ankles. For a moment, her panic washed away with the touch of her beloved water, embracing her skin, soothing the ever-present itchiness. They took another step, down to mid-calf. Then the flash of something below the surface caught her eye. Sparkling silver and gold in the dappled sunlight.

She gasped, drawing back. "What's that?"

Brendan kept tight hold of her hand, not letting her retreat, suppressed laughter dancing behind his eyes. "That's just a young salmon. Nothing to fear. They're harmless and tasty. In fact, it'd be brilliant if you could talk the fish into our nets. We'd have a fine feast for dinner. A dead useful talent that would be."

Anna gave a solemn nod, too nervous to laugh. They took a third step. Now the water caressed her knees. "Is this far enough?"

With a shrug, he said, "Let's give it a go. You said you can talk to the water?"

"Not precisely talk, but I can ask the water to do things."

"Do you ask the water? Spirits in the water? Some sort of water sprite or ghost?"

She shrugged. "I have no idea."

Brendan gave her a half-smile, let go of her hand, and opened his arms wide, making it almost a challenge. "Show me."

Anna took a deep breath, closed her eyes, and visualized the river in front of her swirling. Just a small whirlpool, an eddy past the rocks. When she opened her eyes, the water twisted, round and round, like a flushing toilet. A funnel formed in the river like a miniature eye in a hurricane.

Brendan's eyes grew wide. "That's class, that is! I've never seen anyone that strong before. Now, can you make it stop?"

Pulling in her will, she pictured the water normal again, flowing along with muddy currents. The whirl faded within two seconds.

"Brilliant. Can you draw water up, like a fountain?"

Anna furrowed her brow. "I'm not sure. I've never thought to try."

"Sure and that's one reason I'm here, to shove past your limits. You can never know your power's limits unless you push the edges, right? So, I'm here to help you increase them."

As she quested her will into the water, she prodded into the depths with all the care of someone poking a sleeping lion. She prayed she didn't wake some submarine creature to come investigate who invaded its domain. To her relief, nothing answered, but a small fountain formed.

Brendan directed her through a series of challenges; some easy, some impossible. She made the water leap, freeze, boil, and drip. But when he asked her to make a fountain, it fizzled.

Anna frowned and tried again, visualizing the water spraying up like something from a Las Vegas hotel. The water spouted a few times and then dribbled into nothing.

"No, that's fine. Don't be mad at yourself. We have to find your limitations, and we just found one. That's good!"

She choked back a disappointed sob. "It doesn't feel so good."

Brendan grinned. "Sure, and everyone has their kryptonite, Anna. Knowing what yours is could help you in the future and will help us figure out how these magical powers are manifesting, what forms they can take, and how best to utilize them."

Anna didn't like the sound of the last, as if she were a tool to be used. Still, at least she hadn't cried in front of the Irish man. A great wave of fatigue pulled her down and she sat on the riverbank.

"Anna?"

She waved her hand. "I'm just suddenly really, really tired. Do you need me to try anything else today?"

"No, we can stop here. We'll try again tomorrow, okay? We'll try to refine your control as well as figure out what you can and can't do over the next several days."

Max:

As Brendan dragged Anna off for her test, Róisín appeared at his elbow as if by magic. "Ready for your next assessment? Da's waiting outside."

He wasn't looking forward to any sort of test. Max needed a drink, now. He had a flask hidden in his jacket pocket but didn't want to drink it in public. "Róisín, if I don't find a shitter soon, I can't be held responsible for the actions of my arsehole."

Her expression paled. "Do you mean the toilet? Down that hall to your left."

He hurried into the small room and let out a sigh as he relieved himself. Then he extracted the flask and took a swig, draining almost a third. After several long, deep breaths, he drank most of the rest. Exams had never been his favorite thing, and this one sent him right back into a Hell he kept trying to escape. Rather than finish the flask, he tucked the tin bottle away. He might need the booster later.

When he returned, Róisín raised an eyebrow. "Ready for the fun part?"

He grunted and shrugged. "That wasn't the fun part?" The whiskey had done its job, and he now floated pleasantly along the floor. Róisín brought him out to the back garden, where Colin sat on a stone bench, framed by roses.

When he noticed them, Colin slapped his hands on his thighs and rose to his feet. "Grand! Thank you, Róisín. Can you fetch us some coffee? Now Max, remember, there are no wrong answers. We only need to get a solid idea of your abilities and limits."

Max gave a noncommittal grunt and sat on the bench Colin had abandoned. It still felt warm.

"Tell me more about how you actually command the wind."

He gave a shrug. "They listen to me, more or less."

His host cocked his head. "More or less? What do you mean by that? Can you show me?"

The floating sensation had already gone away, and he clasped his sweating hands. This reminded him of school, another unhappy time in his life. He wiped his hands again, wishing he had taken the third swig from his flask. "I'd have to talk to them first. They don't always listen."

Róisín returned with a tray. "Would you like some coffee for this, Max?"

With a grateful smile, he nodded. "Aye, luv, and thanks. Black."

Colin turned to him. "So, you have to make friends with the wind?"

Max swallowed. "The wind near where I lived helped me out now and then. I never asked for any great favors. When we fought a fire at a nearby campsite, where the only trees for miles grew, they helped out. But, on the trip here, when we landed in Zurich, the winds sassed me."

Colin raised his eyebrows. "Sassed you? How?"

Róisín handed him a cup of black coffee. Would he be able to slip a drop in from his flask? Not with them watching. "I asked them to stop shaking the plane around. They said they weren't my friends, and they could do as they like, the cheeky bastards."

The corner of Colin's mouth twitched. "Do they speak to you with words?"

"They do use words, but not out loud. In my mind like, at least for the last couple of months. They'd never done that. I used to get some sense of what they wanted, but in pictures or feelings. I can talk back in my mind, but I talk to them out loud, if no one else is listening."

Colin frowned and Max wondered why his answer displeased him but decided he couldn't care less. He did what he did. Why should he seek approval on his methods? Could Colin talk to the wind? No, he couldn't. So, he could stuff his stiff disapproval.

Max took a sip of his coffee and almost choked as the burn of good whiskey hit his throat. He hadn't expected it to contain spirits. When he glanced at Róisín, the edge of her mouth curled up. He grinned and took a bigger sip and re-assessed his opinion of the young woman. *She's a right baller, no doubt.*

Colin cleared his throat. "Okay, so let's get started. Ask the wind for help."

Max took another fortifying sip of coffee and closed his eyes. Not that he needed to close his eyes but better than see the judgment in Colin's and Róisín's eyes if the wind decided to be rebellious. "Can you hear me?"

A stiff breeze lifted his ponytail. **We can hear you.**

"Can you do something for me? Uh…" Max opened his eyes, looking around for something to demonstrate with. His gaze fell on the laundry flapping in the breeze next to the third outbuilding. "Can you make that clothing flap?"

The wind didn't answer, but a sudden wind gusted, making the garments snap. Colin's eyes grew larger, and a wide grin spread across his face. "Brilliant! Can you ask them to stop?"

He did, and they obeyed, though he felt some reluctance in their answer. Colin clapped him on the shoulder. "What else can you do with them? Can you make them eddy?"

"Oi, how about swirling around?"

Why should we do that?

"Uh, because it'll be fun? C'mon, mates, work with me, here."

A few dead leaves in the yard rose into an eddy, swirling slowly at first. But the speed increased to the point the leaves disintegrated, and then the wind dissipated, the bits of dead leaf floating to the ground like snow.

Colin took him through several exercises and, despite everything, Max enjoyed the demonstration. Several times, the wind ignored his request, so he asked something else. Most times, though, they complied.

He found himself adding flourishes just to see Róisín's smile, which reminded him of Trina's. When Colin clapped him on the back again, Max jerked, startled, and then grinned with self-satisfaction at a job well done. He hadn't felt so proud of himself in a long time.

"Brilliant, we'll do this again tomorrow, and then the next few days until I've enough information to give PHAE my notes. Why don't you head in for a snack? Working with the wind must be tiring."

Mention of the PHAE soured his triumph. With a sullen expression, he helped Róisín gather the coffee things and trudged back to the farmhouse. Colin hadn't lied; he was bone-tired.

Anna:

By the end of the third day, Anna felt she'd gotten a much stronger hold on what she could and couldn't do, and how to limit her power so the fatigue didn't overwhelm her. She'd finally managed to create a fountain, though a rather modest one. She couldn't hold it for more than a few seconds, but it made her inordinately proud.

As her last effort faded away, Brendan patted her shoulder. "Right. Now, I'm going under the water. I need you to keep the water from drowning me."

"I can't do that!"

"Sure, and you can. Just keep the water from going into my mouth or nose."

She backed away. "Brendan! What if I fail? I don't want you to drown." Anna had been so frightened to practice her powers before. When she had finally given in, she got fired from her job almost immediately. Now Brendan wanted her to push and pull and stretch her limits, and panic made her heartbeat race. Too much change, too fast.

He gripped both her hands. "I won't drown. But I need to know you can perform under pressure."

Anna swallowed and gave a slow nod. "I don't like this."

He smoothed away a lock of hair. "Of course, you don't. You're a gentle soul, and you wouldn't intentionally hurt anyone. But I'm counting on that drive, that basic goodness. The test should impel you to greater depths if you'll pardon the pun. Panicking might make you do things you might be too afraid to try otherwise. Understand?"

Her heart raced as he ducked below the brown surface. When he disappeared, the panic rose in her throat, cutting off her voice. With a frantic thought to the water, she asked it to stay away from the young man swimming next to her. She couldn't tell if anything changed. The water kept its secrets, and when Brandon didn't surface, her concern grew to dread.

She waded into the deeper water, her arms flailing around, trying to find her new friend. Nothing. Her panic overcame her sense. "Brendan! Where are you!"

Something moved behind her, and she whirled. The bushes on the shore rustled. "Brendan?" They stilled, but she kept staring, in case something lay in wait.

After turning back to the water, terror kept her frozen in place. She hadn't talked to the water in minutes. Had it taken Brendan?

Suddenly, the river burst into a fountain next to her. Anna screamed and scrambled to the shore. She couldn't let the monster catch her. Something grabbed her ankle, and her scream turned to a high-pitched screech. "No! No, go away! Leave me alone!"

Finally getting a grip on the flagstones, she dragged herself from the wicked river. Turning to look across the water, she spied Brendan inches from her feet, a smug grin across his face.

Grabbing a rock from the shore, she chucked the stone at him. "Mother*fucker!* You scared the *shit* out of me!"

"Aye, and you did brilliantly despite that. I didn't get a drop in my mouth or my nose. Even when you panicked."

Getting her breath under control, she clambered onto shore and put on her socks. Then she shoved her feet into her shoes too hard, and her toes hurt. "You didn't have to do that."

Brendan put his own shoes on and gave a chuckle. "Indeed, and I did. You might even say that's my job. And we discovered a lot about your talent, what you can do, and what you can't. You did great!"

Anna glared at him, not willing to forgive him. "And that meant you had to frighten the crap out of me?"

"Did my technique work?"

She narrowed her gaze and let out a long breath. Yes, his plan had worked. That didn't mean she had to accept the tactic as valid or considerate. Even in her panic, she never mustered enough courage to jump completely in the river to save him. If the water had been clear, she might have tried.

Clear creeks and swimming pools had never been a problem. But muddy rivers and dark oceans scared the crap right out of her.

In truth, Brendan had just encouraged her to push her talent's limits. He must think her the basest coward, to be afraid of water when her talent controlled it. But she had overcome some to search for him. Until he burst up from the depths like a crocodile, and she ran like a frightened mouse.

As they climbed away from the river's edge, she withdrew her power from the river. With her final feather touch on the rippling surface, something stirred beneath. Something dark and large. Anna sensed the change in her bones and blood, the silt beneath her feet rumbling. She shivered as she stumbled back from the shore. Brendan placed a towel around her shoulders, wrapping her tight. As they walked back to the house, she wanted to hold his hand again, to feel that warmth and tingling from earlier, but didn't dare.

He glanced at her before they reached the back door. "I used to be frightened of the river, too. My Da used to tell me stories of the Dobhar-chú."

"The dover what?"

"The Dobhar-chú, or King Otter. The name translates to Water Dog, an apt enough description for an otter, to be sure. But King Otter is a creature of myth, like the Loch Ness Monster in Scotland. Just a wee bit smaller, is all."

He held his hands a few feet apart, and Anna giggled despite herself, the adrenaline rushing away from her blood and making her giddy.

He spoke in a sepulchral tone, straight out of a bad horror film. "But this creature is a cross between a true otter and a hound. Ferocious. They prey on people doing laundry by the river so, when I had to go to the shore, I kept an eagle eye out for things moving in the murky depths."

Anna cocked her head. "An otter? Is that the most dangerous creature you have here? No sharks or crocodiles or giant squid?"

With a shrug, he cocked his head. "Ireland's pretty tame. Oh, we have sharks in the sea, but they don't bother folks, for the most part. And, sure, you need to steer clear of selkies and the like. You'll have to ask Da about them, though."

Anna hadn't heard of a selkie and couldn't tell if he teased her with the odd word. She didn't want to advertise her ignorance. Besides, she still simmered with resentment over his tactics.

The examination, even if it had been friendly, had drained her. She felt ready to collapse and longed for a nap. However, her stomach growled so loud, she worried that Brendan had heard it, so was glad to see that lunch was laid out in the dining room.

She chose lamb, potatoes, and cabbage and took her seat. Brendan sat in the next chair, his own plate piled with twice as much. He took her hand under the table and squeezed, flashing her a ridiculously cute grin. "Perhaps another day we can go to the sea and find out if your talents differ with salt water."

Panic gripped her, and she had trouble breathing at the prospect, but he squeezed her hand again. "Ah, you'll be fine. I'll introduce you to the resident dolphins."

Dolphins would be fun, and the sea mightn't be so bad if Brendan joined her. She did love looking over the ocean, the height of romantic views. She chided herself for already thinking of Brendan and romance in the same thought but realized she could easily fall in too deep. And then she chided herself for the pun.

She reminded herself about her tendency to have instant crushes, and she was simply reacting to having a safe place after the horrible mob at home. Still, he hadn't even recoiled at the sight of her scales.

Chapter Four

"Love makes the world go 'round? Not at all.
Whiskey makes it go round twice as fast."
– Compton Mackenzie

Max:

Max only had time to scarf a slice of toast before Róisín showed up again. "Ciara's ready to see you. Ready?"

Max wiggled his now-empty cup. "I could do with a bit more fortification."

She narrowed her eyes and placed a gentle hand on his shoulder. "I gave you plenty already. Do you think you can get through this one on your own?"

For a wonder, Max thought he could. He nodded, and she led him into the library. Ciara sat, along with Martin and Paul. "Welcome, Max. Thank you for cooperating with the DNA test and the assessment. Now that we have several days of testing your limits and talents, we can work on placing you."

He gritted his teeth. This sounded a bit too far like the air force for his tastes now. "Placing me? This isn't a bloody entrance exam, luv. I'm not applying to some sort of secret society here."

"You misunderstand me, Mr. Hurley. We will offer you a choice of assignments suited to your abilities and temperament. You are always permitted to decline these offers. Indeed, you're under no obligation to remain with the PHAE at all. You may leave now if you wish. Do you wish to leave?"

Max grumbled under his breath and shook his head. No, he'd hear them out. The recruiter bloke had promised him a plane, and he'd be damned if he quit before he got a chance at that.

Martin handed him a manila folder with several glossy pages inside. As he flipped through them, Ciara explained, "These are different areas within Ireland that could use a man with your talents. Most of them are at strategic points along the coast, but a few are inland, particularly at the turbine farms. Your talent would be a fantastic help with the renewable energy industry, especially when repairs are needed."

Max grunted as he flipped the last page. He glanced up with a scowl. "Not one of these have a bloody plane on them. Hiroki promised me a plane when he got me to come halfway across the world. Is this some sort of bait and switch, then?"

Martin let out a chuckle. "No, we didn't intend any bait and switch. And we do have noted on your file your preference for a plane. However, that needs to wait until you're licensed to fly in Ireland. Once you get that, we can add those opportunities to your list."

"That sounds like a load of shite."

The larger man's shoulders tensed, but Ciara stood. "This is not shite, Max. This is the truth. You have my word on that."

"Huh. Yeah, your word and a dollar might get me a cup of coffee. I've heard promises before. So far, none of them have been honored."

She let out a long sigh. "Very well, I shall make a note of your objection. Unless you have further concerns, we thank you for your time today."

After his assessment, he escaped into the loo again and added the last splash from his flask to the rest of his coffee. Sure, he'd gotten through the test, but now that he'd finished, he needed bolstering again. Once fortified, he could face anything.

The others had gathered for lunch in the dining hall. He couldn't very well call it a room as the place echoed even with the Byrne family, Anna, and him, and the three PHAE reps, a total of thirteen people. Something out of a period drama. The sideboard had fixings for sandwiches and more coffee.

He piled sliced chicken on bread, poured mayonnaise over the pile, added a hunk of cheddar cheese, grabbed some chips, and took the only empty seat. Unfortunately, the only seat was next to Ciara. The tall Dublin woman gave him a knowing grin. He returned her grin with a growl.

She was part of the reason he'd come here, and he wouldn't forgive her so easily for her tricks. He'd been a bit of a bastard to her when they met. To be fair, she hadn't told him she was a PHAE agent. Max only discovered *that* tidbit of important information when they met at headquarters in Dublin. She'd pretended she came on holiday with her husband, Brian. Instead, they'd been scouting for people with talents to recruit for their organization. Hiroki finally landed him, but she'd baited the hook.

On his other side, Róisín ate a green salad with fruit and cheese. She flashed him a smile and he found himself grinning back. *Careful, mate. She's much too sweet and young for the likes of you.*

Max took a huge bite of his sandwich and reached for his cup but drank air. He forgot he drained his drink earlier. When he rose, Róisín stood more quickly and took the mug from him. "I know how you like your coffee. You eat your sandwich."

Max refused to let go, yanking the mug back. As much as he appreciated her help earlier, he wasn't a child to be coddled. "Róisín, you aren't my fucking servant. I can get my own coffee."

Someone made a rude sound behind him. He whirled to see who made it, but no one looked in his direction. Róisín plucked the cup from his grip and strode for the kitchen. He followed, his long stride catching up to her. They entered the kitchen together.

"Róisín, you don't need to—"

She brandished the cup. "My grandfather needed the drink to keep his temper even. He had pain to keep at bay. If you're the same way, I'm happy to help. However, if you tell me, even in passing, that you'd rather quit, I will help you with all the joy in the world. Until that time, I'll help you keep an even keel. I won't let you get plastered but a steady float. Understand?" She glared at him until he relented. Then she reached into an upper cabinet, pulled out a half-full bottle of Tullamore Dew, and poured some into his mug. "Now, fill the rest with coffee."

Chastened, he took the cup from her. "Thank you, luv."

She returned to the dining room, leaving him with his cup of whiskey. Alone in the kitchen, he downed the shot, then returned to the dining room, filled his cup with coffee, and sat. Everyone's eyes stayed glued upon him as he took another bite of his sandwich. Another rude sound came, a mix between a snort and a raspberry.

Max pushed his chair back and stood. "Right. Who's got something to say to me? Come out and say it."

Colin and Michelle exchanged glances, but no one said a thing.

"If you've got a problem, bloody well say it. Unless you're a fucking coward."

The big Jamaican bloke, Martin, rose. "We're more polite to women in this house, Mr. Hurley. We expect our guests to do so as well. Your language is too rough."

Max threw his hands up in frustration. "Did you not just see me try to keep her from serving me? She wouldn't listen! What the bloody hell did you expect me to do, tackle her?"

Ciara stood, as did Róisín and Martin. Paul stayed in his seat, shoveling his food in his mouth as if nothing happened. Max didn't know if they stood for or against him and didn't want to find out. Martin crossed his arms. "Would you care to take this discussion outside?"

Max looked the bloke up and down. He stood at least three inches over six feet, but so did Max. But Martin carried a lot more muscle, and probably weighed in a good six stone heavier. Even if he had no brawling skill, Martin could probably wipe the floor with Max from sheer mass. Still, the physical odds had never put Max off before, and they wouldn't now. The pup clearly needed a lesson in respect.

Ciara cleared her throat. "This seems to be an issue that requires some discussion. However, the dining room is not the right place for such discourse. Outside with you."

The men went outside, as well as Róisín and Ciara.

Max planted his feet and crossed his arms, glaring at Martin. "So, say what you have to say to me, *boy.*"

The younger man took a deep breath. "First, I am thirty-five years old. While I am many years younger than you, I am not a boy. This is part of the respect I spoke of. Women deserve your respect. All of us deserve your respect. You need to curb your language and your attitude. Stop acting the maggot."

Max clenched his teeth and glanced to his side, where Róisín and Ciara stood together. Róisín's eyes turned wide, and she opened her mouth, but then shut it again. Ciara, on the other hand, appeared amused, evidently waiting to see how this all played out. Well, he'd just have to give her the show she wanted, then. "No one here has yet earned my respect, except Róisín. Hell, Ciara lied to me the first time she met me. Where's the respect there, mate? Hmm? Respect is earned, not given."

Martin crossed his arms. The scowl looked menacing on such a large bloke, but Max had stared down big blokes before. "There are different types of respect. When people in power speak of respect, they often mean obedience. When those without power speak of respect, they mean they wish to be treated as an equal. All we're asking is that you treat everyone here as equals."

Max let out a snort. "Bullshit! We aren't equals. You PHAE blokes have all the power, and we're the peons. The testing, assessing, processing, this is just like in the air force. We're just fodder for this PHAE machine, and you are our assigned keepers. We have no equality."

Martin growled and clenched his fists, taking a step forward. His brows knitted with anger, glowering fit to start a thunderstorm. Ciara held up her hand. "Gentlemen, we can talk this out."

Róisín put a hand on Max's shoulder. "Max, you shouldn't believe that. The PHAE is here to help you. We aren't your keepers. You're free to leave whenever you like. The assessment team told you that this afternoon, didn't they? They'll even pay for your passage back home if that's what you want."

He shrugged her hand away, still glaring at Martin. "They're using me. The PHAE mean to create tools for their own purposes. I've been a tool of a government before, luv, and I swore to myself I'd never let that happen again. Even if a pretty face," he shifted his glare to Róisín and then to Ciara, "or two pretty faces, tell me I should. I'm not that much of a wanker."

Some of the anger faded from Martin's expression, but Max didn't care anymore.

"Will you ask me to hurt others?"

Ciara nodded. "That is a distinct possibility. Even a probability if we are attacked or invaded. That is, unfortunately, part of warfare."

He let out a breath. "Can you make me a promise, here and now, that the PHAE won't ask me to kill for them? That they won't order me to do something against my conscience?"

Martin glanced at Ciara, who gave the barest of nods. "I can. The PHAE is a volunteer organization. Unless you've given a further oath to a specific group within PHAE, you're free to leave. Any time you get new information, including a request of service, you can change your mind."

Max's anger huffed out, surprised at the answer. He peered at Ciara, searching her face for deception, but found none. Deflated, he bowed his head and let out a long breath. He glanced at Róisín and, for a moment, he saw Trina instead. The entreaty in her gaze thawed an edge of his frozen heart. He'd give them a chance, for now. But at the first sign of real trouble, he'd have to re-assess. "Fine. I believe you. For now. But that's subject to change."

Ciara crossed her arms. "You believe us until you don't?"

He shrugged and looked her up and down. "That's the best I can do right now, luv, no matter how long your legs are."

The tall woman raised an eyebrow. "You still need to apologize for your language and attitude."

Max rolled his eyes and gave a saucy grin. "Fine. I apologize for my bloody language."

Ciara pursed her lips before giving him a firm nod. "As long as that's the strongest word you use."

Anna:

Ciara came into the office and halted when she noticed Anna already seated in front of the desk. She flashed a perfunctory smile and took the other seat. "I appreciate promptness, Anna."

She just nodded, unsure how to respond to that. She'd only been so early because she wanted to get away from people but sharing those details with Ciara seemed unprofessional.

As she opened a manila folder, Ciara glanced at a page stapled on the left side. "Your file says you did quite well in Brendan's assessment of your abilities. How did you feel about the tests?"

Anna swallowed and shrugged, hands clasped tightly. "They were a bit more intense than I expected."

Letting out a chuckle, Ciara smiled. "So Brendan also reports. But don't blame him for that. I asked him to do so. That sort of test gives us a better understanding of what you can do under pressure. Given your talents, we have several options. I'll list them all for you, and then you can ask questions. Okay?"

Anna nodded, butterflies making her stomach churn. She didn't like the idea of Brendan telling Ciara everything they talked about, but she realized he had to. He would be her mentor and teacher, not her best friend. That made her heart shrink a little.

"We have a station in Galway, up the west coast, as well as one in Cork on the south coast. Then headquarters in Dublin. The first two are right on the coast, while the Dublin office is about a ten-minute drive from the water.

"If you prefer an inland posting, or fresh water, we need someone at Lough Neagh in the north and Lough Dearg in the south. Both are major sources for fresh water for the country."

Anna hid the shudder that went through her at the idea of working in a huge lake.

"Posting locations aside, we need someone who can work with those Unhidden who live in the water."

"Some Unhidden live *in* the water? Like mermaids?" Anna wanted to meet them. In fact, she might end up turning into one if her scales kept spreading.

Ciara nodded, a polished smile spreading across her face. "Not quite mermaids but definitely piscine. Two Unhidden have developed gills and, while they can still breath air through their human lungs, prefer to be in the water. They have no power over the water, like you do. Their talent gifted them the gills and fins."

"Fins?" Anna resisted the urge to tug down her sleeves over her scaling arms. It took every bit of will not to glance at them as Ciara held her gaze.

"Yes, fins. Quite lovely, too. As an alternative, we could use help with water purification efforts. That particular project has been an issue for decades, and this will only get worse as climate change increases."

Anna nodded at this, realizing she could really help some global efforts in that area.

"And, if none of those options appeal to you, we have water-based research and infrastructure projects."

"Infrastructure projects? What are those?"

"Building dams and lochs, things like that. Helping hold back the water during construction, ensuring the tolerances are sufficient. I can get a list of current projects, if you're interested."

The possibilities swam in her mind. The ocean scared the crap right out of her, but also fascinated her. She'd never lived near the sea. However, New York had thousands of lakes so they were both more familiar and less interesting.

Something inside her ached for the sea, despite her fears. The possibilities fought within her, all vying for consideration.

"How long do I have to decide?"

Ciara let out a chuckle. "At least a few weeks yet. You need weeks more of training before you're ready for anything. We just want to give you time to consider the options while you learn to use your talent. These education centers are designed to help you do that, help us learn what you can do, and to help you control any power you get. You know that your power will likely increase, right? Since the magnetic pole shifts, all talents have increased. None have stopped growing, as far as we can tell. They've morphed, shifted, and sometimes even regressed, but they seem fluid."

Now, Anna got completely confused and unsure what Ciara talked about, but not wanting to appear ignorant, she nodded.

"Well, keep the possibilities in mind, and when I speak with you next, maybe let me know which ones seem more intriguing."

As she left, all sorts of notions flitted through in her mind. She didn't pay attention to walking, and she barked her shin on the garden bench as she passed. "Ow! Fuckabiscuit!"

Fiona popped her head from around the rosemary bush. "That isn't a nice word."

Anna chuckled while she rubbed her leg. "I know, sweetie. But sometimes adults say bad words when bad things happen. It helps."

The girl scowled, her freckles bright on her pale skin. "Mam puts a mark next to my name if I say something bad. I have to get two good marks to make up for one bad mark. If I get too many bad marks, I don't get to go to Family Night on Fridays."

Anna rubbed her shin and sat, patting the wood beside her for Fiona to sit. "That's a pretty fair system, Fiona. Things are easier if you do nothing bad in the first place, don't you think?"

As she gave a dramatic sigh, Fiona hopped on the bench. "I suppose so. But there are just *so many* bad things, I can't remember them all!"

"You'll learn. Adults take years, but they learn." Anna glanced at the house. "Most of them."

Chapter Five

"Drunkenness is nothing but voluntary madness."
– Seneca

***Latest** CNN **Update:** Protests on both sides of the Unhidden debate are growing. Demonstrators gather each weekend in Washington D.C., London, Paris, Berlin, Sydney, and Tokyo, as both those with new powers and those against them schedule competing rallies. Several minor incidents of violence have occurred, and national leaders have publicly expressed worries about the consequences of a major incident. Five people died in the insurrection at the U. S. Capitol and, within the following nine days, two Capitol police officers committed suicide. The President of the United States, the Prime Minister of the United Kingdom, the Chancellor of Germany, and several other world leaders are considering more stringent security measures, including bringing military in to help to keep the peace. Similar protests are happening in cities around the world.*

Max:

He'd had a tough day. Max needed to get away, even if just for the evening. Not that he'd been mistreated, but after living on his own for the last thirty years, the sheer press of people drove him mad. Besides, Michelle's attitude reminded him of his former drill instructor. He treasured his solitude and lived alone for a reason. Well, alone except for when he had brief flings with younger women who only wanted to fly in his plane. And the whispering voices wouldn't leave him alone, either.

No, he had to shut those voices up. They niggled at his memory, and he didn't want those images dredged up any more than they'd already been. He never quite made out what they said. He needed way more drink than Róisín had in her hidden stash, and besides, he ached to ride the skies.

This PHAE crew seemed bent on categorizing and sorting him, but not so much on giving him his due. He hadn't even seen a hint of the so-called benefits his recruiter had promised, like a plane of his own. So much for Hiroki and his promises. The bloke had seemed nice enough, but he had obviously been selling a bill of goods when he recruited Max.

Tonight, he'd head down the road to that mythical pub Colin mentioned when he arrived. He could at least find a pint, if not shots of the good stuff. He might even be able to buy a bottle to re-supply. Ireland had a great reputation for whiskey, and Max deserved some recreation time.

And sufficient liquid medicine might quiet the constant voices.

The voices started the day he arrived in Dublin, a week before. At first, mere whispers tickled the dark corners of his memory. Now, they screamed at him whenever he went outside. They sounded like the winds at home, whistling and murmuring around him, almost an affectionate caress. These seemed angrier, more strident in their syllables.

He'd tried to reason with them, to calm them, but they just got louder. Not wanting a repeat of the incident in Zurich, Max stopped trying. But they kept shrieking, just behind his eyes, into his blood, and around his past. Therefore, he needed a drink. Or three. Maybe five.

He ought to bring someone along, though. Róisín wouldn't be his best choice, though she was a class Sheila. Max greatly appreciated her support, but she tended on the preachy side. He didn't need preaching tonight. He needed those seven drinks. Max considered asking that bloke, Brendan, to come with him. He didn't particularly care for the kid, but he looked sturdy enough to help him back if he drank himself legless. He seemed already to be sweet on the American girl, though, so he might not want to go.

Trina's face flashed in his memory, and he shoved the image away. He couldn't face her yet. Not until he'd had those nine drinks.

With a twinge of guilty conscience, he strode to the main house and climbed the stairs. He knocked on the red door, the one Brendan said was his room.

When the Irish man opened the door, he raised his eyebrows. "What's the craic, Max?"

Max gave a casual shrug. "I was thinking of mounting an expedition to the local pub. I'm told the village is about five klicks down the road. Want to tag along? You strike me as a man who appreciates a good drink."

Brendan narrowed his eyes. "I thought you'd become best mates with my sister now. Why me? Are you looking for a babysitter to bring you home?"

He straightened, not wanting to admit the bloke had the right idea. "Not at all. I thought you might need an escape from your parents. But if you'd rather stay…"

"Wait here." He slammed the door, but returned in a few moments, a jacket in hand. "If you're foolish enough to wander around a strange countryside in the dark, you'd better have someone with you who can find the way home."

Max raised his eyebrows as he shut the door. "It ain't even dark yet! And who's to say I can't find my own way back? I've been a pilot for decades, mate. I know how to navigate."

Brendan looked him up and down. While the Irishman stood a few inches shorter than Max's own six-foot-three frame, he had a few more pounds on his bones. "And how well can you navigate on the ground after you've had a few pints?"

This might not be such a good idea. He crossed his arms, glaring at him. "There's just the one road, mate. I can manage."

"Oh, I'm coming. But I'll first let Mam and Da know we're leaving, as they requested."

Max rolled his eyes. "Oh, them. Sure, whatever."

After he returned, they walked out to the one-lane gravel road. Max glanced right, then left. Brendan let out a deep sigh. "Left. You really are an expert navigator, aren't you?"

Brendan walked to the left, but Max crossed his arms again and planted his feet. "Listen, mate, if you're going to cop an attitude like this—"

The other man spun around and cut him off by holding up his hand. "Shut your mouth, Max. You're already on thin ice after your shenanigans. Yes, we want you here, but we're volunteers, too. Mam can decide to kick you out. So, shape up! If you don't, after this long walk, I'll need more drinks than you will."

The bloke had bottle, he had to give him that. A chuckle bubbled up inside. Max let out a snort and strode after him. While he had long legs, so did Brendan, so he had to hustle to catch up. They walked past several smaller farms and a path with a sign for a stone circle. When they came into the village, he spied a veterinary clinic, a grocery, a primary school, and there, like manna from heaven, the pub. The place just needed a sunbeam and singing angels.

The sign declared it The Black Boar, complete with a woodcut illustration of said animal. Max opened the door, and after shooting him another vicious glare, Brendan entered with dignity.

Max had visited many pubs and bars, but the Irish pub seemed to be a unique creation. The sheer atmosphere of the place hit him straight in the chest. Dark wood surrounded them, from the walls, the paneled ceiling, the high-top tables, and the booths. Dark red leather and velvet covered anything padded. The bar gleamed with well-polished mahogany. He inhaled a deep whiff of the delightful bouquet of stout and whiskey, and he wanted plenty of both.

Brendan strode to the bar, and the bartender asked his pleasure. "A pint of stout, Sean."

Max raised his finger. "Make that two, mate."

"Right enough. Will you be sitting here, or at a table?"

Max glanced about, but the tables looked full. "Unless you've got a table hidden under your apron, we'll be here."

As he and Brendan settled on their tall stools, the barman brought over two pints of black stout topped with thick, creamy foam. "Give them a minute to settle, then enjoy."

"Now, that's a gorgeous sight. Cheers, mate." Max, not waiting, lifted his toward Brendan. He returned the toast but put his glass back on the bar. After a long, appreciative drink, Max came up for air. "That's bang on what I needed!"

The barman nodded. "Our national drink, that is. Best stuff in the world, and nothing else like it."

"Right so. Almost as satisfying as whiskey."

Brendan let slip a half-smile and exchanged an enigmatic glance with the landlord. He finally took a sip of his own pint and let out a long, satisfied sigh. "It's been a while since I had one. Mam doesn't approve of drinking, if you hadn't figured that out. But I appreciate a good pint now and then."

Max clinked his glass again, and they worked on finishing the pints.

Shouts rose from the patrons and Max jumped off his stool, eyes darting around, alert for an attack. But they just cheered a game on the telly. Some Irish sport, like soccer with paddles.

Brendan nodded toward the screen. "That's the GAA. Hurling."

"Hurling? That's what you do after too many pints."

The other man let out a chuckle. "Sure, and we've never heard that joke before. But I've heard hurling best described as a mix between lacrosse and football. When women play, they call it camogie."

Max studied the action, trying to make sense of the rules, but gave it up as a bad job. He had more important things to worry about, like his next pint. He drained the first one, and the barman filled his glass again.

Brendan exchanged some small talk with the landlord while Max dulled his pain. The voices faded into an indistinct murmur, tickling the back of his mind.

The Irishman matched him pint for pint and, after four, didn't seem the worse for wear. As his bladder made its presence known, Max peered around for the loo. He spied a sign and lurched toward the door. With the help of the wall, he took care of business and returned to his stool.

However, Brendan had his wallet out with his lips set in a thin line. "I've paid our bill. Let's head back to the farm. I'm not about to carry you back, and any more pints would make that a distinct possibility."

Slightly slurring, Max shook his finger. "C'mon, mate! The party's jusht startin'!"

Brendan scowled and crossed his arms. "I said, that's enough, Maximilian."

The use of Max's full first name drew him up short. His nan called him that when she was about to slap him in the back of his head. How could this man, at least thirty years his junior, remind him so much of his crusty old grandmother? *Hell.*

As they emerged from the dimly lit pub, the daylight had disappeared to velvet black, almost as complete as in Coober Pedy. A faint glow in the distance must be Limerick. He wondered how many pubs the city had and how long it would take to visit them all. A bloke should be able to find a place to live that didn't require a five kilometer walk to get a decent drink.

"This way, Max. Step carefully now. There's a curb."

With exaggerated care, he lifted his knee as he crossed the edge of the sidewalk. He walked toward the glowing city, but Brendan turned him around. "The farm's this way, Mr. Expert Navigator."

He grumbled but allowed the man to lead him in the right direction as whispers drew his attention into the darkness. Max dismissed them as phantoms from the drink and stumbled several times in the dark, but Brendan took firm hold of his arm and kept him from falling.

"Max, what's your deal, anyhow? Why are you so angry all the time?"

Pulling his shoulders straight, Max halted to stare at the Irishman. "Angry? Me? I'm a bloody delight, I am."

Brendan let out a snort. "Right. A bloody delight. Emphasis on the *bloody.*"

Whispers tickled the back of his mind on the return trip. He whipped his head around, trying to find their source, but nothing showed in the gathering darkness. The world tipped and tilted every few steps, and he had to hold on to Brendan's steadying arm more than he liked.

Just before they reached the front gate to the farm, the wind picked up, circling them in eddies. The voices screeched, ululating wails that burned through his brain. Holding his hands against his aching temples, Max cried out, "What? What do you want?"

Brendan, a shadowed form in the night, turned to him. "I want to get you into your room. We're almost home."

He pulled away, clapping his hands over his ears. "No, no, no, stop it! That hurts!"

A door shut and voices called out in query. Brendan answered with growing concern, "I don't know! He's gone completely mental, spouting nonsense about voices. I don't hear anything, do you? Just the wind."

Just the wind, he says. Max crouched, still holding his head as the voices increased. They called him. Where did they call him to? If he obeyed, would they stop? There, down the road. He ran in the darkness.

Brendan's voice faded behind him. "Max! Max, come back! I can't see you! *Feck it all!*"

Gravel crunched beneath his feet as he lurched along the road, stumbling and running in turns. He fell at least three times, his knees and palms growing raw from scrapes. Still the voices beckoned him. He could no more disobey than he could bring Trina back.

Her lovely face swam into his mind's eye, not as he'd last seen her, but when he first met her, an assistant to the civilian consultants on the air base. Trina's French and Vietnamese ancestry melded beautifully together.

Her black hair swept up into a professional bun, but her eyes spoke to his soul like nothing ever had before.

Except the wind.

Now that wind drew him, unwilling and almost unable, down the road. Human voices called his name in the distance, increased desperation in their tone, but he ignored those. He must answer the wind. The wind called into his bones, his blood, and refused to be ignored.

The road rose, his calves stretching as he climbed, up the hill until the voices halted. Then, the air fell still with a snap. Max swayed, falling painfully to his knees as the countryside grew silent. After the roar of the rushing winds calling him, the silence hit him with a striking blow.

Max's breath caught as he spied the river below. Shards of moonlight glittered on the surface and gulls echoed in the night. A fishing boat rocked in the middle of the river, with two shadowy forms and a lantern. Above, stars winked in and out of cloud cover, sparkling like fairy lights above him. The wind whispered in his mind.

We found you.

The winds whipped him hard, bowling over from his knees to the soft grass of the cliff, inches from the edge. They screeched again, but now he screeched back. "Leave me alone! Or listen to me. Just stop haunting me!"

Why should we listen to you? What do you say?

Scrambling back to his knees, his hands wet with evening dew, he shouted into the night, "I say slow the hell down. Fuck me dead, you don't need all this howling!"

The winds eased and then burst forth again with violent speed. On the river, the fishing boat spun in a whirlpool, threatening to capsize. For a moment, Max's mind traveled to that hapless boat, dizzy and terrified. "Stop it! Stop messing with them! Stop messing with me! Just slow down!"

Why?

"Because I asked!"

You did not ask. You told. We do not like to be told.

"Then, for fuck's sake, will you slow down?"

Very well.

The boat steadied, and Max drew a deep breath. His name filtered through the wind, but on human lips. "Max! Max? Are you up there?"

He recognized Colin's deep voice. Torchlight bobbed around in the darkness. "I'm here. Give me a minute, aye?" The light stopped moving. Max took a deep breath and rubbed at his face, still numb from his pints. "Now, listen, wind. I want your cooperation. Will you help me?"

What do you wish?

"Nothing now. I mean in the future. Will you work with me? I'll try to be polite. I'm not very good at playing nice, but I promise I'll try."

We don't like you.

He sat back on his heels and crossed his arms. "Well, why not? I'm bloody likable as hell!"

Their mental voices fluttered. If he didn't know any better, he might think they were laughing.

That is human humor?

"I suppose so. Don't you like humor?"

We do not understand it. We want to.

Whoever thought the wind wanted to laugh? "Aye, I can help you with that. It'll take some time to teach you, but I'll give it a go. Will that help you like me?" Max hoped he could deliver on this promise.

Very well. Until then.

The winds released him, snapping the air with a *crack*. He caught his breath, off balance from the abrupt change. Max did not look forward to explaining this to his hosts. But at least he quieted one of his fears. For now.

Max:

As they half-carried Max into the dining room and set him in a chair, Anna sat across from him. "Are you okay?"

He raised his head, his eyes half-lidded with fatigue, and mumbled out, "What do you think, luv? Do I look okay?"

"No, definitely not."

Róisín returned with a steaming cup of coffee and placed his hands around the warmth. Max held the mug for several moments before taking a sip. "Thanks, darlin'. I owe you."

Brendan came in and sat next to Anna. He bumped her shoulder with his, and she shared a smile with him. "Would you like some tea? Mam's heating up the kettle."

"I'd love some, thanks."

As he left, Róisín came back in with a massive platter of cookies, bread, and butter. "Now, Max, you're to eat at least two slices of bread. You need something in your stomach to absorb all that beer. What were you thinking, running up to the edge of a cliff in your condition? And in a gale-force storm, too."

Max shrugged and stared at the bread. "They stopped when I reached the top. No wind at all."

Brendan returned and exchanged a knowing glance with Róisín. "The wind howled at the base, and we could see you. Wind doesn't work that way."

He still didn't move, cradling the cup of coffee, still staring at the platter. "It did. I swear it did."

Róisín rolled her eyes and grabbed a chunk of bread, slathering sweet cream butter on. She put the slice on a napkin and plopped it in front of the Australian man. "You need to tell us the truth, Max. Lying isn't acceptable."

He leapt to his feet, the action knocking Róisín back. The Irish woman's eyes grew wide as Max yelled, "I'm telling you, the wind bloody well stopped! It taunted me the whole time! Voices everywhere! In my head, in my bones, on that fucking hill!"

Anna gasped as Brendan held his hands out. "Calm down, Max! Just calm down."

"Then stop calling me a bloody liar! Damn it, when I tell the truth, no one believes me!" He backed away from the coffee and bread, until his arse hit the dining room wall. His eyes darted around the room, as if searching for something that wasn't there.

Anna cleared her throat and asked, "Are the voices talking to you now?"

Max sent her a glare. "No, they aren't bloody talking now. We're inside. But they're whispering. Teasing. Tickling my ears. I can't fucking well escape them."

Brendan approached, his hands out. "We can help you find a way to quiet them. The PHAE have all sorts of folks who can—"

Max scuttled out of the way, his eyes getting wilder by the moment. His voice grew louder with each sentence. "I don't give a flying fuck what the folks at the PHAE can do. They can keep their ghoulish claws off me and my talent. And you can keep your fucking hands off me!"

Another voice came from the doorway. Michelle stood, her hands on her hips. "Maximilian Hurley. That language is not permitted in this household."

Like a recalcitrant schoolboy, Max followed his hostess to the outbuilding she used for an office. His blood still raced with terror, and he suppressed an urge to run out into the darkness, to escape this place, these people, and everything PHAE.

Michelle sat behind the large desk while Max took a chair. She clasped her hands together and pursed her lips.

"Mr. Hurley, are you unsatisfied with our hospitality here?"

He shook his head, but his heart ached to tell her yes.

"Please, vocalize your answer, Mr. Hurley. Gestures are too culturally specific."

"No."

Her jaw clenched several times before responding. "And yet you refuse to accept that the PHAE have your best interests in mind. Would you rather be elsewhere? We can arrange your transport to wherever you would like to go. It doesn't have to be Australia."

He swallowed. With his plane destroyed, Australia held little promise for him. But Max couldn't think where else he wanted to be. He just didn't want to be here, now, with these candy-arsed sycophants. He didn't want to be a pawn for this PHAE group. Max just wanted to be left alone. "Brilliant. Why don't you send me to…" but his mind turned utterly blank. Where could he go? America was a right shitshow. Canada had too many goody-two-shoes idiots. England? Too stuffy. Russia? Too cold, and probably even *more* whispering winds.

"While you're contemplating the possibilities, Mr. Hurley, please, consider this. Where else will you receive free room and board, along with instruction in your talents? We have the ability, interest, *and* resources to help you find your true potential."

His true potential sat at the bottom of a whiskey bottle. Max took in a deep breath. He needed a drink for his mind to work. His thoughts had been in such a jumble since he left Coober Pedy. Here, he might break out of his rut. He might stretch his abilities. Sudden shame for how he'd treated Brendan and Róisín made his face flush. Trina always said he acted a right bugger when he got his temper up. He owed it to her to rise above that for once.

He let out a defeated sigh and slumped his shoulders. "Right. You might have a point."

She stood, gripping the edge of her desk as she leaned toward him. Danger alarms went off in the back of his mind. "Then I suggest, Mr. Hurley, that you rein in your natural inclination for cursing, for anger, and most of all, for being a bloody-minded jerk. Are we clear?"

He bowed his head and nodded. She reminded him of his first CO; not a kind assessment.

"I cannot hear a nod, Mr. Hurley. Are we clear?"

At that tone, Max turned twenty years old, at his first day of basic training, and frightened out of his mind. He snapped to attention and said, "Crystal clear, Mrs. Byrne."

"Good. You are on probation until you can prove your determination to change. And prove it quickly. We've gotten some disturbing intelligence, and we may need to rely on you soon."

His stomach churned and he straightened his back. "What intelligence?"

She shook her head. "Nothing official, and nothing I can share yet. But something is brewing. And I'd rather not have to worry about quelling a rebellion in our home. Do you understand?"

Max clenched his teeth. "I do."

"Now, go to your quarters. You're done for now. I don't wish to see your face again tonight."

Well, maybe he should head back to the pub, then.

"And remain at the farm. I don't wish a repeat of this evening's chaos. None of us have the patience for that nonsense."

Bloody hell. Can she read minds? No, Róisín said she could turn time back, or something.

No matter. He had a new emergency supply in his room. The landlord in the pub balked at first, but Max's offer of cash for the bottle of whiskey proved too much to refuse.

Max found the sanctuary of his room, rooted into his bag for his elixir, and held the bottle up. The gorgeous brown liquid glinted in the lamplight. He wondered how long his nectar would last.

He'd encountered too many emergencies since he'd gotten here and must find a cheaper way to re-supply. Did the nearby town have a store?

A knock at the door made him shove the bottle back into his bag. When he opened the door, Róisín stood with her arms crossed and a paper bag in her hand. "Well?"

He set his jaw. "Well, what, darlin'? It's late, luv. I'm bloody knackered. Are you expecting an apology?"

She shouldered past him and placed the bag on his table. "That *would* be the socially correct thing to do. Oh, I know you aren't one for social correctness, but I thought I at least warranted some consideration."

Róisín turned back to him, anger flashing in her eyes. She grabbed his shoulders and stared at him. The gaze burned with intensity, making him tingle from head to foot. Not a tempting gaze, but a strong one, reminiscent of her mother's sheer strength. A shiver ran down his spine. Max stumbled back and fell onto the couch, refusing to look at the woman. He didn't want to do anything stupid, and he didn't trust himself. He mumbled, "Thank you."

Róisín let out a deep sigh and left the room, slamming the door.

As he opened the bag, he found two ham sandwiches, a foil package of roast potatoes, and another of broccoli sprinkled with parmesan cheese. A smaller bag inside held a full bottle of whiskey. Of Tullamore Dew.

Max wiped at his eyes. He didn't deserve her kindness. In fact, she deserved someone much better, younger, and kinder than himself. Maybe, just maybe, he'd be willing to fight for her. Even if the PHAE did the asking.

And oddly enough, he didn't need a drink. Miracle of miracles.

Chapter Six

"A ship is always safe at shore. But that is not what it is built for"
– John A. Shedd

***Latest* CNN *Update:** Several diverse groups have coalesced into a single Pure Earther Movement (PEM) to protest the rising number of so-called Unhidden. Their membership is reported to consist of organizations such as the American Freedom Party, the Aryan Terror Brigade, Stormfront, Faith and Heritage, West Village Baptist Church, and the Alliance of American Klans. One man, named Tiberius Wilkinson, claims to be a spokesperson for the group, and has delivered an ultimatum. They are calling for a curfew for people identified as Unhidden as well as an international registry. In addition, certain factions are asking for a maximum quota of Unhidden allowed in a community, based on a pro rata percentage of total population.*

Max:

With Michelle's commands in mind, Max came to breakfast on time the next morning. He did drink a swallow of his whiskey the night before, but he didn't need as much as usual. Just enough to keep the nightmares away, but not so much that he lost control. Trina still haunted his dreams, but at least she came to him whole and alive, not bloody and broken. Nor did the children appear. He got decent rest without their company.

How long would they have to stay here for more training and education? He'd let someone else ask. Better that than to incur Michelle's wrath again.

Damn, that woman had power. Not Unhidden power, but true, raw, leadership power. She'd make one hell of a drill sergeant. Just the thought of her anger made him crave a drink.

As if he'd summoned her with his thoughts, Michelle entered with Colin, holding hands. He couldn't conceive of a love lasting, what, thirty years?

As he sipped the coffee, Max realized he'd forgotten his flask. *Have I come down with something?* He shrugged and sipped his unadulterated drink, savoring the flavor for once. The bitter coffee soothed the sharp edges of his morning.

When the PHAE suits came in, all conversation halted. Instead of getting breakfast, they stood at the doorway.

Ciara nodded to Martin and cleared her throat. "Listen up, everyone. Thank you for your cooperation yesterday. I apologize for interrupting your breakfast, but we have some news. We'd expected to leave you here for several weeks, learning to control and focus your abilities. However, we have a situation."

Max remembered those words from his days in Vietnam, and his stomach clenched.

Martin glanced around, catching Colin's eye. "We've received reports of plans to attack Ireland."

Brendan and Max both jumped to their feet with a shout. Martin waved them both back into their seats. "Of course, we suspect the PEM, but their leader hasn't said anything directly."

Anna piped up, "PEM?"

Martin cleared his throat. "The Pure Earther Movement. They are an alliance of conservative organizations with an avowed hatred against those with Unhidden talents. They have proposed many solutions, many of them similar to the Nazi's solutions in WWII. Since Ireland is well-known as hosting the PHAE, it has become a rather obvious target for their vilification and rhetoric."

Max furrowed his brow. "Their leader? I didn't know they had organized so much to have a leader."

Ciara gave a curt nod. "In the last few weeks, one man has become their spokesperson. His name is Tiberius Wilkinson. His rhetoric has gotten nastier over the last week, churning up worldwide protests."

After letting out a snort, Max shook his head. "Bloody stupid name if you ask me."

Martin cleared his throat. "I don't recall asking, mate. Look, we aren't certain of the intended target, but our intelligence suggests the most likely site to be Dublin. That's the largest port of trade to Europe and closing the port would severely damage Ireland's economy. We can't be certain Dublin is the target, though, so we need to station talent and defensive arms at several points along the coast. Besides Dublin, which is where we'll concentrate our heaviest defense, we need to bolster Galway, Belfast, Wexford, and Cork."

Martin stepped back as Ciara came forward. "You are, as Michelle mentioned earlier, our strongest talented class to date. We have a half-dozen other talents of your strength with offensive or defensive abilities. We've already assigned them to stations, but we need you to cover shifts. They aren't much more experienced than you, but at least they've gone through the full course here, learning their talents."

Max's throat closed. Despite decades of running, war found him again. He couldn't get out. Sure, the Byrnes assured him he could quit. But they had a name for a man who quit during wartime. He was no bloody deserter. If he didn't quit in the middle of the jungle, holding his lover's charred body in his arms, he'd be damned if he'd quit here.

He didn't want to murder people, but if they attacked, he had no issue with defending himself. And those like himself. With a glance toward Róisín, Max stood, his shoulders squared. "Right. Give me a plane. Give me a bomb. Point me in their direction."

Martin shook his head, his eyes sad. "I'm afraid none of you are ready for that, mate, not as an Unhidden, nor as a plain vanilla bomber pilot. As if the PHAE even had such things. We're not a country and we don't have a military. Even if you had the weeks of training you were supposed to have, we'd have better places for someone of your power. We're assigning you to various defensive points, but you aren't to strike out on your own. You'll have more experienced folks with you, and they'll be calling the shots."

Max's heart skipped a beat when Martin continued. "Róisín, we'll need your healing hands in Galway, at the PHAE central hospital. We have our other healers stationed at hospitals in Dublin and Letterkenny." Max let out a half-breath. He didn't want Róisín anywhere dangerous. Her gentle soul must be kept far away from the front line.

Ciara turned to Anna. "Anna, we're assigning you to Cork, along with Max and Brendan. We've a few folks standing watch already, but they need shift relief."

Offensive talents on the coast, which meant him and Anna. Róisín would be support personnel. That's how war worked.

Max shook his head, annoyed with his military training taking over his thoughts. He hated the idea of being in the military again, and his nerves shook at the idea. But that's what they needed now, right? If war knocked on one's door, only the foolish and cowardly hid under the covers. He just hoped his asshole brain would be up to the fight.

Anna:

The long, winding drive to the southwest corner of the country took them through countless quaint villages and endless farmlands. For over an hour, green hills blurred in her vision. Anna didn't see them. She only saw the angry protestors at the airport, with her brother leading them. They must have been part of the PEM, or at least some similar hate group.

The same folks who Joel had been with in Washington, D. C. People who called her inhuman.

At least Brendan stayed with her. So had Max, but he'd slumped against the car window and fell asleep, so she remained alone with her thoughts.

Anna's upper arms itched. Would her entire body turn to scales? Or just her arms? Her torso, like some reverse mermaid? Not only would she turn into some freak, a monster out of fairy tales, but Brendan would reject her, then, despite his compliments.

The Irishman chatted with the driver. She tried to make out the words, but they spoke in low tones. Over the sound of Max's snoring, words like castle, inlet, lighthouse, and defenders drifted back. She didn't need to be a rocket scientist to figure out the subject.

Anna didn't want to think about what they'd face in Cork. She'd never been a violent person, but she took some self-defense courses in college, and had done well. She'd be fine, so long as whoever attacked did so one-on-one and without automatic weapons. If they didn't follow the martial art rules, she'd be in severe trouble.

She glanced at Max, a line of drool dripping down his chin. Anna couldn't figure out what motivated him, other than drink. She'd met alcoholics before, and he showed all the classic signs. Her dad had a friend who had liked the drink more than his own family. In the end, he'd left them and ended up dead, hit by a semi truck on the highway.

Still, Max had stepped up with his offer to fight. Perhaps not being all alone helped. Or maybe just being in a healthier environment. She didn't know what his home in Australia had been like, but she got the impression he'd lived alone, out in the sticks, and with very few creature comforts.

Her skin tingled as she glanced outside, watching raindrops on the window. Anna fought the urge to fling the door open and jump into the rain. She'd never had a self-destructive streak. Did she feel trapped? A need to escape? Or did she just want to feel the water on her skin? She watched the back of Brendan's head as he nodded to whatever the driver had said.

Brendan gave her hope for the future, even if she turned into a swamp monster.

The car slowed as they entered thick suburbs. She hadn't paid attention to the signs. Had they arrived in Cork already?

Suburbs turned to commercial buildings, strip malls, and neighborhoods. When those thinned, they pulled onto a narrow promontory with a lighthouse. Several white outbuildings and a low wall surrounded the structure, enough space for a dozen rooms.

Several ships moved through the narrow strait, including a commercial tanker and a cargo ship. Cork must be a busy port. She didn't see any docks or cranes, but those might be in Cork proper, hidden behind the headland to the north. Anna could just make out buildings along a distant shoreline.

Max stirred as they slowed to park in the circular driveway to the lighthouse. He yawned, stretched, and unfolded his long frame from the car. "This? This is our stronghold?"

Brendan opened the trunk to extract their luggage. "Well spotted. We're to relieve the current watch."

While shaking his head, Max surveyed the frontage. "This won't do. There's no way this is defensible. I thought you had proper castles in Ireland, with tall, thick walls! Massive bloody things able to withstand a siege of troops? Artillery? This has a laughable outer wall, no killing field, and the water offers easy access from submersibles."

Brendan offered Anna the handle of her carry-on luggage. He hefted the larger case. Max and the driver got the rest. "This is what we've got. Even a *proper castle*, as you put it, won't stand against modern artillery. That's why they fell out of fashion after the seventeenth century. Cannons break through curtain walls and bombs make them useless. With higher technology, the best defense is staying well-hidden. Besides, do you really think this will be a physical invasion force? Modern war is fought more with terrorism and hackers than tanks, especially on an island."

Max waved his hand. "I don't know what the fuck a hacker is. And how do you know there won't be an invasion force? Are the locals going to help the defense?"

"Not many locals around here who can help. Mostly elderly farmers and the like. We've got ships being dispatched, but most are being kept in Dublin to bolster their position. One ship is headed our way but will be some time yet. I'm afraid we're pretty much on our own."

"Guns? Anti-aircraft missiles? You gotta have something, mate."

Brendan shook his head. "Max, Ireland just doesn't have a huge military. Remember, technically we're working for PHAE, not the Republic of Ireland. We're an island perched on the back end of Europe. We haven't had to deal with an invasion since 1760, when the French tried. Unless you count our own Civil War, or trying to eject the English, we haven't fought foreign battles on our shores since then. We didn't even take a side in World War II."

"Then what the bloody hell do you expect us to do? Ask the invaders to leave and come back after teatime?"

Brendan leveled a glare at him. "We are here to keep watch. If someone tries to get into the harbor with ill-intent, we dissuade them. That's all. That's our job."

"Ill-intent. How the hell are we going to know that? Do you have any mind-readers in the crew here already? How about a soothsayer? I might find a deck of tarot cards back in Limerick."

"Max. Just shut up, aye? We're all tired, and we don't have a lot of information yet."

Max threw his hands up in exasperation and stomped off toward the lighthouse door. Anna's anxiety, which rose as Max criticized the palace, ebbed at Brendan's explanation, but simmered below the surface. Brendan hadn't assured them they'd be safe.

Brendan led them to the front door. "Let's get you settled into your rooms, and then we'll take you up into the lighthouse. You've got the first watch tonight. The others have been on for sixteen hours and need a break." He disappeared into one room with his luggage.

Anna didn't unpack her things in the stark room. She just washed her face at the sink down the hall and brushed her hair, pulling the thick mass back into a ponytail. The wind blew fiercely on the coast.

When Brendan returned, he clapped his hands. "All set? You'll have the watch for at least eight hours. We're stretched thin since we had little notice. We have people scattered across the world, so mustering our full strength will take time. And as Mam said, strong offensive talents are rare."

That sinking in the pit of her stomach returned. What use would she be in a lighthouse? Could she light the beacon? That must be automated now. Still, Anna didn't want to complain. Max had cornered the market on complaining.

As soon as they emerged to the yard, Max asked, "So, what exactly are we to do in this thing, mate? Wave our arms? Light the beacons of Gondor? Have a barbecue?"

Anna chuckled, then covered her mouth when Brendan turned to glare at her. "This is no laughing matter."

As they climbed the stairs, Brendan spoke over his shoulder. "Now, as you heard, we're expecting attacks. I just received updated intelligence that they may have more than one planned, but we don't know the details of how or when, and maybe more we don't know of. One is headed toward Dublin, estimated early tomorrow morning. We need a twenty-four-hour watch in case our intelligence is flawed."

Max let out a snort. "How do we bloody know what this attack is going to look like? And what are we meant to do if we see one?"

Brendan gave Anna a sad smile. "That's where Anna comes in. I know we haven't exactly been trained as regular troops, but our talents are valuable resources. She can ask the water to help."

Max coughed as they reached the gallery. "Bloody hell. You're going to stick this little girl on the front lines? Are you fucking serious? Don't you mugs have radar?"

The Irish man crossed his arms. "Max. Do you ever get tired of saying 'bloody hell?'"

As much as she agreed with the sentiment, Anna resented being called a little girl. She fought down her panic at going into the ocean, especially alone, and at night. "I'll do it. Or I'll try. What sort of, uh, creatures live in the ocean around here?"

Brendan gave her a heart-melting smile. "You won't be alone. I'll be with you, with my radio. Yes, Max, we *do* have radar. What should we tell them to search for? Cork is a busy port. We've got loads of traffic going in and out. This is our main shipping connection to Europe."

Max subsided. "Bloody hell. What do you need me to do?"

"You can ask the winds to find things, too. But your wind power will be helpful if we get an air strike. In the meantime, we need to rely on our physical defenses which, as you so rightly pointed out, are hopelessly light, and Anna's power, which is untested and untrained. We may be in for a very long night."

"And what about the rest of the crew, those who are sleeping? What are their talents?"

Brendan pursed his lips. "Jamie can turn dirt red by touch. Useful for signaling someone flying overhead, perhaps. Not much use otherwise. Chen can make stone crumble to dust."

The older man straightened his spine at that news. "Oi, that could be useful! What's his range? How much at once?"

With a shrug, Brendan shook his head. "He needs to touch the stone and can only affect a fist-sized chunk at once. Takes him a few minutes even for that."

Max deflated. "Bloody, bloody hell."

Fear morphed into a heavy lump in Anna's stomach.

Anna:

They'd relieved the previous team of PHAE staffers, Chen and Jamie. Both had almost fallen asleep on their feet. While they stumbled down to the bunkhouses, Max agreed to keep watch while Anna and Brendan tried to talk to the waves.

The sun still hung high in the sky as Anna stared at the dark ocean surface. The solid white lighthouse towered behind her. Rocks scraped against the bottom of her bare feet as waves lapped her toes, and Brendan stood behind her.

Why did the sea seem so calm? The surface should be whipping in furious anger to match her mind's maelstrom.

She'd stripped down to shorts and a T-shirt, exposing her scaled forearms. Her upper arms itched, angry and red, heralding their own scales. Her calves itched, too. She shivered in the biting wind, despite the warm summer sun beating down on her skin.

Anna took a step into the water. A wave splashed up, covering her legs, and her calves itched less. Despite that, fear inched up her limbs, all the way up her body and down her arms. It chilled her skin, which broke out in goosebumps. She rubbed her arms and gritted her teeth. She took another step. The water no longer seemed gentle. It lurked as a dark threat, eager to engulf her.

This time, a larger wave crashed over the rocks, drenching her and shoving her back. She screamed and ran back to Brendan. He held her tight and stroked her wet hair, whispering reassurance into her ear. "You're grand, you're grand, Anna. I've got you."

Turning to make another try, she stepped forward once again.

Another wave splashed. Anna tried to calm her mind by singing, but she forgot every single song she'd ever heard. She turned away again with a sob. "I can't. I can't!"

"Anna? You can do this."

"I can't. The sea is too angry. I can't!" Shoving past Brendan, she clambered back up the rocks.

"Anna!" He grabbed for her, but only caught her ankle, still slippery with sea water. She escaped his grasp and scrambled up the rocks. By the time Brendan reached her, she stood on dry land, staring up at Max in the tower.

"Anna, would it help if I went with you?"

Her fear shifted to anger, and she spun on him. "No, it wouldn't help if you went with me! It wouldn't help if I had your entire family with me. I'm afraid of the ocean! Can't you understand that? Me, the person who can ask water to do things and the water actually listens, is afraid of the ocean. God, I'm such a failure." She covered her face with her hands as racking sobs took over.

Brendan pulled her in for another hug, but she wrenched away. "And save your platitudes! They won't help!"

He backed off, holding his hands up. "All right, all right. What do you suggest we do, then?"

Anna stared at the crashing waves, pursing her lips. Sea spray mingled with her tears, leaving salty trails down her cheeks. The ocean seemed like one terrifying monster, waiting to swallow her into the inky depths. A seagull cried and flew up to the lighthouse, its raucous cry echoing against the white plastered wall.

She followed its flight to the top of the tower and spied a face behind the glass. Anna didn't want Max to witness her cowardice. She didn't particularly like the older man, but she didn't want to look foolish in front of him.

After taking a deep breath, she climbed down the rocks again. This time, she felt determined to at least put her feet in the water, despite the screaming in her head.

Brendan clutched her hand. "That's brilliant, Anna. Can you hear anything from the water? Can you make any contact? I know Max talks to the winds. Can you talk to the waves?"

"Give me a minute, all right?" *Can you hear me?*

The water murmured and thrummed, but she couldn't tell if the waves answered, complained, or just made noise. The seagull cried again.

"I need to go deeper in."

Brendan let go of her hand as she stepped down to the next rock, the water now coming to her neck. Something dark swirled in the water and she almost screamed but steeled herself to remain still until it passed.

She asked the ocean again, and only a thrum answered.

Fuckabiscuit, I have to go deeper.

With one last glance at Brendan's face, pale with worry, she stepped off the last rock and swam under the surface. The humming of the ocean embraced her, vibrating through her body and sparkling off her scales. She surfaced, treading water, and looked back. Brendan crouched on the last rock, his eyes wide.

"Anna, be careful! You're drifting out."

With a solemn nod, she swam back toward the rock, but didn't climb onto the rocks.

If you can hear me, splash this stone with a strong wave. She pictured an enormous wave crashing over the rocks.

A modest spume of water crashed against the stone, but that might just be a coincidence. Anna tried to calm her rapid heartbeat.

Can you do that again, but bigger? Again, she pictured a massive splash.

The second splash gave more credence, this time pushing her back. She swallowed her fear against the success of the command. *Again!*

This time, the wave splashed big enough to drench them both. Brendan spluttered and flashed an accusatory glare. "Did you do that?"

Anna muffled her nervous giggle. "I didn't expect them to answer that well."

"So, you *can* speak to the water? It listened?"

"Seems like. Should I ask them if they can find a strange boat?"

Brendan shook his long hair like a dog, splattering her. She held up her arm to shield her face. "Hey!"

He gave her a grin. "That's just payback. I'm not sure what you could ask about that they'd recognize."

"Have you heard more from Dublin? Do we know if the attack will be a submarine, a boat, or a plane?"

"I'm afraid not. They still say the attack will be in Dublin, not here, but even that is an educated guess. We're sort of flying blind."

Anna frowned. "Well, a sub would be the easiest thing for the water to spot. Let's start with that." She faced the ocean and closed her eyes, questing her attention below the surface. *Do you see a human vehicle, under the water, headed for this island?*

Again, the murmur in her mind could be an answer, or nothing at all. Did she speak to the ocean? Or individual waves? Parts of the water? She'd have to stick to yes or no answers. Anna boggled that it understood her at all. Did the water understand English? Or read the pictures in her mind? As she shut her eyes again, Anna pictured a classic submarine, something out of Hunt for Red October, cutting under the surface toward Ireland.

Nothing happened.

Anna took in a deep breath, only to inhale a spray of sea salt. She coughed and sputtered, Brendan patting her back. For all that she could talk to the sea, breathing water was a different matter. Perhaps her scales would form gills at some point.

What she wouldn't give to be back in the safety of a college swimming pool, presiding over petty college girl squabbles. Instead, she stood on the edge of the Atlantic Ocean, talking to waves and worse, getting sassed by them.

This ridiculous comparison helped to ground her. Anna took in a deep breath, this one thankfully free of saltwater. "I think that's a no. But I can't talk words to it. Or them. Or whatever. Just images in my mind."

Anna climbed out of the ocean's embrace and sat dripping on the rocks, her head hung low. Brendan clenched his fists and growled. She knew his frustration stemmed from the ocean's limited understanding and not her, but she still felt the censure in her heart. "If they can't find a submarine, how do we find a ship? And if the attack comes from the air, I'm useless."

Brendan stared out at the water. Gray clouds drifted in the distance, and the sun dipped lower in the west, about two hours to sunset. The blue-green glittering ocean would turn sinister black at night. Even the deeper water looked darker now. "I don't know, Anna. I just don't know. We need more information."

Max:

The American girl looked so tiny on the rocks. Max dug his fingers into the railing when the waves crashed over her and Brendan. However, he noticed glints of strength in her, hidden by her shyness. She was tougher than she looked. Anna had mentioned she hated deep water, and he'd seen the panic in her eyes when Brendan suggested going down to the rocks. But she'd marshaled forward and did what she had to, like a good soldier. He respected her grit.

In the war, Max learned that courage didn't mean having no fear. Everyone feared something. Anyone who didn't turned out to be an idiot or a psychopath. Those who pushed through the fear and finished their mission, they were the brave ones. Those who completed their duty, despite the heart-stopping fear warring inside their soul.

Of course, that didn't mean their mission was a good one, or a moral one, just that they had the courage to complete the task. That same fear froze some people in place, even when obvious danger fell upon them. Like Trina.

Trina hadn't been brave. She'd frozen with terror. From her body's position, she must have been watching the planes as they rained death upon her village.

He'd cried so hard when he found her that his mates had to drag him away from her burnt corpse. Red and black skin crisped, flaking away at his touch. He didn't even get to bury her. He had to leave her ravaged body in the remnants of her destroyed village, food for crows. Perhaps her bones still lay there.

Max shook his head, trying to dispel the memory. *God, I need a drink. In fact, an entire bottle would suit fine.* He shoved the impulse away and concentrated on Anna and Brendan below. Max considered running down the stairs to help them, but he needed to watch for the enemy.

Max had to admit, this structure looked much more defensible than an inland palace, like that Dublin country manor house. A ridiculous building for war headquarters, despite its poshness. According to the tour brochure, they'd built this lighthouse over two hundred years ago. It no longer had a working foghorn, and they'd automated the light. A low wall surrounded a field at the base with several outbuildings, useless for defense. The rocky shore served as a better barrier.

Max tried to shift his thoughts to something not war-related. He glanced around, still cataloging each feature for its defense capabilities. Rocky outcropping, great elevation, stone walls, all great against a sea attack. Not so great against a sky attack, though. He scanned the skies, noting each speck and cataloging them as different types of birds before relaxing.

His stomach rumbled despite the sandwiches he'd scarfed down. He wanted to fling the window open and touch the winds, speak to them, but not yet. Max didn't feel up to making new friends. Besides, Brendan asked him to wait until he could observe.

On the other side of the lighthouse, small farms formed an irregular patchwork across rocky outcroppings. Brendan said the locals were elderly farmers, no good for helping with any defense. What about at the port itself, though? That lay inland, around the headland, out of sight. They should have at least some marine corps or coast guard troops to help. Unless those were needed for the port itself, which seemed fair enough.

A boat launched from one of the farms. A fishing boat, two men on deck. They headed due south, white smoke spouting from its engine.

A small plane soared to the ground, too small to be a commercial craft. Max perked up and watched the craft land, envy blooming in his heart. Cork must have an airport. He yearned to be in a plane, up amidst his beloved clouds. When they finished this mess, he'd hit Brendan up for that promised plane.

Max leaned against the ancient brick walls of the interior and didn't see Anna or Brendan. *Bloody hell, what happened to them? Where'd they go?*

As images of finding their drowned bodies on the rocks pounded him, Max shoved himself away from the railing and entered the building itself. As he pelted down the spiral steps to the base, his stomach gurgled. Max halted, realizing he hadn't splashed his dwindling supply of whiskey into his coffee this morning. He could use a tot now. He almost ran back up the stairs to retrieve his flask from his pack but hesitated. Maybe he should find Brendan and Anna first.

Three flights of stairs later, he reached the ground floor just as they arrived. They both looked soaked to the bone and shivering, despite their towels and wind-fluffed hair. Each one wore pensive looks.

"Any luck down there?"

Brendan shook his head. "Without knowing what we're looking for, we're at a loss to figure out how to find anything. We'll just have to keep our eyes peeled."

Max let out a snort. "Oi, mate, is the café open? I'm bloody starving."

"No, but we can fix something. We've got sandwich fixings and crisps downstairs. After that, we're famished, too. The Irish Sea can take it right out of you. Go on back up to the gallery to watch. Anna needs to rest after her attempts."

Anna held up her hands. "I'm fine, I really am. I'll come up with you."

As they climbed the stairs, ancient stone muffled their footsteps, swallowing the noise. With each floor, Max's anxiety about the coming confrontation grew. The winds at the farm had listened to him, for the most part. Would these be the same? Cousins or something? He didn't know how it worked, or if he spoke to separate entities, or some elemental power. The voices in his head sounded like several people speaking the same words at once, in stereo, like a trained chorus.

Brendan brought up trays with bread, scones, butter, and canned fish, which gave them sandwiches for now and more for later. He unlocked the gallery door. A stout steel railing surrounded the platform.

As soon as Max stepped outside, gusts buffeted him, making him reel back into Anna. She cried out in pain as he stomped on her foot. "Fuck. Sorry, darlin'."

"That's okay. My fault for standing so close behind you."

They arranged a table on the gallery so they could watch the horizon while they ate. The Irishman turned to Max while buttering his scone. "Eager to start?"

"I wouldn't say eager was the right word, mate. Cautious may be better. Even worried is closer to the truth."

Brendan chugged from a bottle of water. "Worried? What about?"

Max shrugged and looked up at the white clouds. "I've had issues in the past with strange winds. I need to go through a process to make friends, and my process always works. Makes me a bit gun-shy."

"That's interesting. You talk to them, right? With words? What happened when it went wrong?"

Max peered into his tea, wishing the cup held some whiskey. "Sure, I talk to them out loud. They talk back, in my head. But sometimes they sass me, like when the plane landed in Zurich. I asked them to stop tossing the plane around so much. They didn't listen to me, like brats. Instead, they made things worse. I'm not gonna lie, I almost lost my wits there, mate."

Anna choked on her mouthful of scone, spraying crumbs on the table. She hastened to clean them up as Max shot her a glare.

He turned back to the Irishman. "So, Brendan, since you say the locals can't help us, what sort of physical offensive power do we have here?"

"Not much. Ireland has got nine offshore patrol vessels, and they're pleased to let the PHAE use them to defend Ireland. That's in their best interest, obviously. However, they're spread around the island. The closest one is the *LÉ Eithne*, their flagship. She's due to arrive later today, and will sit out about fifteen kilometers south, just inside our territorial waters. The *Eithne* has a Bofors anti-aircraft gun, two cannons, and a machine gun. Not much, but more than the others have. The other eight vessels are deployed around the island at strategic points, with three in Dublin."

Max's eyes grew wide. "Bofors are from World War II, mate. That's all we got?"

Brendan shrugged. "We haven't had to worry about invasion since then as we stayed neutral. The *Eithne* has a helipad. Since you love flying, I thought you'd like that."

He shivered, cold fear running down his spine. The last time he'd been in a helicopter had almost ended his life, and he had no wish to repeat that experience. Or what came afterward. "I bloody hate bloody helicopters. Fucking deathtraps, they are."

Brendan's hopeful face fell. "Oh, sorry."

Max raised an eyebrow. "Oi, speaking of that, Hiroki told me I'd get a plane when I got here. We're over a week in, and no bloody plane. When's that gonna happen, mate?"

The other man shrugged, taking a sip from his mug. "PHAE haven't seen fit to inform me of that. Anything that may have been in the works during your recruitment may have shifted, for obvious reasons. Our planes are preparing for an air attack, should that come next. But, yes, we'll get you a plane when possible. I'll back up that promise."

"Right. I'll hold you to that. Now, unless we get a massive airdrop of troops, which I presume we'll notice, the sea's the only way to get to this island. You'd think that'd convince Ireland to beef up their navy."

Brendan let out a long-suffering sigh. "Sure and it would have been, had we realized Ireland would become the hub of a controversial group of humans. But hindsight is a wonderful thing, Max. We should have, and we could have, but we didn't. The Irish got centuries of grief from England, almost a thousand years worth. When we finally booted them out, we promptly fell into a civil war. After we recovered from that, then came the Troubles, another type of civil war. To tell the truth, we have more weaponry along the Northern Irish border than we do at sea. And remember, these are Ireland's ships, not PHAE's. They're being smart enough to allow us to use them, as an attack on us is an attack on the island. But that's still a tentative agreement."

Max let out a huff of laughter and slapped his hands on the table. "Right. That sucks true bollocks, mate."

Brendan gave an apologetic shrug. "That's what we've got."

"Well, my stomach's stopped growling. Let's see what I can do with the local winds." He stood and gripped the railing, seeking the wind's voices. After taking a deep breath and quieting his concerns about being sassed, he yelled out, "Hello, mates. Will you speak to me?"

Nothing answered as a gale howled around the tower. A stab of fear shot through Max's heart. What if these winds wouldn't speak to him? What if they sassed him like the ones in Zurich, or fought him like the ones near Limerick? His confidence tanked and he needed a shot of whiskey so bad, he could almost taste it.

However, he pulled up an image of Róisín's smile, the one that reminded him of Trina's, but without the lurking nightmares which came with *that* memory. The Irish woman's grin helped him settle his stomach and gave him the bottle to try again.

"Hello, winds! I'm calling you."

Who are you?

He'd never thought to ask for names before. "I'm Max. Uh, who are you?"

We are Gaotha Na Chósta Copair.

"The what? Gweeha nah khoasta copper?" He turned to the resident Irish man, eyebrows raised.

Brendan chuckled. "That's what they said? It sounds like 'winds of the Copper Coast' in the Irish."

"Uh, can I call you Gweeha for short?"

You need call us nothing.

Great. They already hated him. Time to try a different tack. "I made friends with winds farther north. Will you be my friends, too?"

Only silence answered him.

Brendan nudged him. "Ask them to do something. See if they'll listen to you."

Max squared his shoulders and yelled, "Will you dance with me? I love watching the winds dance."

The zephyr grew stronger, tugging his hair from its ponytail. Anna's thick, dark hair danced around her like a halo, whipping in the gale. Even Brendan's shoulder-length hair snapped in the currents. The wind swirled around the lighthouse, and Max got taller. Startled, he glanced down. He no longer stood on the gallery floor. He scrambled to seize the metal railing, worried a gust would carry him off, only to drop him on the sharp rocks below. "Oi! Let me down!"

You said you wanted to dance. We are dancing with you.

He wrapped his arms around the railing as the gale grew stronger. "Not like that! Put me down!" The winds had never tried to bloody kidnap him before. Well, except that time at the fire.

You no longer wish to dance?

"I prefer to dance on the ground, sorry. It's dangerous in the air without a plane."

What is plane?

"A craft where humans can be in the sky. It has wings, like a stiff bird."

We have seen such craft. We do not like them. They make us move aside.

"You can help us with those craft, if you try."

Why should we try?

"Would you try if I ask you to?"

The velocity of the wind eased. Max breathed easier with his feet on the ground, but he didn't loosen his grip on the railing. "What would you like from me? I might be able to help you."

Make the buzzers stop.

"The Buzzers?" Max wrinkled his brow. "Do you mean buzzards? Great, ugly birds eating dead things?

No.

Maybe he could get them to send a picture in his mind. "What do the Buzzers look like? Show me."

The image of a drone flickered in his mind, heading straight for him. Reflexively, he ducked, and then straightened when nothing hit him. He turned to Brendan. "They mean drones, Brendan. Do you think the PEM's sending drones to spy on us?"

Brendan leaned on the railing, staring out to the sea. "I don't know, do I? Loads of people have drones now. They're a huge hit with people photographing the coast. Damned things are everywhere during tourist season. Ireland should make them their national bird."

With pressed lips, Max turned to him. "These didn't look like tourist jobs, mate. They'd be military-grade drones. These could be spies. They can even carry bombs, for fucks' sake. Why don't you ring up your precious PHAE on your bloody mobile and ask?"

The Irishman whirled on him, his face red. "Why do you think they'd know? We're flying blind here, Max. You remember the PHAE is only a few months old, right? We don't have a robust military intelligence branch. We've got us, those PHAE stationed at other strategic points, and those scraps of information the Republic of Ireland deem fit to share with us. That's all for now."

Max threw up his hands and paced along the gallery. "That's just bloody great. We're fucked. We're so bloody fucking fucked."

"Well, why don't you try to unfuck us, Max? You're the one with the military knowledge. Weren't you in a war as an airman? You have access to a point of intelligence no one else has. Ask your precious winds about the drones!"

Max wanted to punch the little snot, but he had a point. After swallowing his temper and wishing to God he had a bottle of whiskey, Max asked the wind, "Where is the closest buzzer?"

One is behind you.

He spun to spy one hovering just above the lighthouse gallery, a high-end machine with a camera orienting on his face. Spitting a curse, he pointed and shouted to any wind who would listen, "Smash it!"

A tiny whirlwind made the drone spin in a tight circle and slam into the side of the lighthouse. The wreckage landed on the gallery floor at Max's feet. A slow grin crept across his face. "Whoa, thanks, mates! That's bloody fine work!"

That is fun. We did not realize they were so easily destroyed. We want to destroy more.

"You can do that with every single one for all I care! With pleasure."

Max:

In the west, the sun kissed the edge of the water. Blazing in brilliant orange, the glimmering rocks below glowed with a ruddy hue. Max, Anna, and Brendan sat in the gallery, gazing at the spectacle.

Anna let out a deep sigh as Brendan hugged her shoulder. Max rolled his eyes and stared at the horizon. The two acted like they starred in a bloody romance novel. He didn't want to have any part in that nonsense.

The winds had destroyed three drones so far, but they had no idea if they missed others. Besides, the drones might just be the first wave for surveillance. They might have demolished them all, but Max had no way of knowing how many they sent, how many remained, or if any got through. If the winds had already been annoyed at them, they must have missed earlier drones. He didn't like not knowing, and he clenched his hands in anxious anticipation.

Anna leapt to her feet, pointing at the darkening inlet. "What's that?"

Brendan peered over the railing, squinting. "A fishing boat, I think."

"What're they pulling behind them?"

"I can't tell. Max, can you ask the wind to describe what's behind the boat? It looks like two smaller craft, but I can't make out any details."

With a deep sigh, Max rose and complied, grumbling under his breath. When the wind brought the image to his mind, he shrugged. "Two zodiacs, filled with square things. That's all they'll show me, mate. Bloody weird thing to be dragging into port, though."

Brendan pulled his mobile out and tried to zoom in to take a photograph, but he couldn't get good focus, even with binoculars. He let out a curse and called headquarters instead.

As he murmured on the phone, Max asked the winds, "Show me the side of the boat." Once he got the name of the boat in his mental image, he fed that to Brendan. "Can you ask the harbormaster if the craft is registered?"

The Irishman nodded and made his second call. He returned with a nod. "Brittany registered. They've been here before, a regular trip once a month. Wait, the harbormaster said this ship isn't due for another two weeks."

Max pursed his lips. "Do you think those blokes'd be upset if those two zodiacs just sort of flipped over all of a sudden-like?"

Brendan and Anna exchanged a glance. She shook her head. "What if they're innocent? Just fishermen trying to bring their catch home? Won't they be upset?"

"Why wouldn't he have it in his craft, then? I don't trust someone dragging boats behind him. That means he doesn't want whatever it is in his boat. Bloody suspicious, if you ask me."

Brendan glanced down again. "Whatever we decide, we'll have to act soon. He'll be past us in a few minutes. But why would they call attention to themselves with something so obvious?"

Max shrugged. "Maybe the boat itself has more, and they couldn't fit everything in? I don't know, mate. Ask him if you want to know the details. I say we scupper the buggers. Anna?"

She stared down at the inlet. "Yeah, I think I can do that. But I need to be down on the shore to talk with the water."

After exchanging a glance, they both rushed down the stairs, almost falling over each other.

Brendan followed at a more sedate pace, wearing a troubled expression. When they reached the bottom, he crossed his arms. "Look, I still don't like this, Max! You're making a lot of assumptions!"

The Australian rounded on Brendan, standing two inches from his face. "Look, *mate.* War isn't perfect. You act on gut instinct, or you die. Don't you get that?"

"Sure, and I get that, but you're making a lot of assumptions here."

"I have to, don't I? We don't have good intel. I don't like making these decisions. I don't like being in charge. I never *had* to be in charge before. But I'm the only one here with military experience, right? This smells to high heaven, and if we don't act, people could get hurt. Are you willing to risk other people's lives just so you can have a clear bloody conscience?"

Brendan backed up a few steps, his eyes wide. Taking his stunned silence as assent, Max ran down the rest of the stairs and marched to the rocks, where Anna communed with the waves. "Right. You make the waves, I'll make a wind. Together, we've got a whirlpool, and we'll drown the fuckers. Got it?"

Anna flashed him a grin. "One Charybdis Special, coming up."

As the fishing craft cruised past their lighthouse, Anna commanded the waters to swirl. They moved slowly, and she gritted her teeth, urging them faster. When they grew swift enough to rock the zodiacs, Max shouted, "Now, mates! Let's make those bloody things dance!"

The inflatable crafts bobbed and pitched in the whirling water. Men on the boat shouted and rushed to the back, trying to haul them in. Anna's waves grew, engulfing the towed vessels into a swirling eddy. Max's winds lifted the water, and the inflatables rose twenty feet in the air, spinning frantically in the tiny tornado. They both flipped, dropping with an enormous splash. All their contents sank toward the ocean floor.

Max and Anna let out a triumphant cheer and shared a hug. Her body trembled in his arms.

As the water cleared, the zodiacs floated upside down. Max flipped them a pair of birds and let out a laugh as he danced back and forth. "Take that, you bloody bastards!" The men on the ship shouted and pointed to them.

He turned to Brendan, the adrenaline rushing through his body and a triumphant grin on his face. "That was bloody brilliant! Right! So, now we head back to your farm?"

The Irish man shook his head. "Not likely. We have no way of knowing that's their only attack, do we? You're the one who complained about lack of intelligence. I'll report this in, and then we await orders. But I'm pretty sure at least one of us will have to stay here for a while. I might send Anna back, and then switch later. With Jaime and Chen, that leaves three of you on watch. Full coverage."

Deflated, Max sat. "Oi, that's just bloody great. But fair enough, that's the smart thing to do. Can't abandon my post, can I? But that begs one question."

Brendan cocked his head. "Which question?"

As a lone seagull cried in the encroaching evening, Max grinned. "Where's the nearest pub, then?"

Chapter Seven

"Nothing in life is to be feared; it is only to be understood.
Now is the time to understand more so that we may fear less."
– Marie Curie

*Latest **CNN Update:** Recent investigations conducted by a Washington Watchdog group has uncovered an extensive network of underground propagandist organizations spreading damaging misinformation. They haven't been able to trace the source of this network but succeeded in shutting down a dozen satellite organizations. The government cautions individuals to double-check the source of any news items regarding the so-called Unhidden and their activities.*

In related news, several prominent leaders have had their social media accounts suspended on grounds of spreading misinformation.

Komie:

After the young girl, Fiona, showed her upstairs, Nokomis Nicholas tested the bed in her room at the Byrne farmhouse. The mattress seemed soft enough to give her old bones good rest. Oddly enough, she felt at home here. While she'd never been to Ireland, the land looked much like her native hills in Maine, the lands her ancestors had called home for thousands of years.

Voices roused her, and when she listened in the darkness, she recognized Anna's American accent. She smiled, pleased that the young woman had returned safe from her battle on the coast. The Australian man spoke as well, so they both must have come back. Eventually, the voices faded.

Komie settled back to her nap, but she couldn't grasp slumber again. Something else called to her, something in the woods. Their whispers beckoned in the mist, and when she went to the window, she spied their shadows in the oak trees.

Thanks to the nasty machinations of her useless daughter-in-law, she'd been run out of her home in Arizona. She'd had to abandon the one thing she still held dear, her granddaughter, Tansy. Sure, Old Tom had promised to keep an eye on her, but Yamka was a piece of work, and would be difficult to deal with. But the experience made her cautious about any strangers. She didn't recognize these voices.

With a deep sigh, she abandoned her nap and descended from her yellow room to the dining room. Sandwich fixings had been spread out on the sideboard, and Komie made herself lunch.

She sat next to the other recently arrival, a mature woman with skin the same shade as her own, aged about forty. She looked six feet tall with a lean, wiry strength. Róisín had informed her that Qacha could control fire. A woman with suspicion and arrogance behind her eyes. But Komie also detected a burning passion, a desire to prove herself. Komie wondered how much of that arrogance was justified and how much stemmed from bravado. She'd seen plenty of both in her time.

Komie gave her a nod and a smile. "I'm Nokomis, but most folks call me Komie."

"I am Qacha."

The other woman returned to eating her sparse meal. She evidently didn't want to chat, so Komie gave a reluctant mental shrug and left her alone.

Once she finished her meal, she must meet with the PHAE representatives to be assessed, whatever that would be. She harbored some worry about this encounter. Growing plants didn't sound exactly like a splashy talent, such as Qacha's control over fire. But that's what she had, and she'd never been one to have pride in flashy things, anyhow. She preferred her well-worn jeans to fashionable outfits, and turquoise jewelry to gold, any day.

As she entered the library, she found Ciara and Martin, two of the representatives from the day before. They bade her to take a seat.

Ciara opened her file and said, "Nokomis Nicholas. Am I pronouncing that correctly?"

"Nah-COMB-ee. Close enough. But most people just call me Komie."

Martin cocked his head. "And you have some control over growing things?"

"That is true. I can ask plants to grow."

He gave her a disarming grin. "And they obey you? How long have you had this power?"

"They do obey me, but I've never asked them to do something they don't already want to do. I just ask them to speed up the process a bit. I've always been able to do this, to some extent, but the ability has increased lately."

Ciara's eyebrows rose. "Really? Most talents have only come into power over the last few months. How long?"

With prim dignity, Komie replied, "All my life. My grandmother taught me."

Ciara and Martin exchanged whispers, but Komie couldn't make out the words. The woman glanced up with a furrowed brow. "How exactly did she teach you?"

Komie straightened her spine. "I'm afraid such techniques are part of our tribal lore and only taught to those who have dedicated themselves to the Great Spirit."

They asked some more questions, pinpointing what she'd done, hadn't done, and any difficulties she'd encountered. Komie told them of the reluctance of the Arizona soil to cooperate with her, compared to the eagerness of the soil in Maine.

She had a host of questions to ask, but decided she'd get better answers from their hosts than from the official representatives. She answered the rest of their questions with dignity and, eventually, they thanked her for her time and dismissed her.

Qacha:

As Qacha Duar hefted her backpack, bag, and cat-carrier, she strode to the farmhouse. The surrounding rolling green hills reminded her of living in her grandfather's yurt in Ulaanbaatar. Windswept fields filled with nothing, but the occasional farmhouse made her homesick. However, different trees and landmarks skewed through her nostalgia, reminding her just how far afield she'd traveled from the familiar.

While she didn't give in to pointless emotion, she missed the aching solitude of the Mongolian steppes, and her summers with her grandfather, learning their traditional ways. The unexpected ache took her by the throat and forced tears from her eyes.

She supposed she should have expected such picturesque locations, with the quaint photographs from the website. But she'd expected that to be all marketing without substance.

Back in Ulaanbaatar, when Qacha initially sent her query email to the PHAE, she half-expected the entire thing to be a scam. But she'd been desperate for a reason to leave her life. Their first response hadn't really disabused her of that notion. They'd only sent a generic response. "We thank you for your inquiry. Most applicants are processed into PHAE through one of our entry centers, and assign them to a local home for assessment, training, and acclimatization to our rules and activities. We base this assignation upon your desires and talents, as well as consideration for differently abled or special needs individuals."

Marketing without substance. As a chef, she'd encountered plenty of meaningless hype. That didn't mean she liked being subjected to such tactics. A yowl from her cat, Manol, made her glance down at the cat-carrier. "Just a little longer, my dear."

After she met the matron and her husband, they led her through the house. Qacha halted when they emerged into the back garden. They looked both ornamental and functional, with vegetables, herbs, and flowers in a pleasant array. She gave an approving nod and followed her hostess to a row of four stone-walled outbuildings.

"Oh, and feel free to browse through the gardens. I have a food garden along the back area, a kitchen garden to the left with herbs, and then some ornamentals along the right."

Michelle pointed out the shower and bath next door, which she'd eventually share as others arrived. After having lived in the dormitories at culinary school, where she shared with three other women, Qacha could handle such privation, providing the others had basic manners.

Their hostess opened the wooden door to the closest one. "This will be your quarters while you stay with us, Qacha. Please, make yourself at home. We shall be serving lunch soon, so if you'd like to come to the main house in an hour, we'll get to know you better over our meal. Remember, listen for the bell!"

As her hostess left, Qacha let out a long sigh for the wonderful silence.

Qacha's assigned quarters had a sitting area, divided from the sleeping room by a three-quarters wall, with a small toilet and sink in an alcove.

Once alone, Qacha let Manol out of his carrier. Then she put her clothing away in the press provided. When she sat on the couch, she calmed both Manol and herself with some cuddle time. Petting the large cat helped to calm her own nerves. The people seemed nice enough, but she preferred her own company, and that of Manol, to any forced society.

As she petted the cat, Qacha studied her quarters. Clean, simply decorated, yet with homey touches for comfort. A painting on the wall of the Irish countryside, amateur but quite good, with a rustic frame. On the coffee table, a vase of yellow wildflowers. A windowsill planter which, upon examination, contained sprouts of rosemary and chives.

A far cry from her utilitarian, modern flat in Ulaanbaatar. More similar to her grandfather's yurt. Nothing at all like her parents' stylish townhouse in the suburbs.

She ached to explore the options and have her hostess share Irish recipes she could practice with. For now, though, Qacha lay on the sofa, petting Manol until he purred her to sleep.

Three peals of the bell made her bolt upright, causing Manol to scratch her as he fled under the sofa. Qacha cursed under her breath and dabbed the blood from her arm. Faint dark red lines traced along her veins from her first fire-working, but they'd faded. She thought the pattern rather striking as she turned her arms back and forth in the light.

She splashed water on her face and took a deep breath. Now, she'd learn the meat of what she'd gotten herself into. Straightening her spine, she cautioned Manol to be good and ducked out the low door.

When she entered the dining room, the rest of the family had already gathered at the table. Food and plates sat on the sideboard, and the patron, Colin, gestured for her to help herself to the offerings.

Qacha had to admit, the Byrne family put on a robust spread for their guests. Qacha sampled several items and took a seat. After a few sample bites, she decided she enjoyed the lamb's marinade. She must find out which herbs Mrs. Byrne used. The food seemed well-seasoned, if simply cooked.

The host, Colin, leaned over and tapped her plate. "You know you're allowed as much as you like, right? No need to ration anything. We've got plenty of food."

Qacha turned to face the man. "I am not given to overeating. I prefer to appreciate flavors rather than over-indulge in plain cooking."

Colin sat back, his eyes widening. "All right so. Well, when you're done with lunch, come with me. I'm to tell you all about what we do here and how you fit in."

"Very well. I shall do so."

The table fell silent after that. Qacha didn't appreciate the assumed intimacy this family seemed determined to impose upon her, but she had elected to come here. She forced a smile at the man, who answered with a grin.

When she finished her food, Colin led her into a library, the walls covered floor to ceiling with books. Leather-bound, paperback, even some scrolls filled the shelves. Heavy furniture, made with dark cherry wood and stuffed red leather, hulked on the carpeted floor. An educated man's retreat, beyond doubt. She perched on one chair, her spine stiff, while Colin lounged in the chair behind the desk.

The man opened a manila folder. "We understand you have traveled here from Ulaanbaatar. Is that correct?"

"That is correct."

"And you have some control over fire?" He lifted his eyebrows in query.

"That is also correct."

"That's an amazing talent. Have you determined how much control you have?"

She gave a bare nod. "I have experimented with the limitations of my abilities, yes."

After that, Colin asked her questions about her life, her experiments, and her desires. She didn't know how to answer that last part, as she had come here as an escape, not a destination. However, she'd never let them know that. Her failures must remain private, not to be paraded across the world.

Silence fell after her last answer, and she glanced up to see Colin staring at her with his head cocked to one side. "What did you hope to find here in Ireland, Qacha?"

She couldn't readily answer that question, at least not in a manner he would wish to hear. However, dozens of job interviews had trained her to answer without saying anything. "I wish to find my place in this society with my powers."

When he finally dismissed her, several hours had passed. Colin said she could rest again, if she wished, before the evening meeting and dinner. Qacha walked quickly into her assigned room. Opening the door, she didn't see Manol. Her momentary panic quelled when she spied his tail swishing from under the couch. He'd already overturned his food bowl, spilling the kibble on the floor. Had he made those scratches in the wood? At least any damage to the rough wood might go unnoticed.

She'd just put everything right when the youngest child, Fiona, knocked on the door. "Hello, Miss Qacha. I've come with a cat bed for your lovely kitty. May I come in?"

Qacha had little experience with young children. Their enthusiasm and bare honesty often confused her. The child's bright smile betrayed a desire to meet the cat as she carried a shipping container with her grandfather's antique horsebow.

Obliging, Qacha let the child in. She went straight to Manol, who had perched on one end of the sofa. Manol's tail whipped back and forth with frenetic energy as the girl pet him with cautious hands. "He's lovely, Miss Qacha! His name is Manol?"

"That is correct."

Fiona placed the round, fluffy pet bed next to Manol and patted the middle, backing away. Manol sniffed the fabric, gave each of them a suspicious look, and settled into the bed, his tail curled beneath his back paws. He closed his eyes.

"Manol appears to have accepted your gift. I thank you on his behalf."

"Very much my pleasure, Miss Qacha! And if you need more food or any treats for him, just let me know, I'll bring them right over! And if you need anyone to watch him, I'd be happy to do so."

After the child left, the room grew blessedly quiet again. Qacha unpacked her grandfather's bow and set the precious artifact on the mantle with care, her shoulders finally relaxing now that it had survived transit.

Komie:

Fiona met Komie afterward, dogging her footsteps upstairs. "How did the assessment go?"

The older woman shrugged. "As well as I expected. The people assessing me didn't seem impressed with my abilities. Helping plants grow isn't very impressive. They do that on their own anyhow."

The girl's eyes grew wide. "Is that what you can do? Wait 'til you see the garden!"

Warmth suffused Komie's heart. "I've wanted to visit the garden since I arrived at your lovely farm, Fiona. May I?"

"Just follow me!" Fiona pelted down the stairs and opened the wrought-iron gate for the Native woman.

Apart from some ornamental benches and a storage shed on the far end, the gardens contained both ornamental and practical plants. The kitchen herb garden sat closest to the house, filled with rosemary, garlic, chive, and others. Beyond that came a small plot of potatoes, turnips, swedes, and parsnips. Along the far edge grew ornamental flowers such as roses and foxglove. Apple and plum trees bordered the pine woods.

Beautiful black marble flagstones formed paths between each section, curving around the plots as if caressing the edges of the roots. Komie longed to get her hands deep in this loamy soil and speak with the land.

Will this Irish land speak to me? Will the soil resist her power, like in Arizona? Or will the land welcome me like Maine?

Fiona placed a hand on her arm. "Want to see the part we're working on? We're trying to get roses to grow here, but they don't like the cold. We even have a stool to sit on."

Komie gave her a wide smile. "That would be delightful."

While disdaining the stool, Komie knelt next to the stunted shoots and placed her palms on the black soil, digging in her fingers and whispering an ancient prayer to the spirits of this foreign place.

Cover my Earth Mother four times with many flowers.
Let the heavens be covered with the banked-up clouds.

The spirits of Ireland spoke within her mind, a chorus of wonder and delight. *We are here. We listen. We honor you.*

Tears of gratitude ran down Komie's lined cheeks. Fiona clutched her shoulder. "Look! Look! I can see the leaves moving!"

After opening her eyes, Komie grinned wide as the rose vines grew toward her, tickling her arms with pale green tendrils, fresh-grown and still damp. The thorns grew away from her skin. She opened her palm, and the vine curled around her wrist, up her arm.

Years of holding her power in secrecy made her worried about showing her power. Komie glanced up at the Irish girl. However, Fiona gasped and clapped her hands. "Oh, that's magical! Wait until Mam sees this!"

Relief swept through her, like a drug coursing through her veins, warming her blood with peace. "This is only a greeting. However, I think I can convince your roses to behave well. Give me just a few moments alone with them."

With obvious hesitation, Fiona withdrew around the bend. Once she got out of sight, Komie dug her hands into the soil again. The cool dampness felt wonderful on her old skin.

Komie called into the earth, down toward the roots slumbering in their cozy beds.

Wake, wake, wake, now. Raise your faces toward the sun. Warmth is waiting for you.

Their stalks stirred and shook, reluctant to answer, but she kept chanting, *wake, wake, wake.* The edge of one split, sending out a questing bit of green. The second one followed, and then each stalk, one by one, peeked open to taste the earth surrounding them.

With a deep sigh, Komie sat back on her heels. She felt drained and elated at the same time. The roses hadn't wanted to obey but, in the end, they heeded her. Her success gave confirmation she'd made the right decision coming to this unknown country. The earth listened to her here, a welcome relief from the difficulties she had in Arizona.

She stood and brushed the dirt from her clothing. The aroma of this land coursed through her like her life's blood. With great reluctance, Komie exited the garden to find Fiona waiting for her on the bench next to the iron gate.

Komie sat next to the child. "Thank you for allowing me to help. Now, I'm exhausted. Do you have a talent with plants?"

Fiona shook her head. "Not really. I mean, yes, I love flowers, especially the beautiful ones, but that's not my talent."

"Do you have an Unhidden talent?"

The girl blushed and stared at her shoes. "I think I do, but I haven't had anything certified yet. Mam said to wait until I'm thirteen in case it morphs into something else. I don't have a very lady-like talent."

Komie's eyebrows shot up. "How intriguing!"

Fiona looked from side to side. "I can tell what's wrong with a broken machine. But my Da won't let me work on most of them until I'm older."

Komie cocked her head. "What makes you say that isn't lady-like?"

With a sullen pout, the girl said, "Because greasy overalls and wrenches aren't for princesses! I want beautiful dresses and tiaras and curly hair!"

As she tried to stifle a chuckle, Komie placed a hand on her shoulder. "You can always take a shower after working on machines to go out to gala balls in the evening, child."

The girl's mouth scrunched into a sour pout. "I suppose."

"What about your parents and siblings, what can they do?"

The girl shrugged. "Liam can move little things, like a paper clip, without touching them. Hugh can see in the dark. Not completely, but better than anyone else. Brendan, he's fast. I mean, he can run super-fast, like the Flash. Róisín can heal with her mind. Not like a broken leg or cancer, but cuts and bruises and things. Mam can curl and uncurl her hair. Then Da, he can make things colder, like a glass of water."

Komie frowned. Some of them seemed so shallow or of minimal use. A glimmer of resentment shot through her. Why should people with minimal talents be considered as useful and eligible as she? "And they're all in the PHAE?"

With a half-smile, Fiona gave her a sidelong glance. "Everyone with a talent can join PHAE, strong or weak. Sometimes, I'm sad for people with little talents. Like I've taken more than my share, somehow."

"What is considered a *little talent?* Have the PHAE created a measurement scale?"

"Mam says they're working on one, but a lot of people are arguing about it. Da says he's fine with being low on the scale, and so does Brendan. Róisín thinks hers should be higher than Brendan. They get into fights sometimes."

"Don't language fluencies get categorized? Perhaps a similar scale can be adapted."

Fiona shrugged. "Maybe. But Mam says it's really important that everyone can be part of PHAE as much or as little as they want, even if their talent is useless, like hers." She gave a silly grin.

But why should useless talents be as important in PHAE as those splashier powers? Wasn't PHAE, as an organization, designed to foster those talents? But if someone's talent had no practical use, that didn't mean the people would be useless to the group itself. The PHAE formed, from what Komie understood, to support the people themselves, not the talents they possessed.

Her words reminded Komie of the blood quantum requirement for some Indian tribes, requiring a minimum percentage of native ancestry to be allowed membership. That arbitrary measure made her angry, as many people who grew up in white families had just as much spirituality, if not more, than those with solid ancestry. This rule for the PHAE would negate that bigotry.

The older woman put her arm across Fiona's shoulders. "Don't be sad. You're granted your power by your ancestors, in a literal sense. They gifted this to you. The best way to honor them is to use that delightful gift with wisdom. Now, I could use a nap. These old bones can't do that sort of work without consequences."

The mention of her ancestors made her think of her granddaughter, Tansy, and old Tom, back in Arizona. Guilt at leaving them ate at her, but she could alleviate that quickly enough. Michelle had told them if they wanted to use the phone, just to ask. Komie meant to cash in on that favor now.

Once she borrowed Colin's mobile, she pulled out her purse and old-fashioned address book, with pencil-written names and numbers. Tom's information had almost faded to nothing, but she made out the digits, dialing them in. As the phone rang, she remembered the time difference. What time would it be in Arizona? She glanced at the clock. She'd never been great at basic math, and time zones confused her. Six hours difference? Seven? Before or after? Before, surely. Four o'clock here, less subtracted seven hours, should be nine in the morning there.

After four rings, she almost gave up, but something clicked. "Hello?" Someone other than Tom answered.

"Hello, is Tom available?"

"This is his son, Jorge. Who's this?"

Relief flooded through her. "Oh, hello, Jorge! Welcome back! This is Nokomis. I used to be your neighbor."

The other man hesitated before answering. "Aunt Komie? Oh, I'm so glad you called."

Komie gripped the phone so hard, the edge bit into her fingers. "What's wrong? What's happened?"

"Dad just went down to your place. He saw the police cruiser speed down the road. Something's happened with Tansy."

Komie's heart jumped into her throat as she tried to breathe. "Talk to me, Jorge."

"That's all I got. I'll have to call you back. I promise, Miss Komie, we'll do everything we can. Dad made a promise to you. I vow to keep that promise."

The *click* on the other line made her stare at the phone, wanting to call back, to get more information from the young man, but she realized that would be useless. Jorge was a good man, and he'd let her know if anything else came up. She must be satisfied with that.

That didn't mean she wanted to be far away from the phone, though, just in case Jorge or Tom called back. Colin spied her perched on the edge of her seat in the library. "Why don't you take the phone with you, Nokomis? It's called a mobile for a reason. I think you might find some peace in the garden, and the signal is stronger. Here, I'll even walk with you."

After swallowing her fear, Komie nodded. "You have wisdom beyond your years, Colin Byrne." She gave his hand a grateful squeeze as she walked outside.

The ornamental gardens buzzed with bees and butterflies in the cool afternoon. Komie breathed in deep of the perfume of growing things. He'd been right, and the serenity of the earth smoothed her jagged worry into a dull ache.

Earth, teach me quiet, as the grasses are still with new light.

Earth, teach me courage, as the tree that stands alone.
Earth, teach me acceptance, as the leaves that die each fall.
Earth, teach me renewal, as the seed that rises in the spring.

Colin stood beside her, a silent, supportive presence. Her husband had been like that. He never spoke unless he had something to say. Too bad her daughter-in-law hadn't been of the same philosophy. If she hurt Tansy, or neglected her… Komie breathed in again, drawing upon the earth to calm her fears again.

"Komie, would you like a project, to take your mind off Tansy? You can stop anytime if they call."

She shrugged. "What sort of project?"

The Irish man pointed to the avenue of trees leading from the garden to the river. "We want to pleach those."

Komie stared at the ancient beech trees lining the lane to the river. "You want me to do what?"

Colin gave her a lopsided grin. "Pleaching. To encourage the trees to meet in an arch over the path, to make a tree tunnel. They're trained over several years, even generations. These trees are already a hundred years old. You can speak to seedlings. But can you speak to older plants?"

Komie had serious doubts. "Do the trees benefit from this?"

"Pleached trees grow taller. They stand stronger against wind. Asking them might be kinder than training them in the traditional way."

"How are they trained to pleach?"

Colin patted the closest trunk. "We tie the tops and weigh them down with rocks, pulled toward the earth. They grow across, forming the arch. Tradition says one of our ancient goddesses, Airmed, taught us pleaching. She's a goddess of healing and herbalism."

The phone weighed heavy in her pocket, but she refused to think about that. "Hmm. I'm pleased you still honor the ancient gods. Do you have a spirit of the earth?"

Colin nodded, his eyes shining with eager interest. "That would be Anú. She's the all-mother goddess. We have few tales about her, but plenty of stories are about her children and their adventures."

"That's intriguing. I shall study this Anú, and she may listen to my prayers. For now, I will ask the trees. I would also ask *you* a favor."

Colin's eyes grew wide. "Whatever you like, if I can grant it."

"I would like to send a few handfuls of this lovely, rich earth back to America. A friend of mine requested a sample."

With a look of utter confusion, Colin shrugged. "That might not get through customs, but sure. We can try."

While shoving away the sudden stab of pain and worry, Komie approached the closest and caressed the rough, gray surface of the first tree. The age pulsed from the heart, years of weathered seasons heavy in its bark and heartwood. Its voice differed from the Maine trees. The Arizona desert held few old trees, only scrubby bushes clinging to life in the unforgiving sun-drenched dirt.

Here, the lush soil pushed growth from the ground, bursting into a verdant haven. As the tree echoed her query with its own, she spoke to it in her mind.

Will you grow for me? Will you do as I ask?

The tree grumbled and resisted. *Why should I listen to you, a mere ephemeral human? Your life will be over in a few brief seasons compared to my stolid tenure. You will flit away like a summer shower. Your commands held no urgency.*

Komie pushed back. *To grow this way is healthy and wise. You would find more sunlight for your leaves, more rain for your soil and soul.*

The tree grumbled again, but she detected a chink in its resistance. She redoubled her efforts and was rewarded with a vibration beneath her hand. The branches above fluttered and stretched, just a few inches, toward their neighbors across the path.

As she panted, Komie leaned against the trunk. "The trees will listen, with some urging. But the results are not dramatic."

Fiona must have arrived while she worked with the tree. The younger girl clapped her hands and jumped up and down. "You did it! You asked, and it obeyed! Can you do the same to another one?"

Despite her weariness, the native woman spoke to the next tree, and then the next, even as the afternoon faded toward dusk. Insects buzzed as the sun dipped lower. Each tree responded with varying compliance, but none resisted like the first. This final one even grew one root over her foot. While she appreciated the gesture, she experienced a moment of panic before she extracted her toes from its grip.

After the fourth tree, Komie's legs shook. She slid down with her back to the trunk. The path and trees swam, as if dancing in the wind, something out of a bad dream.

Colin crouched beside her, a steadying hand on her shoulder. "Komie? Are you ill?"

Trying to regain her equilibrium, Komie held her head in her hands, but closing her eyes made the dizziness worse. She sat with her spine against the tree and dug her hands into the soil, to draw strength from the land. The buzzing power trickled into her arms and shoulders, then into her head. Thin tendrils and roots wrapped around her hands, offering both support and restraint. She couldn't pull her hands away. She shivered and coughed, pain ripping across her throat. The chill now settled into her bones.

Colin stood, his blue eyes growing wide. "Fiona, go fetch Mam. I'll wait here."

As the girl's steps pelted away, Komie struggled to keep her mind from falling into the surrounding mist. The roots pulled at her hands, and she struggled against them. Sure, she'd grown tired working with the land in Arizona, but she'd never gotten so dizzy. Had she pushed herself too hard, or did something else happen? Some sort of illness? With a grunt, she yanked her hands from the soil and placed her palm on her forehead. Sweaty, but not burning with fever.

Her throat remained raw from her cough. Komie curled into a fetal position around the base of the tree, begging for healing without words. A slow pulse of warmth came from the roots below her, suffusing through her skin into her muscles and bones.

Hurried footsteps pounded on the ground toward her. Michelle knelt next to her. "Komie, tell me what's wrong. What happened? How do you feel?"

Her voice came hoarse and thready. "I did too much. Did the phone ring? Did I miss a call?"

Colin shook his head. "The phone didn't ring, Komie, not yet."

Michelle glanced back at Colin. "What did she do?"

Fiona wrung her hands, eyes wide. "We just asked her to talk to the trees, to make them pleach. We didn't mean to hurt her!"

"Darn. Has Róisín already left for Galway?"

Colin nodded. "She left before Komie arrived, Michelle. Don't you remember?"

"Who can remember anything in this madhouse? Darn. We could use her healing touch. Well, needs must. Let's get her up to the house."

Komie let out a deep breath. "I want to sit up."

Between Colin and Michelle, they pulled her to her feet. She still felt shaky, but no worse than after climbing a few flights of stairs. She flashed a weak smile at her hosts.

Colin peered at her. "You're still too pale for my peace of mind. Do you think you can walk? I'd like to get you back to the house and get some tea, if not a good, hot meal in you. If you can't walk, I'll carry you."

With a shadow of her former strength, Komie waved her hand and put steel in her words. "You will do nothing of the sort. I can manage."

Between Colin and Michelle, she got to her feet and half-stumbled, half-walked to the back door and into the dining room. In his deep voice, Colin insisted she sit while he sent Fiona for food. "You need your strength, and it's easier for you to eat here and now. Supper isn't for another hour, so you'll have time. I'll sit with you, if you like."

Fiona returned with a bowl of hot potato soup and a pot of tea, one of the twins trailing behind with a shawl. She cradled the steaming cup in her hands as Colin wrapped the shawl around her shoulders. She drew in the floral aroma of the tea as a salve.

As Colin settled into his chair, he took a sip of his own tea. "A good story can heal the soul, so they say. So, let me tell you what I know of Anú as you eat. Some call her Danú, but others say they're distinct entities. She's also called Anann or Anand. No matter her name, she's the mother of the Good Folk, the Fairies who live beneath the hills of Ireland."

"Do they live below the earth? Or is that analogy?"

Colin shrugged. "Who's to say? We call many caves and wells entrances to the Otherworld. Perhaps they're just portals into an alternate reality." He looked out of the window with a wistful expression.

Komie sipped her tea and raised her eyebrows. "Have you ever entered a cave looking for this Otherworld, Colin?"

He gave a nod, his eyes turning glassy. "Aye, long, long ago, before Michelle and I married, I scoured the countryside, searching for fairy rings and hidden caves, sacred wells and standing stones. Alas, I found nothing I couldn't explain with science and my own over-active imagination."

Komie hid a smile. "And what did you hope to find?"

With a shrug, his mouth curled into a half-smile. "Who really knows? Fame at finding proof of the Fair Folk? A magical trip into the world of Faerie? A desperate need to verify the magic I know in my heart exists somewhere in this mundane life we live? No matter, I never found a thing."

Colin cleared his throat. "Now, Anú. She doesn't, as I mentioned, have many tales about her actions. We've named mountains for her, such as the Paps of Anú in County Kerry to the south of us. She's said to have fed the gods, nurturing them. Therefore, she's their mother. More tales are told of her children, such as the Morrigú, the Dagda, and Ogma, among many others. They had many adventures, battles, and quests, but Anú remains ever-silent, a guardian over the land itself."

Komie already liked this Irish goddess.

Just as Colin started on the next detail, a loud alarm went off and her pocket buzzed. She fumbled for the phone and scrambled to figure out which button to press. Colin pressed one for her, and she placed the phone next to her ear. "Hello? Hello?"

"Komie? Is that you? It's Tom."

She glanced at Colin, who stood and left the room, giving her privacy. "Tom? Tom, tell me what's going on."

"Just a bit of a dust-up here, but first, let me assure you straight away, Tansy's safe and sound. She's frightened and she's just about cried herself sick, but now she's sleeping right here next to me."

While letting out a long sigh of relief, Komie shut her eyes. "Thanks be to the Giver of Life."

"Ayup, she's well enough. Yamka's gotten herself into a bit of a pickle."

Komie didn't care what her daughter-in-law got into. But duty required that she act as if she cared. "What happened?"

"Well, she got mixed up with a rowdy bunch, but you knew that. They knocked over the liquor store in the next village, and got caught the next day, because they acted damned stupid. They told the police she drove them, so now she's an accessory."

No matter her promises in this place, Tansy needed someone to care for her. "I'll be back as soon as I can arrange airfare."

His voice grew firm. "No, no, you stay where you are, Komie. I've got things well under control. Jorge's quite besotted with the young thing, and he's eager to practice his fathering skills. He's brought home a sweetheart, too, you see. Lovely, smart woman by the name of Rukan. He brought her back from Iraq. She worked as a consultant for their base."

As much as it stabbed her in the heart to admit, a proper family would be much better for Tansy than a single grandmother, even if she had no blood relation. "Rukan? What does the name mean?"

"Steady and confident. And she is. I'm a bit in love with her myself. She's everything Yamka isn't. Resourceful, a hard worker, and polite. However, she's got a backbone of steel. She'll do well for Tansy."

Komie swallowed back the tears, but they refused to stay down. "Thank you, Tom. And thank Jorge and Rukan."

"Already have, Komie, already have. You still sendin' me that bit of dirt? I can introduce Tansy to the place you live."

"I just made the arrangements earlier today, my dear friend. You give my heart peace."

Chapter Eight

"Governing a great nation is like cooking a small fish –
too much handling will spoil it."
– Lao Tzu

Hiroki:

With increasing trepidation, Hiroki watched the countryside rush by as they got further from Dublin. While Ireland was completely alien to his experience, he felt bereft leaving the headquarters building after a few days. At least he had another recruit with him and, ideally, the man he'd brought with him, Max, should still be at the Byrne Farm.

The last two weeks had been a jumble for the Japanese man. He'd just started his first professional position in Tokyo after graduating from university when he'd almost been killed. Those events somehow twisted into him being rejected by his parents, recruited into the PHAE, and then, in turn, recruiting *for* the PHAE. He still didn't know how all that had happened.

He glanced at the other recruit, a large woman from Mali. She'd introduced herself as Bintou and had a lovely, musical accent. She wore bright, strong patterns on her clothing, setting off her red-black skin. He appreciated the boldness on her but could never wear something similar himself. Maybe his friend, Masaaki, could have pulled them off. He'd always been the braver, more flamboyant of the pair. Hiroki found comfort in conformity.

They pulled into the driveway and large wrought-iron gates swung open. The farm seemed straight out of the western fairy tales Hiroki had always loved. He glanced around for a witch who ate children, and then his mouth twitched in a secret smile at his own folly.

The driver helped them with their luggage. Bintou exchanged a look with Hiroki, gave him a bright smile, and said, "Are you ready, my new friend? This will be interesting, I think."

He swallowed and fought the urge to run away.

As their hostess, Mrs. Byrne, welcomed them both and showed them to their rooms, Hiroki kept silent. He searched for his recruit, Max Hurley, but didn't see any sign of him. Perhaps he went to some pub or slept in his own room. Could they have moved him elsewhere already? The man had been annoying and difficult to deal with, but he'd have been a familiar face in a world of strangers.

Their hostess said that her husband, Colin, would come get him for an initial assessment, and then they could join the rest of the family for lunch. But Hiroki had already received his assessment, back in Tokyo via video, before he'd ever left Japan. And then more training and testing at headquarters. Perhaps this interview would be another round. Or perhaps the earlier person never passed on his knowledge to this Colin Byrne.

Hiroki sighed at the layers of bureaucracy any institution seemed to multiply constantly. His father worked as a banker all his life, and Hiroki had trained to be the same. Such bureaucracy felt a natural thing to him. That didn't mean he enjoyed dealing with the necessity.

He'd just finished putting his toiletries in their proper places beside the sink when a knock on the door startled him. Wiping his sweaty hands on the towel, he hastily opened the door and bowed to the tall Caucasian man standing before him. In his most polite tone, he said, "Good morning."

"Good morning. You're Hiroki, is that right? From Tokyo?"

"That is correct. I have lived in Tokyo my entire life until these last two weeks. I have been living in the headquarters for the Protectorate for Unhidden Advancement and Education since then. Now, I have been assigned to live here. And will you be my host, Mr. Colin Byrne?"

The man gave an infectious grin. "That's me! I'm here to take your measure. Care to follow me to my library?"

Qacha:

The next morning, as she helped Fiona, Liam, and Hugh clear the breakfast dishes, Qacha studied their kitchen. They had assigned her to food preparation and cleaning up after meals, but she loved working in a kitchen, even in a private home. Qacha always relished the mindless work of cleaning. As the body kept busy with automatic tasks, she could consider thorny issues of philosophy.

She missed the exhilarating rush of a dinner service and the luxuries of a full commercial kitchen. However, this place had a few gadgets she looked forward to trying.

Fiona handed her a stack of cups. "Do you want to plan dinner tonight, Qacha? With the two new arrivals, we'll need a big meal. I asked Mam, and she said I can show you our storehouse and herb garden, so you can see what's available."

A chink in Qacha's mask formed. She pasted it together again. "That would be acceptable. When?"

"After we finish the washing up. I'll take you to the garden, then the meat storage and root cellar. We've got wine, as well. Da says we could open our own restaurant."

Another half-smile cracked Qacha's mask. Qacha had few illusions about her own likability. When she'd arrived at this place, she'd prepared herself to be shunned as a foreigner. Despite their acceptance, she braced herself to being left out of things as a tall woman with little ability to suffer fools or express affection. When that didn't happen, her mask thinned. She'd have to decide if she'd allow her barriers to fade away, something she hadn't done since her grandfather's yurt on the steppes. Only Manol saw her without her mask now.

While the farm had a working dishwasher, seven people exceeded its capacity. Her mind wandered as they washed the dishes.

However, this kitchen wasn't silent. Instead, a sister and two brothers who loved to chatter filled the space with their antics. Fiona washed the cups, as her small hands fit inside even the thin juice glasses. Qacha stood at the huge double sink, washing and rinsing, while the boys dried and put things away.

Since she couldn't concentrate on her own thoughts, she joined the fray. Qacha asked Fiona what meats she had to work with for the dinner plan.

"Lots of lamb and goat, but we still have some beef and pork from the last slaughter in the big freezer. We don't keep as many chickens as we used to, and most are layers because, with so many guests, we need the eggs. We have a few geese hanging to age in the larder."

Liam piped up. "What meat do you like cooking, Qacha?"

Hugh nodded enthusiastically. "Yes, tell us about Mongolian foods! I've never eaten anything from there. This year, Mam's teaching us with food. We have a day for each country. Like, last month we had a day of Jamaican food, and then a day of Cuban food, a day of Haitian. You get the idea."

Qacha raised her eyebrows. "And she does not consider Mongolia worthy of inclusion?"

Hugh screwed up his face. "We haven't studied Asia yet this year."

Ah, just so. "I worked in a commercial kitchen, so I have cooked dishes from many cuisines. I have classical training, which means I understand French cooking, and had to learn both English and French. However, if you are interested in the traditional food we had on the steppes, we ate mutton, goat, and sometimes yak or camel. We made noodles, dumplings, and doughnuts. Often, we ate kebabs or soup with the meat. The first thing I baked was a biscuit from dried cheese. We used a cream similar to clotted cream. We made butter from yak milk, which is saltier and stronger than yours."

Fiona wrinkled her nose. "Didn't I read something about fermented mare's milk?"

Qacha's mask slipped again. She adjusted it with a mental twitch. "Indeed, but that is a drink. You asked about foods."

That earned a high-pitched giggle from Fiona. Qacha frowned at the youngest daughter, which just made her giggle more.

Hugh's eyes grew wide. "What does it taste like?"

Qacha knew full well what reactions mare's milk received from foreigners. "Mare's milk is, how do you say? An acquired taste."

Now, they all laughed. Even Qacha, which surprised her. She'd smiled and laughed more at this Irish farm than she had in the past two years.

Fiona placed the last dish in the cupboard. "If you clean the counters, Liam, I'll take Qacha on that tour."

The girl opened the door and gestured for Qacha to precede her. They walked out to the garden, where Qacha noted the herb varieties. She asked the Fiona to describe the flavor profiles of the few herbs unfamiliar to her.

"I don't know what a flavor profile is, Qacha. But I know this one is salty and bitter. That one's sour but spicy. Is that what you mean?"

Qacha nodded, glimpsing the vein along her hand. The dark lines had grown deeper. She resisted the urge to hide them.

"Mam uses rosemary a lot in baking, especially with soda bread. She also uses garlic in white bread. I love baking. Do you do a lot of baking?"

While shaking her head, Qacha admitted, "Baking is not my best skill. I work better with roast meats, savory flavors. Baking is more exacting chemistry than art form."

She ducked her head to enter the storeroom, which held more meat on offer than many commercial kitchens. Slaughter in the autumn would yield a great deal of meat but must last throughout the year. The root cellar held apples, potatoes, turnips, carrots, cabbage, and beets. Braids of onions and garlic hung from the ceiling.

As they returned to the kitchen, recipes swam in Qacha's head. "I will need paper and a pencil, or a laptop with a spreadsheet program, even better. I need time to plan. Then I will ask you to examine the plan, to ensure I am working within the parameters of your farm's capacity. Does that sound acceptable?"

Fiona nodded. "Sure! But Mam should look this over, too. She's in charge of the food stores, and if you use up all of something, she has to get more."

"That is fair."

The Irish girl brought a computer pad and left her to her work. Qacha made a quick list of her ideas, and then delved into each one.

If she made pork dumplings, instead of yak, the fat would flavor the dough. Mongolian dumplings had thicker, larger shapes than the Chinese type. The dough needed plenty of fat to melt in the mouth. Some chervil would add saltiness, and maybe garlic. Should she add onion, or would that be too much?

Qacha worked for several hours, creating not one, but three meal plans. If the matron accepted all three, they might use the others another day. Qacha detested putting all her eggs in one basket, a metaphor Michelle used earlier. Qacha liked the phrase and vowed to use it more. She spoke English impeccably, but she lacked idiomatic usage. Even the Japanese man, Hiroki, spoke English more naturally than she did. She'd never have the facility of a native speaker, but she improved every day.

As she worked, a knock came from the front door, and then voices filtered through the house. When she glanced up from her notes, a young man walked past the hallway entrance. Tall, with shoulder-length dark hair. He greeted Fiona with a hug and nodded to Qacha. Then they both disappeared. This must be the brother, Brendan. Colin mentioned he'd been sent to Cork with some other Unhidden the day before.

That would bring the total of people on the farm to eight. Qacha felt suddenly glad she quartered in an outbuilding.

She soon forgot about him as she returned to her notes. However, a cry behind her made her spin.

Fiona pelted through the kitchen, quickly followed by one of the twin boys. He carried a stick, and once the girl went past Qacha, the chef stood, blocking the boy's path. "What are you planning, child?"

Confused, the boy looked up at her, then glanced at Fiona, who hid behind Qacha. "Uh, nothing?"

Using her kitchen voice, Qacha asked, "Then why have you invaded my workspace? Do you have no chores to keep you busy? I understood this is a working farm. Why are you not working?"

He backed up a few steps. When Qacha glanced back at the girl, she stuck her tongue out at her brother. The edge of Qacha's mouth twitched, but she schooled her expression back into something more solemn. He retreated to the garden.

Turning to Fiona, Qacha frowned. "And will that assist you to evade from his attentions?"

She gave a saucy grin and escaped into the hallway. Qacha returned to her work, deciding what local herbs might work best with her planned side dishes. She grew so intent in her musings, she jumped when someone touched her shoulder. "Fuck a goat!"

Colin lifted his hands and backed up a step. "I'm sorry, Qacha. I called you, but you seemed in your own world."

Qacha stood to hide her ill-ease. "I am finished with three meal plans. Shall we present them to your wife?"

The man grinned wide. "Absolutely! Would you like to help with lunch, too? We're about to light the grill."

While sniffing the air, Qacha detected wood-smoke. "Grill? You are cooking with fire rather than electric today?"

"We are! Come outside. Michelle's outside chopping potatoes."

Colin walked to the massive grill, smoke trickling through the grate. Qacha smelled lighter fluid along with the wood-smoke, fresh-cut rosemary, and garlic. Michelle sat at a table with a chopping block, between piles of quartered potatoes and whole ones. Several herb bunches lay next to her. The other recruits were not in the garden.

Their hostess turned as they approached, wiping her hands on her apron. "Qacha! How delightful to see you. Isn't this a glorious day for grilling? Fiona said you have a meal plan to run by me?"

Qacha glanced up at the overcast sky and decided Irish sensibilities of what constituted a *glorious day for grilling* must be skewed by their country's penchant for rain. "I have prepared three plans. If they should meet your approval, we can use them on several evening meals."

As Michelle took the tablet to peruse the plans, Qacha strode to the grill, where Colin stirred the wood. "You have just begun the fire?"

The man had a smudge of soot across his brow. Qacha tried not to stare. "I have. The wood won't be ready for the meat for another half-hour."

Qacha peered into metal grill. "Would you like the wood to be ready more quickly?"

He lifted his eyebrows. "Are you offering to use your talent to help? I would enjoy a demonstration, if it doesn't anger Brigit."

"Who is Brigit?" Qacha glanced around as if she'd missed a new arrival.

Colin laughed. "Brigit's our goddess of fire. She's also a hearth goddess, and deals with healing, smith craft, and poetry. She's a talented woman."

"That seems apparent. I will endeavor not to anger her with my efforts."

Colin beckoned Michelle to watch as Qacha pulled in her power. Her blood buzzed with energy as she directed her will into the logs. Tiny edges of glowing red along the wood flowered into licking flame, embracing the dry wood with crackling glee.

Qacha laughed as the fire did, a low chuckle under her breath as the red glow increased to yellow. The flames flared up several feet, an inferno of fury. Even Qacha stepped back from the conflagration, heat flowing off in waves.

Colin's eyes grew wide as he stumbled back several steps. "Careful, we don't want to burn down the garden!"

Qacha's blood flowed hot. She didn't want to quench the flames. They called to her. She stared at their flickering beauty, dancing, beckoning, seducing her with their undulations.

"Qacha? Tone it down, please."

She wanted to make the fire grow, the flames licking everything around her in delicious destruction, but he had a point. She must play nice. With a reluctant sigh, she squared her shoulders and reduced the fire's intensity. Soon, she had the flames down to a manageable size.

The wood crumbled under the fire. The remaining embers pulsed with baked heat.

Michelle gasped, and Colin's eyes widened as Qacha turned, sweat pouring down her face. The surrounding air had chilled as she'd stoked the fire. She was unused to this level of humidity but felt satisfied with her work. "That should suffice."

Qacha:

Qacha had to admit their Irish hosts understood how to cook meat. The marinade Colin used on the lamb kebabs, while unfamiliar to her palate, combined savory, sweet, and salty in a delicate balance. She must ask what ingredients he used. She detected garlic and rosemary, chervil, and perhaps honey?

Between the chunks of meat, they'd spitted pieces of roasted potatoes, turnips, onions, and bell peppers. Several loaves of soda bread, with honey and butter, rounded out the outdoor meal. While the clouds never cleared, the day stayed dry.

Conversation clustered in cliques, mixed groups of hosts and guests. The two new arrivals, Hiroki and Bintou, whispered amongst themselves.

Qacha sat at the end of a table, unwilling to push herself into a group. She wrapped a chunk of lamb in a napkin and placed the morsel in her pocket. Manol would appreciate the treat.

A young male voice at her shoulder startled her. "You know, if you get hungry later in the evening, we have food in the kitchen. You're always welcome to come scrounge."

She turned to find Liam, one of the twins. "This is for my cat, Manol. What is this word, *scrounge?*"

He chuckled and sat next to Qacha despite her warning glare. "To scrounge means to search for something, often with a negative connotation, like a rat scrounging for scraps. Now, if you want cat treats or dinner scraps, I can provide those. Your Manol is a great fluffy beast! I saw him when you first arrived. What breed is he?"

Qacha thawed, content to discuss Manol. "A Pallas cat sired him, with a domestic mother. Pallas cats are a wild breed in Mongolia, round and fluffy, as you say. Their ears are small and their faces flat, so their fluff seems more."

Liam ran his hand through his hair. "He's a grand lad, indeed. Well, I care for the barn cats, and we keep treats in a bin just inside the door. I'm happy to share with Manol. Is he indoor only? Or would he like to explore the grounds?"

She shook her head. "He has never lived outdoors. Even so, he had to endure a six-week quarantine before coming here. I would be worried he'd get lost, or attacked by a dog, or… What predators do you have in Ireland?"

The Irish boy let out a giggle. "Humans are the only big hunters in Ireland. No, really! None of our larger animals lived past the ice age. We have some foxes and shrews, but those won't bother a cat Manol's size. We used to have wolves, but people hunted them out a couple hundred years ago. A few eagles. What do you have in Mongolia?"

Qacha chewed her potato before she answered. "We have wolves, though humans have hunted them. Snow leopards in the mountains. Eagles rule the skies. Sometimes creatures wander into our land from China or Russia. However, that is rare."

The boy's eyes shone with keen curiosity. "What sort of creatures?"

"I recall stories of Siberian tigers, tales designed to frighten children into obeying their parents. They lived wild in Mongolia, but no longer."

He grinned. "I love Siberian tigers! They're class! I saw one at the Dublin Zoo. We had someone visit from the Siberian PHAE enclave, and Da took us all to the zoo on our day off."

Qacha had been about to spear another piece of lamb. "Siberian PHAE enclave?"

Liam nodded. "Sure, a satellite branch. I thought you knew? Didn't they send you to Dublin?"

She shook her head, jaw clenched. "No. I came here straight. I could have gone to Siberia? That would have been a much shorter journey. Much less expensive, and easier on Manol. Why is this information not on your website data?"

His eyes grew wide. "I don't know, Qacha, I'm sorry. We aren't in charge of the website. Siberia's only a small office. Perhaps five people, very low-key."

"Low-key?"

"Under the radar. Uh, they don't like to attract attention, especially from the Russian government. They keep quiet to be safer."

Qacha's fists clenched, her face growing warm. The lines on her arms pulsed with heat. "Are they ashamed of their work? Why are they hiding?"

The boy glanced toward his father, deep in conversation with Michelle. "Because of the riots, the protests. They don't want to be hurt. That's why you should be here, Qacha. Not in Siberia, with just a few Unhidden. Here, in Ireland, where the entire country is your protection. Don't you see?"

Qacha didn't want to see. The PHAE had deceived her, given her incomplete information, which she'd acted upon. Still, Liam had a point.

Even if she'd known about Siberia, they would have just sent her to Ireland. Her anger faded as she chewed the piece of lamb, washing the meat down with soda.

"I apologize for being cross with you, Liam. You are not at fault."

He let out a deep breath, relief washing over his young face. "That's grand, Qacha. Learning new things is hard, especially if you relied on the old stuff. But you're good here now, aye? You're welcome with us."

"Thank you, Liam. For your welcome, and your family's hospitality. Manol and I appreciate this."

He raised his glass of juice. She raised her soda, and they clinked glasses.

By the time she retired to her room, Qacha realized that she'd relaxed with other people for the first time in a very long time. She washed her face, brushed her teeth, and laid out her night clothing, glancing around. Manol wasn't asleep on the couch. Nor the bed. She crouched down to look under each piece of furniture. No Manol.

While tamping down her rising panic, she shook his food bowl. This had always worked in the past, even when he'd been spooked by strangers. This was a strange place in a strange country. She hoped he hadn't gotten out.

Despite Liam's assurances of Ireland's lack of predators, Manol had no outside instincts, and he might not survive a cold, damp night.

Finally unable to find any sign of him, Qacha hurried to the main house to fetch help in searching. Panic making her normally measured movements jerky, she flung open the back door to the kitchen. The four people inside, Colin, Liam, Fiona, and Hugh, stared at her.

Her host rose from the table, concern etched on his expression. "Qacha? What's happened?"

Trying to keep emotion from her voice, Qacha clenched her teeth. "I cannot find my cat, Manol. He is not in my quarters."

"Right. Let me get the lanterns. Wait here." Colin ran into the hallway and disappeared. Liam and Hugh both jumped down from their chairs while Fiona's eyes just grew wide. When their father returned with four kerosene lanterns, he placed them on the table.

Qacha clenched and unclenched her fists in growing impatience while he lit each one, their white glows burning brightly in the kitchen. He handed one each to Liam, Hugh, and herself. "Liam and Hugh will search the garden. Fiona, you look in the house in case he got in here. Qacha and I will search the woods."

As soon as she stepped outside, the darkness enclosed her. The light from the lantern only illuminated a short distance before her. She knew Manol would run and hide from anyone else, but she didn't know what else to do. He had no practice living wild.

Colin lifted his lantern as they reached the edge of the woods. "I know this forest far better than you. Stick to this path and check down near the river. Don't get close to the edge, mind you. If I rustle in the trees, it might scare him back into your arms. At least, that's the theory."

He strode into the trees, shuffling amidst the undergrowth, calling out Manol's name. Colin would never find him like that but his idea that he might flush the cat out had merit, a logical strategy.

Qacha walked back and forth to the river, feeling like a useless fool for what seemed like hours. By that time, Michelle had joined the search. She joined her husband in walking through the forest paths. She improved on the play by bringing pieces of meat to entice the vagrant feline.

Something tugged at her arm, and she turned to see Fiona. "Miss Qacha, I have an idea for you."

Qacha knelt next to the girl, her lantern shining on them both. "What is your idea?"

"You should put Manol's litter box outside. I read once that cats can smell really well, and that he'll recognize that smell."

Another idea with merit. This family seemed to be quite clever. Perhaps she had misjudged them when she first arrived. Qacha hastened back to her quarters to enact the suggestion. With each step back, Qacha's imagination ran wild that they'd discover Manol's poor, dead body.

Fiona accompanied her into the house and helped her carry the box onto the small landing. Would Manol come if people stood nearby? Or would that scare him away? She allowed Fiona to lead her back to the edge of the garden, but then sent the girl back into the house. After all, she had been told to search inside.

About twenty minutes later, Fiona came rushing down the dark forest path toward her. "I found him! I found him!"

Qacha hid her relief behind a stony face and rushed to the house behind Fiona, the entire family in tow. On the kitchen table, content to be munching an enormous bowl of kibble, crouched Manol. Qacha scooped him up to cuddle him close, almost crushing him with her enthusiasm. He purred and rubbed his head against her chin.

Then she noticed the family watching her uncharacteristic show of emotion. With dignity, she carried her cat back to her room, shutting the door behind her.

Anna:

Even three days of rest weren't enough for her, after her efforts at the lighthouse. Every muscle in her ached as she and Max trudged back into the Byrne's farmhouse that evening. They'd finally been relieved of their watch in Cork and a driver brought them back so they could continue their interrupted training.

Anna didn't want any training. She just wanted to crawl into a bed and sleep for a week. Max looked similarly exhausted.

Despite their fatigue, she had to greet everyone and play nice. Normally, she did this as a matter of course, as she needed to be liked by everyone. Now, however, it was a painful chore, and she only wanted to escape so she could sleep.

By the time she met the others and extracted herself, her mind buzzed with fog. As soon as her head hit the pillow, she fell into a deep, healing slumber.

When she woke the next day to birds singing outside her window, she was still tired, but at least could rise, shower, and dress. She stumbled downstairs to a full breakfast room with familiar faces, and she felt almost part of a family, even if she'd only just met some of them.

Anna piled her plate high with a full Irish breakfast and dug in. She buttered her bread and bit into it just as someone knocked at the door. Her hosts exchanged a glance, and then Colin went to the door. Male voices filtered through, and she gritted her teeth. She turned just as the new arrival entered. Her brother, Joel.

Anna choked on her bread, coughing and waving her hand, banging the other on the table. Max leapt behind her and pounded her on the back once, twice, three times. When that did nothing, the Australian man snaked his hands around Anna's sternum and jerked. With a *pop,* the chunk flew out of Anna's mouth and ricocheted across the table, hitting Brendan in the chest. She took in a deep, hoarse breath.

A too-familiar voice at her shoulder sneered, "Always looking for attention, Anna?"

She clenched her jaws, gripped the edge of the table, and pushed herself to her feet. After she turned to her brother, who wore a smug smirk, she rasped out, "Joel, what the *fuck* are you doing here? And after what happened at the airport?"

Michelle's voice came from behind her. "Anna, language."

He rolled his eyes. "I didn't exactly come by choice, Sis. They forcibly recruited me." Max let out a snort as Joel's mouth pinched into a sour expression.

Anna sensed every eye upon them. She spoke through clenched teeth. "This is my brother, Joel. Please, excuse us. We need to discuss some things."

She yanked on his arm, pulling him into the hallway. "Now. Explain."

Her brother shrugged. "Someone from your PHAE group saw us at the airport. They must have been monitoring the protest, researched my background, and found out about you. They believe, logically enough, that if you have Unhidden blood, so do I, so he followed me to my apartment. I got a knock on my door, and three men in black suits, like right out of a movie, demanded to speak to me."

Anna crossed her arms and shot him a glare. "Demanded?"

Joel scowled and glanced back toward the dining room. "Yes, demanded. I told them I had no interest in buying insurance and tried to shut the door, but they shoved their way in. They pretty much forced me to take their DNA test."

"Forced how? Did they hold you down?"

Joel wrinkled his nose. "Nah, nothing so actionable. They threatened to tell my boss I had this Unhidden thing. I know my boss. She went with me to that protest in DC. I've heard her talking about sterilization, banishment, all sorts of solutions to the Unhidden."

While letting out a short laugh, Anna raised her eyebrows. "So, that caught up with you. Imagine that. So, what's your talent?"

He held out his hands, showing her the webbing between his fingers. "Not as spectacular as yours, and I haven't grown scales. But I can make mud into dirt. Great fucking talent, huh? Well, I can make water evaporate. They shoved me through a battery of tests yesterday. Sometimes siblings have similar talents. Since you can do things with water, they say?" He raised his eyebrows, inviting her to share information. "I can't understand why your talent came first. I'm the oldest. I should have been first by any logical measure. Uh, your hands are turning into fish."

Anna yanked her sleeves down. She didn't want to elaborate on her abilities with him. "Yeah, I can do things with water. I still don't get why you're here, in Ireland, on this farm."

"Well, despite me going along with their testing crap, they must have spilled the beans to my boss. When I got to work the next day, she called me into her office, claimed she'd found some errors in my work, and gave me a written warning. The thing is, I know damn well I didn't make those mistakes, but I couldn't prove it." He shrugged, giving a sly smile. "I read the writing on the wall, so I contacted the PHAE. Technically, I'm a volunteer, but I definitely got railroaded."

A mélange of emotions swirled within Anna as she clenched her jaw. "Well, I don't *really* want to say I told you so. But…"

He dropped his gaze to the floor and waved his hand. "Yeah, yeah, yeah, whatever. Listen, Sis, I'm sorry about what I said at my apartment, and then the café and the airport. I felt attacked, but I shouldn't have taken my anger out on you. You didn't deserve that. I'm glad that woman helped you get to your flight."

The ice in her heart melted a little. *Maybe he's growing up.* "That's okay, Joel. Thanks for apologizing, though."

"So, what's the story here? This is all one family? Could they get any more stereotypical? I'm guessing Catholic?"

So much for a reformed Joel. "Try not to be a judgmental ass, Joel. These are kind folks. They don't deserve your bigotry."

In a mocking voice, Joel said, "'They don't deserve your bigotry.' Who's being a judgmental ass now, Anna?"

After throwing her hands up, she rolled her eyes. "You know, just leave me alone. I don't need your crap here. I like these people. They're taking care of me. You know, like *family* should?" As she said the words, she hoped she wasn't lying, that her faith in them wouldn't be betrayed. She'd had enough of betrayal.

"That's a dig at me, right?"

She crossed her arms. "If the scales fit…"

"Fine. Well, I'm here now. They're putting me in an outhouse after today's interview."

Anna let out a deep sigh and rolled her eyes. "An outbuilding, you idiot. A room along the courtyard. Just don't do anything stupid."

Joel raised his eyebrows. "Like selling everything I have and coming here on a whim?"

She'd had enough. "Joel, you're an ass. You've always been an ass. Just leave me alone." Anna stomped away. She didn't return to the dining room as her stomach churned too much to deal with food or any well-meaning questions from her new friends. Instead, she headed to Michelle's office. She'd be due for her assessment soon. At least her confrontation with Joel kept her from stewing over that.

Brendan stopped her as she passed the dining room. "Hey, are you okay? Is that really your brother? Is he always such a prime *amadán*?"

"What's an *amadán*?"

"A fool. A jerk."

She nodded, the aromas from the food enticing her, despite her recalcitrant stomach. "Yes, yes, and yes, he always is. He's just like that." She swallowed and glanced down the hall. "Could everyone hear us?"

He nodded with a grimace. "I'm afraid so. Sound carries along wooden walls. Well, let me know if you need help with him."

"I'm fine. Thanks, Brendan."

The youngest child, little red-haired Fiona, appeared from behind Brendan and tugged on her sleeve. "I don't like your brother."

Anna knelt and smoothed the girl's hair. "That's fair, honey. I don't like him much, either."

Brendan peered down the hall. "Hey, I have an idea. Why don't I grab the rest of your breakfast and mine, and we'll finish it out in the garden? That way, you get a break from people."

Flashing him a grateful smile, she nodded. "That would be wonderful. Thank you."

She escaped out the back door and sat on the stone bench next to the herb garden, breathing deep of the calming chamomile and rosehips.

Fiona knelt at the edge. "Mam said I needed to weed today, so I'd better get a start. She says a job is half-done if it's well begun."

Brendan came out and joined them on the bench, handing her the half-finished breakfast plate. "So, have you thought about where you want to work?"

Anna wrinkled her nose. "Not in the slightest. I've barely considered the options, much less made a life-changing decision. Me deciding to come here felt hard enough. I used up my ability to make major decisions for several months." But at least the options had given her some ideas, some possibility that she could make a new life here, among people who accepted her as human.

He chuckled and took a bite of his eggs. "You don't need to decide right away. Wherever you choose to go, I can visit. Remember, that's my talent, running fast." He put his plate down on the bench and put his hand over hers. Her skin tingled at his touch, even through the glove. She ached to touch him skin to skin, not just through cloth. In a tender gesture, he picked her hand up and kissed it. The electricity of his fingers made her head spin, and she closed her eyes.

"Oh, now I see why you've drunk the Kool-Aid. Back off, Byrne. That's my sister you're pawing."

Brendan jumped to his feet, his face flushing. "Anna can make her own decisions, Joel."

"Yeah? Then why don't you keep your hands off her while she decides?"

Anna shouted, fists clenched. "Stop it! Both of you! Listen, Joel. I have no control over you being here, but you can butt the hell out of my personal life, okay? You never cared when I needed a shoulder to cry on, so you have no right to meddle now. You never played the protective brother role. It just suits your agenda now." She wanted to punch him, to push him, anything to get that smug sneer off his face. Instead, she turned away from him.

"And Brendan?" She swallowed against her anxiety and lowered her voice to something gentler. "I can handle my brother, okay?"

Brendan narrowed his gaze as he looked at Joel. "I won't have him insulting you, Anna."

"I mean it, Brendan! I don't need you to go all white knight on me."

His face clouded, but Anna had just about had enough from both of them. Her blood raged with temper. "Look, if your precious PHAE hadn't corralled him here in the first place, none of this would be an issue. But he's here now, and he's my brother. Which means I deal with him. Me, no one else. Do you understand?"

Chastened, Brendan bowed his head and stepped back while Joel slapped his hand to his chest. "You wound me, Anna! How dare you accuse me of being a terrible brother!"

Fiona stood and crossed her arms, her scowl powerful enough to crack stone. "Brothers don't act like that!"

Joel spared a patronizing glance for the young girl. Brendan straightened his spine and turned to Joel. "I mean no disrespect to you or your sister. My intentions are honorable, I assure you."

"I don't give a flying fuck what your intentions are, or how much you assure me, Byrne. Keep your hands off her."

Anna crossed her arms, placing herself between Brendan and her brother. "Or what, Joel? Are you going to punch him? Pout like a child? Maybe you'll leave? Oh, *please,* let it be 'leave.'"

Joel let out an almost human sigh and placed a hand on her shoulder. "Look, I *am* trying to be a nicer person, Sis, remember? Will you let me?"

Fiona let out a snort.

Her muscles tensed and tingled before she shrugged him off. "A few sweet words now, and then won't cut it, Joel. Actions speak so much louder than words."

"Protecting my sister isn't being a nicer person?"

She glanced back at Brendan, whose face reflected a chain of emotions, moving from anger to worry to determination. "Not if you're a jerk about it. And you are."

He rolled his eyes. "Fine. I'll try harder. Right now, though, I need to punch something." He sent a fierce glare at Brendan before stalking away. All energy drained from Anna's muscles. When she drooped, Brendan put his arm around her shoulders. "Let's get you up to your room. This has been an eventful day already. Fiona, can you fetch some hot tea?"

Brendan led her up the stairs, though he had to half-carry her. Her body wouldn't cooperate. Her limbs shook as if she'd swum a thousand-meter marathon.

When Fiona arrived with a full tray, complete with a teapot, several herbals, and lemon bars, she inched it onto the nightstand. Brendan pulled Anna's shoes off and tucked her into bed. She couldn't keep her eyes open, and her vision swam with gray. "I don't understand what happened. I'm all dizzy, and I feel like I've been hit by a truck. I mean, I was still tired from Cork, but I felt better when I woke. Have I been pushing my power too hard?"

Brendan exchanged a glance with Fiona. The Irish girl set her mouth in a firm line before answering. "Your brother did something. I felt a wave, but I don't know what he did."

"He barely touched me."

Fiona wouldn't say more, but her brother pulled a chair bedside. "Here, the tea is ready. I added honey."

Anna batted the cup away. "No, no honey."

Brendan frowned at the cup. "You should drink something with substance. Would sugar be better?"

"Sugar is fine." Why did she sound like a querulous old woman?

He placed the first cup on the dresser and poured another, dropping in three cubes. He stirred and made her sit up to drink. "The tea's still hot, so take slow sips."

Fiona sat cross-legged on the floor, sipping the first cup. She held a half-eaten banoffee bar, caster sugar smeared on her face. Some strength trickled back into Anna's limbs, and she smiled at the young girl. "Thank you for getting tea, Fiona."

"You're welcome, Miss Anna. Tea makes everything better." She lifted her cup in a salute, which Anna returned. Brendan, now supplied with a cup of his own, lifted his.

She'd forgotten to pull her sleeves down, and her scales flashed in the sunlight. Fiona gasped. "Wow! Your arms are beautiful! Can I see?"

Reluctantly, Anna pulled up one sleeve, revealing scales up to her elbow, creeping toward her shoulders. Brendan turned her arm back and forth and grinned. "The iridescence is gorgeous. You've grown your own jewelry."

Anna let out a breath she didn't realize she held. He hadn't run away, sickened by her impending transformation. They both accepted her as she was. Or what she became, whatever that turned out to be.

Hiroki:

As Hiroki finished off his lamb sandwich, he rose from the table, intent on taking his plate to the kitchen as a Japanese houseguest would. However, like a Japanese host, Michelle took his empty plate and cutlery. "Why don't you relax in the sitting room? We've got others arriving."

"Others? Are these the Unhidden assigned in Cork?"

"Yes, Anna and Max, along with my son Brendan. Did you get a chance to meet them before? No, you arrived after they left. Well, they should be back tonight. Max will be in the room next to your own, and Anna has a room upstairs. I'm sure you'll get along well."

She frowned after her words, though, much like his own mother did whenever she faced an unpleasant task. Hiroki wondered which of them were difficult to get along with but settled on Max as the likely choice. He would discover soon enough. In the meantime, he took her suggestion and left. Before going into the sitting room, though, he perused his host's library for something to read in the meantime.

Mindful of Colin's stories, he found several that looked informative. *Gods and Fighting Men* by Lady Augusta Gregory. Then he pulled *Tales of Old Ireland: Retold* by Lora O'Brien. When he read the back cover, he realized the author was a native and practiced the ancient religion of honoring her Irish ancestors.

Hiroki felt a sudden kinship to this author, even though his own Shinto beliefs had never manifested in dedicated ritual. As a child, he'd helped his parents maintain their shrine, but such practice fell away as the demands of university and everyday life intruded upon his attention. Perhaps he should dedicate some time in renewing his study of Shinto. Or in studying the ancient beliefs of his new home.

The concept of home struck him with pain, as he recalled his father's dismissal of him. How could he honor his ancestors when his own father didn't accept him? Would they also believe him unworthy? And would a dedicated Shinto shrine change that opinion at all?

The door banged open, saving Hiroki from further exploration of this concept, and a riot of voices filled the farmhouse. A tall young man with black, shoulder-length hair and freckles entered the room, a broad grin on his face. "You must be Hiroki! Mam told me all about you. I'm Brendan Byrne, Mam's favorite son. Brilliant to finally meet you!"

Despite the urge to run away, Hiroki shook the man's hand and peered past him to the two other arrivals. Max gave him a grin while standing next to a girl with a pensive expression and thick, dark hair. Brendan turned to the man. "This ray of sunshine is Max Hurley, and this is Anna Taylor."

Max nodded to him, the lines on his face deeper than he remembered. "Nice to see a familiar face, mate."

"It is indeed pleasant, Max."

After Hiroki gave Anna a quick greeting, Hiroki asked for details about the battle. "It sounds most exciting! Did you truly bring the ocean to swallow them?"

Anna chuckled and shook her head. "Not quite like that, no."

Max clapped a hand on her shoulder. "Don't be so modest, darlin'. That's a good enough description of what you did. We worked damn well together. And I'm happy to have you at my back, should we need it again."

Anna blushed as they both begged off to get settled in their rooms, and Hiroki once again stood alone. He let out a sigh and returned to his book. He had just finished the tale of Fionn and the Fianna and began the tale of Queen Medb. A woman of great power, and one Hiroki would never want to cross.

Chapter Nine

"My family is my strength and my weakness."
– Aishwarya Rai Bachchan

Hiroki:

As he settled into a library chair, Hiroki clasped his hands, which made them sweat. Instead, he placed them on his knees, but that seemed awkward. He didn't know what to do with them.

Colin and his young son, Liam, sat across from him on a settee. They exchanged a glance, and Colin took out a clipboard with several pages.

Colin's gaze flicked to Hiroki's hands as he clasped them again. "Hiroki, I'm craving some tea, and am about to ask Liam to make some. Would you like a cup?"

Hiroki nodded, grateful for something to do with his hands.

After he sent his son to the kitchen, Colin put his glasses on, pulled a pen from his shirt pocket, and read the first page. "Your file says you have a gift of persuasion, is that correct, Hiroki?"

Hiroki nodded again and swallowed. He detested examinations of any type, always horrified he'd fail. Not that they would grade him on this exam. Still, he couldn't control his nerves.

Liam returned with a tea tray, complete with scones and jam. Grateful for something to focus on, Hiroki poured a cup and took a scone. He didn't trust himself to cut the pastry without destroying the crust and sending crumbs flying across the vintage rug, so he bit into it.

Colin took his glasses off. "So, persuade me. Tell me you're a spy."

Hiroki almost spewed scone all over the tea tray. He coughed and took a sip of his tea, scalding his tongue. When he got himself under control, he stared at his host. "A spy? Do you think I'm a spy?"

Colin hid his smile behind a sip of tea. Liam grabbed a scone and sliced the pastry in two, slathering it with an indecent amount of jam while his father shook his head. "Of course, not. Which is why you must convince me you are. This would be proof of your magical talent rather than native ability."

Hiroki cleared his throat, searching his memory for the points of persuasion his professor taught him. A hook, an overview, a piece of evidence, a key point of the opposing view, then restate the argument and add supporting evidence.

He took a deep breath and put down his cup. He didn't need any distractions. Hiroki tried to summon the tingling he believed heralded his talent. He focused on both people sitting across from him as they ate their scones. Doubt drained away as power flowed through his veins, building his confidence.

"Wouldn't I be the perfect spy? Inept, clumsy, disarming, and ineffectual in all appearance. However, I will show you how these impressions might mislead you and function as an excellent cover for my true purpose."

Hiroki spoke for ten minutes, giving details of fake qualifications, motivations, and mythical funding. The tingling of his power suffused him with confidence and energy.

Once Hiroki finished his presentation, the doubt flooded back into his brain, screaming that he'd made a horrible mistake. He took a deep breath and sipped his tea. As the power left him, he willed his hands not to shake. He waited on his hosts' judgment and began sweating again.

These people would never welcome him, and he'd made a fool of himself. They'd send him back to Tokyo in utter disgrace and embarrassment, a failure to his family and his culture.

Colin frowned and beckoned to his son, and they left the room. The old farmhouse, however, did a poor job of masking their words.

"What do you think, Da?"

"He makes some excellent points. Do we know for certain this is a lie?"

"C'mon, Da! He's so shy. He can't be telling the truth."

"And yet…"

As they came in and sat, Liam raised his eyebrows and his teacup in salute.

The older man shrugged, his frown disappearing. "You had me convinced, if only for a moment, that you might be a spy for the Japanese government. That is no mean feat, as I've never been one for conspiracy theories. Your ability to make me doubt my own convictions is impressive, even from a talent standpoint.

"Most of our Unhidden powers are obvious, but yours works with elegant subtlety. You could be a fantastic asset to our organization, Hiroki. I'm going to complete my recommendation, and if you choose to join us, I'd be honored to welcome you to the team."

The Irishman stood and held out his hand.

Hiroki stared at it, trying to hold back tears of relief.

Liam leaned forward. "Hiroki? Are you okay?"

After shaking his head, Hiroki rose, bowed to both Colin and Liam, and tried to keep his weakness from showing. "I thank you both for your confidence in me. I hope to be a valuable part of your team."

His heartfelt speech made, he then fled, his scone and tea forgotten, before he disgraced himself in their presence.

Latest **CNN** *Update: Police investigations in Athens, Greece have discovered a group of Unhidden cultists in their home. Their leader convinced*

them to commit mass suicide in order to "call the Gods of the Unhidden," according to the manifesto, published on several social media platforms yesterday. The manner of the suicide has not yet been released to the public, nor the identities of those involved, pending notification of their next of kin and the conclusion of the investigation. The PEM spokesperson, Tiberius Wilkinson, has disavowed any knowledge of this incident.

Bintou:

As they led took Hiroki to one of the outbuildings, a young red-haired girl showed Bintou to an upstairs room. "You get a room inside the house. This one is painted peach, which is my favorite color, the color the sun paints the sky when setting. Sometimes at sunrise, too. You'll see! Do you have colorful sunsets where you're from?"

Grinning at the child's easy chatter, Bintou nodded. "Indeed, I do. Especially when the desert has had a windstorm, the sand can color the sky in brilliant displays."

Her eyes grew wide. "You live in a desert?"

"Well, close to one. Timbouctou is a busy city, but we have a vast desert just outside of town."

The girl pursed her lips in a sour expression. "Ireland isn't a desert. We have lots of rain. Too much rain." That made Bintou want to laugh more. She appreciated this child's easy honesty. She hadn't yet taken the measure of their hosts, but they seemed kind and welcoming. Their house seemed lovely and comfortable, if rustic. After she settled in, the husband said he'd come to assess her talent. As if Ibrahim hadn't already done that when he'd lured her here under false pretenses.

Bintou had wanted to believe Ibrahim still loved her, and so she followed when he called. Only to be handed over to the PHAE like a hunting trophy. Well, she'd discover what she could about this PHAE group. So far, they seemed much more honorable than Ibrahim, despite using his questionable services.

She didn't want to think about Ibrahim. Nor about the reason she'd been so easy to lure. Instead, she gazed out of the window of her room, upon the lovely, lush gardens below, and the woods beyond. She might even see the glint of a river in the distance, through the foliage. A delightful place, if only the weather didn't stay so cold and damp, even in summer. Bintou shivered and pulled her jacket back on. Her clothes would never be sufficient for this climate. She'd gone shopping when she first arrived but only bought a few things. She hadn't found much chance to shop since then, one of her great pleasures. Along with trying new foods, but if she did too much more of that, she'd need to buy all new clothing as her old raiment would no longer fit.

And what a tragedy that would be.

Bintou:

Colin spent all morning with Bintou, testing her on languages. With surprising creativity, he found several obscure dialects she'd never read, including Minoan and Gaulish, and a form of Etruscan she hadn't encountered. He brought out scripts of ancient and medieval Irish, Cumbric, and Norn. Then he surprised her with a modern Gaelic language so laden with idiom and slang it almost stymied her.

Her face tingled as she concentrated on the words themselves. They shifted and aligned, forming pictures that translated into legibility. As the letters tumbled and moved, she recognized Doric and Scots words within the sample, and she identified a version of Scots Gaelic only spoken near Glasgow.

He showed her several personal and place names in another language, but she couldn't extract meaning from them. "What language is this? Do you have samples in narrative form?"

Colin shook his head. "I hoped these scraps would be enough. This is all we have of Pictish, a lost language from prehistoric Scotland. The only other surviving clues are pictographs on standing stones and monuments. But no one's spoken this language since the ninth century. We aren't even sure what the pictographs mean. I did have another set of the pictographs, but I haven't been able to find them this morning." He frowned and looked around, as if they'd popped into existence as they talked.

"I'm afraid I cannot help with the pictographs. I am not Orunmila, the goddess of wisdom. They don't trigger my language talent. Ibrahim tried that when I met with him."

Bintou remained angry at her ex-lover for luring her here with a specious excuse. Her contentment at the Byrne farm didn't assuage her anger nor induce her forgiveness. To think she'd come to Ireland believing he wanted to rekindle their romance only made her angrier. She wouldn't forgive Ibrahim for a long time.

"What about these, then? Do they trigger your talent?" Colin pulled out several photographs of tall standing stones, each carved with groups of parallel lines. Some looked straight, some skewed up or down. Some crossed the center line. Bintou stared at the picture for several moments before shaking her head. "Something is trying to push through to understanding, but I'm blocked. I'm not sure why."

Colin smiled and, without looking down, turned the paper sideways. Now, the lines from left to right popped out at her as words. "Dovaidona, son of the Druid."

As she said the words out loud, her talent buzzed and popped in her mind, and her skin tingled again. The letters jumped and moved, shifting into words she could read. She not only translated the markings into letters, but then the letters into primitive Irish, then English, a triple layer of translation. Her head pounded as she placed a hand on her forehead. "What is that from?"

"That's an Ogham stone, which stands on the Isle of Man in the Irish Sea. These stones stand in the Celtic countries, like Scotland, Ireland,

Wales, even Devon and Cornwall. Most examples are gravestones like this one. Again, we have very few narrative examples, but this is a simple alphabetic cipher rather than a separate language. You already know ancient Irish. Now you can read languages in alternate texts."

Bintou raised an eyebrow. "All this is meant to be a test on the limits of my abilities?"

He answered with a grin. "Yes, like the Pictish. Though, to be fair, I'd have been ecstatic if you translated that. We know the Ogham, but Pictish remains an enigma."

"Do you have ancient texts of mythology from this country? I should familiarize myself with the language and the culture if I'm to remain in Ireland."

The Irishman nodded. "That's a grand idea. I've got many translations in my library, and a few texts in the original medieval Irish. Tales of battles, magic, and betrayal. I'll bring a selection to your room this afternoon."

"And these are tales of those whose blood you believe you've inherited? The Unhidden heritage?"

"That's what the scientists say, but who knows? I mean, to be descended from the Morrigan or Cu Chulainn would be a fantastic genealogy, in the literal sense of the word fantastic. But could that be true?" He shrugged.

Bintou raised an eyebrow at the older man. "Your passion marks you as a lover of ancient languages, Colin."

The Irish man opened his hands, palms up, and shrugged. "Guilty as charged! I love all languages. I studied Irish for my leaving certs and passed with flying colors. And I would die to have a talent like yours." He placed the back of his hand on his forehead in a melodramatic gesture. "But I'll settle for being your assistant and basking in your abilities."

She laughed at his antics. "You are a silly man, but you make me laugh." Her stomach rumbled. "However, I believe my hunger has just betrayed me. Will lunch be soon?"

"Outside, yes. We're having a barbecue in the courtyard."

As Bintou walked outside, the delightful aroma of roasting lamb caressed her senses, reminding her of the Timbouctou market. Except for the missing stink of tanning leather, reek of piss from the public privies, and overpowering redolence of clove and saffron. She missed all such odors, and a sudden wave of homesickness slammed into her, making her stumble.

Colin almost ran into her on the path. "Bintou? What happened? Did you trip?"

She shook her head. "No, I did not trip. I'm just missing Mali."

The older man clapped his hand on her shoulder. "We can be your home if you like. We may not nag you as much as your parents, but we'll support you when you trip. And we'll feed you! Maybe you can ask Michelle about some Mali dishes for a taste of home?"

"I doubt you have access to the ingredients here."

Colin raised his eyebrows. "We might surprise you. Limerick has immigrants from India, North Africa, even the West Indies. Some opened stores to import the ingredients they're used to, so we might be in luck. Also, we have this delightful invention called the internet. You can buy just about anything online."

Bintou awarded his quip with a half-smile. "That is true. I shall speak with Michelle. In the meantime, I am enjoying your foods. Is this preparation of lamb traditional Irish cuisine? Kebabs are Lebanese or Turkish."

"They may have been so originally, but we adopted them wholeheartedly, especially after a night out drinking. Hey, can I leave you with Hiroki for company? Qacha looks lonely sitting by herself. I think I'll go sit with her."

Bintou glanced at the older woman. Qacha did indeed sit alone, in an isolated bubble. She'd met her briefly in the hall earlier, but the older woman remained taciturn. Her severe expression now exuded a desire for solitude. Either Colin didn't read such signals, or he ignored them. Bintou suspected the latter. Most of this family exhibited extreme empathy, if not in natural ability, then by upbringing.

The Native American woman sat next to her, giving her a half-smile. "They sure do like lamb here, don't they? I think this is the third time they've served this meal. Is lamb common in Mali?"

Bintou took a drink of water to clear her mouth before answering. "Very common, though with different spices. Lamb is a favorite of mine. What is your favorite food?"

Komie gave a sly smile. "I know my native tradition should say something like buffalo meat chili or fry bread but, in reality, I love pizza, so long as there're no mushrooms."

"I know what Malian pizza is like, but what is American pizza like?"

She put a finger on her lips and looked up at the ceiling. "Let's see. You start with a flat baked dough, sort of like naan. Then you add tomato sauce, mozzarella cheese, thin pepperoni slices, and maybe garlic, bell peppers, sausage, black olives, that sort of thing."

"But no mushrooms?"

Komie grinned. "Absolutely not. I hate them."

Bintou chuckled and pulled a chunk of potato from her skewer. "That is unfortunate. Mushrooms have a delightful variety of tastes and textures. However, I shall not force you to try them all."

"Try them all? I don't want to try any!"

Pleased at succeeding at teasing the woman, Bintou relented. "I'm afraid I have no way to make you. Therefore, you prevail."

Liam and Hugh joined them, their plates piled with four skewers. Bintou heard about growing boys and their appetites, but these young men were only eleven. One of them, perhaps Liam, sat and took a huge bite. The other said, "Did you hear what Da said?"

Komie shook her head. "No, we have been arguing about disgusting foods." She pursed her lips toward Bintou in an expression of mock anger.

Bintou ignored her and cut up a sizable chunk of potato. "What did your father say?"

"That we gather to sing and tell stories every night, an Irish tradition, making our own pub. Do you have any stories from home? And if you play a musical instrument or sing, that's even better!"

Komie's eyes lit up. "Every night?"

"About an hour after supper, to give time to unwind and do the washing up, in the sitting room. I play the tin whistle. But I found it bent this morning." The boy frowned.

His brother poked him in the ribs. "You probably sat on it last night and forgot."

Bintou finished chewing her potato. "Should I dress nicely for this?"

He shrugged. "We dress casual. We don't dress up much, except for church."

The American woman cocked her head. "Which church?"

The twins exchanged a glance. "We're Catholic, but Mam said guests don't have to attend. In the village, we have an Anglican church. That's Protestant. Or you can stay here Sunday mornings. No judgment."

Bintou glanced at Komie, who frowned at her lamb skewer. "I don't suppose you have a mosque near?"

The young man's face lit up like the sun in a cloudless sky. "Da told me to research that for you! Limerick has four mosques. You'd need a ride, so we can arrange one. We found an Islamic Cultural Center just outside the city, about fifteen minutes away."

An odd mixture of elation and guilt swept through Bintou's heart. She ached to connect to her community but hadn't been a good enough Muslim to inquire when she first arrived. "Four? That is both surprising and gratifying. Thank you for conducting research. You and your family are most thoughtful."

Komie:

Komie had always had a deep affinity for all growing things, even as a child. Her grandmother had taught her to speak with the seedlings, to encourage them to reach for the sun, to grow to their full potential. Even then, her tribe had acknowledged her talent. Now, however, her talent had grown to something almost frighteningly strong.

She questioned how much of her power worked with nature, and how much pushed beyond the limits. Perhaps she should ask her ancestors for their ideas, but she doubted her ability to contact them in this faraway land. The Great Spirit was the same throughout the world but wore many guises and spoke many languages. Anú must be the local mask.

In the three days since her arrival, as Komie worked with the trees on the Byrne farm and learned of the Irish goddess, Anú, she asked Colin for more details. She devoured stories from the Byrne's library. She'd grown to appreciate Ireland's quiet, understated mother goddess. They named mountains for her breasts, founts of nourishment for the people of the land. Anú seemed an appropriate earth spirit aspect for Komie to honor.

As the Native woman worked, she quested her magic for this Anú, but if the goddess heeded her requests, she remained silent. Komie wanted to work with the land's permission, not at odds with it, so she persisted. She experienced a twinge of guilt for working with this Irish deity, this splinter of the Great Spirit, especially as she didn't know how best to ask for her help. She wished she could ask her ancestors for ideas.

In the morning, they visited the first farm on their list. Colin drove them and explained their purpose to the neighbor. A man in dirt-stained overalls, at least twenty years older than Komie herself, studied her with great skepticism. "She's going to do what to my fields?"

Colin placed a hand on Komie's shoulder. "Nokomis will ask them to grow more quickly."

The man narrowed his gaze. "Aye, and I ask them that every day. That doesn't mean they listen."

Komie chuckled. "Other plants enjoy the sound of my voice. Will you allow me to try with yours?"

The farmer grunted before stepping aside. "Mind you, the sugar beets could use some help. The potatoes and oats are doing fine, to be sure."

Komie gave the man a firm smile. "I will make a note of that. Thank you."

The pungent odor of cow dung and hay assaulted her as they walked past the barn into the first field. As she bent to touch the soil, Colin put a hand on her shoulder. "Do you need anything to start?"

Komie glanced up at her host. "I must ask the land first."

She dug her hands into the loamy earth, asking Anú to guide her in helping the plants to grow to their full potential and beyond.

As she came to expect, no goddess answered, but roots stirred in response to her goading. Tiny vibrations buzzed her hands and arms as the beets stretched and cried with literal growing pains, poking their shoots high into the sunlit world.

As Komie pulled her hands free, black soil clinging to her skin, she clutched at her head, trying to quiet the cries. They echoed within her, fading to whimpers. After taking a deep breath, she dusted off her hands, ready for the next crop.

The farmer stared at his beetroot crop, his mouth agape. "Jesus, Mary, Joseph, and the wee donkey, lady! How the feckin' hell did you do that?"

Komie stumbled as she rose to her feet. Her knees refused to obey and buckled. Colin clutched her arm, handing her a bottle of water, and she gratefully chugged the cool liquid.

Colin turned to the farmer. "She's helping in case we need food crops sooner than normal. You have potatoes in the next field? Are they close to harvest?"

With a numb expression, the farmer stared at the native woman. "Aye, a few weeks away."

Colin helped Komie to the potato field. "Do you have people ready to help with the harvest if the crops ripen early?"

The farmer nodded again, staring at his beetroot. "Feckin' hell. Can I rent her next season?"

Despite her fatigue, Komie chuckled. "If I should live so long."

As she coaxed the potatoes into ripeness, they fought her. They didn't love this land like the beets did. They still ached for the ancestral memory of steep mountains of South America. The pain coursed through her muscles as they screeched, lonely for a home they'd never touch.

When she pulled out of the dirt, the world swam gray, and she collapsed.

Voices faded in and out as she floated in a sea of complaints. Tendrils of root grabbed at her, pulling her down, yanking on her limbs. The faceless, dark invaders from last night loomed over her. Several trees argued over who should feed upon her blood as the liquid soaked their roots. A light bloomed in the distance, and a figure approached as she grew entangled in the arguing plants.

A soothing, female voice sang, the tone penetrating Komie's skin where she touched the earth, and through her bones where the tree roots gripped. The song calmed the roots, convincing them not to rip her limbs apart. Komie fell into a peaceful slumber, safe in this woman's gentle arms.

A savory aroma roused her from somnolent bliss.

When she woke, Fiona sat at her bedside, her brow furrowed with worry. "Miss Komie? Did you get some rest? Here, Mam just brought soup."

The older woman struggled to sit up. "What happened?"

The girl gave a rueful chuckle. "You'll have to tell us. Da said one moment you had your arms in the dirt up to your elbows, and the next, you fainted. Da had to carry you to the car and drive you home."

"I must pace myself more wisely."

"Da couldn't wake you up, and I think even Mr. Phelan got scared. He kept asking if we should call emergency."

Komie sipped her soup, savoring the salty heat trickling down her throat. "I'll be better soon. Soup is what my body craved. Please, thank your mother for me."

"She'll be glad. Mam went frantic when we brought you in. Do you think this'll happen every time?"

Scraps of memory floated before her, the woman with the soothing voice. "I don't know. This is difficult to judge. But I believe I have other help now."

Fiona cocked her head. "Help? What sort of help?"

"I believe your earth goddess has heeded my call. She may assist me in future efforts."

The Irish girl crossed herself with a mumbled prayer. "Anú heard you?"

Komie took another sip of the soup. "I can't be certain, but that name seems right. I must sing to her tonight and ask my ancestors for guidance. Do you have an enclosed space to build a fire in? I need a sweat lodge."

Fiona shook her head. "I don't think so. What's a sweat lodge?"

"Have you heard of a sauna? Think of it as a mix between that and Sunday Mass in the broadest of terms. A healing spiritual space."

The redhead shrugged, gathering her empty bowl. "I'll ask Mam."

Komie:

After napping through the whole afternoon, Komie woke, splashed her face, and stumbled downstairs. The house sounded empty. When she spied movement in the back garden, she exited and headed toward the area where they had the barbecue. She couldn't help but glance over her shoulder at the avenue of trees, but the path looked empty.

Komie stared at the firepit, her hand over her mouth. Colin must have worked hard all afternoon to bring rocks from the woods and piled them around the firepit. He'd created a two-foot wall around the enclosure, with a doorway for entering.

He emerged from the barn with a roll of fencing wire. "Will this do for a roof? We can cover the structure with blankets. This won't stand up to a storm, but it should work as a temporary sweat lodge."

Komie fought the tears surging behind her eyes. He must have done research on her native practice to come up with this while she rested. "This is a huge amount of work, Colin. You shouldn't have gone to all this effort just for me."

He wiped his hands on his knees, shaking his head. "This isn't just for you, Komie. Michelle has been wanting a sauna for a long time, and we can convert this when you're done. So, no guilt, all right?"

She should have chosen her own grandfather stones to line the lodge, but she appreciated the effort. As Komie examined those already in place, she had to admit she wouldn't have been able to choose any better. She needed at least twenty-eight, Seven for the virtues, times four stages to the sweat. She counted thirty.

"This is delightful, Colin, thank you. You've done wonderful work. However, you placed two stones too many. Can we remove this one and this one? And we really should have birch and cedar for the roof struts."

As he removed the indicated stones, he furrowed his brow. "I don't think we have any birch or cedar in our woods, Komie. I'm sorry. We've got some withies for a corral we planned, though some of them got broken. Will willow do?"

Komie chewed on her lip. She didn't like using substitutions, but at least the withies were living material, wood harvested by hand. She nodded her approval, and he went to the barn to fetch the materials.

Michelle came from the house, her arms full of thick, wool blankets. With a serene nod, she placed them on the ground and went back into the house.

Colin carried the pile of blankets inside. When he emerged, he crossed his arms, surveying the structure. "Ireland had sweat lodges back in ancient times. Not quite the same thing, but they used them in the Bronze Age for healing, like your tradition."

"Purging and cleansing must be a universal need."

He crossed his arms, surveying his work. "A worthy endeavor, to be sure. C'mon, we'll help you finish up."

For the rest of the afternoon, Colin and Michelle helped Komie construct her sweat lodge. The structure hulked ugly and inelegant but functional. Colin fed the bonfire, lined with rocks. Once they grew hot, Colin would move the rocks into her lodge as a doorkeeper, and she could begin her ceremony. Then he instructed Liam and Hugh to keep her water barrel filled.

She hadn't performed a sweat lodge ceremony for decades. Still, she remembered the blessings of the grandfather stones and the entrance.

Komie entered the lodge, calling the four stations. She would stay within for four sessions, offering prayers to her ancestors, gifts to the spirits, and ask for guidance. First, she offered hickory chips as she had no cedar. The pungent, sweet aroma of the hickory wrapped around her as she placed them on the hot rocks with water, steam filling the lodge.

More water came with each offering, along with herbs or food and songs for the ancestors. By the time she had made her fourth offering, her head swam with scents, smoke, and steam.

In this fugue state, she shut her eyes and embraced the steam. Flashes of light came into her mind, with chanting voices from another age. They spoke in her native language, Wolastoqi'ik. While the voices layered upon themselves, Komie made out a general approval of her course of action. With a deep sigh, she thanked them for their guidance.

After she received her answer, she stayed within the lodge for some time, taking strength from the ceremony and the solitude. Komie emerged from the sweat, her body renewed, and her purpose strengthened.

Komie:

The next day, both Colin and Michelle agreed to the wisdom of Komie staying on the Byrne farm and doing only light work. Still, she felt she must earn her keep, so she insisted on helping in their own kitchen garden. Mindful of the drain upon her energy, she worked in small increments. Colin helped her from place to place, concentrating on the food crops. The seedlings cried while stretching, a painful screech within her mind, but Komie ignored the voices as they pulled on her soul. After each one, she cried against the ground, nourishing the soil with her tears.

The green shoots seemed fragile and out of place in the summer sun, but they'd thrive. By the time night fell, happiness flowed into her tired limbs. Perhaps she'd need to build up to encouraging fields to grow, like building up muscle to work out.

Even this light amount of work drained her energy. When twilight descended on the long summer day, Komie crawled into bed. In her yellow room, Komie drifted into a pleasant sleep as the first drops of an overnight storm pattered on her window.

In the darkness, something tugged at the edge of her dream. The thing lifted her slumber, yanking it off her. Komie sat straight up in bed with a gasp, the echo of her name dying in her ears.

She rose, pulling a robe against the evening chill. Komie opened the window and peered out into the darkness. Had someone called her? Or did she imagine the voice? The trees still dripped with the earlier rain, though the sky looked clear now. The moon's sliver shone against the starlight.

No sound greeted her, but her mind still insisted someone needed help. Komie put on her shoes and traded her robe for a sweater. She padded down the stairs to the rhythm of Colin's snores.

After exiting and closing the kitchen door softly behind her, she walked through the gardens. Garden footlights marked the path under the moonless sky. The call came stronger now, a cry for help.

Now, she recognized the call. Trees chanted her name in the back of her mind. Or perhaps something more than the trees? The very earth below tugged at her soul. Did the earth mother summon her? Had she finally gotten Anú's attention?

She placed a hand on the beech tree she'd asked to grow over the avenue, to pleach. The tree thrummed at her touch but didn't need her help. Instead, it urged her forward. The next one said the same.

Something crunched in the darkness. No tree made that sound.

In horror, Komie froze. A figure dressed in black stood at the end of the avenue, near the river's edge. Her heart leapt into her throat. She should scream, shout, wake up the Byrnes, but her voice died in her throat.

Two other figures emerged on either side of her. Komie's entire body chilled but wouldn't obey her wish to run away.

She had power, though. If her body betrayed her commands, other things would obey her.

Komie dropped to her knees, grunting at the pain, and shoved her hands into the dirt. The close packed soil of the path refused to yield. She dug harder with her fingers, clawing into the dirt.

With her mind, she asked the surrounding bushes to help her, to imprison the attackers. The roots slept, though, and were reluctant to move in the cool, dark night.

Komie pushed through their slumber, her mental voice growing louder and more strident. With maddening slowness, the roots quivered and quested, leaves rustling in the night.

The intruders got closer. One grunted, tripping over something in the woods. Komie swallowed and renewed her efforts. Power flowed through her arms into the ground.

Now, the forms surrounded her as she commanded the vines to twine around their ankles and wrists.

Just as the intruders grabbed her arms, rhododendron vines creaked toward them, shifting and crackling with new life. Startled, the man to her right glanced back. He dropped her arm and stumbled away, losing his footing. Her attacker fell to the ground as the vine encircled his foot. He shouted and tried to jerk his foot free, but the woody branch held firm.

"Hey!" The other man now dropped her arm, discovering his own creeping plant shackle. Other vines gripped their hands and curled around their mouths, keeping them silent.

Komie turned her attention to the first man she'd seen near the river. She peered into the darkness, trying to discern his form. She listened to the night but heard no rustling against the hoot of owls and the rush of wind through leaves.

With growing concern, she stumbled toward the river's edge, searching for the third man. Pain shot through her foot as she kicked a rock in the dark. Komie muffled a cry as she lost her balance and fell into the grass. After catching her breath and regaining her strength, she rose to her feet.

By the time Komie reached the shore, the third man had disappeared. Whether he escaped by boat or by diving under the water, she had no idea. But the other two remained captured, trussed up with rhododendron vines behind her.

She cursed into the inky darkness. If one escaped, he would bring word of their efforts, and the enemy would have information about their defenses.

On shaking legs, Komie returned to her prisoners. Rage and adrenaline rushed through the native woman, something she hadn't felt since she left Yamka and her granddaughter in Arizona. Anger coursed through her blood, anger that demanded action. But what action should she take? She did not care for violence. She couldn't hurt another person. That didn't mean she wouldn't loose this fury in some way.

After resisting the urge to shake the prisoners, she asked the vines to keep them fast as she fetched the Byrnes to deal with them. On her way back to the house, she stopped at the kitchen garden where she'd spent so much of her energy that day. On impulse, she plunged her hands into the loamy soil again, dispersing her ire into the dirt. Nocturnal blossoms of ghostly white bloomed like eyes looking out into the night, winking at her in conspiracy.

The house seemed strange when she entered, as if she were a different person. But she hadn't given in to her aggression, and she remained true to her principles. Gritting her teeth, Nokomis knocked on Michelle and Colin's bedroom door. She didn't wish to wake the household, but she needed to tell them, at least.

After giving Colin the details in a low voice, he gripped her by the arms. "I want to thank you for your actions in protecting us. We'll put the prisoners put in the root cellar for now, but we'll call someone tomorrow to take them to Dublin for questioning."

"I'm glad I found a way to capture them without hurting them."

He swallowed. "As am I. Let's not tell the others. I want their attention on their tasks. Tomorrow, we have three farms along this road toward the south, and when we've helped them as much as you can, we'll move on to their neighbors."

Then he sent her up to her room for a much-needed rest. Though she didn't think she could sleep after all that excitement, exhaustion overtook her body.

Komie:

A sound in the night startled her awake. She rubbed the sleep from her face and went to the window, staring out in the darkness. Were there more invaders? She could see nothing in the black, and the earth didn't speak to her. After a while, she let out a yawn and crawled back into bed, but she couldn't sleep. Something still felt wrong.

She pulled on a robe and padded down the wooden stairs. Perhaps she needed a cup of tea to settle her mind. Another noise, something scraping, made her freeze, but it didn't repeat.

Her nerves were definitely on edge. Should she wake her host? The prisoners might be trying to escape. She walked along the hall, trying to remember which door led to the cellar. Adrenaline surged through her as another sound came from behind. She whirled to see a shape looming in the darkness. With a cry, she grabbed something off the table next to her and threw it at the form. A man cried out and the heavy thing clattered to the floor.

"Hey! Stop that! Who's there?"

It didn't sound like the voices from the night, but it didn't sound very familiar, either. She felt around for something else to throw, and found something heavy, perhaps a candle holder. "Who are you?"

"It's Joel. Who are you?"

Komie let out a shuddering breath. "It's Komie. I'm sorry, but you frightened me. Did I hit you?"

"No, well, not bad. It hit my thigh. Hold on."

In a moment, he had his phone on and a flashlight shone from the back. He flicked it on her face, and she covered her eyes. "Oh, sorry. Did I blind you?"

She bit back an angry retort. He wasn't to blame for her lack of sleep or nervousness. "I couldn't sleep and wanted some tea. Would you like some?"

"Sure."

They found the kitchen and turned on a real light. Komie filled the kettle and placed it on the warming burner while Joel found the tea. She watched him as he opened each of the cupboards. "Were you also unable to sleep?"

He shrugged, his eyes darting to the back door. "Uh, yeah, I'm still on American time."

"I thought you'd been here as long as Anna?"

"No, I came later." He bit off his words, as if uncomfortable discussing it. Then she remembered why he looked familiar. She narrowed her eyes. "Didn't I see you at the airport in New York?"

He spun around, his eyes wide. "Me? Nah, it must have been someone else. I've got one of those faces."

Komie gritted her teeth. She didn't believe him in the slightest. She was certain she'd seen him with the protestors, and likely one reason Anna had been so frightened. Well, she'd keep an eye on this one, especially with PEM prisoners secreted in the root cellar. Hopefully, Colin would have them off the premises and in a more secure place in the morning.

Chapter Ten

"Let thy step be slow and steady, that thou stumble not."
– Tokugawa Ieyasu

Hiroki:

Hiroki rose from a restless sleep the next day. He still hadn't gotten used to the sounds of the rural dwelling, such as neighing horses and clucking chickens. The Byrnes didn't own horses or cows, but their neighbors must. Barking dogs he might classify and dismiss. But his neighbor in Tokyo had a Shiba Inu. The dog hadn't barked often but, when he had, something had gone wrong.

Which is why Hiroki woke every time he heard a bark, or a cluck, or a neigh. The worst was the sound he could only guess must be a rooster, as the creature screamed every morning before dawn. He missed the comforting noise of the city to lull him to sleep, like tires whooshing on the street or a distant ambulance wail.

Of course, now that the other Unhidden had joined them, living with thirteen people meant another set of noises, arguments, questions, laughter. He hoped he'd get used to the noises soon as the lack of sleep made him clumsy. Clumsier than normal, at least.

The sun peeking in through the lacey white curtains meant his alarm would go off soon. Since the summer days grew long here, the mornings came early. Their hostess, Michelle, asked that they arrive each morning in the dining room to help with chores before breakfast at seven. Today would be a series of safety drills, followed by instruction on the structure of the

PHAE and how the organization related to the governments of the world and in Ireland.

This prospect excited Hiroki. He'd studied Japanese governmental structure, especially after his public speaking professor had mentioned going into politics. While he hadn't changed professions, government fascinated him. Now, he'd learn how Irish government differed from Japanese, and how this PHAE integrated. Colin assured them that the PHAE and the Irish government weren't the same. Still, they'd become entwined and pursued treaties and agreements to make that cooperation binding. The PHAE pursued agreements with several sovereign nations. However, such things took time in any governmental process, so the relationship remained honorary for now.

Hiroki still wondered if his talent even registered as PHAE-eligible. He hid his fear as no one else questioned their presence here. Any day now, they'd decide recruiting him had all been a mistake. His dreams of fitting in by being pleasant would be ruined, and they'd send him back to Japan in disgrace. His parents would never welcome him back.

After Hiroki made his bed and started his tea, the alarm for 5:30 buzzed. He shut off the screaming noise and finished his tea, contemplating his options.

Yesterday, Colin asked Hiroki if he'd considered using his persuasion talents for a governmental purpose, such as working with the Oireachtas. After Colin described this group as the Irish version of the Japanese National Diet or the American Congress, Hiroki grew intrigued. The Oireachtas created laws for approval by the executive branch. That seemed like a lot of power to give into a foreign visitor's hands.

Colin had sat in his overstuffed red leather chair and gave a smile. "I must confess, as a schoolboy, I dreamt of getting into politics. My head swam with stories from our revolution. I counted Éamon de Valera as my hero."

Hiroki cocked his head. "Who is he? I am unfamiliar with Irish history. That name sounds Spanish rather than Irish. Or am I mistaken?"

He chuckled. "No, he had a Spanish name, right enough. His mother was born in Ireland, though he wasn't. His father was a Spanish artist. However, de Valera came to Ireland after his father died, at age three, so for all intents and purposes, he had Irish roots, and his mother raised him Irish. He took part in the 1916 Easter Rising, the beginning of our final, successful revolution against the British government. Then, after we booted the Brits, he became our first president."

Hiroki's eyes grew wide. "So, he is similar to the American first President, George Washington? I understand he is much honored in the United States."

"A valid equivalent, to be sure. I wanted to become a lawyer, then a politician, and be a modern-day de Valera. I took several law courses, but then discovered a passion for creating laws rather than defending them."

Hiroki would never have reached such a level in the Japanese government. In order to take part in high-level government administration, one must be born into the right family and possess the right connections. Hiroki came from a banking family, not a political family. He had no such connections.

The Irish government, Colin assured him, worked on a more egalitarian basis, though connections always helped. "Still, as a non-national, you wouldn't be able to participate in an official capacity on the Irish Oireachtas. You might work as an aide to the Teachta Dála or a Senator in the Oireachtas. As an aide, you'd wield considerable influence. Especially with your Unhidden talent."

When Hiroki expressed doubt, Colin moved on. "If you aren't interested in becoming a political aide, what about a press secretary? They make announcements about the Taoiseach and the prime minister and answer questions from the press about governmental issues. You'd not only have the ears of governmental powers, but of the world, as these press conferences are often broadcast. Your powers could work wonders."

This talk about high political power made Hiroki's hands sweat. He clasped them tight in his lap. "Colin-san, I am concerned about the moral implications of using my powers thus. In addition, I am uncertain my talent works over electronic media. They did not work on my parents or friends. My power has many limitations."

The older man shrugged. "That is a valid point, and a question only you can truly answer. As to your abilities to work over different media, how do you know if you don't try? Don't worry, you'll find be plenty of options. You'll see."

Hiroki finished his tea and cleaned the cup, now ready to face the rest of the world, or this small corner of it. Mostly.

Only the eldest daughter of the house, Róisín, stood in the dining room. She smiled as she arranged breakfast plates and silverware on the sideboard. He sat and folded his hands, his back straight, waiting for the others to arrive. He didn't need to wait long as they filtered in one by one. Each exhibited a different level of fatigue or wakefulness. Hiroki classified them as morning people or not, though his own state as a morning person might be in question from his recent difficulty sleeping. Just as this thought crossed his mind, he stifled a yawn.

Michelle and Colin entered, holding hands. Hiroki's parents had never acted so physically affectionate in public. Could this be a cultural difference or a dichotomy between the level of fondness? In truth, he didn't know if his parents loved each other. Of course, they honored each other. But did they love each other? Was his father even capable of love? The notion struck a stark note in Hiroki's heart.

Colin stood at the head of the table while everyone found a seat. One or two headed straight for the sideboard for coffee or tea.

Colin cleared his throat. "Now that we've got a full house, we've assignments for everyone to help keep the farm going and everyone busy. I've created a duty roster for each of you. When the first task of the day is complete, return here for a full breakfast. Then we'll dedicate mornings to classes in using and controlling your abilities. We've assigned another set of chores for either afternoon or evening."

Max stumbled in, his hair sticking up in tangled spikes and his chin in need of a razor. Red creases across his face spoke of a very recent rising. He grunted as Colin paused and made a beeline for the coffee carafe.

Their host frowned. "I thought you understood you must be punctual, Mr. Hurley?"

Max answered with another grunt and a desultory wave toward Colin. Hiroki frowned at his friend's rudeness. The woman from Mongolia, Qacha, entered next, looking as surly as Max, though less unkempt.

Despite the camaraderie they'd formed when Hiroki recruited Max and brought him to Ireland, Max's language toward others made Hiroki intensely uncomfortable. Hiroki had stood by him, but his loyalty wavered when Max spoke such language to their hosts. While he realized that Japanese standards for hospitality and guest behavior weren't universal, other people's reactions to Max's language hinted that he stepped across the line.

Colin sighed and repeated his injunction for promptness. Qacha gave him a polite nod and sipped her tea, her eyes closed. "I offer my apologies, Mr. Byrne. I will endeavor to be on time in the future."

Next to him, the American woman, Anna, spilled her tea and muttered, "Fuckabiscuit!" He jumped up to grab some napkins and helped her mop up the mess. They bumped foreheads, and she cried, "Ow!" just as he cried, *"Chikushou!"*

Anna stumbled back, and Hiroki caught her arm, giving her a chance to recover. Hiroki glanced toward Michelle, expecting a comment about their language, but the matron spoke with her husband. "I am so sorry, Miss Anna."

She flashed a half-smile. "No need to apologize. If I hadn't been such a clumsy mess to begin with, you wouldn't have had to rescue me."

He gave a quick bow. "It is always my pleasure to rescue a lady in distress."

Anna flushed and glanced away, and Hiroki wondered if he'd said something wrong or had been too bold. He felt certain Americans spoke in movies and television shows this way. Had he been mistaken?

To repair his error, Hiroki asked, "I am curious about the thing you said when you dropped your tea. What does the word mean?"

She giggled. "'Fuckabiscuit?' That just means I did something dumb. The word itself doesn't mean anything."

Max sat on his other side and raised his eyebrows, lifting his coffee cup in salute. "Oi, you don't waste time, do you, Hiroki? I would never have thought it of ya. Look at you, the ladies' man!"

Hiroki's cheeks burned as he stared at the floor. He had no wish to flirt with the American woman. He just tried to be polite. Did they mean the same thing in Western culture? Hiroki rose to get his own cup of tea to escape his loss of face.

Anna came up next to him to refresh her own cup. "Pay him no mind. Max thinks there's only one reason for men to talk to women. I can tell you aren't that type. Do you like milk in your tea?"

He shook his head. "I prefer green tea, but this lemon herbal is pleasant. I do not require milk."

The brunette woman grinned. "I brought scads of green tea. They're up in my room. I can get you some, if you want."

A wave of gratitude mingled with homesickness washed over him. Hiroki gave her a polite bow, a silly grin on his face. "That would be most delightful. Thank you for the gift."

"Don't worry, I brought way too much tea with me. I had this crazy notion the Irish wouldn't have enough tea."

Bintou:

Colin and Michelle led their guests to the garden. Chairs, an easel, and a white board had been set up like an outdoor classroom. Brendan and Anna sat next to each other, while Max sat off on one end. Qacha also chose an edge location, while Komie chose a seat front and center. Bintou sat next to her.

The Irish woman picked up a marker. "Now, I'm sure you've heard news about protests and bigotry against the Unhidden. Not everyone is against us, of course, but pockets of people both in the world and here in Ireland are frightened. However, most of the Irish have embraced the Unhidden. Perhaps our strong fairy tradition has something to do with it, or the fact the PHAE set up headquarters here. Regardless of the reason, we are relatively safe in Ireland."

She sat in her chair and crossed one leg over another. "Please note I said *relatively.* As I'm sure you realize, no true safety exists anywhere in this world, even for those of you with offensive or defensive powers. Therefore, as hostilities exist, and there is a possibility, no matter how remote, of a breach in the defenses of Ireland, the PHAE, and this farm, we shall give you defensive instruction."

Bintou's stomach roiled into knots as she raised her hand. "I must inform you, I am not comfortable using weapons against people."

Michelle nodded. "This is understood and accepted, Bintou. Some of you may have personal or religious reasons against violence, and we won't ask you to do anything you're uncomfortable with. However, some instruction in defense, both of yourself and this farm, is prudent. I'm sure others here are more than capable of taking up the burden of violence, should the need arise." She shot a glance at Max, and everyone waited for an objection.

However, the Australian lifted his coffee cup in acknowledgment. "Aye, I can fight to defend the sheilas. That's a cause worth fighting for. Even those almost as tall as me." He gave Qacha a saucy wink.

Qacha glared back at him and shot to her feet. "I do not require defending, Mr. Hurley. Not from you or from any male. I am quite capable of defending myself. Do not make assumptions."

Max waved his hand. "Settle down, luv. I meant no offense to your lovely self. I'm sure you could bugger a man right up if you put your mind to violence. With your bare hands, more likely than not. You're a right Amazon, you are."

She narrowed her gaze at the Australian and sat, her arms crossed. "You are not incorrect."

Michelle cleared her throat and stood again, picking up a marker. She drew a large, skewed rectangle on the whiteboard. "This represents the Byrne Farm. This area here," she drew a wavy line along the top, "is the narrowing end of the River Shannon, our most vulnerable edge. While the river is too shallow to hold a true submarine, invaders in submersible gear might work up the coast."

Bintou, her face drawn with worry, held her hand up. "Why would they target this farm?"

Komie glanced down at her hands as Michelle pressed her lips together. "An excellent question. Unfortunately, or fortunately, the Byrne Farm is known as one of several Irish training locations for emerging talents. We've been teaching since talents first emerged over six months ago. This location is not a secret."

Bintou glanced to Anna, who turned pale at Michelle's words. The American woman tugged her long sleeves to hide the scales on her arms, her glance darting left and right. The Malian woman had glimpsed her scales several times and thought them lovely. She wondered if they kept Anna warm when the cold Irish wind blew. A shudder traveled down her spine despite the warm day.

In a low voice, Bintou quoted, "'Why are our bodies soft and weak and smooth, unapt to toil and trouble in the world, but that our soft conditions and our hearts should well agree with our external parts?'"

Anna turned to her with wide eyes. "What's that from?"

"A Shakespeare play, *Taming of the Shrew*. The words seemed appropriate."

Michelle cleared her throat. "Now, an attack is, as I mentioned, unlikely. But the lessons you learn here will put you in good stead wherever you go after your training, so they won't be wasted. After we finish here this morning and eat lunch, I'll show you where we store the weapons. For those who wish further training, we can instruct you in their use." She held up her hand as Bintou stood, her mouth opening to protest. "And yes, if you are uncomfortable with using them, we understand. However, we ask that you at least attend the instruction so, should you find yourself in danger, and change your mind, you won't hurt yourself."

Despite her strong words, Bintou hadn't always been vehemently against violence. But a childhood memory of being caught in a protest made her heart clench whenever she thought of getting into a fight.

She preferred not to relive that terror, the moment when her parents had disappeared. Fighting had broken out, and she almost got trampled before her parents rescued her. While she tightened her jaw, she refused the memories knocking on her conscious mind. They kept pounding, demanding to be heard, but she took several calming breaths. Perhaps with some training, she might not have been so terrified when Oumar had hammered on her door, demanding to speak with her.

Pulling her attention back to the presentation, Bintou listened to Michelle as she detailed the best vantage points along the river.

When they broke for lunch, Qacha approached Bintou. She hadn't spoken much with this hard-edged woman, but Qacha sat next to her as they ate. After she cleared her throat, the other woman turned to her, steel in her eyes. "If we find ourselves in an attack situation, stand by me. If you help by handing me weapons or fetching water, I can protect you. Especially if they have bows in their arsenal."

"Bows? Like in bows and arrows?"

Qacha flashed a rare smile. "Yes, bows and arrows. I trained with a master of horseback archery. I even competed in the Spirit Tournament but never came close to the skill level my grandfather had. Still, I am an excellent markswoman."

Bintou looked at the woman with admiration and a little apprehension. "You would protect me as my personal Asa? Why?"

Another smile cracked the woman's sun-darkened face. "Because from what I understand, you love and collect beautiful things. I am not a beautiful thing, nor do I collect them, but I do appreciate them. In addition, you need protecting. That is the way of the warrior. For such as you, I learned the art of war. It was ever thus."

Latest **CNN** *Update: Northern Irish authorities report they have apprehended a foreign operative attempting to compromise the water supply at Lough Neagh. While they held the culprit for questioning, he succeeded in taking his own life. Investigations are under way to discover how this breach could have happened, who was at fault, and what organization might have funded the initiative. The equipment and operation were sophisticated, so the possibility that he worked alone is remote.*

Irish Defense Forces believe this foreign operative to be a member of the PEM, Pure Earther Movement. The Dail of Ireland has met to discuss whether to declare the PEM a terrorist organization.

In related news, U. S. Representative Muriel Tinker Browne of Alabama has been outspoken in her support of the PEM as a "God-sent agency to eradicate the threat of the agents of Satan." She said this while giving a speech at a rally organized by PEM leader, Tiberius Wilkinson.

Bintou:

Just as Bintou descended to the great room, the front door swung open. The Byrne's eldest daughter, Róisín, entered. She gave the honey-blonde woman a hug. "Welcome home! I didn't realize you were due back!"

The other woman returned the hug and gave her a grin. "I'm only back for a few days. They've been sending me here, there, and everywhere the last week. I haven't spent the night in the same place twice in a row."

"You've arrived in time for stories, so I am told. Though you've likely heard them all your life and probably tired of them."

"Da's stories? I'll never tire of those. He knows them all."

As they entered the great room, Colin settled into a comfortable armchair and crossed his hands over his stomach. Komie stayed in the sweat lodge while the rest of the group gathered for stories. Some sat on the couch, chairs, and a bench, with the younger children on the floor at their father's feet.

Colin wore an anticipatory smile and caught the gaze of several in his audience before beginning. "Tonight, I shall relate one of the most famous tales of our land. I shall tell you of Tír na nÓg, the land of everlasting youth."

One of the blond twins giggled as the other tickled him, but Róisín sent them a quelling glare, and they subsided.

"Tír na nÓg is a place out of legend, a paradise where no one ever grows old. It's said the Tuatha Dé Danann, or the Good People, go to this Land of the Ever Young when they die, to forever feast, sing, and dance."

When Colin mentioned *Good People,* Bintou straightened. This might be another name for the Yumboes or Bakhna Rakhna in some West African tales. Yumboes were spirits of the dead who came out to dance in the moonlight. They hosted some lucky humans to their feasts and the legends spoke of their benevolence to kind people.

"Many people have tried to find the Land of Youth, mythical heroes with magical artifacts, and some have succeeded. The immram tales give details of these brave explorers beyond our shores, across the Mag Mell, the Plain of Honey. Some of these explorers, instead of reaching Tír na nÓg, found another mythical island called Hy-Brasil, which appears once every seven years."

Colin's eyes glazed over, as if lost in such a land himself. After a long pause, his eldest daughter poked him. He blinked a few times, gave his listeners a sheepish smile, and cleared his throat. "Some tales say you can find Tír na nÓg through passages into the earth, ancient burial mounds, sacred caves, or through magical mist. Such places are considered sacred by cultures across the world, liminal spaces between this world and the next. Ireland is no exception to this tradition. They are often dedicated to a god, goddess, or in more modern ages, saints. I harbor mad fantasies of finding an undiscovered one myself someday!"

As he wove tales of heroes who tried—and sometimes failed—to reach this mystical land of Tír na nÓg, Bintou lost herself in memories of her homeland's supernatural denizens.

That night, after a cozy evening of stories and songs, Bintou dreamed of Orunmila. The tall and powerful goddess of wisdom, draped in green and yellow robes, sat beside her and held her hand. Her triple-layered voice echoed in the small bedroom. "You are home, child. Be true to yourself and all will be well."

Róisín:

County Tipperary, Ireland

As her little sister, Fiona, hummed to herself while peeling potatoes, Róisín studied the recipe for the third time. She needed to get the soda bread right this time. Her last attempt tasted way too floury.

Brendan came up behind her and whispered in her ear, "Want to know my secret?"

Róisín cast her younger brother a suspicious glance. "Only if it's a real secret and not a prank!"

Placing a hand of patent innocence across his chest, Brendan's eyes widened. "Me? Prank you? I'd never do such a thing."

"Not if you thought I'd caught on, you wouldn't."

Brendan dropped his hand and gave a sardonic grin. "Fair enough, Sis. But seriously, do you want my secret ingredient?"

Róisín cocked her head. "Fine. What's your secret?"

"Treacle."

"What? In soda bread?"

Brendan nodded and opened the cabinet, pulling out the dark brown bottle. "Not so much that you can taste the treacle, mind, but a few tablespoons will keep the bread moist with a hint of sweetness. The bread tastes great with salted butter."

With narrowed eyes, Róisín took the bottle from her brother. "You'd better not be putting me on."

He raised one hand, his eyes growing wide with feigned innocence. "May the devil take my spine as a ladder and use it to pluck the apples in Hell, I swear it!"

Fiona piped up from her end of the table, brandishing the potato peeler like a rapier. "Yeah! You better not be putting her on! I'm watching you!"

Qacha:

The next morning dawned with drizzly mist surrounding the farm. Qacha's bones ached with the damp but she rose to help with breakfast preparation. Working in a kitchen, any kitchen, calmed her mind. And as her hostess reminded them, this was a working farm. She and the other guests should assist with the chores.

She didn't mind hard work. People must work to live. But working early in the morning, before most of the others woke, suited her better. With the arrival of the two other recruits, Qacha retreated more often to the solitude of her room and Manol's company. The Japanese man and the woman from Mali might be fascinating individuals, but Qacha had no interest in forming friendships. She would rather do her work and get her assignment.

In the past, she'd allowed her friendships and emotions to define her. She'd vowed never to let that happen again.

And yet, she'd offered to protect the woman. She still didn't know what impulse had prompted her to do that, but a vow offered was a vow kept.

As she kneaded dough for morning bread, Qacha's thoughts sped back to the last time she'd let her emotions take over her life. That disaster had led to her losing the one successful thing she'd ever achieved, her own Michelin-starred restaurant. She might even have garnered her father's approval for that lofty title if he'd still been alive to appreciate the honor.

But one bad decision had led to another, and her heart, her body and, in the end, her restaurant, had all slipped from her control. This disaster started a downward spiral she never recovered from.

Instead of a high-end restaurant, she ended up cooking for some soulless corporate hotel kitchen, working for a money-grubbing manager instead of herself. And even at that position, they tried to squeeze her out.

But she didn't wait around for that to happen. Instead, she dropped everything and fled for this promise of a different life, a place where her talent would be welcomed and appreciated. *More like tested and judged.* She snorted at her own brief flash of optimism. What had she expected? Some sort of Tenggeri on earth, a paradise with no strife?

Qacha hadn't entertained such idealistic notions for many, many years. She should have known better this time. Still, this farm wasn't a terrible place. A far cry from the soulless corporate hotel kitchen she'd left before her decision to come here. Just filled with too many people.

Just as she had that thought, footsteps thundered down the stairs, followed by a high-pitched squeal and laughter. Bracing herself for an onslaught of activity from the younger contingent of the Byrne Family, Qacha pulled out the miniature scones she'd set aside for the children.

She'd brushed them with clover honey and sprinkled them with brown sugar. Perhaps with a sweet treat, she could bribe them to play outside today rather than through the kitchen.

The girl, Fiona, stopped in the kitchen doorway, her face flushed. "Good morning, Miss Qacha!"

Qacha didn't glance up from dicing scallions. "Good morning, Fiona."

"Liam and Hugh said," the girl glanced behind her, "they said that you said that Manol is part wildcat. Did you really say that?"

The edge of Qacha's mouth twitched. "I did not say that. However, that is a true statement. His mother had been a Pallas cat, a breed of wild cat in Mongolia. This is one reason he is so, what is the word, hairy?"

The girl let out a giggle. "Fluffy!"

Qacha gave a solemn nod. "Fluffy, then."

A knock made Fiona's eyes grow wide, and then she disappeared, presumably to answer the door. More voices followed, this time several adults. Qacha washed her hands in the sink in preparation for a kitchen invasion.

The PHAE representatives she'd met before, Ciara, Paul, and Martin, filed into the kitchen. They each wore very grim expressions, almost matching her own.

Ciara glanced around the kitchen. "Qacha, can you please ring Michelle's bell? We'll need to call everyone in. We have some news to announce."

Komie:

Komie dreamt of her son, Mihku, before he'd been deployed. He begged her to take him to the powwow, though the celebration was with a different tribe. With great reluctance, she'd agreed to his begging.

With wide eyes and eager energy, he'd dragged her from vendor to vendor, watched the dances with great interest, and one dancer in particular. In fact, he couldn't keep his eyes off her.

However, instead of a true memory, this morphed into a wish, and the dancer changed from Yamka, the woman who stole Komie's son from her, into a delightful young woman of her own tribe, someone from New Brunswick who honored Komie as a daughter-in-law should.

That's when the bell woke her.

With a deep sigh for what might have been, Komie washed her face and padded down the stairs. The enticing aroma of scones greeted her. Someone must have been busy early in the kitchen for the baking to be complete already. She gave Qacha an appreciative nod as she entered the large dining room but halted when she spied the PHAE people. They didn't look pleased.

Komie fixed herself some coffee, took a hot scone, and sat at the table, waiting for the rest of the residents to filter in. She glanced at Qacha again, and the Mongolian woman held her gaze longer this time. She held tension in her shoulders and in the skin around her eyes.

Hiroki rushed in, a wild look in his eyes as if he had lost his puppy. Before Komie could calm him, Bintou arrived, a wide smile on her face. "Something smells delightful! What did you bake for us?"

When no one answered her, the smile faded. "What has happened?"

Ciara squared her shoulders and glanced around the group. "Please, everyone get something to eat and have a seat."

Now, Anna entered with the Byrne's older son, Brendan, and her brother, Joel, flashed them a frown. Qacha looked around for the final student. Had the Australian slept through the bell? Just as this thought ran through her mind, Max stumbled through the door and to the coffee carafe.

Ciara murmured something to Michelle and Colin, then they went to the library for a conference. They emerged a few minutes later, their hosts now wearing the same grim expressions the PHAE reps wore.

As they all got tea, coffee, scones, or brown bread, the tall dark man, Martin, stood, clasping his hands behind his back. "We've received some disturbing news today. I believe we had briefed each of you on the attack recently made on Cork, and the success our people had in defending against that attack." She gave a nod toward Max and Anna.

"Unfortunately, we've received intelligence that more attacks are planned. Therefore, the council has decided it would be the better part of wisdom to drill each of you in some basic defense courses. After such courses are completed, we shall station you at various places, both for your own safety and to help defend our shores. We are still spread very thin, and the government of Ireland has been reluctant to help us with military firepower."

Bintou raised her hand and stood, her back straight and her face grim. "I've mentioned before that I am a pacifist. I will not attack others."

Martin flashed her a warm smile. "We appreciate that and took your preferences into account, Bintou. We've assigned you and Hiroki to our Dublin location to help with treaty negotiations. Max and Anna, you and Brendan will return to Cork to assist the air and water defenses. Róisín, Joel, and Qacha will join the defenses in Galway."

Komie imagined chaos perched upon the edge of this island, ready to wreak havoc upon them. And yet she wouldn't harm another human unless she had to defend someone else. She stood to address Ciara. "I am also unwilling to do violence."

Ciara nodded once. "We've asked that you remain here at the farm to help grow food. If a blockade is in our future, Ireland will need to feed its own. We expected the need and stockpiled supplies for the last several months. However, your ability to coax quick growth will be invaluable. We may send you to various farms across the county. Will that be acceptable as an alternative to violence?"

Relieved, Komie nodded and sat back down. "That will do. Thank you for your consideration." Ciara's plan sounded better suited to both her temperament and talents, and with one attack at the farm repelled, they should be less likely to try again. She hoped. She would much rather nurture growth and sustenance would feed her own soul. The idea of growth reminded her of her granddaughter, Tansy. How much had she grown?

Ciara turned to Colin. "We're asking you and Michelle to remain here with your younger children. We need your students, present and past, to return to a familiar base if needed."

Colin's face turned solemn while Michelle looked pale. That drove Komie's concern into overdrive. She well understood a mother's worry for her children.

Hiroki rose, his brow furrowed. "Pardon my ignorance, but shouldn't we move the vulnerable to a defensible location?"

Martin raised a bushy eyebrow. "More defensible than an island on the edge of Europe?"

Hiroki swallowed but pushed on. "Iceland. Hawaii. Siberia. Or somewhere else inaccessible. I understand the PHAE have enclaves around the world."

Ciara shook her head. "Your idea has merit, and the council considered such an option. However, those locations don't have the resources to house, feed, and care for thousands of Unhidden, not to mention the logistics of moving them. Most of us are already here, therefore Ireland must be the stronghold, especially as more Unhidden may seek admittance as hostilities escalate."

Hiroki sat, stunned into silence. Komie didn't blame him.

Qacha rose, her muscles rigid. "And if there are thousands of these Unhidden, why are they not assisting in the defenses of the island? Why are we the only ones assigned such a task?"

Ciara gave her a sad smile. "Unfortunately, the vast majority of the Unhidden don't possess strong powers or anything vaguely offensive. We know of perhaps ten strong, offensive talents, and half of those we gathered here in this room, brand-new and untrained. Most are small talents, like being able to change their eye color or lift a sheet of paper with their minds. Not very useful in defense against an armed attack, I'm afraid."

Qacha lifted her chin. "Who is attacking?"

Martin drank a sip of his coffee, and then cleared his throat. "We don't have verification, but we believe the PEM, Pure Earther Movement, is behind the attack. They aren't a sovereign nation, per se, their access to weapons is difficult to assess. However, we must consider the possibility they've stockpiled an arsenal from sympathetic and corrupt governments, through the black market, or even made their own. While these would be crude or out-of-date, they can nevertheless be quite devastating. We must also keep vigilant for any spies. They have obviously been planning something for a while, and might have already sent sleeper agents."

Murmurs swept through the room. Komie stood again. "Are these PEM people the same cowardly bigots who have been protesting on the news? The ones who have been starting riots?"

She exchanged a glance with Colin, and he gave her a bare nod. They were the same as the men who had invaded that night. The men who Joel might have been trying to let out.

Bintou smiled at her description as Ciara nodded. "They are, from what we can tell. Their movement has gained steam over the last months, and their views found fertile ground. The environment of hate and xenophobia encourages their *us versus them* mindset and concept of genetic superiority. Despite our diplomatic corps, the PEM refuse to join us in a negotiation forum."

Qacha jumped up, her face red. "Are we going to allow these criminals to attack us?"

Martin clasped his hands, his face solemn. "That's what they believe. We've been careful to disseminate misinformation about our capabilities. They believe we possess little or no defensive weapons. They're wrong. And a few locals and police have agreed to help us with defense, as their own homes are in danger. The attack on Cork came more quickly than we expected, but we aren't unprepared. Now we must ensure we're prepared for more."

Qacha scowled while Hiroki's mouth pressed into a thin line. The Mongolian woman furrowed her brow. "Weapons. Do you mean us? Or actual physical armament?"

"Both. But we have precious few of either, so our resources are spread thin."

Bintou's eyes darted to each of the PHAE representatives while Qacha stared at Ciara. Hiroki clasped and unclasped his hands. Komie kept her expression calm, but her jaw muscles twitched. Max stared sullenly into his coffee, barely moving.

Martin squared his shoulders. "If there are no further questions, we'll organize your assignments." The three visitors left the room. No one spoke for several moments.

Colin stood, holding his hands up for attention. "We'll arrange transportation tomorrow for those leaving the farm." He shared a look with Michelle. "We had hoped to host you for more than a few days. When the current crisis is over, we'll gather again and complete your training. After you've finished your breakfast, please return to your rooms and pack your things. You can leave items here if you like, and they'll remain safe. And all, please, be careful. Stay strong, stay alive."

He glanced at Liam and Hugh, who both looked unusually solemn. Komie shot a look at the youngest girl, Fiona, whose wide eyes betrayed her fear. She vowed to reassure the young lady after the meal.

Komie finished eating her breakfast, but the delicious food, previously eaten with relish and gusto, now tasted like ash and iron in her mouth.

Chapter Eleven

"The great danger for most of us lies not in setting our aim too high and falling short;
but in setting our aim too low and achieving our mark."
– Michelangelo

Bintou:

Later that morning, Fiona knocked on Bintou's door, her face the picture of shy anticipation. When Bintou invited her in, the Irish girl handed her a big bag filled with warm underclothing. "An earlier student left them. We washed them, so you're welcome to them. Mam said they should fit you. When Anna came back yesterday, we asked if she wanted any, but she said she grew up in New York and had plenty of warm things, so these are all yours."

While Bintou didn't like wearing other people's underclothes, she appreciated the consideration. The few things she'd bought with Ibrahim had gotten lots of wear already, and she'd had no chance to explore the Dublin shopping possibilities while she stayed at headquarters. She'd found no shopping options near the farmhouse. "Thank you for your kindness."

Fiona blushed. "You're welcome, Miss Bintou. It was Mam's idea. I told her I loved your bright colors, and you should always wear those. But she said they weren't as practical for Ireland."

Bintou examined the package, and the clothing looked new or almost new. Perhaps she could wear them after all.

In addition to this largesse, Brendan lent her a soft wool shawl. Bintou wished she'd bought more clothing when she'd gone shopping with Ibrahim. The trinkets and gifts she purchased did her little good in the chilly wind. "Sure, and it's summer, but you can't be used to this cold yet. This is angora wool. While the colors are more muted than your things, this'll keep your arms warm when you're outside in the evening air."

Now, as she descended the stairs to the dining room for lunch, the new underclothing chafed. While large enough to fit her ample curves, they bound her in odd ways, fitting differently from her own garments. The buttoned sleeves looked ridiculous. How could anyone like them?

Despite the chaffing, Bintou now had appropriate garb for this northern country, and she'd be more comfortable. She must find a way to thank both Fiona and Brendan for their thoughtfulness. And her hostess, Michelle, of course.

When she returned to the dining room, the three PHAE representatives stood clustered in one corner, speaking quietly. A few of the other Unhidden sat already, with others hovering along the walls.

Chairs shuffled as Liam and Hugh set food platters on the sideboard. Brendan and Róisín brought in plates and silverware. Everyone served themselves from the pasta and sauce options. Max grumbled first about his chair, then made a nasty comment about the food.

Anna's brow furrowed. "Max, this is the tastiest brown bread I've ever eaten."

"I don't give a flying fuck about what you've eaten."

Michelle narrowed her eyes. "Maximilian. I have warned you about your language."

He shrugged and drank down the rest of his coffee. "Fine, no worries. I won't say a bloody thing. Satisfied?"

Michelle continued to stare at him, while Róisín whispered something in his ear. He brushed her off. "Stop trying to settle me down, Róisín! You aren't my bloody mother!"

With a glance at his sister, Brendan poured his cup full again. "Max, perhaps you'd better have your coffee in your room? You seem like you need some time away from everyone else."

The Australian man growled. "You aren't my mother either, mate." The room fell silent as Max buttered a slice of the much-maligned brown bread. Then he stared at the slice for a moment and held it up like a sign. "The PHAE are using us. Can't you all see that? They're buttering us up to risk our lives in more of these attacks. We're just cannon fodder, I'm telling you!"

Hiroki tried to quiet him, but Max shook him off. "Stop with your wheedling, mate! I get you're trying to use that talent on me. I didn't come down in the last shower!"

Hiroki's eyes grew wide, and his face flushed. He ran out of the dining room. Brendan and Anna exchanged a glance. Fiona fixed Max with a deadly glare. Michelle stood and placed her hands on her hips. "Maximilian Aloysius Hurley, we do not tolerate bullying in this house, either of my family or our other guests. I thought you understood?"

Max threw his napkin on the table and jumped to his feet. "I bloody well do. I'm gone."

Hiroki:

Hiroki wanted to be anywhere but here, under the scrutiny of these strangers. He had just begun to believe he was part of this organization, this family. And then Max yelled at him in front of everyone. Hiroki thought Max was his friend. They'd grown to trust each other. He never used his talent on Max after that first day, and it hadn't even worked then. He'd never do that to a friend. But being accused hurt him more than he imagined.

He sat on a garden bench, staring at the garlic plants without seeing them, his head in his hands. A slammed door made him look up as Max stalked out of the house and toward his room.

The Japanese man tried to make himself disappear, but Max spied him and changed his direction. "Oi, Hiroki. What the hell did you try to pull on me back there?"

Hiroki only shook his head. What could he say that Max wouldn't take as manipulation? Nothing. He could say nothing without being misinterpreted. Would he be doomed to a lifetime of mistrust from everyone he met?

"Listen to me, you son of a bitch. Don't you ever try your talent bullshit on me again, hear? Never again."

Brendan inserted himself between them, his face a few inches from the Australian's. "Leave off, Max. You've no proof, none whatsoever. You're making assumptions and making Hiroki feel terrible. Hiroki's your friend, man! Don't be an eejit."

The Australian puffed his chest, anger in every line of his body. "*He's* feeling terrible? That's just too fucking bad. I feel terrible every fucking day. It's about time someone joined me!"

Róisín and Qacha approached, standing on either side of Max. Róisín put her hand on Max's shoulder, but he shrugged her off, making her take a step back. "Not now, darlin'. I'm in no mood for cosseting by the likes of you. Go peddle your sweetness on someone who needs it."

Qacha pushed Brendan aside and stood nose to nose with Max. She almost matched Max in height. "Silence your mouth, Australian. You are acting like a spoilt child. You have been unjust to three people. Would you care to make that four? Spew your hatred on someone who can fight back, or are you too cowardly for a fair fight?"

He shoved her chest, pushing her back a step. "I'm not interested in your bitterness, either, woman. Get out of my face. This isn't your war."

Qacha's face grew scarlet, and she spoke in a low, dangerous tone. "You dare lay hands on me? Do you have *any* idea what happened to the last man to touch me in anger?"

"No idea, luv. What happened to him? Did you dissolve him with your spite?"

Hiroki tried to sneak down the path, away from the mounting tension. Max and Qacha sparked with anger as their muscles tensed. Hugh hid behind Brendan, peeking out from behind.

The wind swirled, rustling the leaves of the herbs and bushes. Hiroki glanced up, but the late afternoon sky remained clear. This must be Max's talent at work. He glanced back at the two angry Unhidden.

Qacha's smile grew as she spread her arms. Dark lines along her veins glowed red. "Is that how it's going to be, Son of Air? Very well. I shall battle you, as Daughter of Fire."

Róisín held up her hands. "Are you both children? This isn't a playground."

The Mongolian woman shot her a quick glare. "No. This is a fight for dominance. If you prefer to remain safe, return to the house. All of you. I shall not allow my weapons to damage the property. Max will make a similar promise."

Without taking his eyes off Qacha, Max shrugged. "Fine. Right. Everyone, go inside."

Just as Hiroki slunk toward the kitchen door, Róisín stood her ground, her arms crossed. "I will not, and neither will anyone else. If you need to have things out, and we're hurt, you'll just have to deal with the guilt and the consequences. I refuse to make this easier for you to continue this madness." She fixed her gaze on Hiroki and, ashamed of his own cowardice, he returned to her side. Brendan stood next to his sister.

While letting out a deep breath, Hiroki held up his hands. "This is unnecessary. The PHAE has given us no reason to suspect they wish to use us for ill. In fact, they've promised us we can leave if we want. This is not a prison. We are not sworn soldiers, required to enact our commanders' orders despite our misgivings."

Max broke his staring contest to glare at him, but then returned to Qacha's gaze. "I don't want to hear another bloody word from you, Hiroki. I don't trust you to not use your talent. Let someone else talk."

Hiroki swallowed his disappointment and stared at his feet as he clenched his hands into fists. He must do something.

Brendan clapped a hand on Hiroki's shoulder. "Max, Hiroki is right, and I don't understand your anger at him. How can you distrust Hiroki? Do you believe him capable of being that devious? Come on, man, be sensible. This isn't the time nor the place to make a stand."

Róisín gripped Hiroki's arm, squeezed once, and stepped closer to Max. "Both of you, this is unnecessary and a childish show of ego. We don't let Liam and Hugh devolve into this sort of peeing contest, and we won't allow it with you."

Hugh let out a strangled peep, which might have been a giggle.

Michelle's steely voice came from behind him. "Neither do we allow the language you seem to prefer. Mr. Hurley, I have warned you several times about your words, and the respect due to our family and guests. You seem incapable of following the basic rules. Even if you weren't already assigned to leave for Cork, I would ensure you leave our household."

Max gave a shrug. "But I'm going anyhow, aye? Sent on a fool's mission by these buggers. But we're in a war now, and anyone who leaves in a war is a deserter. So, what's your point?"

"My *point* is that you will not be welcome back to my farm when your assignment is over."

The Australian man scowled at Róisín, Michelle, and Brendan in turn, with a final one for Qacha. "Then we finally agree on something."

Latest* CNN *Update: Investigations with MI5 have discovered a hidden weapons cache on the Isle of Man. Local authorities have cooperated fully with the agency, and the UN Security Council has been notified. The authorities have assured the public that no weapons of mass destruction have been discovered within the cache, nor any weapons banned by the Geneva

Convention. However, searches for similar caches are now underway in key areas of the world.

Bintou:

Bintou needed to walk in the garden. If she must leave this delightful haven for the uncertainty of Dublin, she wanted to enjoy the sylvan paradise once more. Cities often had a dearth of growing things, and she would rather get her fill before being bereft.

As she wandered among the buzzing bees and fragrant blossoms, she realized someone stood behind her. She turned to see Anna's brother, Joel. He seemed to revel in lurking in the shadows, always one step behind everyone else, quietly watching them all. She didn't like him but couldn't very well tell him to leave. No matter how much she wished to be rude, she had no control over his actions. Bintou gave him a pleasant nod and brushed past him. Perhaps the woods would be emptier.

He put his hand on her arm. "Bintou, that's your name, right?"

She let out a sigh. "Yes, that is correct."

"I heard about you."

After spinning to face him, she narrowed her eyes. "Heard of me? From whom have you heard of me?"

He shrugged. "Another guy from Mali. Ibrahim, I think he said. He went to Dublin and said he hoped to see you at the bunker. Ciara told him you'd been sent to an education center."

Her mind crashed with too many emotions, and she sat on the bench before her legs stopped holding her. "Ibrahim." Would he seek her out here? Anger and desperation warred within her heart.

Joel sat next to her. "So, you *do* know him? Are you friends?"

Absently, she shook her head. "Not friends, no." Images of Ibrahim in Galway, showing her around the market square. Ibrahim in Mali during their time at university, taking her out to dinner. Ibrahim's warm hand on her waist as they danced. His caress along her waist as they lay in bed together, enjoying the warm feeling after making love. Her skin grew tight as she clenched her jaw.

"Well, he's eager to see you again. He barely stopped to take a breath when he described you. I imagined some dark goddess from what he said."

A dark goddess. He'd called her that once when they dated.

Joel slapped his hands on his knees, rising to his feet. "Well, you'll probably see him in Dublin, then."

Bintou shook her head. "I do not wish to. He has betrayed me too many times."

Joel patted her hand. "Hey, don't judge him too hard, huh? Sometimes people don't mean to betray, Bintou. Sometimes they just make a mistake. Give him a chance, will you? He sounded sincere."

Joel left then, leaving her to stew in her conflicting emotions. She must return to her room and pack for Dublin. She suddenly felt incredibly drained of all energy, as if she'd be happier melting into a pile of goo. At least then, Ibrahim wouldn't have the chance to hurt her again.

Once she regained the temporary sanctuary of her room, she carefully packed her bag. The new clothing she'd received from Fiona made that difficult but, in the end, she fit everything in.

When Bintou tried to haul her bags down the stairs all at once, Colin leapt up to help her. He claimed the largest bag with a solemn nod and met her at the base of the stairwell. A minivan waited outside. Hiroki already sat in the back, so this would be their transport to Dublin. Martin and Ciara spoke next to the passenger door, so one must be coming with them. She hoped Martin would be the one. Bintou really enjoyed his company and his presence made her feel safe.

With Colin's help, she wrestled her belongings into the car's boot. He caught her in a fierce hug and then gave her a lopsided smile. "Stay safe, Bintou, and haste ye back. We'll welcome you with open arms whenever you wish to return."

Unexpected tears pushed behind her eyes. Though they'd only met five days before, she enjoyed the man's stories and appreciated his passion for history. Bintou hoped he and his lovely family stayed safe. War could be dangerous, even away from the battle lines.

She forced a smile and climbed into the vehicle, nodding to Hiroki. Bintou mourned leaving this safe space, despite her own sense of independence. Martin climbed into the passenger seat, waving to Ciara as the car pulled away from the house.

Bintou craned her neck, watching as the farm disappeared. During her vision, Orunmila had told her this should be her new home. Now, leaving ripped her soul. The goddess' triple voice whispered in her ear. *"You will return."*

As the minivan drove toward the capital city, Bintou worried about what might come. She'd traveled on shopping trips to large cities, like Paris and Milan. Cities didn't frighten her. But she'd never been in a city under siege. Nor did she wish to be under siege from Ibrahim's attentions.

Bintou had read countless tomes about ancient battles. Such strategy involved harsh tactics, such as cutting off a population from supplies of food, water, and outside help. Such tactics seldom ended well for the besieged. Cities became prisons as food supplies dwindled, disease rampaged a population, and frightened people rose up in anger and frustration, often harming each other out of desperation and need.

Ireland itself, according to Colin's evening tales, had been host to several horrific sieges. Bintou had no wish to experience another one from the front row.

One evening, their host had told the story of the siege of nearby Limerick, several hundred years ago. A thousand souls died within the city, either by violence or disease. Afterward, most Irish nobles fled Ireland, never to return, a consequence that colored the island's history to this day. He'd called the event The Flight of the Earls, a poetic name to a tragic end to the Irish noble class.

Colin then related a worse tragedy in a town north of Dublin. The English invader, a general named Oliver Cromwell, surrounded a fortified town of great renown, Drogheda. The general battered those walls with superior force and determination. When he asked the town to surrender, they refused.

Cromwell renewed his efforts and stormed the town after a breach. He had everyone slaughtered, including priests, women, and children, even those who tried to surrender to the onslaught. He burnt the priests alive within the church. This brutality echoed even today, in the hatred with which Colin spoke of this Cromwell. Over four hundred years hadn't eased the rage.

That act heralded a decades-long war within Ireland, which resulted in England's dominance over the island. Only a hundred years ago did that dominance end, when the Irish fought off the yoke and gained their own independence.

Had Colin shared these stories of warfare, knowing they might face such situations themselves in the near future? The PHAE may have asked him to prepare them. The instructor in Bintou approved of the method, while the woman in Bintou remained frightened and wished she could flee to safety.

She glanced at Hiroki. He seemed so unsure of himself, and yet his talent might be a great tool for the PHAE. If he could control his anxiety, he could use his talent to great effect. Perhaps she could help him with that. She'd had to learn how to speak in front of others, presenting her findings at university. Over the course of her degrees, often presenting to patriarchal university leaders who didn't believe a Muslim woman could be capable of higher thought, she'd learned some tricks to keep her confidence strong. She resolved to keep her eye on Hiroki and help him when he floundered.

Bintou had no Irish ancestry, but her own land had been subject to countless conquerors throughout history, most recently the French. Mali suffered under French rule for only seventy years, but they still resented that colonization. They only gained their independence in 1960. Even that resulted in several internal wars and coup attempts. They didn't even have a democratic government until the 1990s.

She held little sympathy for invaders. She'd fight for these people who had welcomed her. Besides, according to their scientists' theories, they all shared some common blood bond, a similar ancestry. Where that blood originated, whether labeled fairy or yumbo, they still didn't know, but the bond remained.

As the landscape outside flew past the windows, her breath fogged the glass. Martin and the driver conversed under their breaths. She didn't wish to intrude on their privacy, so she studied the countryside. Small farms disappeared in twinkling flashes of green and gold, the bright sunlight sparkling on dew-wet grass, like diamonds across the land.

Bintou hadn't been in this country for two weeks, yet she'd been so comfortable here. Perhaps she did share some genealogical ties with the people. In a moment of regret, she wished she'd spoken with the native woman more. Komie possessed a strong link with the land itself, and Bintou envied that link. Perhaps after this crisis.

If they *had* a time after this crisis.

Bintou had a healthy dose of optimism, but only in so far as she had control over her fate. She had no control over this land's conflicts, and thus had no well of hope to draw upon. She had confidence in her own competence, but what about those she must rely on? Those gathering intelligence, or those distributing the Talents to strategic points? Of course, she had no strategy training beyond what she'd read in ancient battle accounts. Her education and skills didn't suit any sort of combat. She belonged well behind the lines.

Not in a city like Dublin, ripe for a siege in a pitched war. Certainly, not locked in with Ibrahim. Another shudder ran through her.

To quell her fears, she pulled out her mobile and found a Dublin map. She noted with relief a large river running through the city. Fresh water shouldn't be an issue. Martin mentioned food storage. Modern medicine should be proof against most plagues. Cholera, dysentery, scurvy, these could all be avoided through modern sanitation and nutrition. So long as they had enough supplies to last them through a siege.

As if thought of him got his attention, Martin turned to her. "You came to Ireland through our Dublin office, didn't you, Bintou?"

The memory of Ibrahim meeting her at Shannon Airport flashed in her mind. After shoving her feelings for Ibrahim into a corner of her mind, she shook her head. "An acquaintance procured me, and I landed in Shannon. Róisín brought me to Dublin."

He grinned. "She's a wonder, she is. I can't imagine how difficult this will be for her and her family. They don't like to be split apart."

Bintou gave him a wry smile. "Few families do."

The large man shrugged. "True enough. At least my family did it on purpose. Half my kin still live in Jamaica, but the rest immigrated here a generation ago. And when my own talent showed up, I joined PHAE. Does your family live in Mali?"

She shook her head. "No longer. My parents moved to Cairo when I finished university."

"Did they search for a better life?"

"A cheaper one." They shared a laugh, which died into an uncomfortable silence. Then Martin reached over and squeezed her hand. "Don't worry, I'll stay in HQ. We'll take good care of you."

His hand felt warm and comforting, and the icy hand of fear loosened its grip on her heart. "Thank you, Martin."

Qacha:

The next morning, Qacha left for Galway, along with Joel and Róisín. The drive from Limerick to Galway seemed to take forever, despite being only two hours. Joel chattered incessantly. Qacha decided he must be nervous to be so full of words and yet have nothing of value to say. Róisín attempted to engage with his questions.

Qacha concentrated on the landscape as they passed through green, rolling hills, much like on the website, to a stony, barren place filled with cracked rocks and stunted, scraggly trees. Staring at the land helped keep her mind off Manol, back at the Byrne farm. The twin boys, Liam and Hugh, along with Fiona, promised upon pain of death that they'd take excellent care of her cat. She told them if something happened to Manol, she would lose her powers. Their eyes grew wide. Qacha almost smiled at the memory.

She'd never been fond of children, but she must admit the Byrne offspring had charm.

The countryside reminded Qacha of the steppes, and a pang of homesickness stabbed her heart. Her hands ached to hold her grandfather's bow, to caress the smooth wood and hear the twang of the string, but she'd left the precious artifact at the farm. The antique held more intrinsic value to her than anything in this world, and she'd dishonor her grandfather if she broke it.

Qacha shook off her nostalgia. The Mongolian steppes would never be her home again. She'd become a true nomad, traveling the world. If only her ex-lover, Nugai, could see her now. His provincial heart would be so jealous.

Stony land gave way to green again and faded into suburbs. This must be Galway, a city immortalized in songs according to Colin. A much smaller city than her own Ulaanbaatar, the bustling center still had appeal. As they drove along the bay, the noon sun glittered on the water, sparkling like diamonds across the sea.

Anna would feel at home here, with the ocean embracing the city.

They drove along the wharf and out to a spit of land with industrial structures and a lighthouse. The stink of sewage and rot overwhelmed her. She wished Max had joined them, as he might ask the winds to blow the stench away, but he'd gone to another corner of the country.

The short, white lighthouse had a red-railed gallery and looked about three stories tall. Much of the surrounding bay would be visible from this vantage point. Qacha peered back toward Galway City. No buildings rose above the spire of their cathedral. This seemed like the best place to watch for ocean-bound intruders.

Joel's voice filtered into her musings. "Damn it! What is this, the city dump?"

Róisín wrinkled her nose. "Sorry, the lighthouse is beside a sewage treatment plant. But this is the best place for watching."

Qacha turned to the younger man and pursed her lips. "This is a defensible stronghold."

Róisín opened the trunk. "We've got rooms ready inside. I don't know how long we'll be here, but this is our base for now."

After pulling her purse onto her shoulder, Qacha crossed her arms. "Very well. We should divide the watch responsibilities. Did you say two people are standing watch now? That makes five of us. Four-hour sets, I will take the first watch, leaving two people on the others. That allows everyone to rest in between watches and one person to keep the watcher awake."

Joel held up his hands. "Whoa, who put you in charge?"

She turned to Anna's brother. "I have training in warfare, tactics, and self-defense. Do you possess such knowledge? If so, please share your improvement on my plan."

Joel's cheeks turned an interesting shade of red as his gaze flicked to each person before staring at his shoes. "Okay, that's reasonable. Sorry."

Waves lapped against the shore and seagulls cried out in a chorus of calls.

"Just so. Róisín, show us our quarters."

Joel sulked but followed the Irish woman. Róisín led them past the curtain wall and into the buildings at the base of the lighthouse. They looked in need of repairs, with drywall and raw timber. The four bedrooms looked sparse and functional. However, Qacha had slept in temporary yurts on the steppes of Mongolia.

Joel's voice cut through the silence. "Are you serious? We're sleeping in this dump?"

Everyone ignored his vitriol. Once they stowed their bags, Róisín brought them into the lighthouse. Undressed honey-colored stone walls housed a spiral staircase with a rickety iron railing.

A tall, redheaded man greeted them. "Afternoon. My name's Paddy."

Róisín introduced them and explained, "Paddy's the Unhidden we've had here so far, along with his little brother, Danny."

Joel raised his eyebrows. "Yeah? What's your talent?"

The young man turned and shrugged. "I can talk to seagulls."

The American man's eyes grew wide. "Seriously? Like, with words? And they talk back?"

"I speak words. I can hear their caws as if they use words. They aren't very interesting to talk to. Most of their chatter is about where to find the best people food and the best breezes to glide on. But they have helped keep watch. Danny fell asleep on his feet, so I sent him to bed an hour ago."

Qacha nodded with approval. "Have they given you any useful reconnaissance?"

Paddy shook his head. "Not a fecking thing. They don't know how to tell if a boat has terrorists. That's hard enough for humans to determine, right? Still, I've been awake all night and morning. I'm about to collapse myself, so I'm thrilled you lot showed up. If you'll excuse me, Róisín, I'm off to become one with my bunk. Pleased to meet you." With a tired wave, he descended from the gallery.

The sewage plant dominated the foreground. However, beyond that lay miles of glimmering sea, sparkling in the sunlight. Having never lived near a large body of water, Qacha sucked in her breath in wonder.

Joel coughed several times. "Stinks to high heaven. How long do we have to stay?"

Qacha turned to Joel and fixed him with a gimlet stare. "Joel, if you continue to complain with every breath, I shall take great pleasure in flipping you over this red railing and onto the hard ground below. You will not survive the journey. Do you understand me?"

For a moment, his eyes begged to defy her. She almost wished he would. Qacha did not approve of how he treated Anna, relative or not. She ached for the chance to put the brat in his place. However, his gaze shifted to her feet. "Again, sorry. Look, I'm *trying* to be less of a jerk. But I've got years of practice at being one, you know?"

"Very well. I shall take the first watch. Joel and Róisín, you may rest and come to relieve me in four hours' time. Then Paddy and his brother can return for their shift, and we shall repeat. Róisín, is food available?"

The other woman shrugged. "Sandwiches and fruit in the first outbuilding. I asked them to stock up. Coffee, tea? Water?"

"Coffee and sandwiches."

The two descended, leaving Qacha. She fetched a stout wooden chair from the cupola and Qacha sat staring at the ocean, which soothed her prickly mind. The screeches of seagulls and terns clashed in her ears, turning into raucous background music. The waves became a counterpoint to the birds. A boat passed, its motor adding to the nautical symphony.

What form would the attack take? Before they left, she'd asked Brendan about the details of the Cork attack that morning. Would their invaders be unimaginative enough to try the same method twice? Or would they attempt a different way? If she had charge of the initiative, she'd craft several plans. Each passing boat earned Qacha's regard. She would have preferred holding a weapon, but her grandfather's bow must remain safe.

Qacha cataloged each sound, natural or man-made. Bells pealed from the church spire rising above the skyline. The faint hum from automobile motors rumbled in the distance.

She spied low islands off to the west. Inside the cupola, a wall map named the islands Inis Oírr, Inis Meáin, and Inis Mór. From their profile, they had no mountains or tall buildings, but might disappear on a cloudy day. Like the place from one of Colin's tales, the land of Hy-Brasil. The mythical island appeared once every seven years, but these islands had a real population.

Qacha sat in her chair on the gallery just as Róisín returned with food. Qacha enjoyed her lunch, punctuated by the cries of seagulls and an occasional ship's horn.

If she remained after the current crisis, Galway might make a pleasant home. Even more so than the Byrne farm, though the sea breeze might turn icy in the colder months. The city looked large enough to support several high-end restaurants. Perhaps she could run one herself.

A new sound intruded, one she couldn't identify to dismiss as harmless. She bolted to her feet, half a ham sandwich in her hand.

The sound of a loud bee tickled her ears. She couldn't track its source. Qacha peered over the rail at the ground. No boats came close enough to make that noise. Nothing on the ground, nothing on the water.

A small, dark bird circled the sewage plant. No, not a bird. A drone. Róisín mentioned Max's encounters with them in Cork.

Pursing her lips, Qacha stared at the machine, trying to determine the level of threat. If the drone was a recreational device, a person should be nearby, controlling the movement. Yet Qacha spied no one but them. This must be an illegal surveillance device, as Max and Anna found in Cork. Her hands ached for her bow, and she cursed her decision to leave the weapon behind.

While gripping the railing tight, Qacha drew the heat from the gallery's sun-baked concrete, from the ground below them, and from the very air. As she channeled the crackling energy through her arms, she pointed at the drone. A bolt of fire burst from her hands toward the machine.

She missed. Qacha didn't enjoy missing.

A second time, she pointed, throwing the fire energy through her hands with a primal growl.

She missed again. Qacha gritted her teeth against her rising frustration. She clenched her hands, wishing again she had her bow.

As she glanced at her fists, an idea flashed in her mind.

With a slow smile, Qacha held up her hands as if gripping her grandfather's bow, praying to her ancestors to guide her shot. Her right hand held tight to the invisible string and arrow. When she let fly, her power combined with muscle memory, causing her aim to fly true.

The buzzing drone crackled, popped, then burst into flames on one side. The chunk of scorched metal fell in a smoky spiral, crashing to the ground. The machinery exploded into useless pieces. She panted from the effort, her throat burning.

How many drones scouted in the city? Did they come from other vectors? Had they been sent to other parts of the country? She didn't dare leave her post to rouse Róisín and inform the other teams. She didn't even have a mobile, a serious failure in her planning. *Fuck a goat.*

Hours passed, and she spied three other drones. She destroyed each one with great effort, leaving her panting and weak. She wished Max had joined them. His facility with winds could be an enormous advantage in this style of combat.

Footsteps on the stairs caught her attention, and she spun to face the new threat. Róisín, looking better rested, poked her head into the gallery. "Is all well?"

"It is not. I have spied several drones, as found in Cork. I've destroyed them, but we should examine the wreckage. You will find their carcasses on the ground below."

The Irish woman's eyes grew wide, but she ran down the stairs, returning with a pile of destroyed equipment.

Qacha kept her eyes on the sky. "Do they have identifying marks?

Róisín shook her head. "No, they're purely generic, but all drones should be registered with the Irish Aviation Authority. If they're legitimate, we'll find the owner. If they're from the PEM, I doubt it's registered. I'll take the wreckage to the Galway PHAE office so they can examine the bits."

Qacha crossed her arms. "That leaves me with three sleeping people while you're gone. Will PHAE issue me a mobile phone so that we might remain in touch?"

"That's a grand idea, and I'll put in a requisition. I shouldn't be long."

"If we get attacks from the air, I am not as useful as Max would be. He'd be a valuable asset here."

Róisín furrowed her brow. "I can't call him in. He's assigned to Cork and will have his hands full. We can't assume that since one attack at that port failed, they won't try again. I can put in a request, but that's all."

"That is the best that can be asked."

In the next hour, Qacha destroyed two more drones. After each one, she required lots of water and rest. How many others had been dispatched around the island? How many had pierced their defenses?

The wreckage showed none of the drones carried weapons, so they must be only for surveillance. Qacha ground her teeth at the idea of spies. Spies meant invaders would follow.

She had chosen Ireland as her new home. And these spies intruded upon her home. They would not succeed.

Just as she destroyed a fifth drone, Róisín came back up to the gallery, this time with a tray of coffee. Qacha gratefully prepared a mug and took a long sip of the hot, black liquid. Fatigue already crept into her muscles, and the crimson lines along her veins pulsed with a dull red light.

Róisín stared into the distance as the buzz of another drone tickled Qacha's ears. This one sounded different. The Irish woman glanced around just as Qacha did. When she found the source of the noise, Qacha pulled in a deep breath. This drone looked twice the size of the prior ones. Could this one carry armaments rather than a camera?

She pulled her arm back, despite her aching muscles. With the last dregs of power she possessed, she loosed her *arrow* of fire power at this new intruder. While her power hit the body of the drone, this larger machine wobbled but did not fall.

Instead, the drone shot at her.

Qacha ducked, her reflexes trained for attack. However, Róisín did not duck fast enough, and the bullet hit the healer in the shoulder. She fell back against the railing with a cry.

With a curse, Qacha dropped to her knees and pressed her palm against the bullet wound. Where was the woman's phone? With one hand, she fumbled in Róisín's pocket and pulled it out, but she didn't know the password. She let out another curse. Besides, she didn't know who to call. Would Joel or Paddy be awake downstairs?

A sound behind her made her turn, but she kept her hand in place. Róisín moaned as another drone drifted into Qacha's line of sight. Qacha pointed her free hand at the flying object, channeling all the frustration through her pointed finger. While the power wasn't as strong as when she imagined her arrow, it hit the side of the drone, making it spin out of control and onto the ground below.

Qacha smiled at the crash, but then wondered how many weaponized drones the PEM had acquired. With luck, that had been the only one, but she'd never been particularly lucky.

Anna:

While she folded the few pieces of clothing she'd unpacked, Anna heard the phone ring downstairs. Footsteps and mumbled words, then running and shouting. She crept down the stairs to listen and find out more.

Michelle's voice sounded tense. "Róisín? How bad?"

Anna gripped the balustrade as more footsteps ran through the house, echoing on the wooden floor.

Colin spoke next, his voice wavering. "Sure, I can send someone to help with defenses, but Róisín's our only healer. The other two are in Dublin and Belfast."

Colin paused before speaking again. "I'll send them on, then. Are you sure you want all of them? What about Cork?"

Another pause. "If you think that's best, grand. You send your Kilkenny folks down to Cork, and I'll have Brendan take ours north to Galway. Yes, immediately. Kieran has a plane, down the Foynes Museum. That'll get them there faster."

Anna ran back up to her room. She hoped Róisín hadn't been hurt too badly. If Brendan came, she hoped that meant she'd be with him. He'd been so kind, helping her get used to her talent. She'd feel lost without him by her side.

She wrestled her bag down the stairs. One look at Colin's ashen face, and she knew Róisín had been hurt pretty badly. She didn't even have to tell them she'd heard. They must have been able to tell from her expression.

Michelle sent Brendan to fetch Max who, for a wonder, showed up quickly and without significant complaint. Oh, he grumbled about last minute plans, but he seemed willing enough to get on the road. He gave Michelle a final glare as they went out the front door to Brendan's car.

Anna glanced back at the peaceful farmhouse and wished she could just stay here and not know of any of this. She remembered a Chinese curse about living in interesting times, and found it horribly appropriate.

Even in New York, she'd been content with living in boring times. Settled routine, knowing what to expect from the next day, she found a comfort in that. A reliability on the future. She had friends she could talk to, books she could read, and shows she could watch, none of which would destroy her world view or chip away at her optimism.

Would she ever have such comfort again? Or had that world been forever ripped from her grasp?

Max:

Max caressed the fuselage of the CASA CN-235 twin-engine marine plane, letting out a wolf whistle. *She is a beaut, no doubt about it.* Clean, new, with fresh paint. She'd handle well in sea winds. He couldn't wait to get her into the air.

The flight pad engineer cocked his head. "Hoi, you know how to fly one of these?"

"I can figure it out. I haven't yet found a plane I couldn't fly."

Anna giggled, and Brendan shushed her. "I'd prefer we have a trained pilot at the controls for the first flight, Max. Once we land in Galway, and the current crisis is over, you can try your hand."

He ignored the other man and spoke to the plane. "You wouldn't hurt me, would you, darlin'? I'll take bonzer care of you."

He ached to be in the air so much, he forgot all about needing a drink, and he'd been craving whiskey every waking moment since the last time Róisín added a splash to his coffee. Now, what he wanted, what he needed, was to get behind the throttle of this beauty and point her toward the bright blue sky.

After glancing up, he amended his wish. *Well, the cloudy gray sky.*

A young blond man in a flight suit approached, shaking both Brendan's hand, then Anna's. "I'm Kieran, and I'll be your pilot." He turned to Max, who still stroked the plane. "And you must be Max. I imagine you want to get up in this bird?"

He flashed the young man a look. "More than you can ever know, boy."

"First, I'm not a boy. I'm a licensed pilot. Second, I will be *your* pilot, so I'll thank you to show some respect. Third, I'm to teach you how to fly the CASA. I'm a flight instructor by trade so if you listen, you'll learn a lot. I understand you've got loads of experience with planes, but this one has some new features you may not be familiar with."

Max gritted his teeth. "I don't need someone a third of my age teaching me shit about planes."

Kieran raised his eyebrows. "Sorry, the wind made that difficult to hear. Before you repeat, though, let me add that *I* must approve you to fly, and with that attitude, it'll never happen."

Max stared at him for several moments and swallowed. He glanced back at the plane, his hand still on the fuselage. "Right. Let's go, then."

Anna, Brendan, and Max all climbed in, stowing their bags in the back. The pilot kicked Max out of his seat and made him sit in the co-pilot's chair. "Here are your headphones. Try to keep up."

"Oi, mate, I've been flying planes longer than you've been alive!"

"And this will be the last one if I let you fly. She's got computers you need to understand before you take the controls. Now, watch and learn."

Max grumbled something about infants and diapers but put the headphones on as the plane bleeped to life. The engines purred beneath him, and his blood surged in joy. It felt like years since he last flew.

As the plane rushed down the runway, Max's stomach rose just as the wings lifted them from the tarmac. He wanted to sing, shout, and dance all at once. A high purer than the finest whiskey.

"Max, watch the altimeter as I fly along the coast."

Max got caught up in Kieran's instruction despite his reluctance. His old plane had been a workhorse, with only the bare bones of instrumentation needed for an outback tour plane. This gorgeous creature had so many bells and whistles, his head spun. He paid attention to the younger man and surprised himself by learning. The lad was a decent instructor, he'd give him that.

Soon, Max's mind glided into the sky above the clouds. He didn't dare call on the wind, in case they wanted to be a pain in the arse. Arguing with the wind in this baby could be disastrous. Instead, he reveled in the freedom of the skies and wished he could stay here forever.

This end of Ireland seemed sparsely settled, with rocky hills and farms scattered along the road like drops of water on a tight string.

In no time at all, they drifted down toward a tiny air strip along the bay. He felt as if they might dip into the water before the wheels bit the tarmac on the edge of land. Behind him, Anna whimpered. Max felt more alive than he had since leaving Australia.

He wanted to go up again.

As they exited the plane, he gave Kieran a hearty handshake. "You're a bloody good teacher, mate. I'd be happy to have you in my cockpit again."

The younger man helped them unload their bags. "That's grand. You will, the first few flights. You don't think we're going to let you fly one of our few precious planes alone, do you?"

Max let out a snort and grimaced. "Fair enough."

Brendan practically had to drag Max away from the plane after he loaded their bags into a waiting car, and they drove down the coast. Max kept looking over his shoulder toward the airfield, wondering when he could get back up into that lovely plane.

Once the plane disappeared, however, his focus shifted to worrying about Róisín. As soon as Brendan told him she'd been hurt, he'd demanded to go to Galway. To do what, he had no idea. Protect her? Obviously, he was too late for that. Heal her? That talent wasn't in his wheelhouse. But he felt a responsibility for her that he hadn't had for a long time, and that responsibility translated into a need to help her.

A half-hour later, they pulled onto an inlet, passed a sewage plant, and to another lighthouse.

Another bloody lighthouse. Fucking hell.

With poor grace, Max helped Anna carry her things as Brendan settled them into an outbuilding. Once they dropped their bags, he led them to the red-railed gallery.

Qacha turned as they emerged from the curved stairwell. The Mongolian woman hugged Max in a quick, perfunctory embrace.

He glanced around, seeing no one else. "Where's Róisín? Is she okay?"

"She is resting comfortably in her room downstairs. A medical person has been called to come attend her. She is not to be disturbed. However, I require your help."

Max stared down the stairs as she turned back to watch the ocean. "We have destroyed eight drones through three four-hour watches. Some escaped during Paddy's watch as he had no way to destroy them. Joel discovered he could short out the drones by pulling all the moisture from the surrounding air. We might have missed some before we arrived. They come from all directions. Your help is appreciated."

Right to work, then.

Max positioned himself at a vantage point to scan the horizon. He liked it up here, despite the stink of the sewage. Could he ask the winds to push that away? He'd have to check once he finished with the usual pleasantries.

A buzz caught his attention, and he focused in on the sound. A tiny black speck moved against the wind. *Damn, I still have to chat up the local winds.* He pointed and grabbed the Mongolian woman's shoulder. "Qacha, I see one, over there!"

"I see. That is the surveillance size. The one that shot Róisín looked twice as large. Can you destroy this one?"

"I still have to make nice with the wind before I can ask for their help. How've you been dealing with the drones?"

She lifted her hands as if shooting an arrow. When she let the imaginary missile fly, sparks showered from one side of the drone. The motor sputtered and spiraled to the ground, crashing with a tiny explosion. A satisfying plume of smoke curled up.

His eyes grew wide. "Bloody brilliant work. What do you need me for? You've got this well under control, mate."

"I am exhausted. This takes much energy, and this is my second shift. Joel's method isn't as efficient, and he is resting from his shift. We must keep this place clear."

"Right enough. Give me a few minutes to make myself known to the locals."

Just as Max sent out a call to the wind, a tremendous explosion boomed. Rushing to the other side of the gallery, they watched fire and smoke billow from the downtown area. The concrete floor of the gallery rumbled beneath their feet.

Chapter Twelve

"We seek the fire of the spark that is already within us."
– Kamand Kojouri

Latest **CNN** *Update: Reports are coming in of defensive structures being manned at several key points along Ireland's coast. No word yet if Unhidden enclaves around the world are also beefing up their defenses, but we will report as news is gathered. Most are using previously existing structures, such as medieval castles or Martello towers from the Napoleonic Wars.*

While Ireland signed the Treaty on the Prohibition of Nuclear Weapons in 2017, the Protectorate for unHidden Advancement and Education have signed no such treaties.

Qacha:

Qacha gripped the railing so hard her hands ached. Max ran down to find out what happened while she listened for the telltale buzz of drones and scanned the sky.

Could she douse the fire from here? Her power created fire, but she might also be able to remove flames. She had to try. Thousands of people must live in the city, perhaps tens of thousands. At mid-afternoon, the downtown buildings would be teeming with workers. Did she imagine their cries echoing on the wind?

Her hands still clenching the railing, Qacha drew her power in, like a syringe filling with liquid. As her blood burned and her skin buzzed, her body resisted, exhausted after an afternoon of destroying drones. With aching muscles, she pulled harder. Letting out a scream, she felt ready to burst into fire herself. Qacha aimed her imaginary arrow and shot the energy toward the conflagration, two kilometers from the lighthouse. A shimmer glowed in the air as her power traveled toward the flames, flying farther and farther until the glow disappeared.

Nothing happened.

As she cursed under her breath, she drew up her power for a second try, though she almost forgot to breathe. The power scratched through her blood, fighting her every inch of the way. Buzzing tickled her ears. Qacha spun around to see another drone hovering and watching her.

Furious at being seen and frustrated at being too far away to help the city, she blasted the drone with all her rage, and the machine exploded into bits. Max, just emerging from the stairwell, covered his face. "Bloody hell! You've got this well handled, luv!"

Qacha spun on him, the fire of frustration dancing in her eyes. "What is the news? What has happened?"

He shook his head. "The Galway office isn't answering calls. Róisín mentioned several industrial plants that might have blown by accident. The cell towers must be damaged, so we're flying blind. But she's trying to get through to Dublin on the old land line in the office downstairs. I roused Anna and Brendan, but I can't find Joel."

She clenched her fists. "Joel? How has he disappeared? Did he go for a walk along the seaside? This isn't a vacation."

Max shrugged. "Who knows? Probably took a car for a kebab."

Qacha glanced at the parking lot. Three of four cars remained. "That idea has merit. A car is missing. I might quench the fire if I can get into the city."

"Quench the fire? I thought you made fire?"

She looked back at the fire. "I do not know. I must try something. Can you take the watch?"

Max stared at the billowing smoke. "Yeah, I can do that. Róisín can come. The medic got her patched up and awake, so she worked her talent on her wound. People will need her healing."

"Very well. Do you have a mobile?"

He shrugged. "Never saw the need for one."

"That is unfortunate. I shall have Róisín leave her phone for your use once the towers return to working order. Anna and Brendan can help if we don't return soon."

Max's face turned pale and put a hand on her arm. "Be careful, Qacha. Burns are nasty."

She flinched away and nodded once. His concern touched her, but he didn't understand her abilities. "I shall be."

Qacha hurried down the stairs, her legs stiff from standing on the gallery too long. She caught Róisín just as the other girl emerged from the office.

Tears streamed down Róisín's face. "They bombed us! I don't know how or when, but someone planted a bomb near the Galway office. I don't think anyone could have possibly survived.

Qacha pulled the distraught girl into a tight embrace, careful to avoid her injury. Sympathy had never been her strong point, but Róisín needed support until she rose above the grief. Her healing skills would be in great demand.

"I had friends working in that office! And the city, thousands of innocent people, Qacha! How can anyone *do* this?"

After the Irish woman had subsided to light sobs, Qacha held Róisín at arms-length. "Can you drive me into the city? I might be able to douse the flames, but I must get closer."

Anna's voice came from behind her. "I can help."

She turned to see the young lady, face ashen but her jaw set in stubborn determination. Brendan had turned pale but stood strong. He had a firm grip around Anna's shoulder.

Qacha gave them an approving nod. "Max is in the tower. He will keep watch."

Róisín sniffed in her tears. "I've called Dublin, and they're sending more people. We need all the help we can get."

Anna glanced around. "Where's my brother? He can stay, too."

Qacha pointed to the parking lot. "We can't find him. One car is missing."

Anna stared at the column of smoke. A mixture of emotions flickered across her face. Intense worry, anger, and frustration. "Fuckabiscuit! Is it wrong to hope he got into an accident before he reached the city?"

Brendan squeezed her shoulders. "We'll find your brother. Let's go."

As Róisín drove them along the bay, buildings hid most of the smoke, but then the column rose above the skyline. Once they turned on the winding, narrow streets leading downtown, dust and debris littered the charming pubs and shops. Gray coated the cheerfully painted storefronts. Screaming people ran past them, ash-covered faces haunted with fear and pain. Others stood with shocked expressions, staring at the column of smoke and fire.

At first, Róisín could avoid debris in the road, but soon, chunks of concrete and trash blocked their way. Róisín had to stop the car.

They all climbed out and walked. After scrambling over broken pieces of building and debris, they neared the center of destruction. Flames licked the hulking skeletons of iron, twisted and tangled in the conflagration.

Qacha adopted a power stance, her knees slightly bent and balanced on her feet. She squeezed her eyes shut, questing for the fire. Two blocks ahead of them, the heat pulsed, angry and eager to consume, the center of power.

Once again, she pulled in her power through her bones and into her blood. The energy flowing through her seemed stronger here, close to the blaze. The veins on her arms visibly pulsed with glowing red. Echoes of wailing sirens bounced in her mind.

She sucked the heat of the fire out of the burning buildings and into her body. Flames burned her veins, and she let out a moan as the power coursed through her, funneling fire into the sky where it would burn nothing up there except a few annoying gulls.

Up, up she sent the heat, the destruction, the delicious flames, away from the earth. The crackling energy rushed through her as she arched her back in a blood-curdling, raw scream. The fire passed through her body into the air, a tornado of heat and annihilation. Qacha felt more alive at this moment than ever in her life. Power, flames, heat, all were in her domain.

With a *whoosh,* a sudden gale scattered her column of fire, dispersing the flames across the sky into a shower of harmless rainbow sparks. Her companions stared in wonder as embers floated down, flickered out, and became a sparkling rain of glimmering red ash.

Qacha watched the odd snowfall and decided Max must have finally made friends with the local wind.

As something wet hit her head, she glanced up at gathering storm clouds. The sky had been bright blue, clear, and idyllic before. She glanced at Anna. "Did you call the rain?"

The American woman shook her head, her eyes wide. "I can't do anything like that. Did another Unhidden escape the blast?"

Róisín shook her head. "I know of no such weather talent. If anyone could do this, it would have been the talk of the town."

A siren erupted, and Qacha covered her ears at the sudden sound. They rushed to the pavement as a fire engine barreled past.

The healer put her hand over her heart. "That was close! But we need to follow. We might find casualties still alive."

The healer pelted down the street without looking back. Belatedly, the others ran after her, down the curved street. As they turned the last corner, the epicenter of destruction made them all halt.

The blaze crackled and black smoke billowed in a huge spiral. Qacha hadn't quenched all the fire. The remaining flames laughed at her, taunting her lack of control, her puny power. With gritted teeth, Qacha's temper burned as hot as the flames before her.

Róisín rushed to an older woman lying on the ground, the skin of her face scorched and crackling on one side. The woman reached out an arm with a moan as Róisín laid her hands on her ruined face. "Shh, I'm here to help."

As Róisín worked on the woman, Anna found a teenage boy entangled in the wheels of his bicycle. With Brendan's help, she extracted him and assessed his injuries. "You may have broken your arm. Stay here, and we'll send the healer. I can cool those burns."

As the others dealt with the injured, Qacha faced the tornado of fire before her. She would not allow this fire to defy her so brazenly.

The black column roiled with spouts of flame, caressing the twisted, scorched iron bones of what had once been buildings. Whatever type of bomb they'd used had been most effective. Waves of heat pulsed from the fire. People pelted past as she stalked closer, shoulders squared. Her skin stung with the heat but did not burn, and her arms glowed red even where the lines didn't show.

Qacha halted, blocked by a massive chunk of broken concrete. She had no talent for climbing. This should be close enough for a second attack on the burning, taunting thing. She glanced back toward the lighthouse. Max's assistance would be helpful. Or if she had water support. If only Anna's talent ran toward creating a tidal wave. *No, that would cause more damage than the fire. She must do this herself.*

With a deep breath, Qacha closed her eyes, waves of heat throbbing from the smoldering husk of the building. She drew the fire energy within herself, burning and crackling, dry and dangerous. The flames burned once again in her veins, delicious heat licking her blood. She raised her hands and threw the inferno into the sky like a hose, shrieking as power ripped through her body.

Qacha's knees betrayed her, and she fell to the ground. Someone cried out behind her. A wave of intense pain gripped every muscle in her body as her scream faded to a whimper. When she opened her eyes, frustration shifted her pain into determination.

Her second effort had quenched some of the fire, but not all. Qacha needed to draw the flames again. How many times could she repeat before she collapsed? Thrice? Four times?

A cool, humid wind surrounded her. She opened her eyes to a whirlwind of mist cooling her body. Whether Max or Anna worked to help her, she appreciated the relief. Perhaps she had four attempts in her, after all.

Again, she wrenched the fire through her body, streaming the conflagration into the atmosphere. The humid whirlwind killed her flames and soothed her smoldering skin. The cool mist might even have kept her from bursting into flames.

Qacha felt almost refreshed now. *Once more unto the breach.* With luck, this last effort would reduce the flames to embers.

While staring at the defiant flames, Qacha clenched her fists. She'd always had a short temper. Anger might increase her power. And she had just the source to increase her anger, frustration, and rage.

Qacha pictured Nugai's smug face, smirking at her as he left. His eyes sliding off her body as he called her ugly, how he'd only used her to get ahead in the kitchen. His betrayal made her blood boil, literally. Her veins bubbled and screeched in anguish as the painful memory filled her with furious resolve.

Qacha pulled deep for her last effort. As she drew the flames into her boiling blood, something ripped inside. This time, her screech held more desperation as the fire burned with even deeper pain than her previous efforts. Flames licked the skin of her arms from the red lines along her veins.

Anna:

Anna and Brendan pelted toward the center of the firestorm. They both came to a halt when they saw the flaming mass at the base of the billowing black smoke.

She needed water, but how was she supposed to get enough to quench that monster?

A familiar voice behind her asked, "Can I help?"

Despite her relief in seeing her brother alive and unharmed, Anna rounded on him. "Where the hell have you been? Why did you go running off just when we needed you most?"

He shrugged. "How was I supposed to know we were about to be hit by a huge emergency? My crystal ball is in the shop, Sis."

She swallowed her frustration and gritted her teeth. "Fine. Whatever. We need water. Can you draw it from the air with me?"

He pointed down the street with a wicked grin. "I can do better. I found a fire hydrant."

Hope bloomed in her heart, but then Anna shook her head. "We can't. The firefighters will need to use that and draining the hydrant might endanger lots of people."

He threw his hands up. "Then what about the huge fucking bay behind us? Can't you funnel that over?"

Anna blinked and stared toward the ocean, hidden behind shattered buildings. With Max's help, she might create another water funnel, and direct the ocean to extinguish the smoldering remains from the bomb. Where was Qacha? She should be somewhere near. "Give me your phone."

"Why don't you use yours?"

"It died! C'mon, Joel, stop being a dick."

He narrowed his eyes. "Who do you want to call?"

She held out her hand with a deep sigh. "Max. I need his help to make a funnel. Give!"

Joel's eyes widened. "Good idea. But how do we call him? He doesn't have a phone, does he?"

She'd forgotten Max didn't have a phone. Damn him. "Oh, wait! Qacha said she gave him her phone. I have her number here somewhere." She patted her pants pockets and handed him a paper with scrawled numbers.

After a few moments, her brother shook his head. "Nothing's getting through. The towers must be damaged."

Fine. I'll try this myself. She quested to the ocean, throwing her mind's voice, but the sea lay too far away to listen. Instead, Anna plunged her will deep into the bay behind her, dragging the spirit of the water itself into a low wave, like the exercises Brendan had given her.

Joel put a hand on her shoulder, and she felt grateful for the moral support. Could he lend his strength to her? She drew the water closer, begging the waves to move faster but only got a trickle. In fact, she felt completely drained, as if she'd been running all day. Anna let the wave wash back into the ocean. She took a deep breath, coughed from the ash and dust, and tried again.

A second time, she drew the water from the sea, struggling to keep the sea going forward in a low wave. And again, it fought her, refusing to come more than a few feet ashore. The sea washed back, leaving nothing but damp spots along the seaside streets. Even though she was too far away to see them, she felt them linger, like stains on a cloth.

After three times, Anna had to admit failure. Maybe, if she'd had the months of training she should have received at the Byrne farm, she'd be able to manipulate such a massive amount of water. Without that, she just didn't have the strength or the finesse.

"It's no use, Joel. I don't have the strength to pull from the bay. We'll have to do this from the air. Between us, maybe we can coat the entire area with moisture. This is Ireland, for fuck's sake! We should have plenty of humidity to douse this thing."

She glanced up at the clouds still roiling above. "Maybe we can get them to drop their moisture. Are you with me?"

The fire suddenly whipped up behind him into a tornado, and all three turned to stare. There, at the base of the fiery whirlwind, stood Qacha. They exchanged a glance and ran toward the Mongolian woman.

Just as they reached her, she let out a painful screech and fell to her knees. Anna rushed forward, but Brendan held her back. "Wait! You might burn yourself on her skin. See it glowing? She might be too hot to touch."

Anna gave her white knight a quelling look. "I am a Daughter of Water. I'll survive." She broke away from his grip and ran to Qacha, a hand on her shoulder. With great effort, she tugged water from Ireland's humid, ash-filled air and coated the Mongolian woman's skin with soothing moisture, begging the liquid to quench the flames inside her flesh. Steam billowed from Qacha's skin until the moisture finally penetrated the scorching surface.

Anna prayed that Max could see this from his vantage point on the lighthouse. "C'mon Joel! Help me pull the water in! She needs it!"

Joel sneered at her. "Why should I have to help? You're supposed to be the stronger one. And on top of that, you're my younger sister. I'm older. By rights, I should have more power."

She stared at him, head cocked to one side. "By rights? Whose rights, exactly? Do you think this is something like a democratic distribution of power? Stop being such a selfish jerk. This isn't a competition. We need to work together. Just help, okay?" Anna concentrated on the millions of microscopic droplets in the surrounding air, concentrating them into one place, the blast site.

Joel finally joined her, one hand on Qacha's other shoulder, and one on Anna's. She let out a breath and redoubled her efforts, reaching into her brother's mind for the additional power, but something blocked her. An oily coating, like sludge or slime, keeping her from reaching her beloved water.

The barrier had a familiar feel. She glanced at Joel and narrowed her eyes as he jerked his hand away. "Joel! Stop messing about! Help me with this!"

Her brother shrugged and turned away, crossing his arms, staring at the still-smoldering wrecks of buildings. "It doesn't matter anymore."

Anna couldn't think about him and what that meant. She needed to get this tornado away from the city. Just as Qacha drew the final fire up, she showered it with moisture, and a blast of wind came from the east, blowing the mass out to the sea. Max must have seen them and came through. A flicker of a smile came across Qacha's face as the fire disappeared.

Qacha collapsed in a heap. Anna knelt next to her, coating her still-smoldering skin with water.

A horrible thought formed in her mind. She tried to shove the troubling notion away, but it persisted. She didn't want to believe Joel capable of such a thing. Her own brother? Sure, he had plenty of practice at being a jerk. But thousands of people had just died. "What the hell do you mean?"

Joel gave her a strange, smug smile just as a second explosion erupted. The ground shook so hard Anna fell to the ground. More smoke and dust billowed into the air. Anna's eyes grew wide with both horror at the destruction and death this would mean, and the implications. She glanced at Qacha, still unconscious after her battle. "Were you helping us? Or hurting us? Joel, what the hell did you do?"

She grabbed her brother's arm, and when he tried to pull away, she yanked him back, tears streaking down her ash-covered cheeks. "You knew! You knew about the other one. Did you know about this one? Is that why you disappeared? Joel, did you plant these bombs? Are you working with the PEM? Are you a *terrorist?*"

He didn't break eye contact and didn't say a word, but the truth showed plain on his face. She'd known him all her life. No matter how much he might fool other people, he couldn't keep this truth from her.

Anna wanted to punch him, but her body wouldn't obey her. Instead, all the frustration of the last week, her fear about the ocean, the bombings, and her brother, funneled into a throat-ripping scream.

She fell to her knees, and Joel knelt by her, his hand on her shoulder. She shrugged him away, not wanting him to touch her, but he persisted. "Wait, I can explain."

All her energy drained from her body. Anna collapsed on the debris-strewn sidewalk, curled up into a fetal position, whimpering against the pain in her muscles. Everything hurt, like someone had beat her with a stick in every part of her body. Despite all this, she couldn't cry. No tears would come.

He'd done something , like when he touched her at the Byrne Farm. Had he pulled water from her body? Anna had never experienced severe dehydration, but her mouth felt like the Sahara Desert, and her skin cracked before her eyes. She must get more water into her body.

Drawing upon the surrounding air, she pulled the humidity, the moisture into her skin, into her blood. A wave of relief shot through her, but the pain grew stronger. She pulled more as Joel backed away. Their eyes locked and she saw a parade of emotions flicker across his face. Anger, jealousy, determination, and finally, fear. He backed up several steps before he turned to run.

Rage flowed into her veins. "Joel!"

He pelted down the debris-strewn street and she pulled on the air again. It didn't want to yield any more moisture, but she didn't care now. She yanked everything around her until her arms saturated. Joel had betrayed her and her new family, and she wasn't about to let him get away with that.

Suddenly, her long sleeves felt like they were smothering her. Anna shoved them up her arms, exposing her glittering scales. She pulled all that water into a needle-sharp shot and flung it at her brother's retreating form. It hit the back of his knees and he fell to the ground with a cry.

Both Anna and Brendan reached him just as Róisín arrived. Soot smudged her cheek and blood smeared on her hands and dress. "Was that another bomb?"

She stared at Joel, who still wore a smug smile, despite Brendan sitting on him. "Yes."

The healer knelt next to Qacha, listening to her heart and checking her pulse. Then she placed her hands on the Mongolian woman's chest, closing her eyes. Something shifted within her. Anna couldn't identify the sensation. Perhaps Róisín's healing talent at work? Róisín glanced up, a glimmer of relief and hope in her eyes. "Help me get her back to the car. Reinforcements have arrived. We can't rest, but at least we aren't the only ones here."

When Anna didn't move, Róisín glanced between the two siblings. "What's wrong? Did one of you get hurt?"

Anna stared at Joel, who didn't even bother to struggle under Brendan's weight. A coating of ash made him a gray golem, a monster where her brother had once stood.

Joel, her own brother. The only family she had left in this world. But he was no longer family to her. She had a new family, one who actually cared for her.

Her stomach churned with anguish as her mouth formed the words she must say, despite her tears. "My brother's the traitor."

Her brother's face contorted into a scowl as Brendan lifted him from the concrete, arm pulled back in a lock. He struggled against his captor but couldn't get loose. "You're just angry that I have power, too! Well, I'm the eldest, and I should be more powerful than you. That's only logical!"

Anna just stared at him. Since when did magic have to be logical? If it was logical, it would be science.

"You PHAE asses are so smug, aren't you? You won't win, can't you see that? The world is already against you. You should have stayed hidden, then you *might* have had a chance. But now, the PEM will hunt down every last one of you, except those who have proven themselves useful to their cause. I was supposed to come get you, Anna, and bring you to the PEM. But you screwed even that up!"

Anna swallowed against fear, rage, and disappointment as several other men arrived and took her brother away.

Max:

Still standing on the lighthouse gallery, Max stared at the column of fire. *Damn, that must be Qacha's work.* Calling upon his newly befriended winds, he asked them to disperse the deadly flames into the upper atmosphere. They resisted his request, demanding to know why they should obey.

We don't like fire. Fire is dry. The dry can shrink us.

"You can help us!"

Why should we help you?

With all his will, Max swallowed his pride. He didn't like to beg, but he needed to in order to save his friends. He tasted those words in his mind, *his friends.* He hadn't counted anyone as a friend in years. Decades, even. But now, these strangers, these odd people with powers similar, yet different from his own, filled his heart with the need to protect them. To save them, if he had the power. And he might, if the winds would just bloody listen to him. "Please, we need your help. My friends need your help. Can you help them?"

We do not have friends.

Frustration shot through Max as he threw up his arms. "Yes, you do! I'm your bloody friend, you bloody idiots!"

And why should we help you?

"Because fire can kill my friends."

What is kill?

Max let out a long breath. He was so weary of fighting for every word with these stupid winds. However, he had an idea. "You want to see kill? I'll show you what bloody kill is! I'll show you what fire can do!"

Shoving his terror aside, Max pulled up his deepest, darkest memory. Trina's village in Vietnam, everything burning from napalm, her own body crisp and charred almost beyond recognition. Tears streaked down his face, tears he hadn't shed in years. Tears he usually held at bay with whiskey.

"There, now do you see? That's what fire can do."

The wind did not answer, but they did push the firestorm away. When the city finally looked mostly clear of flames, exhaustion dragged Max to the floor. He'd never pushed so hard in his life, and his muscles protested the effort.

Then the second explosion rocked the city. Max let out a gasp as more fire billowed up, black smoke filling the sky.

No matter how hard he asked the winds to help, they refused to answer his call this time. Had they been destroyed by the dry air? Had he killed them? Max didn't know and couldn't guess. But he could do nothing else from his station.

Why did he need to stay there any longer? He needed to be in the city. The PEM must have completed their attack now. He didn't need to keep watch on this bloody lighthouse anymore. He shoved away the hovering guilt at leaving his post.

Half-stumbling, half-falling down the stairs, Max emerged onto the lighthouse's manicured lawn. He searched the grounds for a vehicle and spotted the one remaining car. Max didn't know who owned it, but he spied a set of keys hanging on a hook on the office wall. A glimmer of an idea in his mind, he grabbed them. His luck held true as the key worked. After several deep breaths, he navigated down the narrow bridge and into the city.

Straight toward the new plume of black smoke.

He didn't want to see the devastation, but he needed to find the others. As he wished to all things holy that he had an enormous bottle of whiskey, he drove closer.

Great chunks of concrete, twisted wires, and burst pipes spewing sewage kept him from focusing on the people. Cries intruded on his concentration, though, cries that echoed his haunted memories. Cries from women who sounded just like Trina.

Max stopped the car and covered his ears, willing the ghosts to bugger off. When he finally quieted the screams, he pressed the gas again. A tire blew, making him whimper. He gave up on the car altogether and walked. A woman ran toward him, her skin black with soot and crisped with burns. He stumbled away from her until his back hit a wall.

His breath turned to panting as her face morphed into Trina's as he'd last seen her. Trina, her beautiful brown skin blackened and charred. Trina, her long, thick hair burnt into singed nubs.

Trina, as she'd been when he killed her. A grisly specter reaching for him with crisped fingers. Her face morphed into Róisín's and he sobbed. Her face morphed into Róisín's and he cried out.

As the woman ran past, Max shut his eyes and clung to the wall, a solid brickwork structure which had survived the blast. Despite the screams echoing in his skull, he opened his eyes and looked around. Shelf after shelf of gorgeous booze surrounded him. Completely by accident, he'd found himself a pub.

And who says God doesn't exist?

Smoke hung in the air. No roof remained, but a line of bottles on the back wall had mysteriously survived the attack.

Max staggered from the support of the wall to each table, then the bar. He yanked down the nearest bottle, Bushmills, and drank deep.

The fiery liquid soothed the pain in his mind, even as the whiskey burned his throat. He tipped the bottle back again.

Outside, the screams and shouts faded into a buzzing blanket of nothing. Inside, he found his old, familiar comfort of oblivion.

Bintou:

They entered through the General Post Office which, according to Martin's running commentary, had been the site of a pivotal event in Ireland's fight for independence. He pointed out pockmarked bullet holes still visible from that time.

They walked into a dimly lit storage room and through a dingy door. After descending a flight of stairs, Martin entered a code on the keypad next to another door, straight out of a spy movie.

As they got deeper into this subterranean space, this system of underground tunnels and offices grew claustrophobic and stank of mildew and sweat. Bintou wanted to run to the surface and scream but gritted her teeth instead, trying to keep her breathing even.

They passed busy offices filled with administrative personnel, and she realized hundreds of people must be down here. She kept craning her neck, searching for Ibrahim's face. When she didn't find him, she let out a breath of relief and ignored the twinge of disappointment.

Martin continued his tour guide role, leading Hiroki and Bintou through the maze. "Over here sits the marketing department, right next to our advertising group, both artists and copyeditors. Next to them, we've stuffed the accountants into their holes, only allowing them to come up for snacks and sleep."

A passing young man with red hair piped up. "And showers!"

Their guide chuckled. "Well, yes, and showers. Very important down here. Next, you'll see one of six boardrooms, with the executive C-suites behind them. The bigwigs only come out at night, like cryptids in a dark forest."

That elicited a giggle from Hiroki, and even Bintou had to smile, tinged with an edge of hysteria. She tried not to think about how many thousands of tons of dirt and rock loomed above them. Bintou couldn't catch her breath, and she stopped to place a hand on the wall for balance. She'd never been particularly claustrophobic and had spent a great deal of her professional life in the underground libraries of the university, structures built to protect the fragile ancient documents she translated but, for some reason, this Dublin bunker filled her with dread.

Hiroki stumbled into her, offering several apologies.

She pulled air into her lungs with slow precision, calming her heart. "I am sorry, Hiroki. I need to catch my breath."

For this day of travel, Bintou had eschewed her native dress for the more practical slacks and blouse this culture favored. While the slacks worked better for climbing downstairs into the depths of the earth, they chafed and bound as she leaned against the wall. She unbuttoned the top of her blouse, the high-necked collar choking her. She unbuttoned the sleeves in a bid for freedom. *Who puts buttons on sleeves? A silly fashion.*

Martin touched her shoulder. "Bintou?" When she didn't answer, he put the back of his hand to her forehead. He turned to Hiroki. "Her skin is clammy. I'll get some water."

As Martin hurried down the hall, Hiroki took her hand. "You have no reason to fear this place, Bintou. How many years has this bunker stood against the city above? The construction's solid, unbreakable. You're safe here."

The assurance in Hiroki's voice caressed her anxiety, rolling her fear up into a warm blanket and shoving it into a dark corner of her mind. Bintou didn't know if he used his talent or not but at the moment, she didn't care. His words helped, and she needed it.

By the time Martin returned with a bottle of icy water, she had more control over her anxiety. She took several sips before reassuring them in a shaky voice. "I am better now. Thank you. Both of you."

Martin led them to an office with two desks, each with a computer, and two doors along the back wall. "This is the diplomatic unit. Well, this and the three offices next to it. You'll be stationed here." He pulled out one of the chairs. "Come, Bintou, have a seat. Would you like more water?"

As she gratefully slid into the chair to ease her still-shaking knees, Bintou gestured toward the doors. "Where do those lead?"

"Bedroom and toilet. One for you and one for Hiroki."

The prospect of staying in this place, day and night, for an unspecified amount of time, made Bintou sweat again. However, Martin held up his hands. "You don't need to stay here unless we have an emergency. We've booked hotel flats above-ground for us all, one for each."

Her breathing eased. "And if we have an emergency?"

His expression turned pinched. "If Dublin should fall under attack, we've designed and stocked this facility to withstand several months of privation. We have our own generators, food, water, medicine, and air scrubbers. We'll be safe."

Bintou still didn't like this situation, but at least they'd made an emergency plan. In the meantime, she needed to establish requirements. She shoved the thought of running into Ibrahim to the back of her mind and shifted into work mode. "What is our task here?"

Martin leaned on Hiroki's desk and grabbed a folder of papers. "The PHAE, as a new agency, must form relationships with a number of foreign government and regulatory agencies. From the Republic of Ireland to the European Union, the World Bank Group, even Doctors Without Borders. Therefore, we require an increasing number of treaties and trade agreements. First, we need to comb through them to improve the diplomatic language and, second, translate them into several languages."

He picked up a memory stick. "Hiroki, we want you to refine the original, drawing on your talent for the greatest impact. Then you can deliver speeches via our social media outlets. Yes, I know your talent is muted over transmission, but you still wield power, and we need every boost we can get. Bintou, the translation is your domain, of course. Your work won't begin until we finalize the language, so you have some free time. Even as much as an entire day." He grinned to take the sting from his sarcasm.

Bintou's stomach chose that moment to growl loud enough to fill the silence. The Jamaican man chuckled, but with no malice. With all the dignity she could muster, she glanced between Martin and Hiroki. "Would one of you fine gentlemen be interested in taking a lady to dinner in this calm before the storm?"

Chapter Thirteen

"Normality is a paved road: it's comfortable to walk, but no flowers grow
on it."
– Vincent Van Gogh

Hiroki:

Hiroki wished to be anywhere but here, in the bowels of Dublin. He felt suffocated in the underground tunnels despite the many comforts built into the space.

However, having a task helped keep his mind off the thousands of tons of dirt and stone over him. Bintou cleared her throat. When he looked up from his work, they locked eyes, and then peered at the ceiling. They exchanged a look and a sad smile and returned to their writing.

He read through the seventh version of the International Agreement between the PHAE and the Pure Earther Movement. Each had different clauses, and Martin asked him to compile the differences into a summary checklist so the PHAE board of directors could evaluate them.

Bintou worked on the same task, independently, as a double check to his work. He felt grateful for this reinforcement, as a second set of eyes eased the pressure on his own skills. He'd still need to be perfect, of course, but at least they could compare notes and work out discrepancies before presenting to an outside party.

Such teamwork created camaraderie, and he had already worked with Bintou enough to know her own standards were as exacting as his own. This gave him a measure of peace to work with someone he could rely upon.

Martin entered the bunker room, carrying a tray with their lunch. Steaming bowls of soup and thick, crusty bread filled the room with enticing aromas. Hiroki still hadn't grown used to western foods and flavors but loved lamb stew and Irish soda bread. They'd become his new favorite and seemed a common meal.

The savory, salty soup had chunks of onion, potato, and carrot, as well as some other root vegetable he didn't recognize. They had the same texture as potato but a slightly different flavor. The novelty occupied him as he ate, keeping his mind off the ceiling.

As he wiped the last of the breadcrumbs from his desk, Martin's phone rang. He answered it, said, "Yes," a few times, and then hung up. Then he gave a huge grin and placed his hands flat on the table. "Hiroki, we've got a surprise for you."

Swallowing a chunk of bread, Hiroki cleared his mouth with a sip of tea, his eyes wide. "For me? What is the surprise?"

"I think you mean, who is the surprise?" The PHAE man rose and opened the door with a wave of his hand like a game show presenter.

His pure white skin almost glowing in the bright fluorescent light, his old friend, Masaaki, walked in, his arms wide. "Hiroki!"

Hiroki had thought he'd lost his best friend, back before Hiroki knew he had Unhidden talent. Back before he'd known he'd become part of the same chaotic world Masaaki had escaped to. Now, he couldn't jump from his chair fast enough to embrace Masaaki as Martin escaped the room with a wave, his phone ringing again. "Masaaki! *Chikushou!* You're here!"

"Of course, I'm here! Where else would I be? I told you I would go to Ireland. I'm glad you came. And with such a useful talent, too! Mine is just ornamental, but I'm good at administration, so they've made good use of me. When I heard you had been assigned here, I asked to be assigned to help you. Will that be acceptable?"

A lump in Hiroki's throat wouldn't let him speak. In a rare show of affection, he clutched his friend in a tight hug. As kind as his hosts had been, seeing his friend from Japan threw a stab of homesickness so strong into his heart he forgot to breathe.

Memory of their parting had weighed heavy on Hiroki. He'd said some cruel things to his friend and didn't think he'd ever have the chance to correct that wrong. Now, however, Masaaki seemed to have forgiven him for his earlier censure. He sniffed back tears as they threatened to flood him.

Hiroki sat, taking a drink of his now tepid tea to clear his throat. "Bintou, please, meet my friend from university, Masaaki. Masaaki, this is Bintou. She can read any language and comes from Mali."

Bintou stood, shaking hands with Masaaki. "I must work hard to live up to an introduction like that. I'm quite pleased to meet a friend of Hiroki."

"Same to you." The other man walked to the mini-fridge, pulled out a can of Coke, and settled in the fourth chair. "How long ago did you arrive?"

"Just yesterday. They've already put us to work."

Masaaki grinned. "That's why I'm here. I helped analyze the previous agreement drafts so I can offer insight. I've become well-familiar with the terms, and which ones the PHAE find acceptable."

Bintou spread butter on a piece of bread. "How long have you been working with the PHAE, Masaaki?"

"Three months. I came a week after this happened." He gestured at his face. "Unlike Hiroki's talent, this white skin made my Unhidden status obvious to anyone who saw me, and life immediately got difficult in Tokyo. After only one thrown bottle, I realized I must act. Someone from PHAE contacted me, so I moved here and never looked back. They've taken great care of me."

Martin returned, his expression solemn. "I have news from Galway."

Bintou turned, worry etched on her face. "Galway? Isn't that where they sent Anna, Max, and Qacha?"

Martin's dark skin looked ashen as he took the fourth chair. "Yes, along with Joel, Róisín, and Brendan. We set them on watch at the lighthouse, but something breached their defenses. Two bombs have exploded in the city itself."

Hiroki's skin pebbled, despite the warmth in the room. "Bombs? Are people hurt?"

With a silent nod, Martin covered his face with his hands, his elbows propped on the table. "Thousands must have been killed. They smuggled two bombs into the center of the city. They may have planted more, but only two have detonated. Our office in the city... We don't think anyone survived."

The silence spread around the room, except for the fizzing from Masaaki's can of Coke. Eventually, even that died.

Martin's phone rang again. With dread in his eyes, he answered, "Yes?"

He stared at the table as he listened to the speaker. "I understand. Sure. I'll tell them."

When he ended the call, he glanced from Bintou to Masaaki, and then Hiroki. "Our team from the farm have survived, but Qacha is badly hurt. She tried to destroy the fire, burning herself in the process."

The fire must have been massive to burn a Daughter of Fire so. Hiroki wasn't a religious man, and though his parents raised him Shinto, he hadn't dedicated himself to the Shinto way in many years. However, he sent a brief prayer to the *kami* that Qacha's *taishitsu* remain strong and heal quickly. She had a very strong *ki,* from what he could tell in their brief acquaintance. He just hoped her strength would be enough. But she had Róisín with her, and Róisín had healing power. She must be in good hands. "Did anyone else get hurt?"

Martin cleared his throat. "Not that we know of, other than minor injuries. We now have a new mandate from the PHAE regarding to your documents." He tapped the data stick plugged into Hiroki's laptop. "We must ensure that a cessation of hostilities is rock-solid in all finalized agreements. Stop their surveillance and all attacks, under threat of retaliation."

Bintou gave a somber nod. "Will they need to send reinforcements to Galway? Have any other cities had attacks?"

Martin covered his face again. "I don't know. So many people lost, I can't even comprehend. I had friends in the Galway office. Dermot and Jaime, Justine, Shannon. So many people."

Bintou laid a hand on Martin's shoulder, and he gave her a sad smile.

Hiroki felt the loss of these people, and he'd never even met them. How would he feel if someone he knew and loved had been killed? What if his parents had been in the blast?

Latest **CNN** *Update: Authorities have discovered several new enclaves of the so-called Unhidden around the globe. Groups have formed in Hawaii, Peru, Iceland, Greece, Siberia, China, Denmark, and Finland. Other locations are being investigated, though the efforts have been hampered by local resistance to interrogations. Wilkinson, leader of the PEM, has called for extermination of these enclaves. Certain governments, such as Indonesia and the United States, are being investigated for using methods of interrogation by the International Criminal Court.*

Hiroki:

After Bintou took Martin out of the office to get his mind off the casualties, Hiroki stared at his phone. He should call his parents. Despite their last words to him, he remained their only son. What if they heard about the attacks? His parents would have no idea if he had been in Galway when the bomb went off. They'd certainly be worried about him.

With all the news reports on social media speeding across the internet, he didn't want his mother to worry about him. He also didn't want his father to spy his son in this group of foreigners without Hiroki first explaining his new position to him. He touched his phone to call home, but then pulled his hand back again. What if his father rejected him again? He didn't think he'd be able to handle that.

Hiroki reached for the phone again, and once more pulled back.

"What are you doing?" Masaaki's voice behind him made him jump. He'd thought his friend had left with Bintou and Martin.

"Nothing."

His friend crossed his arms. "Right, nothing. Hiroki, I've known you since childhood. Call me paranoid but, for some strange reason, I don't believe you."

Hiroki kept his expression as flat as possible. "No, really. I thought about looking something up, and then decided I didn't need to."

Masaaki's white-blond eyebrows shot up. "Seriously? You expect me to believe that? We aren't in school anymore, Hiroki-chan. Tell me the truth."

Hiroki let out a deep sigh. "I want to call my mother."

His friend's eyes grew wide. "Are you insane? Didn't you tell me your father shut his door on you when you told him of your plans?

Miserable, Hiroki nodded.

Masaaki downed the second half of his Coke, squeezed the can, and tossed it into the recycling bin. "Then your path is clear. That family has disregarded you. You have a new family now, these people, this PHAE organization. They have welcomed both of us into their trust, without question and without condition. Why wouldn't you accept that?"

While shaking his head, Hiroki jumped up and paced around the small room. "That's not fair. I need my family, Masaaki. I can't just throw them away like you did yours!"

After a moment of stunned silence, Masaaki lifted his chin. "That was a cruel thing to say."

Hiroki halted, turning to face Masaaki. "I didn't intend to be cruel, but I told the truth. You wanted the truth, didn't you? Or have we grown so far apart I must be a polite stranger again?"

Masaaki grabbed a second can of Coke from the mini-fridge and chugged half down as if he didn't have a care in the world. "I can't stand around and watch you torture yourself like this."

Hiroki waved his hand toward the door. "Then, go. I didn't ask for your advice or counsel."

The other man shook his head. "Nope, you're stuck with me."

Frustration bubbled inside Hiroki. He just needed to be alone to think, think about what he would tell his parents if they answered the phone. He needed Masaaki to leave. While pulling his power through his fingers, his skin tingled, and his blood roared in his ears. He shoved that persuasive talent into his words. "Go."

A startled look came across Masaaki's face. Still holding the Coke, he walked out with a stiff gait, as though a puppet on a string.

Once alone again, Hiroki locked the door and dialed his home. The phone rang several times, and he prayed his mother would pick up. He almost shouted with joy when the line clicked. "Moshi Moshi?"

His mother's voice had never sounded so beautiful. "Okaa-san, it's Hiroki."

Dead silence greeted him for several seconds. "This is not wise, Hiroki-san. You shouldn't call here."

Once again, he pulled on the power that had so recently banished his friend. Hiroki put all the passion he had into his words. "Okaa-san, please, listen to me. I cannot live with being so rejected. Please tell me you'll speak to father about me?"

"Hiroki, you know I cannot."

This wasn't how the conversation should have gone. His mother was supposed to help him. Desperation filled his tears as he choked back a sob. "Mother, you're all I have."

For a moment, even through a mobile phone and halfway across the world, he sensed his power working on her. And then a door closed on her end of the line. "Your father is home. Don't call again!"

After the line clicked, Hiroki stared at the phone for a very long time, until the tears dried on his cheeks.

Hiroki:

After his phone call, Hiroki didn't wish to speak to anyone. He rebuffed all attempts from both Masaaki and Bintou to discuss what had happened. When they both stopped trying, Hiroki felt both relieved and disappointed.

They worked through more iterations of the agreements, eventually coming to a consensus on the best combination of clauses to present to the PHAE Council. Ciara agreed with their choices, and they all took the afternoon off as a break.

Martin brought them out of the bunker, and Hiroki breathed in deep of the clear city air. While Dublin, as a city, felt different from Tokyo, all cities possessed a sameness, a homogeneity that comforted him. The sound of traffic, chatting people, and planes from the nearby airport combined with the odors of automobile exhaust, sun-baked concrete, and the ever-present tang of the ocean. He almost felt at home.

The residents of the city seemed barely affected by the bombing in Galway, almost as if they hadn't even heard of the disaster. But Hiroki watched the news reports, and they showed horrid footage of the destruction. Still, people went about their daily lives on this coast, seemingly unconcerned, which baffled him.

Once he started looking, though, he noticed a heavy military presence. Armed soldiers were stationed at street corners, watching the crowd. Police vehicles seemed around every corner. And from what Martin said, the crowds in the streets seemed half what they would normally be on a sunny summer weekday.

Every time a plane flew over them, Hiroki stopped and watched, intense dread rushing through him. He knew the first attack in Cork had been by sea. The attack in Galway seemed to have been by land, someone planting a bomb in the center of the city. That left the air as a third attack venue, and he couldn't rid himself of that notion.

Bintou insisted on doing some shopping, so Martin and Masaaki tagged along with them as she entered shop after shop on the high street. They all agreed to carry her bags as she bought clothing, gifts, and samples of local foods. She made them all try local foods at lunch, such as *coddle* and *boxty*. While Hiroki loved the first, a stew with potatoes and sausage, the *boxty* wasn't as much to his taste. The potato pancake seemed dry and flavorless.

They'd just about finished their afternoon, and came close to the General Post Office, with its hidden bunker door in the back storeroom. Martin had assured them this wasn't the only entrance, but it had the advantage of lots of traffic in and out of the GPO and, therefore, coming and going would go unnoticed amongst the crowds of tourists and regular business.

Just as they reached the front steps, Martin's phone rang. By this time, Hiroki tensed every time he heard that ringtone. He recognized it as Ciara's, and she'd shared bad news with each call. As Martin listened to her information, Hiroki watched another plane soar overhead, flying south from the Dublin Airport. It banked, heading inland. Would it be heading to Galway? Or an international flight?

Something made him look back toward the airport. Another plane was coming. It seemed so close behind the last one. It didn't seem right. He grabbed Masaaki's sleeve, pointing to the second plane. "Masaaki, look."

His friend glanced up and shrugged. "It's a plane. You've seen planes before, Hiroki. Do you want to go flying or something? Don't tell me, you want to go back to Japan to talk to your parents."

He shook his head. "It's not that. Something's wrong with it."

Masaaki squinted into the bright sky. "What's wrong with it? It looks fine."

The plane hadn't risen as high as its predecessor. In fact, it looked like it was descending. Straight toward them. Masaaki's eyes grew wide as his mind registered this information.

The white-skinned man grabbed Martin's arm, interrupting his phone call. "Martin, I think we need to get into the bunker. Now."

Martin stopped mid-sentence to stare, and his eyes grew wide. He shouted into the phone, "Ciara, bogey attack! Commercial flight. Scramble code 71!" Then he grabbed Bintou's hand and pulled her into the General Post Office. Hiroki and Masaaki followed, and they ran to the storeroom.

Hiroki's breath came short as they ran down the stairs, the bags of shopping bouncing on his knees in the small space. Something in his mind screamed at him to drop everything, but his hands wouldn't let go.

By the time he reached the small, crowded concrete landing, Martin frantically punched buttons to open the bunker door. He glanced up the stairs several times, but everything stayed silent. He finally wrenched the door open and shoved Bintou, Masaaki, and finally Hiroki through, along with their shopping bags.

As they all piled through, Bintou turned to Martin, gripping his arm. "But what about all those people?"

The man shook his head. "We cannot save them all. We must keep PHAE headquarters safe. I'm sorry, Bintou."

Martin shoved the door shut and turned the lock, leaning against it with a long sigh just as the ground rumbled. The ceiling shook. Hiroki sank to the floor, his back against the cold wall, and covered his head with his arms. Bintou, Martin, and Masaaki did the same, waiting for the concussive explosion to die away.

Then the lights went out.

Bintou:

Bintou couldn't breathe. The world pressed down. Black surrounded her. Someone coughed. "Hiroki? Martin?"

Someone's hand touched hers. She grasped tight, relief for the human contact flooding through her. Martin's voice crept from the darkness as the hand squeezed. "I'm here, Bintou. Masaaki? Hiroki?"

Masaaki said, "I'm here. Hiroki is next to me."

The sound of their breath echoed in the shadows as the rumbling had ceased. The faint sound of sirens wailed.

Martin rose, pulling her to her feet. She held onto the wall, drawing comfort from its solid presence. The other two men must have risen, as well.

His voice wavering, Martin's phone glowed. He touched a few buttons, shining the spotlight in each of their faces. Though fear gripped each of their expressions, no one seemed hurt. "Okay. Let's move deeper in. We need to find out what happened and find a safe spot."

Bintou let out a bark of laughter. "Safe spot? A safe spot? Are you making a joke? Did we not just get bombed? There is no safe spot. The surface will be a war zone. We'll be stuck in a siege, like in the ancient battles. We'll die here, starving! Or we'll suffocate!"

She sank to the ground again, her body shuddering with fear. Martin knelt, gripping her by both shoulders. "Bintou! Snap out of it. We'll be fine. These tunnels are solid concrete. We have plenty of food and air."

Shaking her head, she pulled away from him. "No, no, we won't be fine. How can we be fine? Things will never be fine."

On one side of her, Hiroki shook his head in the gloom, repeating the word, "Fine. Fine. Fine." Beyond him, Masaaki held his hand, a glimpse of his gleaming white skin reflecting the edge of Martin's phone spotlight.

Her breath came in gasps. Her heartbeat sped as she clenched her fists so tight, her nails biting into her palms. "Safe. We have no safety. We have no air. We're going to perish here."

Martin pulled her in for an embrace, but she shoved against him. "No! I cannot breathe. You will suffocate me."

"Bintou! Bintou, listen to me. We will be safe. We will survive. We have air."

She pummeled her fists against his chest, but she had no strength to fight. Finally, she let him hold her as he rubbed her back and whispered reassurances in her ear.

Slowly, her breathing slowed, and tears replaced her frantic fear. She sobbed into Martin's shoulder as the siren wailed in the distance.

Hiroki and Masaaki stood, and Martin drew her to her feet again. He shone his phone down the hall. "We need to check in and find out the extent of the damage. Let's get you all back to your rooms."

As she stumbled after him down the hall, he kept hold of her hand. She clutched his warm flesh like a life preserver, refusing to let go. Dust floated in the corridor, dancing in the light like shining motes. The supernatural silence unnerved her. She'd gotten used to the thrum of the generators, lights, and conversation. Now, all that had silenced, except for murmurs from the few rooms they passed.

Martin halted at a boardroom, peering inside, but the space seemed empty. He moved on to a breakroom where a few people had gathered. Someone else had the spotlight on their phone shining up from the middle of a table, lighting up the room in an odd glow. Bintou's relief at seeing other humans alive came out in a long sigh. Something loosened its tight grasp on her heart.

He held up his phone, the spotlight playing across the ceiling. "Does anyone have signal?"

Bintou recognized Paul, one of the PHAE agents from the Byrne Farm, as he shook his head. "Not one bar. Towers must have been damaged.

And our generator got knocked. We sent Darryl down to check things out. He can do wonders with machines and should fix them up soon."

Bintou swallowed. "You have only the one generator?"

Paul shrugged. "We have three. But one was down for scheduled maintenance, and the other hadn't come online yet. We had scheduled the new one to come on next week, after the city inspection."

Another rumble shook the concrete beneath their feet. Dust swirled in the cone of light. Bintou flattened against the wall, her heartbeat racing again. Martin pried her away, enfolding her in his arms until the tremor passed.

Ciara's voice cut through her panic. "Martin! Martin, are you down here?" His comforting hug disappeared, but Bintou had control of herself again. She concentrated on breathing as Ciara entered the room, counted the people, and made notes on her tablet. "Right, that's everyone, then. Thank all the Gods. I worried about you lot, as you went to the surface this afternoon."

Martin coughed a few times before answering, "We had just gotten to the GPO steps when Hiroki spotted the plane."

"A plane? What about a plane?"

Martin and Hiroki exchanged a glance. Hiroki gave Ciara a small bow. "I noticed one plane coming from Dublin Airport, with a second one very close behind. Neither rose high in the air. In fact, they descended toward the city. That's when I alerted the rest of us to the anomaly. We then rushed to the bunker entrance."

Martin frowned. "Didn't you hear me on the phone? I gave you the scramble code."

She shook her head. "Your call just cut off. I couldn't hear a thing. I'm just glad you're safe. But we'll need to debrief you. The council's gathered in the south boardroom."

Martin glanced at Bintou. "Do you need all of us? We're pretty shaken. Bintou could use some rest, I think."

The Irish woman shook her head. "No time for rest, I'm afraid. I'm still taking stock of the damage, then the council needs all the information they can gather. Then we need to start clean up."

Bintou laid a hand on Martin's arm. "I am all right, Martin. I shall accompany you to the council. If my viewpoint can help, I am happy to relate my experience."

Even as she said the words, another rumble shook the ground. She swallowed against the fear rising in her throat.

Qacha:

Qacha dodged between fumaroles of flame bursting forth from the black, pitted ground. She had to hop back and forth. The eternal landscape filled with fire and dust. Her eyes teared from the acrid smoke. She dragged her exhausted body forward from one tiny island of safety to the next.

Fatigue overwhelmed her. She didn't care any longer. Qacha lay down across three fumaroles and ignored the pain as they spit forth burning tendrils of angry flame. The heat flayed open her skin. The edges cracked and shrank into ruinous tatters. Fire burned through her veins and ripped into her muscles.

A soothing voice intruded on her agony, ice across her world of fire. "Qacha? Qacha, can you hear me? Qacha, squeeze my hand. Squeeze my hand."

The pain screamed as it receded. Fire and smoke faded to a gray blanket of clouds. "What?" Her voice croaked with pain. "What?"

"She's awake! Brendan, quick, bring water. Her throat must be scorched."

A blessedly cool liquid trickled down her throat, making her cough. Someone helped her sit up, but her muscles screeched in protest. Qacha coughed again, craving more water. Someone held a cup to her lips, and she sipped with tender caution. Someone cried out in the darkness, and someone else soothed with calm words.

A damp cloth patted at her face, making her skin ache. She opened her eyes, seeing nothing but darkness. "Don't talk yet, Qacha. You're burned, but I'm here to help you. You remember me, right? Róisín? I'm a healer. I can heal your skin and eyes, but even my power will take time."

Another croak burst from her. "Fuck a goddamned *goat*! What… what happened…"

"I said don't talk! But if you must know, bombs went off in Galway and Dublin. I think our group from the farm is all alive. Anna sustained some minor injuries, and Max, well, he got stinking drunk."

Qacha wanted to laugh about Max's misadventure, but a laugh would be a horrible idea with her burnt throat. She just hoped the older man survived his attempt at self-destruction. Not everyone did.

"You're at Galway University. We've commandeered a few buildings as a hospital. Look, I need to tend to other patients. I'll look in on you as soon as I can. You've got a catheter hooked up, so if you need to go to the toilet, just let go. I promise, I'll be back soon."

Other patients cried out or moaned. Footsteps echoed along a wooden floor, all fading into background noise. Pumping air became a rhythmic background noise. The acrid scent of charred flesh warred with antiseptic and blood.

Qacha ached to open her eyes, but if she'd damaged her face, that would make things worse. She'd seen enough burns in the kitchen to respect them.

How had she gotten so burnt? She'd thought her skin impervious to fire. Her power must have limits to withstanding heat. She touched the veins along her arms, where the red glow had been. She felt deep grooves along her blood vessels on the underside of her arm, hot to the touch. They pulsed with the rhythm of her heart.

Would she spend the rest of her days as a burn victim, covered with ugly scars? Not that she'd ever held pride for her appearance. At almost two meters tall, she'd long since adopted the attitude that she'd never be attractive in the classical sense. Qacha's last lover had stood eight centimeters shorter than her.

Someone sat beside her. "Qacha, Brendan here. Are you thirsty? We're working out an IV option without power. You can't have solid food, but we have a cold broth and juice, which would be best for your throat."

After she nodded assent for broth, his footsteps walked away.

They had no power? That would explain the air pump sound. She heard no beeps or hums from electric equipment. How did they run a hospital without electricity?

The prospect of being an eternal invalid revolted her. She'd take her own life if she had no other options. But her old cooking scars had healed when her talent first showed, along with the cut on her arm from archery. Perhaps her ability to heal her damaged skin would grow, as well. She'd need to give her talent more time to work.

Brendan returned with the promised broth and fed her in awkward silence. While she detested depending on others, Qacha resigned herself, for now, to the necessity. Once the cool liquid coated her parched throat, she didn't mind the indignity.

"There, you did grand. Do you need anything? If not, I'll be back in a half hour to check on you."

Once he left, Qacha steeled her will to heal her damaged skin. As she laid back on her bed, she reached into her soul's center, to find the healing power.

She found only angry fire.

Flames still burned and flickered within her veins. She wanted to cry out, but her parched throat refused. Only a pained whimper escaped. Writhing on the hospital bed, she shoved away the magic.

Not yet. Maybe never, but definitely not yet. Qacha drifted back into an exhausted sleep, filled with nightmares about spurting fire and burning screams.

Hiroki:

Hiroki wiped the sweat from his brow and stared at the podium. Bintou gave him a long hug. "You'll be brilliant, Hiroki. We have worked hard on your speech and examined every nuance. When you deliver this missive with your unique talent, and we cannot help but succeed. You shall see."

The last five days had been mind-numbing and exhilarating at the same time. After Ciara and Martin organized the PHAE personnel in the bunker, they determined the extent of the damage. Of the three entrances, two seemed blocked from the outside. The third wasn't blocked, but it had been warped from the blast. After two days, the rescue people found the right equipment to remove the door.

Once they had access to the outside, things got worse. The Dublin Dockyards quarter had been utterly destroyed by the bombs, as well as the East Wall and all the way south to Ballsbridge. West Dublin survived better, and nothing to the north was attacked. Unfortunately, the Docklands destruction included Trinity College and the eastern edge of downtown.

Thousands of people worked to remove the rubble but, in five days, the job had barely begun. Hiroki, Masaaki, and Bintou at least escaped the bunkers for a while and breathe fresh air.

This helped both Hiroki's and Bintou's anxiety a great deal. But when they had to return to the underground tunnels, she dug her heels in. "I will not return to that place, Martin. I refuse."

The PHAE representative raised his eyebrows. "Bintou, we must. Can't you see, the bunker is far safer than Dublin itself? For God's sake, look around you! The tunnels survived better than this has."

She shut her eyes, shook her head, and crossed her arms.

Hiroki raised his hand. "The idea of working from hotel rooms has merit. Perhaps we could all benefit from staying outside while the necessary repairs underground are completed?"

Martin's eyes grew wide, an edge of desperation in his voice. "Hotel rooms? Do you really think that our hotel survived in the slightest? The whole building is nothing but a pile of rubble now!"

In the end, they decided they'd find an intact hotel in the west part of town. However, with destroyed cell towers, the internet would be unstable. In order to work on the speech Ciara wanted him to prepare, they'd all need access to the documents, and the only way to do that with no internet was to be in the same room.

Once they found a base of operations, they worked throughout the next few days with barely a break for rest or food. When the words swam on his screen, Hiroki pushed back from the hotel room desk and rubbed his eyes, wishing they would stop aching.

He glanced at the curtains, drawn against the destruction outside. How many people had lost their lives, here and in Galway, because the Unhidden had chosen Ireland as their home? How many people had they destroyed from that decision?

He suppressed an urge to fling the curtains open. They wouldn't see anything but city lights and the surrounding darkness, anyhow.

Once they finished working on the agreement options, he delivered those to Ciara and Martin. Then they had to work on the speech Hiroki would deliver to the world, a prospect that filled him with more dread than he'd ever before imagined. He'd never enjoyed giving presentations, but knowing his talent helped him be more persuasive helped his own insecurities. But this would be on television, broadcast to the world. He was well aware his talent diminished over broadcast media. He shoved aside that anxiety for now, diving into the work of crafting the words.

They hammered out Hiroki's speech with Bintou's knowledge of precise language. She'd explained that she'd read thousands of historical documents, including Roman and Greek speeches. She understood the masters of rhetoric and persuasion, and she offered examples from writings from Mansa Musa, Muhammad, Qu Yuan, and Shakyamuni Buddha. Hiroki sat in awe of her immense store of knowledge.

He glanced at Masaaki, who gave him a jaunty thumbs up. After swallowing so hard his throat hurt, he tamped his printed speech, so the papers stacked neatly, and walked next door, to the room Martin and Ciara had secured.

When they settled upon the final language, as a group they traveled out of the hotel and to Leinster House, the governmental building where the Dail of Ireland met. Luckily, it lay on the other side of Trinity College from the bombing sites and escaped most of the destruction. They still had to wend their way through several repair crews working on the college buildings before arriving.

Protestors stood outside, carrying banners, and shouting their concerns. Hiroki couldn't understand their words as they yelled over each other, but he felt relieved once they rushed past the crowd and into the relative safety of the building. Martin and Ciara led them down several pompous hallways covered in oil paintings of old white men. Finally, they came to a press room.

Behind the podium, the PHAE flag hung from the ceiling. Three stylized figures of various sizes in brown, yellow, and white held hands, superimposed over a simple green globe. White olive branches surrounded the globe, all on a deep blue field.

Reporters and PHAE officials sat in the small audience. Cameras trained upon Hiroki from several directions. He'd never been on television and tried not to think about how his failure might mean disaster to his new family. Would his old family, his mother and father, be watching? Would they be glad that he survived? Did they even care? Hiroki didn't know if that made this easier or more difficult.

Ciara nodded and the lights flicked once. She held up three fingers and counted down with them. They would be on the air in three, two, one.

Hiroki stared at the camera across from him. "Good afternoon, citizens of all nations. My name is Hiroki Kubo, and I have a message from the Protectorate for unHidden Advancement and Education."

So far, so good. His glance flickered to Ciara, who wore a broad, encouraging grin. Bintou stood behind her with Masaaki and Martin. For a moment, he wished Max had been there, as well, but Max did important work, defending this island's shores. If Hiroki could convince the world that the PHAE, and Ireland itself, were worth defending, he could relieve Max, and all his PHAE family, of that responsibility.

His friends had his back, as they said in this country. With that support, he could do this.

"First, we want to thank everyone watching. We appreciate your attention and willingness to listen. Second, we wish to be clear about who we are. We, the Unhidden, are a people who have developed, by genetic fluke, previously undiscovered talents. Throughout human history, similar genetic flukes have resulted in blue eyes, straight hair, or freckles. None of these changes in genetic material has changed the fact that we are all still human beings."

Hiroki stared at the massive CNN camera as if addressing the equipment like a person. "Let me restate that. We are *of* the human race. We are not alien, we are not animals, we are not evil mutants. We are humans. Any species must have diversity to survive. Scientists have proven that inbreeding causes reinforcement of genetic errors. Our talents will strengthen humanity. We can enrich our race, make the population stronger as a whole and more able to excel."

Hiroki emphasized the similarities between the Unhidden and everyone else, and how the PHAE might help the world. He mentioned their willingness to work with governmental bodies and international organizations to fight against poverty, hunger, and disease. He'd originally included the phrase "to help maintain world peace," but Bintou removed those words in case people misinterpreted that as an offer to act as a worldwide police force.

As Hiroki spoke, he glanced at each reporter, gauging their reaction. Each person sat rapt, hanging upon his every word as if he recited an intense thriller and they wanted to discover who the murderer would be.

Hiroki drew confidence from this evidence of his talent working. The words tingled in his blood when he used his power, though experimentation had proven his audience weren't aware of being manipulated, even when the effect eventually faded. However, he remained aware his talent didn't work as well with an electronic filter. Would his persuasive talents come through the broadcast at all?

He couldn't think about that now. He wouldn't fixate on the people who'd died while they crafted the perfect speech, those in pain across the country. Those who might have to continue to fight if he didn't convince the world that the Unhidden were innocent victims and deserved worldwide protection against the terrorists who continued to attack them.

"In conclusion, we must demand the violence against our locations halt. This war of aggression is illegal and immoral, an international crime. The hostilities are unwarranted and go against the principles of peaceful life in our modern age."

As he let out a deep breath, Hiroki gave the CNN camera one last lingering look, and then each of the other cameras in turn, before bowing and retiring from the podium. Ciara thrust her fist into the air in a gesture of victory. As the last camera shut off and he stepped off the stage, he collapsed into his friends' arms.

Masaaki pulled him in for a fierce hug. "You did fantastic, Hiroki! I knew you could do this!"

Bintou drew him next, her ample curves enveloping him like a blanket. "*Al'ama!* You would have made Cicero and Nelson Mandela proud."

Martin looked up from his laptop with an infectious grin. "Early results look good, Hiroki. The polls are already showing a wave of goodwill from all parts of the world. Not everyone, but a massive improvement over previous impressions. We'll compile more data as reports come in."

Hiroki only wanted to sleep for at least twelve hours. And drink a beer. That speech took more energy than running up ten flights of stairs.

Would his father be proud of him now?

Bintou:

Bintou sniffed back tears as Hiroki delivered their speech. Those words had been her finest creation. Sure, she'd cobbled together tricks from many of the great orators of the world. She'd borrowed turns of phrase from Douglass, Roosevelt, Gandhi, and Mandela, even Churchill and Sojourner Truth. But the result grew into a unique creation, a thing of intense beauty.

She hoped the speech would remain in the records as the first true missive from the PHAE to the world. Bintou enjoyed the idea of both her and Hiroki being part of the historical record, to be learned by future students of history. Hiroki's inspired delivery had caressed the words and shaped them into efficient tools to carve the world's opinions.

Now, they needed to wait and see if the carefully crafted seeds they'd sown would bear fruit. Any harvest took time and patience, even if Komie helped them grow faster. That didn't mean Bintou cared for waiting. Their talents didn't have splashy power like Anna, Max, or Qacha, but they might create longer-lasting results.

Hiroki looked ready to collapse, and she didn't blame him. He'd given a stellar performance, and his phrasing and timing had been flawless. Pride for his success made Bintou smile. They'd made a fantastic team.

As Hiroki rested, Masaaki and Martin sat with her in their office, back in the bunker. She hadn't wanted to return and begged them to go back to the hotel, but Martin insisted. The communication network had been restored in the bunker, as well as all the generators. They needed to be on hand and close by. Finally, Bintou agreed.

However, agreeing in mind didn't mean her body wanted to comply. As they came to the bunker door, panic gripped her muscles, and they refused to move forward. Her breathing grew difficult, even as Martin hugged her shoulders and moved her step by step toward the door. Finally, she squeezed her eyes shut and let him drag her in, her body completely limp. When she finally opened them again, they were within the bunker.

He agreed to leave the tunnel door open until they turned the corner, and that gave her a measure of peace.

When they returned to their office, they got Hiroki to his bed, and then Bintou, Martin, and Masaaki spent some time cleaning the concrete dust from the surfaces, set lamps upright, and restored the space to its prior condition. Once the room looked like it had before the bombing, her breathing finally slowed to normal levels.

Martin clapped his hands together. "Right. Who's for a spot of supper?"

Memory of the hot, savory stew they'd had during that day of shopping came to Bintou. "Can we have some of that coddle? That would be quite warm and filling."

He gave her a grin, but Masaaki frowned. "I didn't care much for that."

Martin patted the Japanese man on the shoulder. "Never fear. We'll rustle something else up for you. Now that the place is set to rights, will you be fine if I fetch food, Bintou?"

She nodded, grateful for him checking with her. "I shall be fine, Martin."

He returned about a half-hour later, his tray filled with three types of soup, including her requested coddle, bread, and butter. They ate in relative silence as data trickled in.

She didn't want to think of the devastation above ground. Bintou shivered, thinking of how terrified she'd been when the bomb hit. The ground had shaken and rumbled, and she thought an earthquake had hit. The reality turned out to be so much worse. An earthquake would be a natural occurrence, something not fueled by malice and violence. The deliberate attack made her feel so vulnerable, like she stood alone on a field with a firing squad aiming at her heart.

And she couldn't escape that feeling easily. Two of the three exits to the surface had all been blocked by rubble, and the third required equipment to remove.

Bintou prayed to Allah that everyone remained safe at the Byrne farm, as well as those in Galway. Róisín had an inner strength she admired. Fiona would be a formidable woman someday, someone who fought for herself and others. Brendan seemed to be an excellent support for Anna. The world needed more like them.

Martin sat up straight. "Something's coming in!"

Bintou's heartbeat raced as she gripped her chair's arms. "Do be more specific. Data or another bomb?"

"Data! Data's coming in. The PEM backed off! At least physically. No more submarines are coming. Italy, France, and Germany all offered to sign a treaty with the PHAE. So have several other governments. Australia, New Zealand, Canada, Poland, and Estonia so far. Oh, and Iceland."

Masaaki walked to the mini-fridge, pulling out a soda can. "Not Japan? Or Great Britain?"

Martin shook his head with a snort of derision. "Not yet. You'd think the Brits would want to prove their goodwill after nine hundred years of foreign occupation in Ireland, but there's no accounting for colonizer mindsets."

Bintou pursed her lips. "We would be unwise to conflate Ireland's government with the PHAE, even in our minds, Martin."

He waved the suggestion away. "Sure, sure. Wait, I'm getting a call from Róisín."

After putting the phone in the middle of the table, he pressed a button. "You're on speaker, Róisín. Martin and Bintou are in the room. How are things in Galway?"

Her voice crackled and sputtered through the poor connection. "Well enough, though a few of our patients aren't healing as fast as they should. I've never dealt with burn victims, so they pose unique challenges. Many are still coughing up smoke, with burns in their lungs and throats. How're things in Dublin?"

"Above? Getting repaired. The blast destroyed much of the Docklands and some to the north, but the heart of the city received only minor damage. No casualty reports yet. The radio's full of logistic chatter, getting people to where they're needed. Our local tower had repair priority, so we have service now. When did yours return?"

"They shunted the signal to Connemara. Who would have believed Connemara would help Galway with a tech issue?"

Martin rolled his eyes. "Huh! They'll never let us live that one down, will they?"

Róisín paused before asking her next question. "Have you heard from my Mam?"

"I have, and everything is well at the farm. How's everyone there?"

She paused, and Bintou wasn't certain if she'd fallen off the call, but her voice came back on. "Qacha has been badly hurt, but she's alive. We've lost track of Max again."

Bintou's disdain for the man fled as she sent a prayer to Allah that he hadn't been killed.

Latest **CNN** *Update: The organization known as the PEM, or the Pure Earther Movement, has issued an ultimatum to the PHAE, the so-called Protectorate for unHidden Advancement and Education, as well as to the government of the Republic of Ireland. They have demanded registration for all people with the Unhidden mutations in an international database for tracking. If they refuse, the PEM want them taken for re-education and removal to work*

camps. As of the time of this report, the PHAE have given no response to this demand.

In response to the recent attacks, Ireland has declared a no-fly zone across the entire island.

Anna:

Anna coughed and winced, her throat raw. How much came from smoke inhalation and how much came from allergies, she didn't know. She glanced at Brendan at the next makeshift cot, feeding Qacha after her latest setback. Just as the Mongolian woman's burns showed rapid signs of healing, she'd contracted the flu. So had half the ward in the hospital. Coughing and hacking filled the room with echoes. Róisín, Brendan, Max, and Anna all joined those recruited to help nurse the sick and injured.

A few patients coughed up blood, but the doctors assured them that happened with some burn victims. A few also showed fever and nausea. Allergy season compounded other injuries. More patients came in every day. While most had been injured during the initial blasts, repair and rescue efforts created more injuries along with those rescued.

As the days passed, though, hope of finding living victims dwindled. Now, a full week after the initial explosions in Galway, a sober mood fell upon the city as people realized missing loved ones might be buried beneath the rubble.

And her only *loved one,* Joel, had been taken away by the PHAE, a traitor to their organization. Sure, he'd tried to run after she discovered his treachery. He even gave them a merry chase through the rubble-strewn streets of Galway, but the PHAE agents caught him. Not that they had any love lost between them, now.

Violent retching behind her made Anna spin, and she rushed to grab a basin before the patient threw up all over the floor. However, she didn't move fast enough. Resigned, she placed the basin next to his bed and fetched the mop and bucket.

Just as Anna reached the closet, she fell to her knees with another coughing fit. She gripped hard to the doorway to keep herself from collapsing further.

Brendan rushed to her side, grabbing her arm and shoulder. "Anna? Here, let me get you to a bed."

Anna glanced at her hand and saw specks of blood in her sputum. She grew dizzy as she stared at it. When she looked up, she locked her gaze with Brendan.

His eyes grew wide as he glanced between the blood on her hand and her face. "Your status just changed from nurse to patient."

Brendan supported her shoulder as she stumbled to the ward wall. She sank to the floor as he gathered supplies. Since they'd run out of cots, he had to create a new one. First, he went to the supply closet and pulled out several blankets and a sheet, along with a pillow. The local hospital supply depot had been destroyed, but they'd extracted as many things as they could to help with the hospital operations.

Then he set these up like a bed and led her to lie down. Once he ensured she was comfortable, he turned to fetch a doctor.

His phone buzzed, and he held it up to his ear. "Yes, Mam? No, I'm grand. Anna's a bit ill, but… No, I haven't heard anything."

He fell silent as he listened to the other side of the conversation. "What? Are you certain? Fecking hell. Oh, sorry, Mam. Tell me what you know? I'll inform the doctors here."

After he ended the call, he blinked a few times and turned to Anna. "I've got some news."

She swallowed against the ring of pain in her throat. "What news?"

"Nothing good." He stared out the window at the wreckage of Galway. "Reports of illness in Dublin."

"Smoke inhalation, like here?"

Brendan shook his head. "No, they don't think so. Sure, the smoke made it worse, and may have hidden the effects for a while, but this seems to be something else."

Anna's throat closed, and she coughed again.

Komie:

Five straight days of extracting power from the land left Komie in a permanent walking daze. She possessed energy for only three fields a day without collapsing, but she'd increased the yield of all the neighboring farms. Colin, with Fiona's help, brought her around to each in an ever-widening spiral.

The last field had proved difficult. Something in the ground resisted her, pushing her back. Nothing seemed wrong with the land. But a force slumbered beneath the soil, something powerful, which stirred when her power touched. Whatever stirred did nothing but grumble, but the potential concerned her. Komie tried not to poke. This prolonged activity might be getting to her. Either that or she'd come down with something. Or maybe she was just growing too old for such sustained efforts.

When she asked Fiona if she looked ill, the young girl shook her head. "No, you look fine, Miss Komie. Sure, and you're tired. We all are. But you don't look pale or anything." The girl covered her mouth with her hand. "Oh, I'm so sorry! I didn't mean to say it like that."

"Like what?"

"Uh… pale. Like in paleface? Isn't that an insult to your people?"

Komie gave a tired chuckle. "An insult from our people to white people, child. I am not offended in the slightest. You may rest easy."

"Oh, thank Mother Mary." She crossed herself.

Komie cleared her throat and coughed a few times. Perhaps she *was* coming down with a cold. Her breath came shorter today than before. When the time came that she could take several days for self-care and rest, she would welcome them.

When they returned to the farm, she pulled Colin aside to ask some questions. He led her to his office, sat in the green leather chair and steepled his fingers. "Now, how can I help?"

"Do you have any more stories in your lore of your earth goddess, Anú? I believe I have touched her, or someone like her. It is possible that something is sleeping below the hills. Do you have tales which speak of such a possibility?"

He let out a long, hearty laugh. "Do we ever! That describes half of our lore."

Komie bit at her lip. "Can you be more specific?"

He leaned back in his chair, putting his hands behind his head. "To put the stories in a very simplistic nutshell, The Tuatha Dé Danann lived on the surface, as we do now, until the human Milesians came from Spain and stole their land. They moved beneath the hills and became known as the Sídhe, fairies and nature spirits, though they aren't quite the same. Many people in Ireland still believe in them."

Komie nodded, considering the implications. "And what are the consequences of rousing one of these Sídhe?"

"Ah, now, that depends on the tale. Sometimes the person gets the best of the encounter. But that's a rare accomplishment, indeed. Common results are curses upon seven generations of descendants, hunched back, clubbed foot, madness, even death. The list is epic. Accepted wisdom says to leave them alone. If you do encounter one of the Good Folk, give them a wee gift to appease its angry temper. If not, you're in for a world of hurt."

"You call them the Good Folk?"

He nodded, tapping his nose. "We use over-polite terms to avoid the risk of insulting them with a more accurate description of their dangerous natures."

"Are they powerful?"

"They can be, depending on which one you encounter." He sat back, entwining his fingers together. "Komie, does this inquiry have a purpose? Have you met a Sídhe?"

The native woman pursed her lips. "I can't be certain. I've sensed something powerful sleeping beneath the soil. Whatever I sense moves when I use my power but hasn't woken up. Yet. If I touch them too many times, I fear they will rouse and wreak havoc."

He leaned forward. "Truly? A real Sídhe! Oh, what I wouldn't give to encounter one."

Komie narrowed her gaze. "I thought you said no one wished to meet one?"

He waved his hand in dismissal. "To be sure, to be sure. But I'm a folklorist. I collect stories of such creatures. I know how to deal with them. Can you imagine what I might learn from meeting one?"

Komie shook her head. She'd thought Colin possessed more wisdom. Her own tribe's lore contained dangerous creatures to avoid at all costs.

"You think me foolish, don't you?"

She gave him a sad smile. "Earth power can nurture and heal but can also be dangerous and destructive. While the soil grows food to feed us, the ground can also rip apart with earthquakes. One doesn't rouse earth spirits without paying the price for foolhardiness."

"Very well. Tell me more of this presence you sensed. Did they speak?"

Komie shook her head. "Not with words, but I heard grumbling in my mind. A female voice, I believe. Something powerful but asleep. Almost sleeping, as I may have roused her."

"I believe I told you already about our Anú. She's the mother goddess to the Tuatha, which is why they are the Tuatha Dé Danann, the people of Anú."

"Yes, you spoke before of Anú and Danu. These are the same entities?"

"For the most part, yes, though some debate that correspondence. Most tales speak of her children, such as The Morrigan, The Dagda, Brid,

Aine, Boann, or Lugh. They're the ones who battle, form courts, and go on adventures. Anú is the quiet power beneath them all."

"And if I have touched a lesser god, would they also be dangerous to wake?"

He lowered his glasses and peered over the frames at her. "Any Irish god is dangerous if woken, Komie."

She glanced at the shelf of books lining his office wall. "I sensed an entity. I have no context to identify which one. To my People, the Great Spirit is the same throughout the world. We don't break them up by geography."

"I am both excited and cautious, Komie. I'll tell you what. When I take you to the next farm, I'll stay by your side as you work your talent. Maybe together we can figure it out."

After dinner, she staggered to her room. She'd barely had the energy to eat, but the household cooked hearty meals designed to stoke her constitution to maximum strength. She appreciated the effort, but craved rest.

That, however, eluded her. Memories of her son, Mihku, invaded her thoughts. And Tansy, left all alone in Arizona, cared for by strangers. No matter how many times she tried to meditate these visions away or shove them into a locked hole in her mind, they returned.

Eventually, she gave up trying. Komie surrendered to tears of grief and exhaustion until she fell asleep.

The next day, when Colin and Komie approached the farm in the Limerick suburbs, apprehension gripped her. This presence terrified Komie, and she didn't frighten easily.

Waking any Irish god or goddess would be dangerous. They didn't seem to have pure evil or benevolent entities. Instead, each god or goddess had complex motivations and actions, some benefiting humans and some harming them. In a way, their gods seemed more human. And while her own ancestors had granted her permission, even their blessings, to work with these local gods, that didn't mean they wanted to work with her.

As she sunk her hands into the soil, she swallowed her fear and drew the power up into the soybean roots, encouraging them to stretch, grow, and flourish.

The rumble shook through the earth, stronger than before. A mix between a child's hungry cry and a bear's growl.

"Colin, put your hand on my shoulder. Can you feel the vibration?"

The Irish man did as she bid, his hands warm and steady. The entity yawned within Komie's mind, crackling with energy and irritation.

An echoing voice rumbled through the dirt. ***"Who calls me?"***

Colin jerked his hand back, his eyes round. "I heard that. Did you hear that?"

Komie collapsed into a blanket of swirling gray.

*To be continued in **Much Ado About Dying***

**She needs ancient magic to prevent more deaths.
But messing with the gods could get them all killed.**

Will Róisín's perilous covenant plunge them all into darkness?

Buy ***Much Ado About Dying*** to banish the blight today!
books2read.com/MuchAdoAboutDying

Thank You!

Thank you so much for enjoying Taming of the Few. If you've enjoyed the story, please consider helping others find Anna, Max, and the rest of the Unhidden by leaving a review.

If you would like to get updates, sneak previews, sales, and FREE STUFF, please sign up for my newsletter.

Monthly Newsletter Signup and homepage:
www.greendragonartist.com

Other Books by This Author

**See all the books available through
Green Dragon Publishing at**

www.greendragonartist.com/books

About the Author

Christy Nicholas writes under several pen names, including Emeline Rhys, CN Jackson, and Rowan Dillon. She is an author, artist, and accountant. After she failed to become an airline pilot, she quit her ceaseless pursuit of careers that began with the letter 'A' and decided to concentrate on her writing. Since she has Project Completion Compulsion, she is one of the few authors with no unfinished novels.

Christy has her hands in many crafts, including digital art, beaded jewelry, writing, and photography. In real life, she's a CPA, but having grown up with art all around her (her mother, grandmother, and great-grandmother are/were all artists), it sort of infected her, as it were.

She wants to expose the incredible beauty in this world, hidden beneath the everyday grime of familiarity and habit, and share it with others. She uses characters out of time and places infused with magic and myth, writing magical realism stories in both historical fantasy and time travel flavors.